Captives of Minara

Eric E. Wright

CAPTIVES OF MINARA

ISBN-13: 978-1-926676-38-8

Printed in Canada

Printed by Word Alive Press
131 Cordite Road, Winnipeg, MB R3W 1S1
www.wordalivepress.ca

WORD ALIVE PRESS
Just Write!

This work of fiction is written in appreciation for the rich culture and generous hospitality of the Pakistani people.

It is dedicated to all those who fight to eradicate the scourge of human slavery.

ACKNOWLEDGEMENTS

I acknowledge with deep gratitude the encouragement and suggestions of writing colleagues from the Apple Way Writers' Group and the Word Guild Revision Group. First and foremost, however, kudos go to Mary Helen for her reader's eye and her continuing support and encouragement.

I saw the tears of the oppressed—
and they have no comforter;
power was on the side of their oppressors—
and they have no comforter.

ECCLESIASTES 4:1

TABLE OF CONTENTS

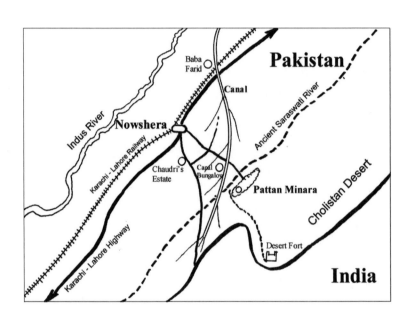

PROLOGUE
Abduction

NOVEMBER 22
A PAKISTANI VILLAGE HALFWAY
BETWEEN KARACHI AND LAHORE

A breeze off the desert sent dust devils skipping ahead of Chandi's sandaled feet. With one hand, she steadied the huge bundle of fodder balanced on her head. With the other, she adjusted her headscarf to hide her face as she passed the Punjabi section of the village.

Down one of the dirt avenues, several fat, black water buffaloes chewed their cud beneath the shade of shesham trees. She glanced toward the whitewashed mosque in the village square and grimaced. Two boys, kicking a soccer ball back and forth, stopped to stare as she strode past.

Chandi knew that the distinctive blue-bordered, red calico of her dress set her apart from the Punjabi women. And so it should. Not for her a life of bowing to every demand of an uncouth husband. She was a Marwari, daughter of the desert, worshipper of the ancient gods, no slave of Allah. And soon, very soon, she'd announce her status by exchanging her imitation ivory bangles for silver ones. Wasn't her father in Karachi making final arrangements for her wedding?

Her skirt swept the ground as she passed the stagnant pond that separated her village from the main part of Dhera Mundi. Her tribe's allotment might be on derelict land rendered sterile by salt peter, but to her it was home. She strode through a gap in the compound's wall of thorn brush and called for her younger brother to come to her aid.

Kalu dropped his crude cricket bat and ran to help her lift down the load of fodder she'd brought. Leaving Kalu to chop it into feed for their brace of skeletal oxen, Chandi stooped to dip water from one of the terracotta water pots. Empty. Both empty. She picked up the pots and headed toward the well.

A couple of hundred yards beyond the thorn brush wall lay the debris of what had once been a working Persian water wheel. The Punjabis, whose water came from a modern well in the village square, had long ago abandoned this one to Chandi's tribe.

Chandi set one pot down, balanced the other on her hip, and reached for the rope to bring up the leather bucket full of water. The sound of a vehicle made her turn. She watched a Toyota Land Cruiser approach slowly along the dirt road that separated the two parts of the village. She dropped the rope and pulled the corner of her shawl over her face.

Just when she thought the Toyota would pass, it swerved to a stop in front of her and two men jumped out. Chandi stumbled back, dropped her water pot, and turned to flee. One of the men grabbed her roughly around the waist. The other tried to seize her feet, but she twisted and kicked to get free. Her shawl flew off and her blouse tore. She screamed like a wounded jackal as she pounded the face of the man in front of her. He clamped his hand over her mouth to stifle her screams, but Chandi bit down until she tasted blood. With a howl of pain, he wrested his hand free and slapped her hard. The other grabbed a handful of her hair and yanked so hard that her eyes watered. He caught her in a choke-hold and dragged her into the Land Cruiser. With the salty taste of blood in her mouth, and the smell of stale sweat in her nostrils, she tried to spit out the tape they pressed over her mouth. The last thing she saw before the vehicle ground into gear and sped off was her younger brother running down the road toward her.

CHAPTER ONE
Flight to Pakistan

Stepping onto Pakistani soil after an absence of thirty-one years awakened the demons I'd spent years stuffing into my subconscious. The late arrival of my jumbo jet from New York had set them sharpening their knives.

And here I was stuck in an endless line-up at customs while on the verge of missing my flight upcountry. I glanced around as I loosened my collar and fanned my shirt in an attempt to dry the sweat that trickled down my back.

Clusters of submachine gun-carrying Rangers guarded every exit.

When my turn finally came, the immigration officer examined my documents then looked up at me through the fly-speckled glass of his booth. "You are Joshua Radley?"

"Yes, sir."

He waved my immigration form in one hand and my passport in the other. "Then, why is this form made out for Josh Radley while your passport says, Joshua H. Radley?"

I stifled a chuckle. "It's just a nickname—short for Joshua— most people call me Josh. I use it without thinking."

He arched his eyebrows. "Without thinking? Well, you should think more carefully. I see you didn't fill out the name of your father either. Why? Are you really who you say you are?"

My face began to heat up. I wanted to tell this petty bureaucrat where to go. What did it matter who my father was? Instead, I bit my lip and said, "*Janab*, an oversight. My father's name is Lawrence Radley."

He scowled at me for a few moments, then winked. He motioned ever so slightly over his shoulder as he handed me my stamped passport. Out of the corner of my eye, I caught sight of his supervisor, a heavily bearded man with the grim look of a religious zealot.

By the time I'd reached my gate, I was beginning to smell like a locker room. Fortunately, delay seemed the order of the day, so I dashed into a washroom and, using a couple of packaged towelettes, tried to freshen up.

Back out in the waiting room, I saw that the flight had not yet been announced, so I strode over to a bank of phones and called Stephanie. She answered on the fourth ring.

"Sweetheart, I'm already missing you," I said.

"Me, too. Are you calling from Karachi?"

"Yeah. This'll have to be quick."

I reminded her to set the timers when she left to join me and be sure to turn down the thermostat. She told me how excited Janice, our daughter, was about coming. I warned her about the gruelling nature of the trip and suggested they take a sleeping pill during the flight.

"Mr. Grumman will meet you in Karachi," I said. "He'll help you get on the upcountry flight. I'll meet you at the Nowshera airport."

Maybe things would work out well after all. Didn't they say absence makes the heart grow fonder?

I joined the back of the line forming for the flight to Nowshera and idly glanced around. Through the windows, I could see troop carriers and armoured Hummers patrolling the tarmac. The terminal looked like a building in a war zone.

I lifted my digital camera to snap a couple of photos. Suddenly, a burly sergeant spun me around and demanded my camera. "No photographs of important installations, *Munna*."

I lowered my camera and addressed him politely. "*Janab-e-ali.* No problem. I'm a journalist here to report on Pakistan's archaeological heritage."

I leafed through the junk in my wallet and extracted my press card. The sergeant shook his head and scowled. "No exceptions. Your camera."

Unwilling to surrender my camera, I extracted the memory chip. Since it was a new chip with few images, I offered it to him. He took it, waving his finger in my face. "Western media. Very bad."

I took a deep breath and fanned myself with my passport as I watched him walk away. A man in front of me in the line turned toward me and smiled. "Don't worry," he said. "This state of emergency will soon be lifted. The police are bullies; they like to throw their weight around."

A few minutes later, we boarded a PIA turbo-prop for the flight north to Nowshera. From my window seat, I glanced around, thankful the seat beside me was unoccupied. Quite a cross-section. A couple of men with their faces buried in newspapers; probably government officials. Two rows of army officers. A woman, fashionably dressed in a silk sari, trying in vain to get her three children to stay in their seats. A scattering of businessmen with briefcases. Two tall, bearded Sindhis wearing distinctive skullcaps covered with embroidered bits of mirror.

I settled back and turned to the Herald magazine the attendant had handed me. Long articles analyzed threats from suicide bombers, the turmoil on Pakistan's frontier with Afghanistan, and possible candidates to take Benezir Bhutto's place in the next election. What impressed me most about the monthly magazine was its size, a hundred and fifty pages, and the breadth of content ranging from poetry through book reviews and fashion into the changing role of women and the spread of technology.

I continued to leaf through the magazine until I found an article about Pakistan International Airways' poor maintenance record. Uh-oh. Evidently the European Union had suspended PIA's landing privileges in Europe until they improved their aircraft maintenance procedures. Not a good sign.

The last person to board was a turban-wearing tribal man in a billowing white shirt and white baggy pants—*shalwar-qamiz*—balancing a huge bundle tied up in a cotton sheet. He stopped, dumped the package on the empty seat beside me, pulled out his boarding pass, and smiled as he looked at the number. Opening the overhead compartment, he tried to stuff his bundle inside. A flight attendant strode down the aisle shaking her head. After a heated exchange, he threw up his hands and surrendered his bundle. He carefully put his turban in the overhead bin and took the seat next to me.

To say he sat down would not do him justice. He removed his handmade, embroidered shoes and, with his feet tucked under him, perched on the seat in the lotus position with his arms crossed in front of him.

I stared at him out of the corner of my eye. How could he do that? He had to be at least fifty, but as agile as a monkey. He sat like a Buddha on a lotus flower. Even the businessman across from us stared with his mouth open.

Buddha-in-white turned toward me. His expressive eyes—a rich shade of chocolate brown—seemed to say that the whole world was mad. I couldn't understand a word of the torrent he unleashed in some tribal language. Finally, he paused, and said, "*Angrez*—English? No speak."

I smiled and replied in Urdu that I was a Canadian.

"*Acha ji,*" he said, although I doubt if he knew anything about Canada. He pointed to himself. "*Mah,* Raju."

"*Mah,* Josh."

When he leaned over, I noticed a heavy silver medallion hanging around his neck on a thick red string. It looked like it might be a Hindu god. I wondered if he was a member of one of the nomadic Hindu tribes left behind in Pakistan after the partition of India. I pointed to him. "Marwari?"

He nodded his head slightly, then looked around to see if anyone had overheard. The Marwaris I had known as a child growing up in the Nowshera area had been used as cheap labour by Muslim landlords.

Beyond smiling and gesturing, we seemed to have come to a dead-end as far as communication was concerned. Who was Raju and what life or death issue had him on a flight from Karachi when Marwaris were almost invariably poor?

The overloaded plane lumbered down the runway. I could actually see the wings flexing up and down like a fat beetle trying to become airborne. A couple of the overhead bins flapped open. I turned from the window and stared at the space between my feet. That didn't help. The whole plane seemed alive.

I took a deep breath, leaned back in my seat, and tried to breathe normally. The businessman across the aisle continued to read the Dawn newspaper as if he faced death every day. I was glad to see that Raju had put his feet on the floor and begun fingering his pendant.

With a bounce, the plane hobbled into the air. I took another breath and tried to forget that wags called PIA, Pakistan *Insh'allah*

Airlines. The moniker was taken from the phrase that concluded every statement by flight attendants about arrival times. "Allah willing, we will arrive at..." My mind returned to the article I'd scanned, not that air travel really worried me. My nightmare hadn't involved an airplane.

As the plane settled down into level flight, I continued leafing through the Herald until I came to an article on the abduction of women. The article documented the kidnapping of women and children in Baluchistan and outlying areas of the Punjab province, including Nowshera District. Case histories told of victims being sold into sexual slavery in the Middle East and Europe. Depressing.

I set down the magazine and stared through my window at the changing landscape. Desolate patches of slate gray. A string of trucks on a black ribbon of highway. The sun glinting off the Indus River. The crumbling walls of an old fort. Clusters of palm trees marking mud-walled villages. A toy train chugging north on the Grand Trunk Railway.

Not long now. The lump in my stomach tightened. I clenched and unclenched my hands, swivelled my head from side to side, and practiced deep breathing. It wasn't the flight, but the destination that made me jittery.

Perverse, because scores of writers would stab their best friend to get the plum assignment that had dropped into my lap. Later today I'd be at the site of the archaeological scoop of the century: the excavation of one of the lost cities of Asia. Pattan Minara might become as famous as Ankhor Wat in Cambodia.

And I'd be coming home. Then why had the very thought of returning set sirens wailing inside my head? I'd asked myself that question a thousand times. I ought to have been euphoric about returning to the town where my parents served as missionaries and I'd spent my childhood. I had so many happy memories: eating *pakordes*, hot and spicy from a vendor in the bazaar, being wakened by the brassy tinkle of a string of camels ambling by our house... but...

Josh, you're an idiot. This trip is a dream come true... and your financial salvation... If only your parting with Stephanie had been smoother. Were we doomed to fight... and then make up... only to plunge again into acrimony? I opened my wallet to her photo and tried to connect with the woman I had loved... did love... would love forever.

"*Ap ki bivi?*"

Startled, I turned toward Raju. "*Mu'af karna*—sorry?" My Urdu was coming back.

He pointed at the picture of Stephanie. "*Bivi?*"

I nodded yes and pointed to another picture, that of our daughter, Janice, and our son, Jonathan. "*Meri beti aur mera beta.*"

Somewhere from the folds of his *qamiz*, he pulled out a creased picture and offered it to me. Using signs and Urdu, he explained that the girl in the photo was his daughter and that she was to be married soon.

I learned he had been in Karachi to finalize arrangements for her wedding. He shook his head as he explained how expensive it was to arrange the wedding of a daughter. "*Bahut rupeah.*"

I could understand now why he had taken the plane. It embellished his reputation. Even the poorest in Pakistan borrowed heavily for weddings and funerals lest they lose face in their village.

The flight attendant interrupted our attempt at conversation by announcing our imminent arrival at Nowshera. I turned from Raju to gaze out the window. The desert began to give way to a patchwork of lush fields laced with canals.

Despite my misgivings about a rough landing, the turbo-prop touched down lightly and taxied to the small terminal building.

A swirl of dust and a blast of heat hit me as I joined others swarming down the stairs to the tarmac. My mouth fell open as I gazed at the ornate marble front of the terminal building—so out of place in this dusty provincial town. Gulf oil money at work. The Sheik of Abu Dubai must still use the airport to ferry in his hunting parties.

Not much military presence here; just a couple of soldiers with submachine guns and two local policemen with old Enfield rifles. I looked around for the Chinese archaeologist who was to meet me.

"Mister Radley!"

An erect man with a military bearing waved as he came toward me. His baggy cotton *shalwars* billowed in the hot wind, revealing black oxfords. His hand went to his sheepskin Jinnah cap in a salute. Who could this be?

CHAPTER TWO
Chaudri Gujar Mohammed

The tall, clean-shaven man who came toward me across the tarmac appeared to be in his late fifties. He held out his hand. "Welcome to Nowshera, Mr. Radley. My name is Chaudri Gujar Mohammed."

I paused before reaching out to shake his hand. "I'm sorry, sir... *Janab*, I was expecting someone from the Pattan Minara excavation."

"Ah, yes, so right," he said. "The chief archaeologist, Mr. Wu, asked me to meet you. He cannot leave the site today. Since I'm chairman of the local Preservation Committee, I came in his place."

I must have still looked puzzled, for he went on: "The full name is, the Punjab Committee for the Preservation of Ancient Sites, but it has such a long name, we just call it the PC."

He waved his hand toward the terminal. "We're delighted to have serious archaeologists finally digging at Pattan Minara."

"I'm very excited to be here."

I followed him past two submachine gun toting Rangers. Inside the terminal, a uniformed guard saluted him. "*Salaam alay kum*, Chaudri Sahib." Further along, an airport official repeated the greeting. So did a member of the flight crew.

"You have how many bags?"

"Two," I said.

"If you'll give me the baggage claim tickets, I'll have Bahadur fetch them." With a toss of his head, he signalled to a man in a gray *shalwar-qamiz* who stood off to one side. Bahadur stood six foot four and weighed at least 250 pounds. Except for his luxurious black beard and white skullcap, he had the physique of a running back for the Pittsburgh Steelers.

I fumbled in my pocket. Could I really trust this Chaudri character? Obviously, he was used to giving orders and having them obeyed. From his lamb's wool Jinnah cap to his Italian brogues, he projected power and wealth of a modern, idiosyncratic style. A Blackberry protruded from the pocket of his hand-embroidered vest. A Rolex glinted from the loose sleeve of his white *qamiz*. His dark obsidian eyes hinted at a barely restrained temper made more sinister by a one-inch scar over his right eye. In his correspondence, Mr. Wu had not mentioned a local contact.

He smiled. "Ah, quite right to be suspicious, Mr. Radley. We must be careful whom we trust—no?" He threw up his hands. "I should have brought a letter of introduction... but I never thought. Everyone in Nowshera—indeed everyone in the Punjab—knows me."

He beckoned to a man in a pinstriped suit. "Salamat Sahib, can you vouch for me?"

The businessman set down his briefcase, embraced Chaudri, and began to chuckle. "Vouch for you?" He pointed in my direction. "Have you fallen afoul of the American CIA?"

A ripple of laughter spread around us in the terminal. Chaudri's slightly protruding belly shook as he joined in the general merriment.

I grinned at the quip and pointed to the Canadian maple leaf on my briefcase.

The businessman smiled at me. "Sir, Chaudri Gujar Mohammed is a member of the provincial parliament and the largest landlord south of Bahawalpur—what is it now, Chaudri? Twenty-five thousand acres, or fifty? He owns Punjab Poultry, among other businesses. He is a great benefactor of arts and literature. He built the new library. I could go on."

I passed Chaudri the baggage claim tickets. "Sorry. I didn't know."

"How would you?" He gave the tickets to his shadow. "Come. We'll let Bahadur pick up your bags and follow us in the Land Rover."

At the curb, in front of a no parking sign, stood a silver late-model Mercedes. His chauffeur—another giant wearing a gray *shalwar-qamiz*—held the door open for us.

Soon after we were seated, Chaudri's cell phone rang. "Excuse me," he said.

I turned to stare out the window as the Mercedes eased through the airport traffic onto a well-paved road lined with emperor palms. I could see the touch of Abu Dubai's oil-rich sheik in the whole ornamentation and layout of the airport. It hadn't even existed during the time my parents had served here as missionaries.

My amazement didn't last long. The driver turned off the airport road onto the town's main thoroughfare. A brightly coloured bus with several passengers clinging to the roof almost deafened us with a long blast of its air horn. The chauffeur made an obscene gesture out his window. We narrowly missed a motorcycle carrying five: a father, three children, and a woman clad from head to toe in a black *burqua*. Here was the land I remembered.

Traffic slowed to a crawl. A two-wheeled *tonga* pulled by an emaciated horse with red tassels hanging from its blinders cut us off. Garishly painted trucks, piled high with bales of cotton or sugarcane, bulled their way through. Cycles flirted with trucks. Three-wheeled rickshaws flitted in and out of the snarl. Women in dingy white full-length *burquas* followed turban-clad men who sauntered along as if they were rajas. Like an eddy around a rock, traffic flowed around a blind beggar who stood partway into the traffic holding out a battered metal dish for *baksheesh*.

Horns blared. Donkeys brayed. Camels gurgled. People cursed. Dust rose in stifling clouds under a relentless sun, creating a scene straight out of Dante's Inferno.

And I smiled. This was it. The Pakistan of my memories. I sighed. The gut-wrenching anxiety that had made me clench my shoulders and pop antacid pills began to subside. I wanted to be in the melee, wandering through the bazaar, sampling the *pakordas*—deep-fried potatoes in thick, chickpea batter—sniffing the aromas perfuming the air around the spice shop, stopping for a cup of *chai* and a pastry.

Suddenly Chaudri raised his voice. I caught the word *afeem*. I frowned... why was he talking about opium? What was he arranging? Some hanks for his *hooka*? I kept looking out the window, but I listened more carefully, trying to remember the Punjabi I'd learned so easily as a kid and just as easily forgotten.

Pakistan was divided into four provinces, two on the west, Baluchistan and the North-West Frontier Province, and two on the east, Sindh and Punjab. Urdu and English were spoken widely, but each province had its own local language. Since Nowshera was in the Punjab, near the Sindh border, most spoke Punjabi, with the exception of small tribal groups.

Chaudri spoke another word I remembered, *godom*—warehouse. Then he used the word for trucks, recognizable in any language. Did this mysterious landlord also run a fleet of trucks? Of course, he'd have trucks to haul his crops. And yet...

Free from the bazaar's gridlock, the driver accelerated into a quieter, residential area. We crossed a large feeder-canal and picked up speed on a two-lane, well-maintained asphalt road out of town. Fields of wheat and sugarcane alternated with patches of alfalfa.

"Excuse me," said Chaudri as he put away his cell phone. "There's no escape from business."

"I shouldn't be taking up your time," I said. "I could have found my way to the dig."

"You must allow us the pleasure of extending hospitality." He pointed ahead. "We're almost there."

A mansion rose like a mirage from the surrounding fields. To the left stretched a dense orchard. On its right stood a series of single-storey barns.

A veranda marked by fluted Corinthian columns fronted the house. Deeply recessed, arched windows graced the second floor. A false front soared above the second storey. In the center, a blue, stylized "M" held pride of place. A profusion of peach-coloured bougainvillea cascaded from the veranda's roof. The overall impression was that of a jumble of styles: a mixture of Grecian, gothic, and Islamic.

Our driver pulled into the circular driveway. "Come," said Chaudri. "Let's enjoy some refreshment after your trip."

I got out of the car, and then paused when I caught sight of the elaborate rose garden that had been hidden by a perfectly trimmed hedge. Chaudri came around the car. "Ah, you like my garden? Let me show you some of my prize specimens while they steep the tea."

He led me down into the sunken garden and began to point out various specimens—row upon row of roses of every conceivable hue. I'd forgotten how congenial the climate of Pakistan was for their cultivation. He waxed eloquent about the differences between varieties and pointed proudly to those he had personally grafted. He urged me to smell the fragrance of one and admire the size of another.

Chaudri Gujar Mohammed seemed to be a very complex man: a landlord and farmer, an entrepreneurial businessman, a member of provincial parliament... and a gardener. Everyone in town seemed to know him and like him. And although I'd only just met him, I found myself already charmed—in spite of his taste in architecture.

"Chaudri, Sahib," I said. "Your garden has captivated me. May I bring my wife to see it when she arrives next week?"

"I would be honoured," he said. "Visit it any time. Consider it your own. But we mustn't keep the *Begum Sahiba* waiting. Our tea will be ready. Come inside where it's cooler."

As we left the rose garden, Bahadur arrived in the Land Rover.

"Ah, your bags," said Chaudri. "I'll have him drive you to your bungalow after we have refreshments."

We entered the mansion through a huge carved wooden door. The tiled floor of the living room—it looked more like an audience chamber—was almost completely covered with Persian carpets. Clusters of brocade settees and inlaid Kashmiri endtables encircled the room. A crystal chandelier lit the interior.

He waved me toward the far end of the room. A young woman in a pink silk *shalwar* and matching *qamiz* stood behind a table laden with at least a dozen covered dishes. "I want you to meet my wife, Noorani," he said, indicating the young woman who inclined her head toward me and smiled. I caught the vague scent of some exotic perfume.

Self-conscious in my wrinkled and sweat-stained shirt, I bowed. "I'm honoured to meet you, *Begum Sahiba*. Please excuse my appearance."

"The honour is ours." She lifted the covers off the various dishes. "Pleased to help yourself. You must excuse me. My English. Not good."

I smiled in return. "Much better than my Urdu."

Chaudri handed me a plate. "Please eat up. I have the best cook in the area and I've asked him to go easy on the chillies in your honour."

I stuttered. "Wow, this looks wonderful. More like a feast than tea with a few refreshments."

"You must be very hungry. Airline food is very bland." He proceeded to heap my plate high with enough food to prepare me for a two-day fast. "Here, try some of this butter chicken... and some pool-gobi... a little korma. You must try the sag-paneer. My cook makes the best sag in Pakistan. Here, have a couple of lamb chops..."

I laughed out loud. "Enough, enough."

With his own plate piled high, he pointed through an arch into a dining room. We sat at a table that looked like something from Buckingham Palace. I waited for his wife to be seated first, but she bowed and slipped away. I eased myself onto a gilt chair and turned toward the bounty on my plate. A servant set a goblet of mango squash in front of me. I felt awkward in the midst of such ostentatious luxury.

"Eat up, my friend," he said. "Tea will arrive shortly."

Between mouthfuls, he inquired about my flight, my family back in Canada, and my childhood in Pakistan. I enthused about his garden and asked about his farm.

I pointed to my plate. "This is the most delicious butter chicken I've ever eaten."

He signalled to one of the servants hovering in the background. "More chicken for Mr. Radley."

"No, please." I covered my plate with my hands. "I can't eat any more."

He let out a dignified belch, a sign of culinary satisfaction in this culture, and clapped his hands.

A servant came in bearing a silver tea set, which he placed on a small side table. I looked around at all the signs of wealth and, in the light of the mention of opium, wondered how much Chaudri had earned legitimately.

Chaudri broke into my thoughts. "How much sugar, three... four?"

"One, please."

The servant brought me tea in a gilt-edged porcelain teacup.

When he brought Chaudri's tea, he slipped, slightly sloshing a few drops of hot tea onto the saucer and Chaudri's hand.

"*Bevukoof!*" Chaudri bellowed.

The servant offered a towel and bowed low. "*Ma'af karna* Sahib—please forgive me, sir."

With a scowl, Chaudri turned back to his tea.

He was in the midst of telling me about a few of the sights I should see during my visit when another servant whispered something in his ear. He replied to him in Punjabi, then turned to me. "Some delegation wants to see me. But it's nothing important."

I had been looking for an excuse to take my leave. The long trip, combined with the meal, left me struggling to stay awake. "Chaudri, Sahib, I've been greatly honoured by your hospitality..."

Chaudri touched my arm. "Say no more. I'm forgetting my duties as a host—to get you to your accommodation. You must be very weary." He stood up. "Come."

I inclined my head toward his young wife, who had appeared in the doorway, then followed him outside.

On the veranda, six turban-clad tribal men sat as if chairs were alien to their experience. The nearest man, who reclined in a lotus position, looked familiar. When he turned toward me, I recognized him as Raju, my Marwari seatmate from the flight up-country. Furrows of anguish obscured the smile I remembered. He started when he recognized me, then nodded his head slightly in acknowledgement.

Chaudri swept by the men and led me toward a Land Rover. "Bahadur will drive you to your bungalow and get you settled in.

The Land Rover is one of the expedition vehicles and will be at your disposal for the duration of your stay."

"Chaudri Gujar, sir," I said. "You have been extremely kind. I'm very grateful."

He waved his hands in a sign of dismissal. "It is my duty, a duty commanded by the prophet, peace be upon him."

As we drove away, I watched Chaudri turn to the group of tribal men. He gestured with his hands as he addressed them in what appeared to be an angry manner. What could Raju be doing here?

CHAPTER THREE
Canal Bungalow

We drove for half an hour along a single lane asphalt road before turning off on a dirt track. Dust swirled behind us and seeped inside. The vehicle's air conditioning couldn't stop the sweat from soaking my shirt. I wrinkled my nose as I caught a whiff of my own odour. My kingdom for a cool shower.

The rough track led through a village and ended at a broad canal lined with shesham and *kikar* trees. Bahadur turned onto the canal road and drove with care. He soon had to pull over to let a huge flock of sheep and goats pass. Farther along, he yielded to a couple of young boys driving a herd of water buffalo across the road to their soak in the canal. I envied the boys as they leaped into the canal after their charges. I'd loved canals ever since my childhood in Nowshera.

Besides the occasional jeep or tractor and a rickety bus, vehicle traffic was light. The waterway appeared to be a large feeder canal that channelled life-giving water from the Panjnad Barrage. Panjnad, named after the five rivers of the Punjab, was an amazing piece of engineering. Before its construction this whole area had been largely trackless desert right up to the Indian border, thirty miles away. Access to water had transformed much of the district into fertile farmland and brought on a land boom.

Ten or fifteen minutes along the canal, we turned down a lane and stopped in front of a weathered bungalow beneath an encircling grove of trees. At the sound of our vehicle, two men appeared from the side of the building. They saluted us as we got out, deferring particularly to Bahadur. Did I detect fear in their attitude toward him? Bahadur introduced them as Mohammed and Musa. How would I remember all these new names? M & M? Okay, I'd call them M&M.

Tall and burly, Mohammed sported a luxurious beard and a waxed moustache twisted into points that extended a good five inches on either side of his face. He wore a dark gray *shalwar* and *qamiz* and carried a thick, metal-tipped bamboo nightstick. Bahadur introduced him as the *chaukidar*—the night watchman. I wondered if he was in Chaudri's employ.

By contrast, Musa was short and slim with wispy hair reddened by a touch of henna. Laugh lines radiating from his raisin-eyes broke his leathery face, as if laughter waited just below the surface. Years of washing had dulled his white *shalwar-qamiz* until it looked the colour of whitewash after a monsoon. Like most of the men I'd seen since arriving in the Nowshera District, both wore the typical squashed turbans wound from a long narrow strip of unstarched cloth.

Mohammed saluted, but kept his distance. Musa stepped forward. "Welcome, *Sahib*," he said. "We very happy to serve you."

Bahadur turned toward me. "Besides these two, a sweeper will come every morning to clean the floors, disinfect the latrines, and tidy the yards. If you have any problem, need anything, Musa will get word to us. Chaudri Gujar Sahib wants to make your stay as pleasant as possible. Here are the keys to the Land Rover. Mr. Wu will visit you in the morning."

Bahadur was an enigma. On the one hand, he radiated a certain aura of menace—as if he dared anyone to challenge him. Mohammed and Musa avoided looking directly at him. On the other hand, Bahadur's English was quite good and his manner toward me infallibly polite.

Bahadur gestured toward the dusty Jeep that had followed us, then inclined his head toward me. "Mr. Radley, it has been a pleasure. I must now take my leave. Mohammed and Musa will care for your luggage and get you settled. I trust you have a good rest after your tiring flight."

"*Bahut mihrbani,*" I said. "Thank you very much for all your help."

After a burst of rapid Punjabi directed at M & M, he got into the Jeep and was driven off.

As soon as Musa had shown me around the bungalow, I pleaded fatigue, closed the door to my room, took a quick shower, and collapsed on the bed. That's all I remembered until I awoke hours later in a tangle of sheets.

Something had awakened me. Some sound? No, a nightmare. I had been screaming as a herd of black water buffaloes closed in on me. I broke free from the tightening circle and ran and ran through a labyrinth of narrow dusty streets until I could run no more.

I shivered as I stared at the high ceiling where a fan slowly circulated. Why a fan? Where was I...? Pakistan... in a canal bungalow. The light from the narrow ventilation window near the ceiling seemed subdued. A glance at my watch told me it was five-thirty in the morning. I'd slept through the night.

While I gazed around the room, I took deep breaths to calm my racing pulse. On the bedside table was an intricately decorated camel skin lamp. The room had shuttered windows, plaster walls tinted a pale green, and a concrete floor with a dusty rug. White streaks of flaky salt peter climbed the wall below the windows. A framed photo of Pakistan's founder, Mohammed Ali Jinnah, stared at me. To my right, near the washroom door, stood a tall wooden wardrobe, an *almiri*. Across the room, my laptop lay on the wooden desk beneath a shuttered window. A worn armchair rested nearby, next to my unopened suitcases.

My accommodation was ritzy compared to the tent I'd expected to occupy. I should have felt thankful and excited, but instead I felt... what did I feel? Uneasy? Worried? Scared? No, not scared! Perhaps frustrated that circumstances had forced me to take an assignment when all my instincts screamed against it. At least now I could stave off bankruptcy.

I rubbed my eyes and shook my head to clear it. *Come on, Josh, smarten up, you're a big boy. Stop whining.* Stephanie wouldn't be complaining—she'd be working, to keep us solvent.

Asian Archaeology's assignment even had the potential to launch me into the big time. Six articles on one of the most sensational archaeological discoveries of the century. With such a plum assignment, being back in Pakistan wasn't so bad, except...?

I flung off the sheet and padded over to a window. Throwing open the shutters, I stood there a few moments, breathing deeply of the cool air of early morning. In the bathroom, I rinsed the sleep from my eyes and took a swipe at my unruly hair. Back in the bedroom, I threw on a shirt, jeans, and a jacket.

I wanted to give Stephanie a call, but I couldn't see a phone.

In front of the bungalow, a couple of flowerbeds with woody roses and a few stunted geraniums bracketed the straggly lawn. The clink of pots drew me around to the back of the bungalow. When M number one, Mohammed, saw me come around the corner, he sprang up cradling a bowl of *chai* in his gnarled fingers. "*Salaam alay kum*, Sahib," he said.

"*Waalay kum as salaam*, Mohammed."

M number two, Musa, peered around the jamb of a door that led into what must have been the kitchen. "Good morning, *Sahib*. You sleep well?"

I yawned. "Too well."

"You be wanting cup of *chai*?"

"Do you have any coffee?" It seemed a bit early to face the local brew—tea leaves thrown in boiling water along with buffalo milk and raw sugar.

Musa shook his head. "No, Sahib. But I will purchase from bazaar today."

He looked so dejected to have failed in his first test as cook that I hastened to reassure him. "*Chai* will be wonderful."

"And I make you big breakfast. Omelette. *Prata*—fried buttered nan. Flench flies..."

I smiled and held up my hands in protest. "Whoa." I pointed to my watch. "One hour." I mimicked holding a phone to my ear. "Musa, is there a phone around?"

He shook his head. "Sorry, Sahib, no phone."

I should have known that this far from town and out on the edge of the desert there might not be a phone. These old canal bungalows had been built to accommodate travelling canal inspectors and officials when there were no other accommodations nearby. The occasional visitor didn't merit a permanent landline. What would I do for e-mail?

I rubbed my hands to ward off the chill of early morning. "Musa, could I have some of that tea?"

Cradling a bowl of *chai*, I returned to the front veranda, sat down on the steps, and let the warmth from Musa's potent brew work its magic. Birds flitted in and out of the trees. I recognized a parrot in the date palm opposite and a hoopoe bobbing up and down in one of the beds. Stephanie would love it here. I made a mental note to look in town for an Asian bird book so she could continue her hobby.

When I finished the tea, I set out to explore my surroundings. Climbing the bank to the canal road, I set off at a brisk pace. Steph would be impressed if I got in a good half-hour walk, or more, before breakfast. Not far from the canal bungalow, three men washed in the chocolate-coloured water of the canal. They stood and stared at me as I walked by. A half-mile further, two boys who couldn't have been more than eight or ten, splashed water on half a dozen water buffaloes. Like the men, they too stopped what they were doing to stare in my direction.

Before the end of the day, the news about the arrival of the *angreez*—the foreigner—would be telegraphed everywhere. I hoped it wouldn't inspire hordes of curious children to hound me on my walks.

On the far side of the canal, fields stretched to a line of sand dunes notching the horizon. On the near side—the inside of a long curve in the canal—stunted thorn trees dotted a huge patch of land rendered snow-white and useless by salts brought to the surface by the rise of the water table. The *whump, whump* of tube wells in the fields beyond the barren patch laid down a steady rhythm. The miracle of water in the desert had brought with it the problem of rising soil salinity, which led to plummeting productivity. The tube wells lowered the water table and flushed away some of the deadly salts.

A *milkwala* approached on a bicycle laden with three huge milk cans, one on each side of his back wheel, and another on a carrier in front. He raised one hand in greeting and almost wiped out as he passed. Obviously, I was going to become a local curiosity. Stephanie and Janice would find the stares intimidating.

Ten minutes farther on, at the junction of a single-lane paved road that crossed the canal, I came upon a village. The mud-walled compounds of Punjabi farmers made up the largest portion of the community. I caught a glimpse of the twin minarets of a mosque and heard the *tak, tak, tak* of a diesel engine—probably operating a water pump or flourmill. Three Punjabi women balancing water pots on their heads came into view from the general direction of what must have been the village square. How could they carry those pots without spilling water? Amazing. I was soon distracted by an unsettling wail coming from somewhere on the edge of the village.

The ululating keen emanated from a small collection of thatched mud huts with peaked roofs nestled within a protective wall of interlaced thorn branches. I recognized the compound as typical of Marwaris. From my elevated position on the canal road, I could make out a circle of several dozen men seated on mats under a huge baobab tree. At their head sat Raju, his swarthy face a mask riven by deep lines of grief. The howls of anguish seemed to come from within one of the thatched huts. Must be a death.

Uncomfortable about my intrusion on a family's grief, I turned back in the direction I'd come.

CHAPTER FOUR
Pattan Minara

B ack at the canal bungalow, I asked Musa, the cook, about
the grief I'd observed in the tribal village.

He shook his head. "At Dhera Mundi village? Very
much bad. Men kidnapped young woman."

"Was she Raju's daughter?"

His face furrowed. "Yes, his daughter... but how you know
Raju Moro?"

"I met him on the plane from Karachi."

Musa's eyes widened. "On plane? Where he get money?"

I could understand his puzzlement at someone from a very
poor tribe being able to afford an airline ticket. "I don't know. But
why would Raju's daughter be kidnapped?"

He wiped his hands on his apron. "She young, pretty. I hear
this. Fetch many rupees—dollars—in Gulf, even Europe."

"She'll be sold?"

He sighed. "She not alone. Many poor families lose daugh-
ters... and sons. Some sell children to get out of debt."

"That's terrible. Can't the police stop it?"

Musa snorted. "Police? Hah. Very corrupt. Earn big money."

I slumped into a chair while Musa kneaded whole wheat dough for breakfast *pratas*—thin, unleavened disks cooked with clarified butter. How would I feel if someone kidnapped my daughter? I thought about phoning Stephanie and telling her not to come. At least not to bring Janice. It looked like I would have to go back into town to contact them unless the area had wireless internet.

"More *chai*, Sahib?"

"What? Oh, yes, please."

"Is very much sad." Musa brought me a cup of *chai*. "I hear Raju's daughter was to be married soon."

"Can't Chaudri Sahib do something? I hear he has much *rasookh*—influence."

Musa's eyes darted toward the doorway. "Chaudri Gujar Mohammed is great man. Please, Mr. Josh Sahib, you not mention this conversation." He walked away quickly and busied himself whisking a bowl of eggs.

When I returned to the veranda with my bowl of *chai*, I found a short gnome of a woman sweeping the driveway with practiced gusto. The broom she used was constructed of a bundle of broom straw bound around a short handle with wire. Stray locks of gray hair peeked out from her *dupatta*. Lines creased her dark face. She seemed to have a permanent stoop from bending low to do her sweeping.

She'd probably finished the inside sweeping while I was on my walk. I wondered if I would ever feel comfortable about having so many servants. Stephanie would be aghast. Especially when she found out about the disdain with which the rest of society viewed sweepers. Pakistan pretended not to have a caste system, but it seemed almost as entrenched as in India. Like many of her kind, this woman would probably be a nominal Christian, a descendant of the mass movement to Christianity from among the Hindu outcastes of the Punjab during the nineteenth century.

As soon as she saw me, she stopped, tucked her broom under her arm, bowed to me, and let loose a torrent of speech, none of which I understood. I bowed in return and, indicating myself, said, "*Main Joshua hun.*"

From her reply, I gathered she was called Naomi.

I nodded and went back inside where I found Musa laying out breakfast. He brought in a spicy omelette and *pratas* plus sliced melon, oranges, and more *chai*.

The sight of all this food made me realize how hungry I was. I sat down and dug in. Partway through my omelette, I heard a vehicle approaching.

Musa went to investigate. He returned with a short Asian man wearing worn jeans and a plaid shirt. My visitor extended his hand. "Mr. Radley, I'm Lok Wu. We're delighted you've come."

I wiped my hands on a napkin and stood to shake his hand. "Great to see you. I'm looking forward to this assignment. Have you had breakfast?"

Mr. Wu threw his broad-brimmed hat on the table and settled into a chair. "Breakfast! That would be wonderful."

Musa came and poured Mr. Wu a cup of *chai*. I instructed Musa to prepare another omelette and more *prata*.

Mr. Wu looked young, too young to be the supervisor of such an important archaeological dig. Of course, the age of people from the Far East had always left me mystified. This man had to be in his mid-forties, about my age, and yet to my eyes he seemed to be in his twenties.

"I apologize," he said, "for coming at this early hour, but I was anxious to make up for my lamentable absence yesterday. We had a problem at the site."

"No need to apologize, Mr. Wu. Chaudri Sahib was most hospitable."

"Please, call me Luke. That's what my friends call me. So, will these accommodations be adequate?" He didn't give me time to respond, motoring on. "How was your trip? Is there anything you need?" He spoke perfect English, but at warp speed.

I laughed. "Yes, long, and yes."

"Sorry," he said. "Even my mother accuses me of talking too fast and not listening."

"The accommodations are much better than I expected. The only thing I'm missing is a phone."

"Ah, unfortunately, there is no regular phone service this far from town. But cell phones seem to work everywhere—at least for local calls. I'll get you one. And for emergencies, I have a satellite phone at the dig."

"What about internet?"

"You may be able to make a wireless connection, but it's very erratic. We get power outages all the time that seem to affect the service. Plus, this close to the Indian border the military may block service at any time—especially if they are planning manoeuvres."

At that point in our conversation, Musa brought Luke—Mr. Wu—an omelette and more *prata*. As we ate, Luke filled me in on events at the excavation.

"We've had a catastrophe."

"Catastrophe? Anyone hurt?"

He broke off chunks of *prata* and scooped up portions of his omelette. "Two workers killed. A trench we've been digging collapsed." He picked up his cup of *chai* and looked off into space. "Two of our best workers. Tragic."

"That's terrible. Shoring give way?"

He nodded. "Yeah, but I don't know how. I inspected it myself. I'm sure it was solid."

"Must be sandy soil out there. Hard to tunnel through."

"Away from the mound, it is sandy, but we were in the tell itself."

"The tell?"

"The debris mound. Quite solid. Even though there was little chance of a cave-in, we roofed the tunnel as we went." He frowned. "It's an ominous way to start a dig. The workers have gone on strike. We'll have to pay them more to return, but that's not the worst of it." He took another bite of omelette. "They say the cave-in was caused by *jinn*."

"Evil spirits?"

"Yeah. *Reasitis*—a local tribal group—claim that Pattan Minara is cursed. They allege that disaster has befallen everyone who tried to explore the mound. Fortunately, we have a Pakistani student from Oxford with us. She persuaded the workers that those old stories were just fables."

I pushed my empty plate away. "I did notice in the briefing material you gave me that a British archaeologist abandoned exploration here in the late 1800s. Does anyone know why?"

"Not exactly, but being an archaeologist in the 1800s was like letting a kid loose in a candy store. They had so many sites to pick from. If he didn't find anything valuable at Pattan Minara, he probably just left to make his name at one of the thousand or so other sites in India and Pakistan."

"So what can you do about persuading the workers to come back?"

He took a piece of melon. "I've given them three days off to grieve and offered a bonus for every week of work they complete. We won't have any problem getting more workers—there's too much poverty for that—but it's the loss of time. We'll need to train two more workers up to the skill level of those we lost. And we'd already unearthed some fantastic pieces. Potentially revolutionary."

I finished my omelette and took a sip of tea. "Pottery, that kind of thing?"

"Not just pottery, but seals and trade goods. So far the pieces are not as impressive as those unearthed at other sites, but they may give us the clue we need to interpret their language. Have you finished the background paper I sent you?"

"Not quite. I've absorbed the basic facts: that the Indus civilization rivalled cultures in Egypt, Mesopotamia, and China, that it thrived between 2600 and 1900 BC, the stuff about city layout—that kind of thing. But I'm stumbling over the technical language."

"That's why we need you," he said, "to translate our jargon so that the general public can get as excited as we are. In the days ahead, just ask me about any term you don't understand."

I laughed. "Like Early Bronze Age? Steatite beads?"

"All in good time. But why don't we drive out to the dig?"

When we got to his vehicle, he rummaged in the glove compartment until he found a cell phone. "Here, you can use this for calls within the country."

We drove about fifteen minutes down the canal road before turning east along a sandy track. Five or ten minutes later, the site came into view. Off to one side stood a row of tents, empty now with all the workers taking three days off. Beyond the tents, I could make out the single, stubby tower that rose from what looked like a rust-coloured ridge of sand dunes. From my childhood explorations, I knew they were not sand dunes at all, but miles of brick and terracotta debris—one of the lost cities of the Indus civilization.

Luke pointed ahead. "See that depression? That's the dry bed of the ancient Saraswati River. The mounds beyond it are what's left of the city."

I nodded. "I remember it from when I was a kid."

Luke turned toward me. "You were here as a child? How?"

"My father was a missionary in this district. We came here for picnics or when my dad visited one of the local Christian families."

"I wondered how you spoke Urdu so well. I heard you speaking to the cook, though I couldn't understand a word."

I smiled. "You mentioned the ancient Saraswati River. Do we know what happened to it—why it dried up?"

"That's another mystery. Probably a seismic convulsion changed the courses of the rivers in this area. Presto, we get the Cholistan Desert."

The Land Rover dipped as we drove down into the dry riverbed. "This is incredible; it's so wide," I said.

"At least two miles at this point."

"To think that we're driving in the bed of a river that had cities and farms up and down its length. I still find it hard to believe."

"The evidence proves it. The Saraswati River must have supported a huge population. Five hundred sites have been identified along its banks and others along the Indus."

I leaned forward in the seat. "I can't wait to see what you've found."

Luke jabbed me on the shoulder. "Now that's the kind of excitement we want you to convey to our readers."

Halfway across the riverbed, we came to a barbed wire fence with a gate manned by a guard holding a walkie-talkie. He saluted Luke, opened the gate, and waved us through. The fence extended out of sight to the north down the middle of the riverbed. To the south, it climbed the debris mound near the ruined tower that gave Pattan Minara its name, separating it from the mud walls of a Punjabi farm compound that encroached on the site.

I pointed. "Do those farmers have permission to build on the site?"

Luke screwed up his face in a grimace. "No, but there's nothing we can do about it. A big landlord owns that compound and he has influence with the District Commissioner. It took us five years to negotiate an agreement with the government to excavate here, and another two years to get them to agree to a fence around the site. You would understand better than I do the power of *zar, zamin,* and... I forget the other z."

"*Zan*—women; gold, land, and women." I looked around. "Where are your student interns?"

"They're using the opportunity to visit Mohenjo Daro, the Indus site near Karachi." Luke parked, jumped out, and beckoned me to follow. "Let me show you what we've found. We've already excavated a couple of city streets and the foundations of the wall along the river."

Luke strode ahead on the remnants of a mud brick wall that must have been fifteen or twenty feet wide.

I adjusted my floppy hat to shade my face from the sun. "I thought they didn't have many enemies. Why such massive walls?"

"To protect against floods. The river was unpredictable."

"So their main enemy was the river?"

"That's right. And it's the same at all the Indus sites. There's no evidence of warfare. Everything points to a thousand years of peace." He turned toward an extensive excavation that revealed the remnants of walls of burnt brick on either side of what looked like a street. "We've already uncovered one of the main avenues and eight or ten houses. The streets seem to be laid out in a grid roughly following the four points of the compass. We found a treasure trove of objects in one of the houses—probably a house belonging to a merchant."

I pointed to a line of burnt brick along the side of the cleared roadway. "Is that a covered drain?"

"Exactly, just like those discovered at other sites."

I knelt down to get a closer look. "This is incredible; just like your briefing paper described. More advanced than the drainage systems in most of the towns around here today." I got up and looked around. "And a thousand years of peace. No wonder this culture rivalled those in Egypt and Mesopotamia."

"Well, I wouldn't say rivalled," said Luke. "It was larger in extent and probably population than either of those. Indus sites have been discovered in Afghanistan, the mountainous areas of

Northern Pakistan, and India. But since it didn't leave the massive monuments we see in Egypt and Iraq, it doesn't appear as impressive."

We climbed out of the excavation onto the debris mound. Beneath my feet, and as far as I could see, the mound was covered with broken shards of terracotta pottery and brick fragments. I could feel sweat trickling down my back. I pulled out a handkerchief to mop it up. It came away streaked with dirt.

Luke noticed my discomfort. "Two things we can't escape out here: sun and sand. I'll show you the site more thoroughly later. For now, let me show you some of what we've found."

We clambered down off the mound and walked toward a series of brick sheds. He paused in front of the largest, extracted a key from his pocket, and unlocked a steel door. In the dim light, I could make out a long worktable and racks of shelves, most of them empty.

Luke lit a lantern and hung it from a hook. It threw light on carefully numbered objects filling several shelves. The shards didn't look very impressive, but Luke almost danced with excitement as he pointed from one to the other.

"We believe this cube is a weight used by merchants. These are carnelian and agate beads... and these terracotta models of a dog and a boat. A shell ladle. Terracotta bangles. Look at this: an almost perfect pot with a gazelle design on the side... and these, you've got to see these."

Luke fell silent as he knelt down and began to search around the floor below the shelf. "Impossible!"

"What is it?"

"The elephant seal and the tablet. Gone!"

CHAPTER FIVE
Padri Fazal's Request

L uke searched the shed. He looked under every rack of shelves and sorted through the shards on the workbench. Then he collapsed on a chair in front of it.

"They were very important?" I said.

"Important?" Luke began to curse.

He threw a fragment of pottery against the wall and began to pace up and down. "Those two objects were the most important artefacts we've discovered. The tablet came from the merchant's house and had what appeared to be symbols in both the Indus script and Sumerian."

I remained silent.

"Archaeologists have discovered some 3700 objects inscribed with the Indus text, but no one has been able to decipher it. The tablet we found was the first one with a parallel text in a known language." He stopped pacing and took a deep breath. "It could have been our very own Indus Rosetta Stone."

He picked up a clay tablet and held it out to me. "See, this one is covered with Indus symbols. The missing one had parallel lines of hieroglyphics that I'm sure were from Sumer in the Euphrates River area. It makes sense that merchants trading between Mesopotamia and here would record transactions in both languages."

I pointed to one of the symbols on the tablet. "This looks like a fish."

"Yes, a fish, but what about all the others? We have nothing to compare them with."

"Do you have a photograph of the tablet?"

"Yes, at least we have that." Luke squeezed the bridge of his nose as if a headache was coming on. "But without the actual object, scholars will tend to doubt the authenticity. Photos can be faked."

He got up and went to the door, punching it with his fist as he went out. "Look. I'm going to leave you to wander around the site while I talk to the guards. See if I can get to the bottom of this."

Luke locked the door and strode away toward the guard post at the gate.

I spent the rest of the morning wandering along the dry riverbed, climbing the debris mound, and exploring the trenches. A dust devil danced around me, flinging grit in my eyes. I wet a corner of my bandana from my water bottle and tried to clean out the grit, but only succeeded in making the irritation worse.

With the workers gone, silence hung over the buried city. I could almost see boats plying the river, smell the smoke from kilns used to bake brick, hear artisans hammering copper into knives, and merchants selling their wares. But I had no idea what the ancient people might have been saying. Did their language sound like one of the old languages of India? Would we ever find out? It would be tragic if Luke couldn't recover the lost tablet or find others like it.

At noon, Luke found me and offered to drive me back to the canal bungalow. "How'd it go?" I asked. "Were the guards able to narrow down the time of the theft?"

He slammed the door as he clambered behind the wheel. "No. Both of those on duty swear on their grandfather's grave that they were awake all night. They assured me no one has entered the shed since the day of the cave-in."

"When was the tablet discovered?"

"Just three days ago."

The drive passed in silence. Luke seemed lost in his thoughts. Occasionally he ground his teeth. When we arrived at the canal bungalow, he turned to me. "This is a real blow. But we press on. I'll see you in the morning. Can you find your way now?"

"You bet. Maybe you'll find another Rosetta Stone."

He slumped over the wheel. "Yeah, and after that we'll find the Ark of the Covenant."

With a wave, he drove away.

I spent most of the afternoon settling in, working through two research papers Luke had given me and trying to connect to the internet. Partway through the afternoon, the electricity went off, so I gave up, not wanting to run down my laptop battery.

After a meal of curried chicken and *chapaties*—flat, round, unleavened wheat bread—I went for a long walk along the canal road in the opposite direction I'd taken in the morning.

I was glad to see the canal and the fields beyond free of human activity. Farmers had returned to their compounds for the evening meal. I couldn't see a single water buffalo soaking in the canal. Except for a tractor pulling a trailer overloaded with sugarcane, the road was empty. So peaceful.

I pinched myself and smiled. Here I was at the very site that had fascinated me as a boy, while five thousand years of history peeled back like layers of an onion. Most writers would have given anything to be in my place.

Perhaps being back in Pakistan would work out for the best. Musa's curry made me realize how much I'd missed its cuisine. And the countryside. I gazed toward the horizon. There was something serene about being set down in farm country a thousand miles from the nearest skyscraper. Instead of the din of traffic, I heard the occasional bleat of a lamb and the distant *tuk, tuk* of a diesel engine powering a tube well.

True, something was amiss at the dig. Two dead in a cave-in and now the theft of a key artefact. Coincidence? The farm compound at the end of the mound, built so close to the standing tower, looked suspicious. I wondered if Luke had checked for rubble piled outside the compound's surrounding wall. People after artefacts could easily have dug into the mound from inside those walls.

Two or three miles along the canal, an acrid, sulphurous smell hit me. A brick kiln sprawled beside the canal at a crossroad. People were still at work in spite of the late hour. The oval hump, about fifteen feet high and half a football field in length, belched black smoke. On top of the pile, a man shovelled coal through a hole to replenish the smouldering fires within.

Three or four men slogged back and forth in mud up to their knees. I looked again. They weren't men, just children of maybe ten or twelve. Their shoulders slumped as if they could hardly force themselves through the slurry. A supervisor in starched, white *shalwar-qamiz* shouted at them to pick up the pace and pointed to areas where the pond of goo needed more mixing.

On a level patch beside the pond, five or six more children bent to their work. Using their hands, they rhythmically plopped mud into wooden forms, wiped off the excess, and laid the newly formed raw bricks in even rows. Their handiwork would dry in the sun and then, after the kiln was emptied of its current batch, these would be stacked in their place and fired.

I frowned as I turned back the way I'd come. No laws here against child labour—or were the laws just ignored? Two or three were girls who kept fussing with their long *dupattas*—gauzy scarves—lest they seem immodest. So much for my ramblings about a pastoral paradise.

As I walked back, I wondered if Pakistani commerce would grind to a halt without its infusion of child labour. How many farmers sent their children to school? Was there even a school nearby for them to attend? I knew that a host of employers, including weavers, tanners, and even butchers, used children. Of course, so did a lot of family businesses, even in the West.

The growl of an approaching motorcycle interrupted my reverie. I stepped off the road and turned to watch it, but instead of going by, it stopped in front of me. The grizzled driver wore dark sunglasses, a western style short-sleeved shirt, and chocolate brown pants. On the pillion seat sat Raju, holding onto the motorcycle with one hand and his turban with the other.

The driver turned to me and smiled. "Mr. Radley, Sahib?"

I paused before answering, wondering how to respond if they appealed for money or help in getting a visa to America. "Yes," I said. "But I'm afraid I have not met you. Mr. Raju Sahib, I know." I bowed toward Raju and he folded his hands together and reciprocated.

The driver engaged the kickstand and got down from the motorcycle. *Uh-oh, what next?* But he extended his hand and said, "Joshua, Sahib. You don't remember me? I am Padri Fazal Masih. As a child, you often played with our son, Yunis."

I stared at him with my mouth open. A thick thatch of snow-white hair crowned his head, but—yes—he did look like Padri Fazal. I reached out for his hand as I stuttered, "Padri Sahib? How... where...?"

He pumped my hand and roared with laughter. Who could forget that great belly-shaking laugh? After pushing the motorcycle to the side of the road and parking it, he came over and smothered me in a crushing embrace, which I tried to reciprocate. He stood back with his hands on my shoulders and shook his head from side to side. Using the Urdu idiom, he exclaimed, "Seeing you is like seeing the Eid moon."

I staggered a little as I tried to ease the kink his embrace had left in my back. "And you... and seeing you... here."

Raju leaned against the truck of a nearby tree.

Padri Fazal's dark eyes probed mine. "How is your father?"

"*Teak hai*—Okay," I said. "He has a heart condition, but it's under control."

He nodded his head. "We all grow older. The doctor wants me to avoid salt and fat." He laughed as if that was a joke, then his eyes moistened and he looked away. "Ah, your father was a dear brother. We had wonderful times together. And your mother? Is she well?"

"Yes, she is also *teak hai*." Memories of my childhood rushed back. "But tell me about Yunis. How is he?"

I thought back to the old house in Nowshera where I'd grown up. Yunis and I had been collaborators in mischief: stealing mangoes from the neighbour's yard—only to get sick; liberating a donkey and riding it through town; conning a shopkeeper to give us candy out of fear that the Sahib would stop buying there. The children of missionaries and pastors were supposed to be good examples, not little rebels. Not that I didn't love my parents; I did—and respected them. I'd respected Padri Fazal, too. In fact, as a kid I'd been a little afraid of him and his thunderous preaching. I remembered once being sure that the earth would swallow me up and deposit me into the fires of hell.

"Yunis is married with four children," said Padri Fazal. "He works in a Karachi bank."

He went on to tell me about the rest of his children, but didn't mention his wife, so I asked, "How is *Yunis ki Ammi*—Yunis' mother?"

A cloud came over his face and he looked away. "She died last year. Diabetes."

"Oh, I'm sorry." I scuffed at the dirt on the road. "Why don't you and Raju come and have a cup of tea? I'm in the canal bungalow down the road."

Padri Fazal nodded his head. "Good. We were hoping to talk to you."

Back at the bungalow, I motioned them toward a couple of chairs on the veranda and asked Musa to make us some *chai*. I told Padri Fazal about my parents, showed him pictures of Stephanie and our two kids, and learned more about his family. As Padri Fazal and I caught up on family news, I smiled at Raju as a way to include him in the conversation. Did he understand much of what I was saying? I finally turned to him and said in Urdu, "I'm very sorry to hear about your daughter."

He glanced at Padri Fazal, looked down at the floor, and in clear Urdu said, "Thank you, Sahib."

Musa served tea. When he left, Fazal turned to me. "We want to talk to you about the kidnapping of Raju's daughter. We hope you can help."

"I'm delighted to see you, but I don't know what—"

Padri Fazal reached over and touched my arm. "I believe Chaudri Gujar Mohammed met you at the airport and entertained you in his home."

I wondered how they knew so much about my movements when I'd only just arrived. True, I'd seen Raju on Chaudri's veranda, so I replied, "Didn't Raju already request his help?"

Padri Fazal's face screwed up in anger. "Hah! He had his *goondas*—thugs—send Raju and his friends away without even listening to them." He took a deep breath. "Joshua Sahib, please let me explain. Chaudri Sahib chairs the local branch of what I believe they call the Preservation Committee. His committee supervises the excavation of Pattan Minara, where we've heard you will be working. As a foreigner, you have *rasookh* with the Chaudri Sahib. Nothing can be accomplished without influence."

I took a sip of tea. "I doubt if I have any influence, but even if I did, what good would that do?"

Raju and Fazal exchanged looks. "Chaudri Gujar Mohammed," said Fazal, "owns flour mills, most of the area brick kilns, chicken farms, a fleet of trucks, the cinema in town, and more land than anyone else. He's a member of the Provincial Parliament and a personal friend of the Sheikh of Abu Dubai."

"Yes, I've heard he's very powerful."

Fazal looked around to make sure Musa was not listening. "And very corrupt, but don't tell anyone I said so... although everyone knows."

I frowned at Fazal. "Corrupt? The people at the airport seemed to like him."

"Many do. He throws a lot of money around. He endowed the college and built the new library. He pays for *madrassas* that train Muslim *maulvis*. But where does the money come from?"

Raju's expressive eyes flashed fire as he broke out in a mixture of Urdu and English. "Cheats his sharecroppers, exports drugs, steals land, and..." He turned away. "Kidnaps *bacce*—children."

I poured them more *chai*. "If this is true, why don't the police arrest him?"

Padri Fazal let out a grim laugh. "The Superintendent of Police,"—He looked around again—"is in his pocket. He is protected; no one can touch him. Chaudri Sahib even appointed one of the most important district judges."

"But surely—"

Fazal interrupted. "When two police deputies started an investigation three years ago, they disappeared."

Child labour didn't surprise me. I'd seen it all around me as I grew up, forcing people ensnared in debt to indenture their children to work in a brick kiln, or knot rugs, or labour in a factory. But kidnapping children? Girls? "Do you have any kind of proof?"

Fazal turned to Raju, who answered. "My son ran after the Toyota Land Cruiser they used. He is sure it was one of Chaudri Gujar's vehicles, the one with the damaged back bumper."

Fazal reached over and touched my arm. "Sahib, thousands of children go missing every year. Especially from minority groups whose families are poor. Some end up working in brick kilns or illegal factories. Some are sold into slavery in Saudi Arabia or one of the Gulf States. Still others become prostitutes in Europe or America." He looked at Raju. "Raju's daughter was to be married. You could appeal to Chaudri for mercy in this one case. Raju will pay two hundred thousand rupees for her safe return."

I caught my breath. "Isn't that half a year's wages?" The thought of Raju's daughter in the hands of thugs sickened me. Could I march up to Chaudri's house and demand justice? I hardly knew him. This could jeopardize my whole assignment, and maybe even get my visa revoked. Yet how could I refuse to help? What if it had been my Janice? I looked from Raju to Padri Fazal, and back to Raju. "Can you come back in the morning? I'll think about it tonight and let you know."

Raju put his head in his hands and stared at the floor. How many times had he heard that kind of answer?

Fazal put his hands on my shoulders, stared into my eyes. My gaze went to the cross hanging around his neck. "Joshua, Sahib," he said. "We need your help urgently. The longer we wait, the less chance we have of finding Chandi."

I forced myself to look into his eyes. "Okay, I'll talk to Chaudri."

Fazal squeezed my shoulder. "I knew you'd help. You're just like your father."

Raju came over, touched my knees, and bowed. "*Mihrbani*, Sahib. Thank you, very, very much."

CHAPTER SIX
Human Trafficking

After Padri Fazal and Raju left, I paced the veranda. Why did Fazal have to bring up my father and his blasted compassion? I wasn't my father. I was pragmatic, hard-nosed, and not even a good Christian. Sure, I had feelings for the downtrodden. I had done stories for the Toronto Post on the victims of family violence, drunk drivers, and... lots of stuff. You had to have some sense of outrage to be a good journalist. But...

Had I become a hack, motivated more by a desire to further my career than really help people? I shook my head to banish the memory of an argument with Stephanie over why I didn't write more about the oppressed.

Okay, maybe it was the voice of conscience. Maybe it was the influence of Stephanie. Or maybe it was the effect of my father. I couldn't sort it out, but I'd try to get Chaudri Gujar Sahib to help. He could use his connections. No way was he involved. One of his men must have used his vehicle. Or was I being naïve?

I strode inside, picked up the cell phone Luke had given me, extracted Chaudri's card from my wallet, and punched in his number. On the fourth ring, I heard, "*Salaam, Gujar Mohammed bol-ra-hun.*"

"*Salaam alay kum*, Chaudri Sahib. I apologize for calling in the evening."

"Mr. Radley. No problem. You are welcome to call at any time."

"Could I take a few moments of your time around eight o'clock... or nine... whatever time is convenient in the morning?"

"Certainly. Why don't you come at seven-thirty and have a bite of breakfast?"

"Oh, I don't want to intrude on your family."

"No intrusion. Seven-thirty then?"

"Okay."

"Wonderful. You can give me your first impressions of the archaeological dig. By the way, what did you want to talk to me about?"

I paused before answering. "I'd prefer to tell you in the morning."

I breathed a sigh when I put the phone down. No harm could come from asking for Chaudri Gujar's help. But then why did I feel so jittery? Must have been too much tea. I'd have to limit my intake.

I picked up the background paper Luke had given me on the Indus civilization and sat down to make notes. After ten or fifteen minutes rereading pages, I gave up. My mind refused to focus on anything but Raju's daughter.

I booted my laptop and had it search again for a wireless internet connection. Success! First, I retrieved my e-mails.

Among the spam were two from Stephanie and one from our son Jonathan.

Jonathan wrote about how jealous he was that his mom and sister were getting to go to Pakistan. The first one from Steph provided her flight details and gushed about how excited she and Janice were. The second one sent a quiver of alarm through my system.

> *Dear Josh,*
>
> *I miss you tons and can't wait to get there.*
>
> *Unfortunately, when I come we're going to have to go over our finances again. I've had to deal with two problems with Eagle's Eye that suddenly arose. Why couldn't these things have happened while you were here? The water pump packed it in. I had to get it taken care of. And the insurance company sent an inspector. He took one look at the woodstove and said the chimney had to be upgraded to meet current code—whatever that means. Without the upgrade, the insurance company won't renew the policy. Since we couldn't leave the house without insurance while we were away, I had to call in a workman to install a new insulated chimney.*
>
> *The repairs leave us with no wiggle room.*
>
> *Anyway, we'll talk about it when I get there.*
>
> *Lots of love. See you soon.*
>
> *STEPH*

I fired off a reply expressing concern over the bills, giving a general description about the weather, the beauty of the roses in Chaudri's garden, the canal bungalow, and how exciting things were at the archaeological site. I briefly mentioned the kidnapping of Chandi, but didn't give them any details for fear I'd have them worrying unnecessarily. Besides, I was concerned about electronic eavesdropping.

Still restless, I began an internet search for articles on the modern slave trade. My jaw dropped. 1,850,000 hits. Many sources, including the UN, estimated there were twenty-seven million slaves worldwide, bought and sold at an average price of a hundred bucks. Unbelievable, more than the number of slaves seized from Africa in four centuries! Russian women sold to brothels in Europe. Children locked in musty hovels and forced to weave carpets in India. The stories staggered me.

Haitians forced to work in Dominican sugar fields. Three hundred thousand Japanese sex tourists a year visiting the brothels in the Philippines, where this trade had become the country's fourth largest source of GNP. According to the U.S. State Department, up to ninety thousand blacks were owned by North African Arabs, and often sold for as little as fifteen dollars apiece.

The more I read, the queasier I got. I opened the jar of instant coffee that Musa had bought and made myself a mug.

I grimaced at the taste of instant coffee whitened with powdered milk. Yuck. I should have had Stephanie bring some ground coffee. I set down the mug as a thought struck me. Had the hands that picked the beans for this coffee been those of a slave? I returned to the internet.

One article described Sri Lankan women traveling to Lebanon believing they were being offered jobs. They ended up hungry, imprisoned, abused, and raped. Another told of Indonesian maids enslaved in Malaysia.

What about Pakistan? I quickly discovered an article on bonded labourers in Sindh Province. Some were shackled in leg irons lest they flee. Often small debts were the pretext used to force them to labour in cane fields.

Next I spotted an article on brick factories. The story described the freeing of seventy-eight people, whole families, who had been held as slaves at a kiln in India. My thoughts went to the children I'd seen labouring in the hot sun not five miles from where I sat.

I learned that Canada was not immune. Every day, Canadian customs discovered six or seven slaves being transported across the border, usually in shipping containers.

I reached for my coffee, but it was cold. Would Chandi end up in some brothel in Karachi? From what I was learning about slavery, more likely it would be Dubai or Saudi Arabia.

I needed some ammunition to use in talking to Chaudri Gujar, so I set up my portable printer and ran off two of the most horrific stories.

The disturbing information kept me restless, unable to sleep until well after midnight. When I did sleep, I had troubling dreams—different from my usual nightmares. I was stiff when I woke up, although a rushed shower helped somewhat. I arrived a few minutes late at Chaudri's house. The drive in the unfamiliar Land Rover had taken longer than I thought.

"Good morning, Mr. Radley," Chaudri said as he strode toward me from the direction of the rose garden.

I greeted him with an apology. He shifted the bouquet of roses he held to his left hand and clapped me on the back. "Late? Come, come, the guest is never late." He laughed that deep-seated laugh I remembered and gestured toward the house.

Over a breakfast table laden with an enormous array, we chatted about a variety of topics. Finally, he turned to me. "You had something you wanted to ask me?"

I pushed away from the table. "I'm sure you've heard about the kidnapping from the village near the canal bungalow?"

He nodded his head. "Yes, such a lamentable affair. Very sad."

"Apparently, the young woman was to be married quite soon."

He frowned. "I had not heard that. How do you know?"

I paused, wondering how much I should say. "Padri Fazal—do you know Padri Fazal? He brought the woman's father to see me last night."

"Yes, I know Padri Fazal—good man—but how do you know him?"

"Well... you see, I knew his family years ago. My father worked with him." I paused again, wondering why I was so hesitant to acknowledge my father's ministry to this staunch Muslim land-owner. "My father taught Christians, set up schools and clinics. He was a missionary."

Chaudri arched his eyebrows. "Oh, I see. That's why you know some Urdu."

"Yes, I remember some of what I learned as a child."

"Do you understand Punjabi, too?"

"I played with Punjabi children as a child, so I absorbed the language, but I seem to have forgotten everything I knew. That was over thirty years ago."

Chaudri narrowed his eyes as he looked at me. Was he re-membering his phone conversation in Punjabi on the way from the airport—wondering if I had understood? I began peeling an orange. Why did he seem to be more interested in what I knew and whom I knew than in the kidnapped girl?

"Amazing," he said. "Luke Wu picked the ideal man for this job."

I put down my orange and smiled. "I'll do my best. Anyway, about Padri Fazal. He brought Mr. Raju to see me last night and appealed for my help. But what can I do? So I thought of coming to you."

"What can I or anyone do to catch these miscreants?" He rubbed his forehead. "These *budkar*, criminals, run circles around the police: outgun them, outsmart them. Too much money to be made and too many poor people to exploit. I should know, I'm the District Representative on the Human Rights Commission of Pakistan. The Commission gets complaints every day and not one in twenty can be resolved. With terrorism the main threat, the Commission has few resources to pursue their domestic agenda."

I savoured a segment of orange. This guy seemed to be every-where. Was he sincere... or was he like most others of his class? I wondered if I should mention the children I'd seen working at the brick kiln near the canal bungalow. Better not. Instead I said, "Chaudri Sahib, perhaps you could use your influence to inquire, get the word out and..."

He interrupted me. "Joshua Sahib, you overestimate my influ-ence. These kinds of villains operate in a dark underworld invisi-ble to the rest of us. Coming from the West, you should under-stand. In spite of billions of dollars and years of effort, neither the U.S. nor Canada—nor Europe, for that matter—have been able to stem the flow of drugs and prostitutes and illegal weapons. How can what your people call a third-world country be expected to do what the G-8 cannot?" He sat back and laughed. "Excuse me, that was a bit of a rant."

"No, you're right about Western problems and hypocrisy." I grimaced. "I just thought I'd ask. Mr. Raju is so concerned he has offered a two hundred thousand rupee reward for his daughter's return. No questions asked."

Chaudri arched his eyebrows. "Two hundred thousand rupees. Where would Raju get that kind of money?"

"I don't know. Money lender, I guess."

"If he pays, he'll never get out of debt. Such a sad, sad busi-ness. You say she was engaged?"

"Yes," I said. "To be married within the month."

"All we can do is try. I'll get the word to our labourers. Per-haps they have heard something or can pass the news about a re-ward around. Tell Raju Moro I'll do my best. Now, can I get you any more *chai*, *prata*, anything?"

"No, thank you." I held my hand up to my eyes. "I'm stuffed up to here. Your hospitality is so gracious that I feel like I won't have to eat again for a week."

"Nothing. It is nothing!"

I'd decided not to give him the printouts on slavery. Chaudri walked me to my vehicle. As I went to get in, I noticed two heavily loaded trucks parked on the far side of his U-shaped driveway. Four men from the North-West Frontier, identified by their dress, lounged in the shade cast by their vehicles. They must have been the drivers and their *cleaners*—glorified labourers who catered to every whim of those who drove. They were all smoking *bidis*— hand-rolled cigarettes. Mud and dust from the journey couldn't obscure the bright scenes painted onto the woodwork of the paneled trucks' bodies. A depiction of the winding road leading through the Khyber Pass, gateway into Afghanistan, decorated one truck, while a scene of mountains and lakes adorned the other. I'd forgotten my childhood fascination with this brand of Pakistani pop art. On long trips, truck art had provided a welcome diversion from miles of gray desert.

I pointed. "I love the way Pakistani trucks are decorated."

Chaudri didn't seem to share my enthusiasm. He shouted something at them in what must have been Pashtu and pointed behind the house. Then he turned back toward me and said, "Very garish, not good art."

"Bright and cheerful, though," I said. "Thank you again, Chaudri Sahib, for your hospitality and willingness to help find Raju's daughter."

As I drove away, I eyed the vehicles in my rear-view mirror. They were piled high with huge bundles sown shut with burlap. Must be some merchandise from the North-West Frontier. But what could Chaudri possibly do with anything imported from the frontier—unless it came from beyond the border?

All the way back to the canal bungalow, I pondered the complicated persona that Chaudri Gujar Mohammed projected. What had the trucks been carrying? Rugs? Wool? Drugs? Was he the epitome of evil, as claimed by Padri Fazal and Raju? I could understand their point of view. Those who struggled with poverty and injustice all their lives found it easy to blame their troubles on the rich and powerful. And they could be right. My dad had trusted Padri Fazal's judgement. But Chaudri seemed such a nice guy. Urbane. Hospitable. Sophisticated. How could he have any connection to the disappearance of Raju's daughter? And yet there was the matter of the vehicle Raju's son had seen speeding away from the kidnapping. What about the mention of opium I'd overheard?

I felt uneasy, but what more could I do?

CHAPTER SEVEN
Cave-In

After leaving Chaudri, I drove to the dig. With the workers back from their strike, the mound looked like an anthill that had been poked by a giant.

As soon as I arrived at the gate, I could tell that security had been tightened. Poles topped with floodlights had been installed at intervals around the site. A guard at the gate waved me to a stop and handed me a clipboard to sign. After signing, I drove to the shed Luke used as his field office, parked, and went inside. I found him leaning over a light table looking at some rough sketches.

He looked up. "Good morning, Joshua. Have you caught up on your sleep?"

"I'm getting there." I didn't want to tell him I'd stayed up late researching the modern slave trade. He had enough to worry about. "Any leads on the missing artefacts?"

He sighed. "Nothing, though I have a feeling some of the men know more than they're saying."

"What are you going to do?"

"I've limited access to this building and installed floodlights and motion sensors linked to an alarm in my tent. And since it's the Chinese government that's sponsoring this dig, I've also requested Chinese guards."

"I'll be surprised if Pakistan grants permission for Chinese guards."

"Well, they haven't yet. But allowing a few guards is a small thing. Think about it. With nuclear-powered India always a threat on Pakistan's eastern border, and Afghanistan in turmoil on the west, it makes sense for Pakistan to cultivate China's help."

I nodded. "Both have a stake in preventing the spread of Islamist terrorism."

"Exactly. The disorder in Tibet may encourage agitation among Muslims in China's western provinces."

"Pakistan and China make natural allies."

Luke shrugged. "Normally I wouldn't give a thought to all this geopolitical wheeling and dealing. I'm just an archaeologist. But if a little politics helps us do our job, then so be it." He turned back to the light table. "Give me a few minutes to plot a position on this street grid, then I'll meet you up at the main excavation."

I left the office, climbed onto the mud brick dike that had been cleared, and paused to watch the giant anthill up close. A stream of labourers—both men and women—trotted back and forth between the various trenches cut into the mound and a growing pile of discarded debris in the dry riverbed. Their darker complexion and the burgundy colour of the women's clothing flagged them as tribal. Probably from one of the non-Muslim desert tribes. These women not only exposed their faces, but also flaunted an abundance of silver jewellery. Their conduct seemed strange in a Muslim country.

There were no signs of automation, not even a wheelbarrow. Workers carried debris in shallow baskets, woven from willow baskets they balanced on their heads. The seemingly effortless way the tribal women sashayed back and forth over the surface of the mound had me shaking my head in amazement.

I followed one file of labourers to a deep gash cut in the mound. The sloping trench—seven or eight feet deep at the far end—exposed what Luke had told me was one of the main streets of the ancient city. A blue plastic tarpaulin shaded that part of the dig where workers continued to burrow into the mound. Their excavation had unearthed rough brick walls on either side of an exposed roadway. Doorways, some cleared, some still choked with debris, punctuated the wall at intervals.

Beneath the tarp, a young woman, dressed in a loose cotton shirt and jeans with her dark hair peeking out from beneath a scarf, worked in front of a screen. She appeared to be sifting through shards brought from the face of the dig. I took her to be one of the archaeology students employed to help with the detail work. From time to time, she picked up a fragment, brushed it clean, and examined it closely. Some she placed carefully in a shallow box beside her; others she tossed onto a pile of discards. Two young men, covered in reddish dust, worked beyond her at the face of the trench.

"I see you've found our A-team," said a voice behind me. I turned to see that Luke had joined us. "Guys, this is Joshua Radley. He's going to write up our discoveries." He gestured toward the young woman. "Josh, this is Parveen, our Ph.D. student from Oxford." She extended her hand to me, but I hesitated a moment before reciprocating. Men didn't shake hands with women in this culture.

She laughed. "Some of us are quite liberated."

Luke pointed to the two men. "And those two dust-covered devils are Scott and Darren, both students from my alma mater, Penn State."

Scott grinned. "You've already met our slave driver then."

Seizing this opportunity to take a break, several of the tribal men who had been clearing discarded debris pulled out *bidis* and lit up. After we'd chatted a bit about our respective backgrounds, Luke turned to go. "Carry on. I'm going to show Mr. Radley the rest of the site."

I followed Luke out of the trench back onto the surface of the mound. He pointed out several other trenches being dug at intervals. "By digging trenches on the mound, we can plot the direction of the original streets and establish a rough map of the city. I was plotting coordinates on a map of the mound when you arrived. We hope to find clues to the location of public buildings, temples, granaries, that kind of thing."

I indicated the brick tower that gave the site its name, Pattan Minara. It was the only feature that rose above the surface of the mound. "How does the existing tower fit into the city scheme?"

"It doesn't. It was built much later over the ruins of the earlier city. Even so, we don't want to damage it. We're positive it's all that's left of one of the oldest Hindu temples in existence, comparable in age to the Durga Temples in India."

I wiped my face with a bandana I'd taken to carrying. "What about that trench leading to the tower?"

"We think the tower stands over some of the most important ruins. So we have to tunnel beneath it." Luke sighed and looked away. "That's where two workers died. We're repairing the shoring to make it doubly safe."

Luke spent the next hour introducing me to the men he had supervising the excavation of each of the trenches. Then he turned me loose. "Josh, I want you to become familiar with every aspect of the dig. Spend time getting acquainted with the techniques involved. Ask me about anything you don't understand. Take as many pictures as you like. We'll call you if we make a major find. In that case, I want pictures showing the whole process of discovery, including cleaning the artefacts."

"What's the deadline on the first article?"

"A week from Wednesday," he said. "That means I need to see your draft on the Monday of that week, so we can get it off to the magazine in time."

"Do you have a theme in mind?"

He turned over a shard with the toe of his shoe. "I thought we'd leave that to you. We want a fresh approach, something that will appeal to the general reader."

Suddenly, a rumble followed by wild shouts interrupted us. I turned toward the sound and saw an enormous cloud of dust rising from the trench leading to the tower and completely obscuring it.

"Oh, no," shouted Luke as he ran toward the scene.

I ran after him past labourers who had laid down their baskets to gaze at the billowing cloud. Five or six figures staggered out of the trench coughing and spitting. Their *shalwar-qamizes* were streaked with dirt and dust. All of them collapsed on the ground. I saw that one was a tribal woman. Her hair was caked with dirt and her *dupatta* was missing. An unpleasant, mouldy stench hung over the scene.

Luke gestured toward the nearest cluster of water pots. "Quick. Water."

While a couple of labourers ran to fetch water, Luke spoke into his walkie-talkie, requesting a guard to bring up the van carrying the first aid supplies. Then he turned to me. "Josh, can you ask them what happened?"

I spoke to the nearest man. "*Kya hua?*"

He answered with a garbled stream of words that didn't make any sense to me. I folded my hands in appeal and said, "Please slow down and speak in Urdu."

His eyes wild, he glanced over his shoulder toward the trench. "*Jin*, Sahib." He shuddered. "*Jin*."

All of them began to talk and gesture at once. I translated as best I could. "They say evil spirits are angry about the excavation.

That this is a very bad place. Haunted. They were clearing debris when suddenly, with a loud boom, evil spirits rose through the floor, grabbed three of their women, and dragged them down into the bowels of hell. These men say the demons grabbed at all of them, but they managed to escape."

Luke waved at the men bringing water, urging them to hurry. "You say, three women? What's holding up that truck? We've got to get in there fast."

The three student archaeologists ran up just as the water arrived.

Scott pointed toward the trench. "What happened?"

Luke scratched the stubble on his chin. "Sounds like a collapse under the tower. Evidently, three of the workers, women, have fallen through."

I indicated the six tribal workers gulping down water or pouring it over their heads. "They think the place is cursed. That evil spirits snatched some of their women and took them down to *jahunam*—hell."

Luke snorted. "Just what we need. Another rumour about evil spirits."

The van roared up and the expedition's medical aide jumped out. He immediately began to treat any of the workers that needed his help.

Luke was rummaging in the van when suddenly the sound of muffled screams coming from the trench stopped everyone in their tracks. The six workers who had escaped jumped up and dashed away, stopping at some distance to stare at the tower that was now beginning to appear from the dust cloud.

The crowd of workers that had gathered from all over the mound began to murmur and move away.

"*Roko!*" shouted Parveen. "Are you children or men? *Jin* are nothing before the power of Allah. Is God not almighty? *Allah-hu-akhbar!*"

Here and there, men began to look at the ground or glance around nervously. From one or two, I heard a weak response. "*Al-lah-hu-akhbar.*"

But in a moment or two, everyone in the crowd began to shout louder and louder, extolling God's power. *Allah-hu-akhbar. Allah-hu-akhbar. Allah-hu-akhbar.* Even the non-Muslim tribal workers seemed to take up the shout.

Before my eyes, the ancient Islamic rallying cry that has galvanized Muslims for centuries began to do its work. Nervous labourers became chest-pounding peacocks.

Luke appeared from the van holding a coil of rope and a couple of heavy-duty flashlights. He held up his hand and asked for volunteers. Scott tied his kerchief over his face, took the rope and a flashlight from Luke, and strode toward the trench. Three tribal men stepped forward to join him. Darren, Parveen, and I followed them.

Luke held up a roll of the twine. "Wait. Scott, tie this to your belt so the rest of us will have something to follow. When you get to the break, fix it to something on the wall and we'll have a guide so none of us gets lost. I'm going to get a generator and some lights."

With our faces covered with moistened scarves, we followed Scott single file into the dust cloud. The crowd that had gathered let out a cheer; *Yah, Allah! Yah, Allah*—in the name of Allah!

I kept a few steps behind Parveen and passed the twine to one of the tribal men who followed me. The cloying stench of mouldy, stale air grew stronger. Parveen kept shouting in their tongue to have courage, that help was coming, but the screams seemed to be weakening. The dense fog of dust closed in so thickly that the figures in front of me metamorphosed into phantoms. The deeper we went into the tunnel burrowed beneath the tower, the harder it became to breathe. Suddenly, something above our heads creaked. The man following me jerked the cord as he paused. I flashed my light toward the ceiling, but the timbers seemed solid.

Even so, I had the terrifying feeling that the tower above us would come crashing down at any second, burying us alive. Two men had already died in here.

I had never liked confined spaces. As a child, I'd been called a sissy for refusing to join the other kids exploring a bat cave in the Korakhorams. But this was worse than anything I could imagine. Scott's bravery and the dim sight of Parveen in front of me shamed me into gritting my teeth and carrying on.

Just when I felt I could go no farther, Scott passed back word that he'd reached the break. We edged forward gingerly to gather behind him. He played his light around the edges of the collapse, where bits of rubble looked ready to tumble. A feeble voice reached us from somewhere in the darkness beyond the reach of his light. "*Khuda ka shukr. Juldi kuro.*"

"Stay back a ways," he said. "It looks unstable. Darren, hold the light while I tie this rope. Parveen, can you talk to them? Keep up their spirits?"

Scott took the rope, tied a double bowline, slipped it over his shoulders under his arms, and instructed us to anchor him. He lay down on the floor of the tunnel and slowly crawled toward the gap. Parveen kept up a steady patter of encouragement in Punjabi.

"Darren can you grab my legs?"

With Darren holding his legs and the rest of us gripping the rope, Scott inched his way along until he was looking over the edge of the break.

"There seems to be a pillar holding up the floor where we're standing and one on the other side. So it shouldn't collapse any further. I can see the women who fell, but it must be twenty feet down. Hard to tell. One of them looks unconscious. We have to hurry."

"Parveen, will you take my place and explain to them what we're going to do? Shine the light on your face so they can see you."

"You got it," she said.

When Parveen was roped up and had crawled to the edge, where the women could see her, Scott began giving her instructions. "Tell them to move to the far side away from us in case our movements loosen debris. Explain how to put their legs through the two loops of the rope and grip it tightly with both hands while we bring them up. Ask them about the woman who appears unconscious. We should bring her up first."

Parveen explained things to the women, then shouted over her shoulder. "All of them are badly hurt. One is unconscious, one has a broken leg, and the third woman thinks her arm is broken. They're not going to be able to hold onto the rope."

With a final shout of encouragement, Parveen crawled back to the group of us. "What are we going to do?"

"Someone is going to have to go down there," I said.

CHAPTER EIGHT
Rescue

The six of us, the three tribal men plus Darren, Parveen, and myself, gathered around Scott. Our breathing was laboured, most of us had hacking coughs, and one of our flashlights had died. The stink of tension enveloped the group. Scott wiped his face. "Mr. Radley is right. One of us has to go down to help get them up."

Darren grabbed the rope Parveen had dropped and stepped into the two loops. "I'll go. I've had first aid training."

One of the tribal men touched my sleeve. "What is happening?"

I explained to him in Urdu that someone needed to go down to help the three women.

He stepped toward Darren. "*Main jata. Meri bivi.*"

Scott must have caught the implication that the man's wife was among the women who had fallen for he shook his head. "Parveen, please explain to him that Darren has medical training."

Using Punjabi, the main local dialect, Parveen described to the men what they planned to do.

Another creak had us all looking over our heads. I felt myself instinctively tighten my shoulders as I flashed my light around. Ahead of us, across the cave-in, farther down the tunnel my beam caught a trickle of dirt cascading from the ceiling.

Darren moved toward the edge. "Time is running out. Lower me down."

"Wait." Scott looked around. "You may need some kind of sling."

Parveen pointed to the turbans of the men and broke again into Punjabi. They mumbled to each other something unintelligible, then reluctantly unfurled their *pagardis* and handed them to Darren. Scott passed Darren his water bottle. "Take a sip, then moisten the cloth you have over your face. Give what's left to the women."

Scott grabbed the rope. "Everyone get a good grip so we can let Darren down slowly. No jerks."

I could hear the fall of pebbles loosened by the rope as we let Darren down. I gulped as the rope rasped, then jerked. A few minutes later, the hollow echo of Darren's voice reached us. "Okay, I'm down. Give me some slack."

Scott turned to me. "Mr. Radley you take one of the tribal men and go back to the entrance. We'll keep your flashlight here, but you ought to be able to find your way back by following the cord we unravelled. Tell Mr. Wu what's happening and send back a couple of men, a stretcher, and more flashlights."

I picked a tribal man named Manu. We grasped the cord in our left hands and stumbled back the way we'd come. By the time we got halfway, I was struggling to breathe through the dust-choked cloth covering my mouth and nose. Then I began to sense some slight air movement and hear the hum of a generator. We staggered up the incline leading to the surface, past two small fans, and broke into the bright sunlight, where we collapsed.

Someone passed me a bottle of water, which I half-drank and half-poured over my face. Luke grasped my arm. "What happened? Where are the others?"

Between gulps of water, I filled him in on the situation. "They've lowered Darren through the breach to help the women, but they need more help and more flashlights, as fast as you can send them. The women will have to be brought out in stretchers."

"We don't have more flashlights." Luke pointed to a couple of men bringing floodlights and spools of electrical cord from one of the trucks. "We're going to set up a string of floodlights. And the fans should clear the air soon."

I shook my head. "Those fans won't help much. It's almost impossible to breathe in there. And they need bottles of water."

Luke picked up a case of water, grabbed one of the labourers, and thrusting it into his arms pointed toward the tunnel. Then he ran over to the van, pulled out a stretcher, and a bottle of oxygen.

Manu, the man who'd accompanied me out, had been talking to a group of men. He slapped a couple of them on the shoulder and loped back toward the tunnel. Two of them followed him.

Luke ran back to my side. "You stay here. I'm going in." He shouldered the stretcher, hooked the bottle of oxygen to his belt, and passed me the satellite phone. "You're in charge until I get back. I've called for an ambulance from Nowshera. Just make sure that generator doesn't conk out. And try to keep these idiots from talking about evil spirits."

The crowd of workers had become restive. It would only take one troublemaker to convince the rest that angry *jin* inhabited the whole place. The situation was ripe for another walkout.

I stood up and motioned for the workers to gather around. In rusty Urdu, I praised Allah that the three workers were alive. Then I proceeded to embellish the discovery of the vault beneath the tower. I described it as a long lost palace. I told them how news of this discovery would make not only their children proud, but also the whole of Pakistan. Drawing on dim remembrances of tales

told to me by my father, I talked about a lonely princess whose
betrothed had been killed in battle. She had retreated to Pattan
Minara to nurse her grief. The rediscovery of her palace would
make Mr. Wu so happy, he would throw a big celebration with as
much curried goat at they could eat.

I went on to describe the feast he would throw. A huge *deg*—
pot—of savoury chicken curry. Another of goat curry. Palao to
feed an army. Sweet rice full of juicy raisins and coconut. Gallons
of the sweetest tea. Pakistani fudge by the ton. And a bonus for
everyone.

Smiles began to outnumber scowls and nervous glances toward the tower. Here and there a *wah, wah* of delight broke out.

I had to keep them from thinking about demons, so I went on
to describe the ancient Indus civilization. I pointed toward the dry
riverbed and asked them to imagine a wide river full of boats of
commerce and a land of great cities and prosperous farms up and
down the river. A couple of men snickered, but most appeared
intrigued. I told them how fortunate I was to be visiting a country
with such a proud history.

I was beginning to run out of material when a shout went up.
I turned to see two men emerge from the tunnel bearing a
stretcher.

The expedition's medic pointed toward the shade cast by the
van, where he had laid out some blankets. The men carried the
injured woman over to the makeshift pallet and gently laid her
down. Then they ran back into the tunnel.

When the medic tried to wipe the grime off the woman's face
with an antiseptic cloth, she groaned and pointed to her head
where a huge gash still oozed blood. At least she was alive.

Ten or fifteen minutes later, the other two women were
brought out, one carried by the man who had volunteered to take
Darren's place. By the tender way she laid her head on his shoulder, I could tell he was her husband.

The three women's injuries could have been much worse. One had a probable concussion. Another had two broken legs. The third nursed a broken arm. All of them suffered from assorted cuts and bruises. I learned that they'd been fortunate to fall not onto a brick floor, but onto sand and dust that must have drifted into the building in the centuries after it was abandoned.

Scott, Parveen, and the others emerged from the tunnel and collapsed on the ground. Luke came last. As soon as he appeared, a cheer went up from the crowd. *"Allah-hu-akhbar. Woo Sahib zindabad. Allah-hu-akhbar."*

Luke gripped my shoulders with both hands. "I'm not sure what you did, but they seem happier than when I left."

Parveen, who had been talking to one of the tribal women, laughed. "Mr. Radley didn't do much. Just promised them a huge feast and a bonus."

I stared at the ground. "Well—"

Luke dropped his hands and turned toward Parveen. "He what?"

"I had to do something," I said. "They were getting real nervous, so I—well, yes, I thought you'd want to celebrate. You can tell them I was crazy—or something."

"And have them go on strike again? What else did you tell them?"

"Oh, you know, just stories about Pattan Minara. That kind of thing."

Parveen chuckled. "Why don't you tell us the story about the lonely princess whose betrothed was killed in battle?"

"Hey," I said. "I had to use my imagination."

Luke slapped me on the back. "Good job. We'll hear the story later. I don't mind putting on a feast." He grinned. "As for the bonus, we can take it out of your salary."

I threw up my hands and groaned.

"A celebration may well be in order," Darren said, as he tried to wipe the grime off his face. "I wouldn't be surprised if that room the women fell into isn't part of the citadel we've been searching for."

"We'll find out soon enough," Luke said. "But first, why don't you all get cleaned up. Take the rest of the day off. I'll wait with our medic for the ambulance."

Later that day, I learned that the three women were making a good recovery in the municipal hospital in Nowshera.

When I returned to the site the next day, things were almost back to normal. None of the workers seemed to have deserted the project. In fact, a cluster of men looking for work squatted under the shade of a shesham tree near the front gate.

Luke, instead of focusing his resources on exploring the room exposed by the cave-in, had sent everyone back to their original tasks. Evidently, he was working out a careful plan of exploration before he had anyone return to the tunnel. He had a locked gate installed at the entrance and two engineers brought in to gauge the tunnel's safety and the stability of the tower beneath which it burrowed. A hundred yards or so from the gate, he'd had a shelter erected to house the generator so he could power a string of floodlights when necessary.

I spent the rest of the week becoming familiar with various trenches being dug across the mound and planning a series of articles. I took zillions of pictures and drank hundreds of cups of *chai* with the workers. I must have consumed crates of bottled water. Thirst dogged my footsteps every day but I avoided the workers' water stations. They drank from communal cups out of *ghardhas*—large terracotta water pots covered with wet burlap. Better a bit of thirst than typhoid or dysentery.

By noon each day, the fresh clothes I'd donned had a tawny reddish cast from the clouds of dust thrown up by work at the site. By late afternoon, I felt filthy, gritty, and ravenously hungry.

Back at the canal bungalow each evening, I took a long shower before sitting down to a meal fit for a prince. Steak. Chicken. Goat curry. Fish. Sometimes Luke joined me. Once he brought the three students, Parveen, Scott, and Darren, to get a taste of civilization. I gathered that the cook at the site couldn't compare with Musa.

Musa had become indispensable, and not only as a cook. He could get a shoe repaired, find a spare battery for my computer, or mail letters. He even had my clothes laundered and pressed; and it cost a pittance. He seemed surprised when I turned down his offer to get some *sharab*—alcohol. Where he would find it in supposedly dry Pakistan, I had no idea. I began to suspect he padded the *hisab*—the accounts—and hoped that securing *sharab* would keep me happy. But he was so enthusiastic and helpful that I didn't mind if he pocketed a few extra rupees. He had a huge extended family to support.

We had irregular power outages that made connecting to the internet very erratic. When I was able to get my e-mail, it turned out to be all spam except for one from Stephanie that gave me no further details on our financial situation.

My nagging concern about our finances, along with my anxiety about being back in Pakistan, receded as my interest in the site grew. Occasionally I'd find myself worrying about Raju and his daughter's plight, but I heard nothing further about them. Moreover, I was so tired at night that I gave up doing any further research on human slavery. After supper, as soon as any guests left, I'd collapse on my bed, read a chapter or two from a mystery, and fall into a deep, dreamless asleep. In the morning, I'd drowsily reach beside me for Stephanie, only to wonder where she'd gone. Then I'd sit up, remembering I was alone. Only a few more days and she and Janice would arrive.

Several times during the week, Luke had me photograph workers unearthing unusual artefacts. One was an unbroken piece of painted pottery. Another was a brass seal with a raised representation of an elephant.

On Friday afternoon, while many of the workers offered *namaz*, Muslim prayers, Luke had me accompany him to the most distant trench where workers had exposed a grave. A cluster of terracotta pots lay grouped around the skull of a complete skeleton. The three archaeology students knelt in the trench, carefully brushing away dirt and lifting bits of debris from their find.

Buried beneath the out-flung legs of the adult skeleton, Parveen had unearthed the skeleton of a baby. "By the pelvis, a female," she said. "Probably died along with the child during delivery."

Scott held up a couple of beads from a cluster scattered beside the skull. "An important woman if her jewellery is any indication. High quality beads. I would guess carnelian, jasper, agate, possibly steatite."

Darren pointed to a bangle encircling one of the arms. "I'll bet a week's pay that bangle is gold."

After taking pictures from every possible angle, I sat on my haunches and tried to imagine myself walking the streets of Pattan Minara in 3000 BC. Who had this woman been? Had she lived in one of the houses on the main street? I imagined her husband and children standing around her grave, weeping. Was her husband a priest or perhaps a merchant trading in far off Sumer? Perhaps her family had offered animal sacrifices at her death.

Or had they worshipped the Creator God? A common religious bond might have existed between the citizens of Palestine and those along the Indus. Unlikely, but possible. If so, their worship could have been monotheistic like that of Melchizedek, described in the Bible as priest of the Most High God. I recalled reading that before sorcery and sun worship took over, the Santal of India had worshipped one good god, Thakur Jiu.

According to earlier research, primitive monotheism was quite common in the ancient world. The Austrian researcher Dr. Wilhelm Schmidt claimed that monotheistic beliefs permeated ninety percent of the world's folk religions.[1] I decided to follow up

---

[1] Don Richardson, *Eternity in their Hearts*, Ventura, California: Regal Books, 1981, p. 44

that line of inquiry for an article on the religion of these ancient people.

But first I had to get cleaned up for the feast I'd forced Luke to promise.

When I returned, the site had been transformed. On a level section of the dry riverbed, a huge wedding tent had been erected, divided into two sections: one for men and one for women. Cotton rugs covered the ground beneath the *shamiana*. Coloured lights swayed in the light breeze off the desert. A trio of musicians sat on a raised platform playing tablas and sitars.

Although the women were out of sight, I could hear their laughter. The men, wearing their best outfits, stood around smoking and talking. A few wore western clothes—long sleeved shirts and dark trousers—but most had on white, starched, *shalwar-qamizes*. Here and there, I saw an elaborate turban or a mirrored skullcap.

The tantalizing aroma of curry and pilaf reached my nostrils and set my taste buds tingling.

Luke strode to a point where both men and women could see him, beckoned for Parveen to join him, and clapped his hands. "Friends, I want to thank you for being such a good crew of workers." Parveen translated into a mixture of Punjabi and Urdu as he spoke. "I am proud of the work you are doing to unearth a great city from long ago. Your country is proud of you as well. The provincial governor has sent his best wishes.

"This could have been a tragic week, but it wasn't. The three women who were injured are making a full recovery—and they are back with us."

He pointed toward the women's side of the tent and the three injured tribal women appeared, two of them on crutches. A cheer went up.

"As a token of appreciation for the good work you do and your commitment to stay with us until this excavation is complete, I put a little something extra in your pay packets this week."

A deafening cheer arose. "*Woo Sahib, zindabad.* Long live Mr. Wu."

"Thank you. Now enjoy the meal."

On Saturday, I stayed at the canal bungalow collating pictures and working on the rough draft of my article.

Sunday, I woke early—excited at the prospect of meeting Stephanie and Janice at the Nowshera airport around noon. I planned to visit Padri Fazal's church for the morning service, but first I took a leisurely stroll along the canal road. The air was cool and fresh. Parrots flitted in and out among the trees along the canal. The sound of a gristmill laid down a soothing background sonata.

I continued my stroll toward the village at the crossroads. As I approached, I saw that something was wrong. A bulldozer sat beneath a baobab tree. I stared. Raju's village had disappeared. Nothing remained but raw earth and one tree.

CHAPTER NINE
A Pakistani Church Service

Incredible! The whole Marwari village had vanished: fence, huts, animals, cooking pots, laughing children, men, women—everything, even their god-house. The only remaining witness, the massive baobab tree, lifted indifferent branches to the morning sun, as it must have done for half a millennium.

I scanned the raw earth for clues. On one side of the defiled ground, I saw several broken pots and a torn strip of red cloth. Bulldozed off to another side lay a huge pile of charred debris.

I considered possible scenarios as I hurried back the way I'd come. The Marwaris could have moved to another location. After all, they worked as migrants—a precarious existence. And yet the Marwari villages I'd known as a boy seemed quite permanent. Perhaps Raju's people had been evicted. Could the kidnapping have been intended to warn them off the land?

Back at the bungalow, I sought out Musa. I'd come to depend on his high-speed connection to the local grapevine. He was preparing breakfast, another huge repast by the look of it. In spite of my appeals to cut down on the quantity, he still cooked too many eggs and squeezed enough oranges into juice for a troop. I suspected that him and Mohammed, the night watchman, and their children enjoyed the leftovers.

"Musa, what happened to the Marwari village?"

He cracked six or seven eggs into a bowl. "Police bring paper—three, four days ago. Tell them to go. Owner needs land for a warehouse. Day later, bulldozer come. Push down fence. They go."

"But they must have been there for years! Surely, they should have a month's notice, at least."

"Notice," he snorted. "Sahib, you know *mahavrah,* di wun with big club, he own water buffalo?"

"Might is right—but it isn't." I sipped from the cup of *chai* Musa handed me. "Where did they go?"

He shook his head. "I not know. Pack everything on bullock carts and camels. Left."

After breakfast, I drove to Padri Fazal's village. Maybe he'd know where Raju's people had gone.

As a boy, I'd gone with my family to the church in his village where my dad had often preached. I remembered it as a mud brick shelter built against Padri Fazal's courtyard wall.

The church I saw when I arrived could hardly have been more different. I pulled into a brick-floored courtyard and parked beside several dusty cars and six motorcycles. The single-storey brick church was about fifty feet wide with a veranda across the front. A short bell tower topped by a simple wooden cross proclaimed, in modest terms, the nature of the building. From the wide-open double doors, the sound of exuberant worship brought back long buried memories. For a village, the building was surprisingly substantial.

I was not alone in arriving late for the service. A couple, trailing three children, smiled at me as I climbed the steps to the front door.

The sight of scores of men's shoes in the hall leading into the sanctuary reminded me to doff my sandals—something I'd almost forgotten. I stared in bemusement at this cultural mosaic. A couple of pairs of highly polished black oxfords: school teachers, bank clerks, or government employees? A dozen or more pairs of loafers in a variety of states of repair: merchants? Three pairs of beautifully crafted and decorated Bahawalpuri shoes: tribals, possibly Marwaris? The scattering of scuffed, handmade heavy leather loafers must have belonged to farmers or sharecroppers. Even three or four pairs of cheap rubber thongs: labourers or street sweepers? But most surprising were the name-brand sneakers that proclaimed the presence of young people or jocks.

The shoes on the women's side reflected a similar cross-section of economic classes, ranging from the quite well-off to the very poor, but with a vital difference. Aside from a couple of pairs of flats and one pair of mules, all were thongs in a rainbow of colours and styles.

I slipped into the sanctuary and sought an inconspicuous spot. Like many rural churches, rugs took the place of pews. The men squatted on the left side and the women on the right. Most of the men wore white shirts with dark trousers, while the women, their heads covered with gauzy *dupattas*, wore a more colourful array of clothing. Quite a few favoured silk or satin *qamizes* over white *shalwars*. I spotted a couple of women in *saris*. The clothing of the majority, however, was sewn from cotton in a variety of prints. Off to one side of the women's section sat a group of Marwari women in their distinctive flaring red dresses.

The whole congregation clapped in time to a mini-orchestra seated in a semi-circle on the slightly raised platform at the front.

An older man with a thatch of grizzled hair madly pumped a harmonium while nodding his head from side to side. Like animated drummers in a rock band, two young men—their hands a blur—beat out the rhythm on *tablas*. Beside them another man kept time on a terracotta water pot. Padri Fazal sashayed back and forth across the platform, belting out the words of the song while marking time with his tambourine.

Jai, jai, Jesu ki jai. Praise, praise, may Jesus be praised.

I eased myself onto a vacant square of rug and ducked my head to avoid Padri Fazal's gaze. I wanted to talk to him later without being singled out during the service. I tried to squat like everyone else, but only succeeded in plunking down and kicking the man in front of me. He turned with a scowl, but seeing that I was a stranger, and *angrez* to boot, he smiled and scooted forward, giving me a little more room. I nodded my head in thanks.

The young men playing the *tablas* slowed their rhythm. Padri Fazal signalled the end of the song. Here and there, hallelujahs rang out.

Padri Fazal pointed in my direction and launched into rapid-fire Punjabi, most of which I missed. I did catch the words, Radley Sahib. People turned toward me and smiled. He motioned for me to rise and urged me in English to bring greetings from my father and the Canadian Church. Since I felt more like a prodigal than a disciple, I stumbled through some clichés, hardly knowing what I was saying. No matter. Everyone clapped as I sat down. This could get dicey. Next time, he might ask me to preach. He had no inkling of the struggle I'd had with scepticism.

The service continued. Padri Fazal led everyone in reciting the Lord's Prayer and then announced a psalm. The musicians immediately launched into a rousing introduction. I found myself carried along by the enthusiastic singing, nodding my head in time with the music, and clapping with abandon. I smiled as I imagined the shock some of the more staid members of my church back home would express at hearing this rendition of one of the Psalms of David. No plodding, melancholy melody this.

One could be excused for assuming this church was Pentecostal. In enthusiasm it was but, as my dad had explained, in format it was more a mix of the best from Anglican, Presbyterian, and Free Church traditions. From the letters Padri Fazal had sent to my dad over the years, I knew he combined a sharp mind with a tender heart. Perhaps the apparent dearth of this combination in my experience with the western church was the cause of my struggles with the faith—or maybe I was too critical.

Padri Fazal interrupted my reverie with the introduction to his sermon. During the next hour, he wooed his listeners with gentle entreaties only to plunge them into terror by thunderous indictments designed to pierce their consciences. He pounded the pulpit, he paced up and down, and he told stories that had the congregation laughing uproariously. I shook my head in admiration at his rhetorical skill.

How could he concentrate on his sermon given all the distractions? Mothers nursed their babies. Amens and hallelujahs rang out at the strangest times. Men went outside to spit. Children came and went. Stragglers arrived and demanded to be noticed, often marching right up to the front with their offering.

At the end of the service, I tried to slip away, hoping I could collar Padri Fazal away from the church. However, before I could leave the sanctuary, a bevy of elders surrounded me and took turns crushing me in bear hugs while they fired questions at me in their dialect. They obviously assumed that I must have inherited my father's linguistic ability. I could do little but parrot the one Punjabi phrase I knew, *mainu Punjabi nahih aundi*—I don't speak Punjabi. Finally, with a lot of laughing and shaking of heads, they let me go. When they moved on, a large part of the congregation seemed to descend on me. The matrons patted me on the head and clucked approvingly. I couldn't stand being patted on the head. Like my sister, I'd been the object of that kind of Pakistani endearment too often as a child. So I nodded my head, muttered *mihrbani*—thank you—and forced my way outside.

Padri Fazal strode over to where I waited. "You must come to our home for a meal."

"I'd really love to, but I can't. My wife and daughter will be arriving shortly by plane from Karachi."

He grinned. "Wonderful. Bring them, too. My daughter-in-law will be happy to meet them. We'll have chicken curry ready, along with kabobs. You do like curry... if you don't, we can make an English dish?"

My stomach rumbled at the thought of a good curry. "We love curry, but Stephanie and Janice will be very tired after their flight. Please, can we come another time?"

"I understand," he said. "Friday then?"

I nodded. "Sounds great... Padri Sahib, can I talk to you privately for a minute?"

His brow furrowed momentarily, then he motioned me to follow him around the corner to his office. When we were seated in his book-lined study, I asked, "Padri Sahib, what happened to Raju's village? I went by there this morning and it was gone—completely levelled."

Padri Fazal spit something out in Punjabi that I didn't catch. He took a deep breath. "May God have mercy. The police came on Wednesday with a court order for them to vacate the land in two days." Fazal's eyes blazed. "Some trickery about the land being owned by a merchant who needed it to build a cotton mill, or warehouse, or... something."

"But even if the order was legitimate, two days, is... is... inhuman. Couldn't they get a lawyer to secure an extension?"

"They tried. No lawyer would take their case. Someone had warned the lawyers to stay away from them."

I shook my head. "That's unbelievable, especially after the abduction of the girl."

Fazal gripped the arms of his chair. "I think it's connected. When Raju couldn't persuade Chaudri Sahib to do anything to help, he used a lawyer to register a complaint with the District Commissioner. That set the cat among the pigeons. It made the DC duty bound to bring in investigators from Islamabad."

"But why didn't Islamabad act?"

"The gears of government turn very, very slowly. When investigators come, if they ever do, they'll find nothing but bare land. On Friday, the local police came in force with a bulldozer and began levelling the village. The villagers pled with the police to give them another day. By that time, I had arrived to plead their cause, but all I could secure for them was an extra hour. Raju and his people ran around packing everything onto camels, camel carts, and a rented truck I'd arranged. The women and children stood off to one side weeping as police torched their houses and bulldozed their god-house. It was a scene from hell."

I looked down at the floor as the images stabbed my heart. In a strained voice I said, "Where did they go?"

"I'm not sure, but the last I heard they were staying with relatives in the Sindh."

"What can we do?"

"Joshua Sahib, I'm sorry to say there is little we can do beyond praying for God to intervene—restore the land to them. Things like this happen all the time." He got up and paced the room. "Few care about the poor and powerless. Little has changed in a hundred years. Certainly, things look different. We have TVs and DVDs and cell phones and camcorders and refrigerators and air conditioners—but people are the same. Lusting after power and property."

I drove to the airport in a sombre mood. I kept seeing images of Raju and his people being driven from their village by police and bulldozers. But gradually my anger dissipated as I thought about welcoming Steph and Jan. I really missed them.

Inside the terminal, I was told the plane from Karachi would be at least thirty-five minutes late. I took a table in the tiny restaurant and ordered a Coke and a plate of *biryani,* which turned out to be lukewarm. I tasted a mouthful before pushing the plate away. While I idly drew patterns in the mound of rice with my fork, I thought back over the last year. Thank God our separation hadn't ended in divorce. Fights, yes. Talks into the night. Silence from Steph. Shouts from me. Periods of brittle armistice broken by one of us asking for forgiveness. But in spite of disagreements, at least we were closer than we'd been before the separation.

The depth of my loneliness since arriving had taken me by surprise. It wasn't just the sex that I missed; I missed her... her warm brown eyes, and the way she prayed as if God was really in the room. I mean, he was, but...

I took a forkful of *biryani* and made a face. In the last week, I'd had a chance to ponder our disagreements. I'd come to the bitter conclusion that they were rooted in jealousy over Steph's success. I had lost my job at the paper just when she was hired full time. Her career was spiralling upward while I was struggling to keep afloat.

I drained the Coke. *Josh, my man, I think it's deeper than that and goes back further. Strong women threaten you. Especially when they exude competence and self-assurance. And her success at work has given her a huge infusion of self-confidence. Admit it, Josh, you've always been insecure. No wonder you react the way you do. You're so driven to prove yourself that the sparks fly... but all the sparks do is ignite your insecurities.*

A garbled announcement broke into my musings. I dropped some money on the table, hurried to the arrivals area, and watched as a small PIA turbo-prop taxied up to the terminal. Steps were wheeled up to the door and passengers began to straggle from the plane. My pulse quickened as I searched among them for my first glimpse of Stephanie and Janice. What if they'd missed the plane?

CHAPTER TEN
Stephanie and Janice

Steph and Janice were among the last to deplane. In defer-
ence to local custom, they'd changed into *shalwar-qamizes*,
but no one would mistake them for Pakistanis. With a
steady breeze off the desert, both struggled to keep their heads
demurely covered by the *dupattas*.

The hollow feeling brought on by wild thoughts that they
might miss the plane, or that their plane might crash, or a hundred other scenarios, was swallowed by a crescendo of joy—
especially at seeing Steph. I stood on tiptoe and waved. Janice set
aside her grown-up sophistication for a moment and waved back,
becoming quite a spectacle. Stephanie whispered something to
her and she lowered her startling blue eyes to the tarmac. By this
time, my daughter's blonde hair, revealed by the fluttering
dupatta, had caught the attention of most of the men in the ter-

minal. Uninhibited by western constraints against staring, they followed her progress toward the terminal.

I hurried forward to meet them. I couldn't envelop them in a great bear hug like I wanted to, so we stood awkwardly for a few seconds. I'd warned them that Asians, certainly Pakistanis, frowned on public expressions of affection between men and women. In this culture, men hugged men and women, women.

"How... how was the trip?" I stammered.

Stephanie smiled. "Tiring and scary. We're sure glad to see you."

"Me too!" I said, winking at Steph and steering them toward the baggage claim area where we ran another gauntlet of staring men.

"Whew, I'm glad to be on the ground," said Janice. "We thought that puddle-jumper wouldn't make it from Karachi." She shuddered. "You should have felt it vibrate when we took off."

"I know what you mean. I came on the same plane."

We claimed their bags and fled the circle of curious onlookers.

As I manoeuvred the Land Rover through traffic, I fired off questions about their trip and our friends at home.

"Josh! Watch out for that cyclist."

I blew a series of hoots on my horn. I hadn't realized how quickly I'd adopted Pakistani driving habits until Steph shouted a warning. "Don't worry about him. He'll get out of the way. You have to drive aggressively to survive here."

"That truck," said Jan. "It's so colourful... Mom, look at the cloth shop. Can we stop, Dad?"

I arched my eyebrows. "You've just arrived and you want to go shopping?"

Stephanie turned to Janice, who sat in the back seat with their carry-on luggage. "Sweetheart, what I need is a bath and a good night's sleep."

"Dad, this is so exciting." Janice pointed. "What are they selling in that shop?"

"I doubt if you want tobacco for your *hooka*."

Janice screwed up her face. "Yuck. What's a *hooka*?"

"A water pipe."

"I want to see everything. When can we come back and explore the bazaar? When can you take us to the dig?"

I laughed. "How about we get you settled before planning the week?"

Stephanie leaned back in her seat. "Good idea."

We wove our way through town into the countryside, where the traffic thinned. A couple of miles outside of town, I pulled under a shesham tree and set the brake. I glanced in the rear-view mirror to make sure no one was coming, then leaned over and kissed Stephanie. To Janice I said, "I didn't have a chance to properly welcome your mother."

"Go to it, Dad."

Steph's soft brown eyes opened wide. She smiled and touched my face, tracing the contour of my jaw. "I missed you."

Pulling back onto the road, I headed toward the canal bungalow. When my hand was not engaged in shifting gears, I rested it on Steph's knee. She reciprocated by gently tracing each of my fingers. Janice kept up a steady stream of questions about everything: what the farmers planted, how they tilled the soil, where their children went to school, why their houses had flat roofs.

At the bungalow, I introduced them to Mohammed and Musa and showed them the layout of the house. As soon as Jan was settled in her room, Stephanie and I closed the door of our bedroom. We'd no sooner fallen into each other's arms than I heard a scream.

Jan flung open the connecting door and cried, "Daddy, there's a lizard in my room!"

I'd forgotten to warn her about the little house lizards that scooted around the walls. "Sweetheart, they're quite harmless. They're called *chipkillis* and help keep down the insect population."

I pointed to one near the ceiling in our room. "See? We have one, too."

Stephanie frowned. "Can't we get rid of them? What if one falls on us at night when we're sleeping?"

Jan shivered. "Yuck."

"They're not going to fall on you. They have suction cups on their feet. We don't want to get rid of them. They're beneficial. Like bats, they catch tons of insects."

"I don't like bats," said Jan.

As soon as I mentioned bats, I knew I shouldn't have. We'd once had a bat incident back home. I went up to Jan and put my arms around her. "Sweetheart, when I was a boy I was afraid of *chipkillis*. Then my dad made a game of it. He called them Oscars and suggested that every night I say good night to Oscar, who would keep watch for bad insects that might bite me and give me malaria."

Jan frowned. "Sneaky."

I accompanied Jan into her bedroom and pointed out the suction cups on the feet of her *chipkilli*. She seemed reassured, although she kept glancing at it from time to time.

When I returned to our room, I saw that Steph was sound asleep. I stood there, looking down at her. Tousled brown hair framed her face. A tiny mole stood out on her right cheek. Pencil thin lashes hid her hazel eyes. Her lips were parted in a smile. She lay with her slender arms out-flung on the bed as if she'd collapsed from exhaustion. She'd kicked off her shoes, exposing delicate feet with red painted toenails. I'd often marvelled at how aroused I could get just massaging her feet. A slight thickening of her waist was the only sign of the babies she'd carried. What a woman!

All I wanted to do was enfold her in my arms and make passionate love. Instead, I retrieved a book and slipped out onto the veranda. After giving Musa instructions about supper, I settled down to read *A Thousand Splendid Suns*. I found it hard to concentrate, so I wandered around the garden. In a far corner, I spied Mohammed in front of his quarters puffing on his water pipe. I wandered over to say hello.

He motioned me to a seat and offered me the pipe. "Smoke, Sahib?"

I declined as politely as I could, then, to practice my Punjabi, I launched into a series of queries about his family. Mohammed looked mystified by what I thought were well-practiced phrases. Finally, he laughed and said. "Sorry, Sahib. No speak English."

I threw up my hands and laughed in return. Between English and Urdu, which I did know fairly well, I learned about his wife and five children, three of whom were employed by Chaudri.

When I returned to the veranda, I saw that both Stephanie and Janice had changed into fresh clothes.

"Feel better?" I said.

Stephanie rubbed her eyes. "The shower helped, but I think I could sleep for a week."

"Could we eat first?" Janice said. "I'm starved."

Musa had laid out a feast: a platter piled high with thin, breaded tenderloin steaks, a dish of chicken curry, a mound of mashed potatoes, green beans smothered in butter, two loaves of freshly baked bread, and half a dozen *chapatis*. For dessert, he'd baked a chocolate cake.

Jan filled her plate. "This is incredible."

Stephanie stared at the bounty with her mouth open. "Do you eat like this every day?"

"No way," I said. "Never two meats. I think he's worried about you taking over the kitchen."

We did our best to show appreciation for Musa's culinary skill. Between mouthfuls, I laid out a tentative plan for the week including morning visits to the dig and a trip to the bazaar. I told them about Padri Fazal and his connection to our family, then mentioned his invitation to have dinner at his house on Friday. I described some of the other people they'd meet, including Luke Wu and Chaudri Gujar Mohammed.

"Dad," Jan said, "I have something to tell you. I only have a week before I go to Lahore."

"Lahore?" I said. "How come?"

"You remember Faria, my friend from college?"

"Yeah."

"She's back in Lahore with her family and she's invited me to visit."

"But that must be five hundred miles north. I don't think I can take time off to drive you that far."

Across the table, Stephanie winked. "You don't know your daughter very well. She's got it all arranged."

I sputtered, "Arranged how?"

Janice reached over and touched my arm. "I made reservations in Karachi—on the Khyber Mail. A first class, air conditioned compartment from Nowshera to Lahore."

I frowned. "Jan, honey, all by yourself? This is not Canada."

"Dad, you worry too much. I'll be all right. Besides, it's in a women's compartment and I'm twenty-four—not fourteen! Faria's family will pick me up at the station in Lahore. And I'll be back for Christmas."

My fingers drummed the table. "But suppose they don't pick you up? Suppose the train breaks down. Suppose... Sweetheart, I don't like this."

Steph pushed a lock of hair behind her ear and smiled. "I don't think there's much you can do. She's made up her mind."

I rose from the table and began to pace back and forth. "Neither of you understand. Too many things can go wrong. Women don't travel alone in this country, especially on a train. Rail travel can be a nightmare. And, if I remember right, the Khyber Mail gets into Lahore late at night. I'll worry the whole time you're gone."

Janice got up, came over to me, and put her arms around me. "Daddy, I didn't know you'd feel so strongly about this. I'll be fine. Besides, didn't you tell us when we were kids that God would send his angels to watch over us?"

"Talk of angels is fine, but God expects us to be careful."

"You were hardly careful," Stephanie said, "when you tackled that terrorist in the basement of the Rogers Centre."

I thought back to the Lightning File affair, my discovery of the terrorist cell and their Arabic file. The authorities had been sceptical until my translation pinpointing their first target proved accurate. Still, it was too late to save the first lock on the Welland Canal. Fortunately, that shock had galvanized them into action in time to stave off an even worse incident. But the struggle beneath the Roger's Center? It still gave me chills.

"That was different," I said. "I had no choice. It was either tackle him or die in an explosion and take thousands with me."

Stephanie arched her eyebrows as she refilled our coffee cups without saying anything.

I sighed. I should have learned by now the impossibility of budging my strong-willed daughter and her stubborn mother from any path they chose. It was two against one. I didn't have a chance, but that didn't stop me from feeling uneasy.

Janice yawned. "Dad, let's talk about this tomorrow... after I catch up on my sleep."

She kissed us goodnight, then went off to bed. We lingered over our coffee. Stephanie reached over and gripped my hand. "I'm not overly thrilled about seeing her go to Lahore either, but we have to let her make her own way. Didn't you tell me that you gave your mom and dad gray hairs when you backpacked through Europe?"

"Yeah, I guess you're right. It's part of growing up."

Stephanie set down her cup. "Josh, could your misgivings be affected by your own reluctance to return to Pakistan?"

I took a sip of coffee and stared at the motionless fan over our heads. "I suppose."

"How are you feeling now that you're back?"

"More or less as you predicted. On the one hand, I feel like I've come home—not that Canada's not my home. It's just that I spent a big chunk of my life here. I feel comfortable here and the language is coming back. Except for sandstorms, the weather is great. Who wouldn't love roses in December? Plus, the people are friendly. But..."

"What? Panic attacks?"

I took another sip of coffee. "No, nothing that intense. Sometimes—for no reason—I feel anxious, as if something terrible is about to happen."

Steph toyed with crumbs of cake left on her plate. "What about that nightmare you had at home? Has it come back?"

"Once, but the dream was different." I leaned back and closed my eyes. "I was playing soccer with a Pakistani boy on a village street. I kicked a highball that bounced into a stagnant pond. The boy—he seemed familiar somehow—ran after it. Then, he just disappeared... into the pond. I woke up in a cold sweat. Couldn't get back to sleep."

"Did something here trigger it?"

I didn't want to spoil her first day in Pakistan by talking about Chandi's kidnapping and the destruction of her village, so I changed the subject. "Maybe, but one thing is certain. What they're discovering at Pattan Minara will blow your mind."

Steph looked around to make sure Musa wasn't listening, then reached over with her right hand and traced my lips with her fingers. "Sweetheart, you look much better, more relaxed than when you left. I can even see some of that excitement you had in your twenties."

I kissed her fingers. "I am excited. I can't wait to show you the dig."

With a glance around, Steph extracted her fingers. "I don't think I'll get as excited as you about archaeology. Just being here with you is enough to get a real sense of what you've talked about for years."

I smiled at her. "After we visit Pattan Minara, we can see the sheikh's palace, the Bong Mosque, have a picnic on the bank of the main canal..."

Steph pushed away from the table. "Can we talk about all that tomorrow? I'm beat."

I laughed. "Sorry. You go on to bed. I'll join you after I thank Musa."

When I told Musa how much we'd enjoyed his meal, he fairly glowed with pleasure. By the time I got back to our room, Stephanie was curled up in bed, sound asleep. I felt disappointed and, since I wasn't sleepy, took my book into the den. After a few attempts to banish thoughts of her comforting curves, I began to get into the story of life under the Taliban. Finally, about eleven o'clock, I slipped into bed beside her and dropped off to sleep.

It must have been about two in the morning when Steph whispered in my ear. "Are you awake?"

"Huh?" I groaned.

"Did you hear that?"

From some distance came what sounded like the hysterical laughter of children. I turned toward her and yawned. "It's nothing, honey. Just jackals, miles away."

She snuggled against me, reached under my pyjamas and began to massage my chest. "I didn't want to wake you, but my clock is out of kilter."

I murmured. "You can wake me like that anytime."

CHAPTER ELEVEN
Quarrel

Stephanie brought her coffee and joined me on the veranda. I zipped up my jacket to ward off the chill of early morning. The call to prayer sounded faintly from some distant village.

"I wonder how many Muslims actually pray five times a day," Stephanie said.

"In my experience as a kid here, not many," I said, setting down my mug. "Could be more now with the rise of fundamentalism."

She pointed to a couple of birds frolicking in the shesham trees along the canal. "What kind of birds are those?"

"Myna birds. Amazing mimics. We'll have to get you a bird book next time we're in the bazaar.

"Let's do that soon. Jan is dying to go and I'd love to be able to identify all these new birds."

"Sounds good. By the way, how are you handling having servants?"

"No problem. This is like being at a resort—without the sea-shore."

"Wouldn't have put it that way, but that's a great attitude. Just so you're prepared—there's another servant due soon."

"Another!"

"Yeah, the sweeper."

"Sweeper?"

"An older lady comes every morning to sweep the floors and disinfect the bathrooms. I think she also gets rid of trash. Once or twice a week she tidies the yard, sweeping up fallen leaves, that kind of stuff."

"I don't much like the idea of her puttering around in the bathroom. Can she be trusted?"

"Hard to know. Just keep valuables out of sight, locked away."

Stephanie drew in a deep draft of the cool morning air. "I could get used to this lifestyle. And it seems so peaceful out here. I pictured crowds and noise."

"There's a tranquility to the countryside. Deceptive really."

"Deceptive?"

"There are tensions below the surface." I touched her arm. "I was so glad to see you and Janice that I didn't want to spoil your first night in Pakistan."

She reached over and took my hand. "Josh, what have you not told us?"

I leaned over and kissed her. "Just a week ago, two men died in a cave-in at the archaeological site. A day later, someone stole a couple of valuable artefacts. And..."

"And what?"

I drained my coffee. "You know the kidnapping of the tribal girl I mentioned in my e-mail? She was engaged to be married next month."

"That's horrible. Do the police have any leads?"

"Padri Fazal thinks the police may be implicated. A couple of days ago, they helped enforce an order destroying her tribal village."

Stephanie's mouth fell open. "You're kidding."

"Wish I was. They delivered a paper to vacate, came back two days later, and gave them an hour to pack up and leave, then they brought in a bulldozer and levelled the whole village. Best guess is that the father's appeal to the District Commissioner stirred up whoever is behind the abduction of girls in the area."

"You said girls, as in plural?"

"There seems to be a human trafficking ring operating in the area. If this girl isn't rescued soon, she'll probably be sold as a sex slave."

Stephanie grimaced. "A sex slave?"

I told her what I'd learned about men, women, and children being traded like commodities on the international market.

"Josh, is there anything we can do about this girl?"

"I asked Chaudri to help find her. He promised to try, but I have my doubts about his sincerity. Padri Fazal thinks he's also involved. The girl's brother is sure that Chaudri's Land Cruiser was used in the abduction."

"Josh, all these names are confusing. Who is Chaudri?"

I grimaced. "Just the combined Warren Buffet and Rockefeller of the area."

I filled her in on all I knew about Chaudri Gujar Mohammed, including his position heading the local committee supervising the dig, and Padri Fazal's suspicions. "I'd like you to meet him, get your impression. He comes across as sophisticated and benevolent, but I wonder. He invited me to bring you to see his rose garden any time. Just don't be shocked by the number of wives he has."

"After what you've told me, I guess I shouldn't be shocked at anything." Stephanie pushed stray locks of hair behind her ears. "I've got some bad news to share, too."

I frowned. "The bills you were telling me about?"

"Right. After I paid the bills for the new water pump and the woodstove upgrade, there was no money left for the mortgage company. We were so far behind in payments that it was the last straw. They told me there would be no more extensions and demanded I settle the arrears or they'd liquidate the property."

I leaned toward her. "Nothing left from the advance I got from Asian Archaeology?"

Stephanie looked away. "Nothing. I had no choice... I had to put Eagle's Eye on the market, at a reduced price."

I jumped up. "What?"

"Josh, please, keep your voice down."

I glared at her. "Surely, you could have put off the woodstove upgrade or—"

She broke in. "I tried everything. I even tried to get the money back for our air tickets. No deal." Her voice rose. "My whole salary goes for living expenses and the mortgage on our Mississauga place. In our present state, trying to carry two houses doesn't make sense."

"But..."

"Hear me out. For our whole married life, you've left me in charge of the accounts. You run out and buy something, then expect me to work magic. Well, this time you went too far." She looked away. "You drained everything allowable from our retirement fund. All you left me is an overdraft and two mortgages."

"That's hitting below the belt. You initiated the separation. I needed some place to live. That's why I bought Eagle's Eye." I stood frowning at her and thought about the log house on the lake I'd bought when we were separated. The perfect writing retreat. A dream come true. "There's got to be some way."

Stephanie's voice softened. "Look, Josh, I understand how much you love Eagle's Eye. I love it, too. But the mortgage company gave us one month to sell or they would foreclose."

I began to pace the veranda. She jumped up and reached out to restrain me. "Josh, it's not like we'll be without a roof over our heads. After all, it is a second house. Once we sell it, we'll be back in the black. And we already have a purchase offer... all we need to do is fax our acceptance."

I flung away her hand and stomped across the garden, flinging words over my shoulder. "I bet you're happy. You never wanted me to have it in the first place."

"Josh..."

Janice came out on the porch as I strode toward the canal. I heard her say, "What's the matter with Dad? Did you have another fight?"

Before I'd gotten half a mile along the canal road, I regretted my outburst. I knew that Stephanie had been doing her best to keep us solvent. I just found it hard to think about losing my log retreat.

For the rest of the day, a silent wall rose between us. I wanted to make up, but somehow couldn't. Janice filled the silence with cheerful comments and questions about everything around us. She'd become adept at dealing with our spats—forcing us to talk. I answered most of her questions with the kind of overly hearty responses people make when they're pretending nothing is wrong. Inside I felt dark. We had been doing so well; we hadn't had a real argument for months. And following such a tender reunion...

After breakfast, I drove them out to the dig and, since it was a safe topic, blabbered on about the Indus civilization. Janice wanted to know everything: why the Saraswati River dried up, how old Pattan Minara was, why there was a barbed wire fence around the site, what had been found, and why the only visible structure was a crumbling tower. Even Stephanie began to perk up and ask the occasional question.

On the mound, I led them toward the excavation where I'd found the three archaeology students working earlier in the week. A steady stream of workers balancing baskets of debris on their heads exited the trench.

Parveen, the Ph.D. student from Oxford, stood near the entrance to the trench, turning something over in her hands. She looked up as we approached. "Good morning Mr. Radley. Lots of excitement today."

I introduced her to Stephanie and Janice, then asked, "What's going on?"

"During the excavation, we discovered the walls of what might be part of the central citadel. In one of the side rooms, we uncovered a trove of objects. Look at this bull seal, for example."

She held out a four or five inch square of terracotta with the raised figure of a bull and a line of Indus characters. She traced the animal's hump and horns with her finger.

As Janice peered closer at the seal, her *dupatta* came free, revealing her blonde hair. "Wow," she said. "Is it really four thousand years old?"

"Maybe older," said Parveen.

Men began to stare at Janice. One of the tribal women reached over and touched a strand of her hair. Stephanie wound her *dupatta* tighter and whispered something to Jan, who immediately readjusted her own headscarf.

Under a barrage of Punjabi from Parveen, the men shuffled away with their heads down. She turned to Janice and smiled. "Ignore these barbarians. They'd think your blonde hair is more interesting than old tablets any day. And blue eyes. They must imagine you came directly from Hollywood."

"I don't know what you said, but it sure was effective," said Janice. "I don't like people staring at me or touching my hair."

Stephanie changed the subject. "How do you know where to dig?"

Parveen beckoned us to follow her to a rough table set up under a tarp. On one end of the table, a map of the excavation was pinned in place. The rest of the surface was littered with shards of pottery, a couple of tablets, and what looked like an array of beads.

She pointed at the map. "Our first step was to excavate a series of trenches across the mound. Here, and here, and here. The trenches began to reveal the layout of the city. See these dotted lines? They represent what we believe to be streets of the original city. Once we have a rough plan of the city, we can concentrate on excavating sections that seem more promising. And that's why we began focusing on this trench and the area around the tower."

Janice pointed toward it. "So that's all that remains of the old city?"

"No," said Parveen. "That's not part of the ancient city at all. It's much more recent, but very old, an addition—all that still stands of a Hindu temple built on the ruins of the ancient Indus city."

Stephanie remained unusually quiet, but Janice almost vibrated with curiosity. "And these? What do you do with these?" She pointed to the shards laid out on the table.

Parveen explained how designs painted on the pottery and their style helped them date the site and gave them understanding about the daily life of the people. She showed how the shards were numbered and logged. "See? Here's a painted Indus pot we're piecing together. And these are carnelian beads from the room we just excavated. The Indus craftsmen must have been very skilled to drill such tiny holes."

Janice's almost Nordic appearance contrasted sharply with Parveen's honey-coloured skin and midnight black hair, but there seemed to be an instant rapport between the two.

"Can I come back tomorrow and watch you work?" asked Janice. "This is fascinating."

Parveen laughed. "The romance of archaeology? It's really about grubbing in the dirt and breaking fingernails and getting hot and sweaty."

"I don't care about that," said Janice, as her *dupatta* slipped off her head again. "But show me how you keep this dumb thing on."

"It's dumb and dangerous..." Parveen looked around to make sure no one was within earshot. "Necessary as long as those bearded dinosaurs in their black shrouds are on the prowl."

"You mean...?" said Stephanie.

"*Maulvis*, Muslim priests. The Taliban and their Wahabi masters have everyone looking over their shoulder."

Parveen showed Janice how to knot her *dupatta* behind her head to keep it in place.

Stephanie tried to follow her instructions. "Why did you say these were dangerous?"

"Every year, dozens of women get badly burned when their *dupatta* catches fire while they're cooking a meal."

Luke came striding across the mound toward us carrying a cloth bag. "Parveen, they need you at the face of the excavation, but first have a look at this."

"I'm sorry," he said, turning toward my wife and daughter. "I'm forgetting my manners. You must be Stephanie, and you, Janice. Joshua has told me a lot about you. Welcome." His words tumbled out. "Exciting time. Let me show you."

He took a dusty figurine about twelve inches high out of the bag and laid it carefully on the table. Beside it, he placed a long metallic band and two thick bangles.

Parveen took a brush and dusted off the female figurine, then gently rubbed one of the arms. She gasped.

"Gold," said Luke. "Near as I can tell, the bangles, the head band, and the figurine are all solid gold. And there's more in the room we're excavating."

"This is astonishing. These pieces must rival those found at Mohenjo Daro." Parveen glanced around. "Do the workmen know?"

"No," said Luke. "I have Scott and Darren working alone in that room. They'll bring out every important piece in cloth bags. But we've shown the workers enough artefacts to realize it's a major find. And we'll keep them motivated by giving everyone a bonus."

I pointed toward the storehouse cum office where Luke kept the relics they discovered. "Have your Chinese guards arrived? I didn't see any when we came in."

"Not yet," said Luke. "They arrive in a couple of days."

CHAPTER TWELVE
A Threatening Slogan

Over lunch at the canal bungalow, Janice kept up a steady chatter—mostly one-sided—about the excavation. A wall of silence had descended between Stephanie and me. By the time our meal was over, I could stand it no longer. I beckoned Stephanie to join me on the veranda.

"Steph, I'm sorry I got angry... said things I shouldn't have said..."

Stephanie cut in. "Josh I understand how hard this is for you. And I should have found some way to give you more information but—"

"Connections have been haywire. I reacted badly. I should have trusted you."

"Josh, I tried everything to get more credit. There was no other way. If we don't sell the property ourselves, quickly, we lose out completely. The mortgage company will just take it over and liquidate."

"So what do we do?"

"We've got to sign the agreement I brought with me and fax it to the real estate agent."

During the drive to Nowshera, I said little. Janice kept up a running commentary about everything she saw. My mind was back at Eagle's Eye, sitting on the back porch of the log house, watching fish surface on Rice Lake. It had been such a tranquil place of healing after Stephanie and I got back together. And I'd done some of my best writing there—not that I'd been able to sell much. I thought of family barbecues. The warmth from the fireplace during the winter storms. An eagle soaring over the lake.

By the time I pulled up to the post office, the anguish I felt was almost like the grief experienced in losing a friend—in this case, a dream.

I sat there a moment in silence, until Stephanie touched my arm. "You want me to send it off?"

"No."

I took a deep breath, opened the car door, and strode into the post office.

After faxing the agreement, I drove Stephanie and Janice to the cloth bazaar. We must have wandered into a dozen cloth shops and some stores that sold ready-made outfits. We kept hearing, "Very cheap, *Memsahiban*," and by our standards everything seemed to be. Each shopkeeper tried to ply us with tea, which we politely refused. Stephanie and Janice, however, couldn't pass up the bargains. They purchased yards of cloth, a couple of *dupattas*, a satin sari, and two ready-made Pakistani outfits. In a bookshop, Stephanie bought a bird book.

The only jarring incident occurred when a black-garbed Muslim *maulvi* followed us muttering curses and calling us *kafirs*—infidels—destined for the fires of hell. The only way we could escape the malevolent gaze of this Taliban look-alike was to flee into a restaurant, where we indulged in *samosas* and chicken puffs.

The week passed quickly. Janice went to the dig every day where she learned from Parveen how to clean and catalogue artefacts. Some days I went with her, and at other times I worked on finishing my first article. Stephanie made friends with Musa and Mohammed's families. Musa's wife helped Stephanie sew a new *shalwar-qamiz* from some of the material she'd bought.

We didn't hear anything back from the real estate agent. To me, that seemed like good news. I hoped for a miracle. Steph and I were talking to each other again, but in a skittish way like boxers who had each received stunning blows and were trying to avoid another wallop.

The weather turned cool and cloudy, threatening rain.

On Wednesday morning, I took Steph and Jan to visit Chaudri's rose garden. Chaudri's youngest wife, Noorani, met us at the front door of their mansion. Her eyes were outlined with kohl and her lips with a bright red lipstick. She wore a silk *shalwar-qamiz* with a matching *dupatta* and silver sandals. Her fingernails and toenails were painted with the same red as her lipstick. She looked as if she'd just stepped off the set of a Bollywood movie.

"Chaudri Sahib leave very sudden," she said. "Welcome. I show you *ghulab*."

After I'd introduced Stephanie and Janice, Noorani led us into the sunken rose garden and began to point out various specimens. "You see this? Is it not beautiful?"

"The whole garden is amazing," Janice said.

Stephanie knelt to smell a fuchsia-coloured rose. "Exquisite."

I wandered away from the women and sat down in a gazebo, watching them. Stephanie and Janice seemed to be bridging the cultural gap better than I was, even though I'd grown up here.

Sure, the *Maulvi* in the bazaar had freaked them out, but who wouldn't be intimidated by his malevolence? And here they were laughing and chattering, in spite of the language problems. They'd obviously made a friend.

After making a circuit of the whole garden, Noorani led them to the gazebo. "You have seat. I fetch tea."

"Isn't this incredible?" said Janice. "A rose garden that rivals the one in the Butchard Gardens—and yet it's five hundred miles from any major city."

"There's probably another one nearby that's even more astounding," I said. "The Sheikh of Abu Dubai maintains a hunting lodge out in the desert not far from Pattan Minara. It has twin marble palaces separated by a garden with fountains; one palace for the prince and his men, and the other for the women."

Stephanie shook her head. "I can't come to grips with the contrast; unimaginable wealth in the midst of dire poverty. Did you see those shacks we passed on the outskirts of Nowshera?"

Janice pointed to Chaudri's mansion. "That's no shack."

Stephanie frowned. "A bit garish... but I guess if we lived where almost everything is brown or gray, we'd welcome some colour. Even the trees are gray with dust."

"We should get rain sometime this week," I said. "That'll wash everything off."

Janice stood up. "I saw some horses in the paddock when we drove in. I'll be back in a minute."

Stephanie blew a wisp of hair out of her eye. "Jan is having a ball. She's just so excited about everything.

"And you?"

"I wouldn't say excited. More like... thankful for the opportunity to absorb the culture. I could never understand why you hung onto those Urdu phrases, why you kept telling the kids the same stories about your childhood. Now I have more of an idea. We've only been here a few days, and Pakistan has already grabbed a corner of my heart. If only..."

"You could do something about the poverty?"

"Yeah, and the child labour."

Noorani arrived leading two servants with covered trays. Stephanie gasped when she saw them spread out a huge array of Pakistani treats plus a plate of delicate cucumber sandwiches.

Janice hurried to join us. She pointed back over her shoulder. "Such beautiful horses."

Noorani nodded as she poured our tea. "Arabians. You ride horses?"

Janice nodded. "Yes, a little."

"You come. Ride with me." Noorani passed around a plate of Pakistani fudge. "Distant field. Away from men."

As we finished our tea, a dusty Land Cruiser arrived. Chaudri got out and came toward us. As he strode into the gazebo, Noorani adjusted her *dupatta* and lowered her gaze.

"I apologize for being away," he said. "I hope Begum Sahiba has taken good care of you."

We answered almost as one. "She's been wonderful. Very hospitable... extremely kind."

"Good, good," he said, sitting down.

Noorani poured him a cup of tea. After we'd chatted awhile about his rose garden and the state of his crops, he asked me how things were going at the excavation. Before I could answer, Janice exclaimed. "They've made some exciting discoveries—a gold figurine and—"

I broke in. "Quite a small figurine. Lots of pottery shards, that kind of stuff."

Chaudri stroked his chin. "A gold figurine?"

Sensing my unease at giving Chaudri too much information, Stephanie said, "We love your rose garden. Your wife said you grafted some of the roses yourself. Can you explain how you do that?"

Chaudri launched into a detailed description of grafting. When he seemed about ready to return to the subject of the excavation, I suggested we take our leave, pleading my need to work on my articles.

As we drove away, Stephanie turned in the seat to look back at Janice. "Jan, honey, even though you love horses, I don't think you should go back there. I don't like the way that man looked at you."

"It's my blonde hair. I wish everyone would stop staring at me."

"It's more than your blonde hair. I don't trust that man."

Janice let her *dupatta* drop and shook out her hair. "Noorani is so sweet. I'd like to see her again, but I don't know if I want to go back there anyway. I saw something in the stable that shook me up."

"What'd you see?" I said.

"A young woman was cleaning the stalls. She had a huge bruise on the side of her face and one eye was black and blue."

I honked at a flock of sheep blocking the road. "Maybe she got hurt by one of the horses."

Janice began twisting her hair into a braid. "No horse would have given her bruises like those. Besides, one wrist had an iron manacle and the other was rubbed raw."

Stephanie braced herself as we skirted a huge pothole. "Are you sure it wasn't a bangle?"

"I've never seen a bangle like that. Too heavy and rusty. Besides it had a loop welded to it for a chain. Could she have been the kidnapped girl?"

"What was she wearing?" I asked.

"The usual *shalwar-qamiz*. A bit dirty and torn."

"If it had been Chandi," I said, "she'd have worn the distinctive long red skirt of the Marwari tribe.

"Daddy, whoever it is, we've got to do something. Tell the police."

I blasted my horn at a jeep racing toward us down the middle of the dirt road. "That may be a problem."

●●◆●●

On Friday afternoon, we drove to Padri Fazal's for supper. As we turned down the dirt road leading to the village, I pointed out how the compounds of Punjabi Christians clustered together around the church, the Christian school, and the Padri's house. Also on the outskirts, but farther east, an interlaced fence of thorn branches enclosed a cluster of Marwari huts much like Raju's vanished village.

As we approached the village, an *azan*—call to prayer—rang out. I glanced at my watch. *Two hours until sunset, must be the third of the five azans.* On the road leading to the center of the village where the local mosque stood, I could make out a few men in clean, white *shalwar-qamizes* making their way there for prayer. Others would feel sufficiently religious to ignore the *azan* altogether, having attended the earlier Friday communal gathering.

Padri Fazal met us in front of his house. "Joshua Sahib and his charming family. *Khush amdad.*"

After introductions, he bid us follow him. As we entered his courtyard, I noticed a splash of whitewash applied over what appeared to be Urdu letters scrawled on the outside wall. Strange. Inside, he presented his youngest son Caleb, his daughter-in-law Rahima, and their two boys. According to Punjabi custom, a married son often lived in the home of his parents. In this case, since Fazal had lost his wife, it made a great deal of sense.

Fazal led us to seats of honour. The courtyard, which was about a hundred feet square and surrounded by a mud brick wall, was typical of village compounds. Padri Fazal's house, with its three rooms all opening off a large veranda, seemed more substantial than most. A water buffalo lounged under a *neem* tree to my left. To my right, a woven stick fence surrounded a small vegetable plot.

Fazal invited us to make ourselves comfortable on two *char-pais*, portable beds constructed in the Pakistani manner using a tightly woven mesh of string upon which a thin cotton mattress was laid. He'd spread hand-woven cotton coverlets over them. Rahima brought us tall glasses of mango squash.

"This is beautiful," Stephanie said as she fingered the intricate needlework on the coverlet. "Who did it?"

Rahima pulled her *dupatta* more tightly around her head. "It's nothing. I have much better pieces I can show you after we eat."

As soon as Janice heard Rahima speak English, she began to ply her with questions. "What do you cook on? The other day, I saw some village women cooking over an open fire, burning round patties of some kind."

Rahima pointed toward the thatched shelter against one wall of the compound. "I cook on that stove. I'm lucky to have bottled gas so I don't need to use dung cakes for cooking."

"Dung cakes?" Stephanie said. "What we used to call cow flops?"

Padri Fazal laughed. "If you wander down our street, you'll see rows of dung cakes plastered to the courtyard walls, drying in the sun. They still show the finger imprint of those who made them."

Sensing Stephanie and Janice's shock, Rahima smiled. "Dung is valuable, not to be wasted. Dung cakes make a very hot fire. And quite useful. You may wonder why our dirt courtyard is so smooth and dust free. It's regularly plastered with a fresh coat of dung."

Janice lifted her feet. "But..."

Padri Fazal nodded. "I understand. You find some of our customs unsanitary. Let me assure you that the sun makes it quite sterile."

I pointed toward the mud brick compound wall. "I imagine that wall is plastered inside and outside with a mixture of dung and mud."

"Exactly," Fazal said.

Janice pointed toward the house. "The plaster on the house?"

"No, not the house," laughed Fazal. "It's built of burnt-brick covered with cement plaster."

Janice pointed. "Why do you have a brick stairway leading to the roof?"

Caleb had been listening with a quizzical expression on his face. "We sleep on roof during hot weather. Take beds up and down every day so we need regular stairs."

"And we dry grain and spices on the roof." Rahima rose to her feet. "Now, will you please excuse me? I have to prepare the meal."

Caleb also excused himself. "I must take water buffalo to canal." His two sons followed him.

The squawk of a hen, quickly cut short, told me that Rahima was preparing chicken curry from scratch. My salivary glands began working overtime.

I turned to Fazal. "Padri Sahib, what was that scrawled on your wall?"

His eyes narrowed. "You mean the one that says, 'Death to those who blaspheme the prophet Mohammed'?"

"That's terrible," Stephanie said.

I leaned forward. "Does it mean your neighbours accuse you of blasphemy?"

Fazal shook his head. "Some troublemaker wrote it, but I doubt if it was my neighbours. We get along well. Without my help, there would have been no school in the village. They've even voted me onto the village *panchayat*—the council."

"But isn't it dangerous even to be accused?" Janice asked.

"It could be, but not this time. The *maulvi* from our village mosque came by yesterday to assure me that no one from the village was responsible. They'll keep an eye open for miscreants."

"If not someone local, then who?" I said.

"Maybe terrorists seeking a pretext to promote instability?" He shrugged. "Anger over American involvement in Iraq? Militants from the radical mosque in Nowshera looking for someone to target after the republication of the Danish cartoons? Who knows? It's nothing new. We usually get along well with our Muslim neighbours, but from time to time some fanatic stirs up trouble about the very existence of Christians in Pak... istan—this so-called holy land." He snorted in amusement. "As if there haven't been Christians here for a century or more."

I reached over and gripped his arm. "Padri Sahib, this is no laughing matter. Aren't people using the blasphemy law as a pretext to target their enemies? On the plane, I read of a pastor being murdered after being accused of blasphemy. You probably know of more."

He ran his hands through his mane of gray hair. "It's true there have been more incidents, but there's little chance of it happening here." He waved his hands as if shooing away flies. "This is an unpleasant subject. Let's talk about something else. *Memsahib*, your husband told me that you work in a home that cares for older people. In Canada, don't grown up children take care of their parents?"

I listened to Stephanie trying to juggle that hot potato while, out of the corner of my eye, I watched Rahima preparing our meal in the open kitchen across the courtyard. With one hand, she stirred onion and spices in a brass pot on the two-burner propane stove. With the other, she tended a fire in the *tuva*, a beehive-shaped clay oven set into a raised brick platform. Those families who had a *tuva* used it to bake the bread that went with every meal.

My mouth watered at the thought of chicken curry and crisp *chapaties*. *Chapaties* cooked in a *tuva* were always the best.

As ordinary as the scene appeared, my mind was on edge. By how quickly Padri Fazal changed the subject, I could tell he was more worried about the slogan than he let on. I replayed the news items I'd read about what happened to people accused of blaspheming Mohammed. Arrested. Murdered. Set on fire.

CHAPTER THIRTEEN
The Superintendent of Police

By Saturday morning, Stephanie and I were somewhere in the middle ground between strained civility and passionate reconciliation. Every day saw a little more thawing of our relationship.

We'd settled into a morning routine. I joined her on the veranda with coffee for both of us. She read from one of her inspirational books while I just sat there sipping my coffee and letting the sounds of early morning wash over me. The *tuk, tuk* of a distant tube well. The trill of some unidentified bird. The heehaw of a donkey.

I'd often turn to Stephanie and ask her what she was reading. She'd share some thought, which I would chew over. Saturday was no exception.

"Josh, listen to this," she said pointing to the Bible lying open on her lap. "'I looked and saw all the oppression that was taking place under the sun: I saw the tears of the oppressed—and they have no comforter; power was on the side of their oppressors—and they have no comforter.'"

"Is that from Proverbs? It sounds so contemporary."

"It's from Ecclesiastes, written over three thousand years ago."

I poured the cold remains of my coffee onto the flowerbed. "Nothing much has changed. A girl from a poor family kidnapped, and when her father protests his whole village is bulldozed."

"An aging pastor accused of blasphemy."

"According to Janice, a woman with massive bruises cleaning a stable."

Stephanie's eyes misted over. "We can't just throw up our hands. We've got to do something."

"Like what? I tried to get Chaudri to help find Raju's daughter."

Stephanie reached over and gripped my arm. "Why don't we call Nadia? She has connections at the highest levels of the Pakistani government."

Thoughts of Nadia brought back uncomfortable memories. A Pakistani psychiatrist living near Toronto, she moonlighted for the Canadian Security Intelligence Service. I'd run into her during my attempts to convince CSIS to take the Lightning File seriously. My background in Pakistan had created an almost instant rapport between us, and her allure, combined with the tattered state of my marriage, had nearly precipitated an affair.

I shook my head. "She certainly has connections, especially in the Pakistan Intelligence Service, but we can hardly expect her to change a centuries-old system. Besides, didn't she leave Pakistan in disgust?"

Stephanie slumped in her chair. "There must be something we can do."

"What?"

She stood up. "We should march into the police station and demand they act."

I snorted. "Fat lot of good that will do. They'd resent our interference."

She began to pace up and down the veranda. "As foreigners, they'd have to listen to us, especially since you're connected to the Pattan Minara excavation."

I didn't like where this was going. Stephanie was like a mongoose after a cobra whenever she sensed injustice. Besides, she was right. We should try to do something, except... "You can't go marching into the office of the Superintendent of Police. Big cultural boo boo."

"You could go."

My stomach fluttered at the thought. Police always made me nervous. The thought of confronting Pakistani police, probably on the take, set the acid building in my stomach.

I took a deep breath. "I suppose being connected to the dig might help. The excavation could put Nowshera on the map and encourage a flood of tourists. They won't want to jeopardize that."

After breakfast, Luke arrived to drive Janice to the dig. She'd spend the morning with Parveen continuing her initiation into the mysteries of archaeology while Steph learned to sew Pakistani clothing from Musa's wife.

I drove into Nowshera to visit the Superintendent of Police. On the way, I popped a couple of antacid pills to try and still the churning of my stomach.

The SP's office was a colonial-era bungalow with a boxy addition on one side. Dirty streaks marred the institutional yellow of the rambling building. Budget constraints must have postponed the repainting that usually occurred after the rains.

A throng of petitioners jostled each other in a ragged line-up in front of the veranda. Police officers brandishing *lattis*—riot sticks—appeared to be fighting a losing battle to keep order.

More petitioners sat cross-legged in clusters under the ancient shesham trees shading the park-like grounds. Here and there, flowering jacarandas and *gul mohars* struggled to lend a cheerful appearance to the chaotic scene.

I groaned as I parked. This could take all day. Maybe I should have just turned around and gone home, but one of the officers spied me walking up the circular drive and waved his *latti* in my direction. I guess he could tell from my height that I was an *angrez*. True to Pakistani custom, he beckoned me to the head of the line. For once I was glad to be a foreigner, glad it gave me special privileges. As the officer ushered me through the door, dark looks and grumbling followed me.

Inside, another horde of petitioners sat clutching files and dog-eared papers. The officer turned me over to a *babu* behind a scarred desk. This receptionist peered at me over the top of a dirty-gray computer monitor covered with flyspecks. Tufts of gray hair poked out from either side of his Jinnah cap like wings. Smallpox scars dotted his puffy cheeks. His lips were red from chewing betel nut. Behind him, dusty shelves stuffed with files lined the whole wall from floor to ceiling. I stifled a hysterical chortle as I imagined him being buried beneath an avalanche of files.

"Yes, what can I do for you?" he said, in passable English

"Sir, my name is Joshua Radley and I need to speak with the SP about an important matter."

He gestured at the crowded benches and smiled, showing red-stained teeth. "The whole world wants to see the SP about an important matter."

"I'll only take a few moments of his time."

"I can arrange an appointment for next week if you'll tell me the nature of your request."

How much was this guy raking in from bribes? "It's not so much a request as a concern."

His thumb rubbed his fingers in the universal signal for *baksheesh*. "A concern?"

I glanced at the open door leading to a cellblock to my left as I pondered how to explain my concern and get in to see the SP without offering a bribe. Before I could answer, a slim man with a carefully trimmed beard wearing a blinding white, starched *shalwar-qamiz* threw open the door to the SP's office and bellowed. "*Sardar, chai kahan hai?*"

The *babu* jumped up and, folding his hands in supplication, replied in Urdu that the tea would be there in a moment. He went on to blame a servant who had forgotten to get sugar.

The bearded man, who must have been the Superintendent of Police, caught sight of me standing there. "And who is this?"

"Mr. Joshua Radley, sir," said the *babu*. "I'm arranging an appointment for next week."

The SP beckoned me to follow him. "I'll see him now... and the tea *jaldi, jaldi*—very quickly."

The SP's spacious office contrasted sharply with the crowded anteroom presided over by the betel-chewing *babu*. Not a speck of dust appeared anywhere on the furnishings. Bright windows looked out on a well-tended flower garden. A huge desk dominated the room. The desk was clear except for an onyx elephant, a single khaki-coloured file folder, an expensive pen set, and a thin, modern Apple computer. A large Kashmiri rug covered the floor in front of the desk. Behind the SP hung two portraits, one of Pakistan's founder, Mohammed Ali Jinnah, and a smaller one of Pervaiz Musharraf. On another wall hung an oil painting of K2, the second highest peak in the world.

Leather settees and armchairs hugged the walls opposite the desk. The only furnishings that seemed out of place were a semicircle of quite ordinary wooden chairs arranged in front of the desk. The layout of the room projected power and sophistication—while humbling petitioners.

The SP sat down behind his desk and motioned for me to take one of the wooden chairs. "Please have a seat, Mr. Radley. You're here covering the Pattan Minara excavation?"

"Yes, sir."

"Astounding, really. We're quite proud of our heritage."

Encouraged by this opening, I described some of the finds without mentioning the more precious artefacts. "But you are very busy. I wanted to ask you about another matter."

He stroked his beard with his right hand. "And what would that be?"

I sat on the edge of my seat. "I've been very concerned about the kidnapping of a young woman from Dhera Mundi village—Chandi, daughter of Raju Moro."

His bushy eyebrows came together in a deep frown. "What is your interest in this tragic affair?"

A bead of sweat trickled down my chest. "Nothing personal. It's just that Raju Moro seems to be such a fine man... and right after the kidnapping their whole village was destroyed. I—"

He broke in. "Not destroyed. Demolished by its rightful owner to reclaim the land. Mr. Radley, you don't understand our laws or customs." He leaned forward over his desk and skewered me with his dark eyes. "Raju Moro's tribe illegally occupied private land. They ignored official letters warning them to vacate. Marwaris are a tribe of *kafirs* who always cause trouble."

I doubted the SP's explanation, but was sure that a file would be manufactured to substantiate his story. Even if Raju's tribe had been served papers, they should have been given more time to evacuate. Coming so soon after the appeal Raju had filed with the District Commissioner, the destruction of the village was very suspicious. I was about to pose a few more questions when the SP continued.

"As for the kidnapping, I have no doubt it concerns a marriage arrangement gone wrong. You have no idea what kind of emotions are generated in jilted parties when a girl is promised to a rival family. Be assured that we are looking into the matter very carefully."

He signalled the end to our interview by opening the file on his desk and picking up a pen. Beads of sweat formed on my brow. But when I thought of the slogan scrawled on Padri Fazal's wall, I sat up straight and said, "Sir, I'm quite conscious that I'm a guest in your country. Chaudri Gujar Mohammed has shown such a delightful example of Punjabi hospitality that I don't want to take your benevolence for granted or waste your time. But I do have one other very small request."

Had I laid it on too thick? I could tell by the sudden lifting of his head that the mention of Chaudri Gujar had gotten his attention.

"What might that be?" he said.

"Would it be possible to station a police officer outside Padri Fazal Masih's house at Chak 75 for a few days? There's a slogan on his wall accusing him of blaspheming the prophet Mohammed, peace be upon him. I know Padri Fazal would never do anything like that. Extremists might take this opportunity to do him harm."

The SP tapped his pen on the desk. "Are you telling me how to do my job?"

I cringed. "No, sir. I just thought you might not be aware of this situation."

His voice rose and he pointed his pen at me. "I know all about Chak 75 and every other village in the district. And I know all about Padri Fazal and his ilk. Where there's smoke, there's fire. Look at this..."

He rummaged in his desk until he found a pamphlet, which he threw across the desk at me. As soon as I saw the title, *The Danish Cartoons and the Jewish-Christian Conspiracy*, I knew there was no point in further discussion. I needed to leave without doing anything to alienate him further.

I couldn't resist one comment. "But sir, Padri Fazal has no connection to Denmark. Those cartoons were not even produced by Christians. Christians proclaim a gospel of love."

He leaned back in his chair and took a deep breath before replying in an ominously soft voice. "You want to lecture me? Perhaps you want to try and convert me to Christianity. Well, don't bother. I know all the arguments. Let me give you a little advice. Stop sticking your nose where it does not belong. Leave the police work to me while you write stories about life at Pattan Minara five thousand years ago. That is the condition under which you received a visa, is it not?"

"Yes, sir."

"Show me your passport."

I grimaced. "I... don't have my passport with me."

"A foreign national?" His lips betrayed a tight smile. "And you don't carry your passport? Then show me your residence permit."

"Residence permit?" I was sure there was no requirement for foreigners to have a residence permit. I figured he must have made this up to show his authority. I gnawed on my lip as I pondered how to overcome the antagonism I seemed to have aroused.

He held out his hand. "Yes, your residence permit."

Using the honorific, I replied, "*Janab-e-ali*, Chaudri Gujar Sahib and Mr. Lok Wu, superintendent of the excavation, took care of all my paperwork. But I don't remember them mentioning a residence permit. I'm very sorry if this has been neglected. I'll immediately ask them to secure that document."

He indicated by a slight tightening of his facial muscles that my mention of Chaudri Gujar had given him pause. "You will do nothing. I will ask him directly." He stood and pointed toward the door. "You have wasted enough of my time. Stick to the job you came here to do. There are those who do not take kindly to people who snoop. We cannot protect you around the clock."

I inclined my head to indicate that I understood his implied threat and turned to go. Before I could exit, he added. "And you better tell Padri Fazal not to do anything to incite a riot. If we have trouble in Chak 75, I'll know whom to blame."

I closed the SP's door behind me, took a deep breath, strode toward the exit, and wiped my face with the kerchief I carried. I received several dark looks as I hastened from the building. I was shaking so badly by the time I got to the Land Rover that I could hardly get the key into the lock.

As I drove away, I pounded the dashboard with my fist. Instead of helping, I'd made things worse.

CHAPTER FOURTEEN
The Khyber Mail

On Sunday morning, Stephanie and I had already finished our breakfast when Janice appeared. We cut short our discussion of my visit to the SP.

She stretched her arms toward the ceiling. "You two look gloomy this morning."

"We're worried about the Lahore train," Stephanie said. "You're going to miss it if you don't hurry."

"I need coffee. Bad. There must be something in the air here." She yawned. "I'm sleeping like a hibernating bear."

I poured her a mug of coffee. "Probably all that grubbing around at the dig."

Janice flexed her fingers. "Hard work, but fun. Parveen is teaching me how to clean and catalogue artefacts." She gulped some coffee. "I never thought archaeology could be so interesting. Mom, will you pass me that plate of *chapati*... thing-a-ma-jiggers?"

Stephanie passed her the plate of flatbreads stuffed with curried hamburger that Musa had made especially for her departure. "Why don't you phone your friend in Lahore and postpone your visit? We could go with you later."

Janice took a couple of bites of *chapati*. "If I'd known this archaeology stuff was so fascinating, I'd have planned to go later, but I'm not going to throw away the ticket. Hey, this *chapati* is good."

I passed the jam. She smeared it on everything. "Sure we can't change your mind?"

"No way. Parveen has been telling me all about Lahore: the Fort, the Shalimar Gardens, the Badshahi Mosque—I'm not going to miss that stuff. Plus, I promised Faria. But I'll come back in plenty of time for Christmas."

"Can you hurry, honey?" I asked. "If the Khyber Mail is on time, we've got to leave here in twenty minutes."

All the way to Nowshera, Janice chattered about what she'd learned of the Indus civilization. I concentrated on driving, honking like a seasoned Pakistani driver. After a near collision with an oxcart, I finally lurched to a stop in front of the railway station. Half a dozen coolies in faded red shirts immediately surrounded the Land Rover. I chose a burly porter to carry Janice's suitcase and promised the head coolie a handsome reward—think bribe— to guard our vehicle.

There was a definite hierarchy among coolies, a sort of coolie-mafia with a boss who controlled the men who carried luggage and extorted *baksheesh* from harried passengers at every station. The gratuity would ensure I wouldn't be missing a wiper or headlight when I came back.

By the time I'd purchased platform tickets, allowing Stephanie and me to help Janice find her berth, the blast from a diesel horn signalled the arrival of the fabled Khyber Mail. Chaos reigned as the green and yellow coaches of the express train clanged to a stop. Coolies immediately led wedges of passengers toward carriages already bursting with humanity. One coolie balanced a huge tin trunk on his head. Another slouched forward under the weight of a bedroll and two cardboard suitcases. Anxious families with women in head-to-toe *burquas* struggled to keep track of tribes of children as they hurried after coolies charging through the crowd like halfbacks in a wild football game. Their men-folk shouted warnings. "*Yar, jugah do! Dekho bucce!*—Friend, give us some space. Watch out for these children!"

Businessmen in designer suits or spotless white *shalwar-qamizes* forced their way through the press toward the upper class carriages. Hawkers harried people at the fringes of the crowd selling sections of sugarcane from dirty blocks of ice, sweetened buttermilk, kabobs, Coca-Cola, roasted corn on the cob, bangles, combs, and even Danish ice cream and cell phones. Above everything rose the chant of the tea-vendor: *Chai, garm, garm chai.*

Our coolie jogged toward several first class carriages, where the crowd was thinner. The coolie forced his way onto the train, elbowing a family out of the way in the process.

"*Bevakoof!*" the man shouted, indicating his evaluation of the coolie's mental prowess.

I joined my hands together in an expression of apology to the man. "*Mu'af kejea janab.*"

Seeing that we were foreigners, he shrugged his shoulders and replied in English, "These coolies have no manners."

Janice's berth was in a *zenana*—women's—compartment, so I left Stephanie to help her settle in while I dealt with the coolie.

When I handed him a fifty-rupee note, he threw up his hands and began to wail. No doubt he'd imagined this rich foreigner paying in dollars.

In a mishmash of Urdu and English, he protested. "Sahib, you very rich man. I very poor—*bahut garib.*" He lifted the hem of his shirt. "Look. Very old."

I turned away, but he wasn't going to let me get away so easily. "Allah, have mercy." His lamentations began to attract stares. "*Mere bucce*—children hungry, Sahib. Please."

In disgust, I threw him another bill. He caught the money, stuffed it somewhere on his person and joined his hand together in thanks. "*Sahib. Bahut mihrbani.*"

I joined Stephanie, who stood below Janice's open window giving her last minute instructions. "Jan, honey, don't drink any water. Use those purification tablets if you have to, but be sure and wait fifteen minutes. Tea is okay."

Janice wound her *dupatta* more firmly around her face, hiding her blonde hair. Nothing could obscure her startling blue eyes. She leaned out the window, arching her eyebrows in excitement. "Don't worry, Mom. Dad already warned me a hundred times."

"And don't get off the train except in Lahore. You're sure you have your friend's phone number?"

She rolled her eyes at me. "Dad, can you get her to stop?"

I reached up and patted her arm. "Honey, we're parents. We love you and don't want anything to happen to you. Don't forget to lock your compartment door at night." My voice dropped to a whisper. "And keep your passport and money belt hidden at all times. Better sleep on them."

"And your malaria medicine," said Stephanie. "Don't forget to take it. You've seen what malaria did to your father."

Janice fiddled with her *dupatta* again. "You guys worry too much. I'm a big girl, remember?"

A half-dozen shrill blasts from the diesel horn stirred the crowd into renewed frenzy. A scratchy and unintelligible blare came from the station speakers. The few coolies who hadn't yet forced their way into second and third class carriages tossed their load through doorways into the crush of passengers already filling the cars. Women shouted. Men cursed. The hawkers' spiels rose in urgency. The guard blew his whistle. Once, twice, then waved his flag at the engineer. Slowly the train slipped from the station. Last minute arrivals ran frantically for their carriages.

We jogged beside Janice's coach until we ran out of platform. We blew her a kiss. She waved. We watched the Khyber Mail until it became a distant speck.

"Do you think she'll be okay?" Steph said.

Keeping my voice level to hide the lump in my throat, I said, "She's a trooper. She'll be fine."

"She'll make friends with everyone in the compartment before they get halfway to Lahore."

We exited the platform through a rusty iron gate guarded by two police recruits with ancient Enfield rifles. An officer with a holstered handgun and swagger stick waved us through the thinning crowds. Outside, a blind beggar implored us for *baksheesh*. Three taxi drivers barred our way to the parking lot, emboldened by visions of American dollars. "Ver cheap, sahib!" "Look. Modern taxi!" "Vher you go. I take you. Special price!"

I pointed toward the expedition Land Rover and smiled. They turned away, looking crestfallen.

The head coolie in his unfaded, bright red shirt saluted us as we approached. He pointed to the vehicle. "Look, Sahib, perfect condition."

Knowing I'd be setting a bad precedent, but wanting to forestall a tedious argument, I gave him a handful of rupees and jumped in the car. Ignoring his appeals for even more, we slowly threaded our way down Station Street through a tangle of rickshaws, taxis, and horse-drawn *tongas*.

On Jinnah Avenue, we stopped at Mohammed Zahir's Emporium to pick up groceries, then headed out of town. Stephanie seemed fascinated by the commercial bazaar while I concentrated on avoiding mayhem from traffic and merchants whose wares encroached on the street. We passed mountains of tin trunks and vendors of every kind including a vegetable market with geometrically arranged piles of carrots, potatoes, eggplants, and cucumbers. A sweet shop. A bakery. A cluster of stationery shops, then a row of shops selling fabric.

I blasted my horn at a *tonga* stuffed with carpets. The driver of the horse-drawn, two-wheeled taxi ignored me. Slowing to a crawl, I reflected on the vivid nightmare I'd had the night before. I'd been playing soccer again with a Pakistani boy... on a city street... no, it was a dirt road winding through a village when... something... I strained to remember... something terrible happened. From there, my mind was blank. My return to Pakistan hadn't banished all my nightmares, but lessened their frequency.

Ahead of me, the *tonga* turned onto a side road. We passed the Habib Bank and a cinema with a garish three-storey false front depicting a dashing hero rescuing a heroine from certain death in a flooded river.

"Watch out, Josh," Stephanie screamed above the sound of a blaring horn. I swerved to avoid a truck barrelling down our side of the street.

I sighed as we finally broke free of the bazaar's congestion. But I still drove with care through a residential area of walled compounds, watchful of children playing on the street. Finally we turned along the canal road leading into the countryside.

Stephanie pulled off her *dupatta* and flung it into the back seat. She tossed her head from side to side and fluffed the natural curl of her brown hair that had been crushed by the headscarf. "I'll never get used to this traffic. Every driver flirts with death."

"A nation of offensive drivers."

"At least we have a bungalow out in the countryside and don't have to endure this every day." She pointed toward a field of yellow flowers. "What's that?"

"Mustard. They crush the seed to get oil. You remember the *pakordes*—the fried slices of potato in chick pea flour you had yesterday?"

"They were good."

"Well, they were fried in mustard seed oil."

"What's that...?" The ringing of her cell phone stopped her in mid-question. She retrieved the phone from her handbag and pressed it to her ear. Her face turned pale as she put it on speaker.

"Mom, Dad, what should I do?" I heard a quaver in Janice's voice. "Bandits have stopped the train. Waving machine guns."

Stephanie gripped my arm. "Pull over. Jan's in trouble."

Through the speaker we heard screaming and then the staccato sound of automatic weapons. "Mom," Janice whispered. "They just shot some men... oh," she whimpered softly as more shots rang out. "They're just killing people... demanding money... ripping gold bangles from older women... throwing the younger women off the train."

I snatched the phone from Stephanie. "Jan, can you slip off the train?"

"No, Daddy. They're at both ends of the carriage and all along the tracks. SUVs or something." Her voice trembled. "I'm scared."

I pulled to the side of the road. "Quickly, Jan. Try to tell us where you are."

"I don't know," she wailed.

"What do you see out the window?"

"Ca—big canal... fields... blue dome of a mosque or something..."

Jan shrieked and the phone went dead. "Jan! Jan! Are you there?" Silence.

I turned in a tight circle and accelerated back in the direction we'd come.

CHAPTER FIFTEEN
Race to the Train

Stephanie braced herself against the dashboard as I roared down the canal road, struggling to control the Land Rover on the sandy surface. With her free hand, she snatched the cell phone off the seat.

"Nothing! What if Jan is...?"

I drew in a long breath. "Jan will be okay. Got to be."

"What can we do?"

My fingers tightened on the steering wheel as I accelerated. "We're going to find the train."

"Find the train? How?" Stephanie bit her lip. "It'll be miles from here."

I reached over and patted her knee. "Not so far. Jan saw the blue dome of a mosque. That has to be the shrine of Baba Farid. About twenty-five or thirty miles from Nowshera. It's the only shrine I know of near a big canal on the railway."

Stephanie's head was bowed. She was probably praying. No harm in that. We needed divine intervention... a miracle.

Prayers mingled in my mind with questions and a lot of re-crimination. *Father, protect Janice... send your angels to guard her... but why, Lord? Why Jan? I'm the prodigal! Please, Lord, don't let her be harmed... I shouldn't have come to Pakistan, shouldn't have been so stubborn, so proud, so determined to become a stupid, freelance writer.* I felt moisture form at the corner of my eyes and I swiped it away with my right hand. *I should have taken the job offer from Stephanie's father... We'd be safe in Tennessee. Just rescue Jan, Lord... please.*

I swerved around a bullock cart and entered a long curve.

Stephanie screamed. "Watch out!"

I saw the flock of sheep filling the canal road too late to do more than stand on the brakes and swerve. We lurched off the road into the scrub, where we slammed into a shesham tree with a jarring thud. Sheep had scattered in every direction.

I turned to Stephanie. "Are you okay?"

Stephanie rubbed her knee. "I think so."

A turbaned herdsman stood in the middle of the road, waving his staff and shouting at us in Punjabi. I jumped out and responded in Urdu about roads and cars and fields and livestock. I pointed to our vehicle and threw up my hands. With a final epithet, the herdsman turned away and began gathering his scattered flock.

I walked around the vehicle to assess the damage, then jumped back in. "Looks like just a dented bumper. The brush we mowed over slowed us down. I turned toward Stephanie who her head in her hands. "If we rock the Rover a bit, we can get back on the road. Could you..." She looked up. A cut on her forehead oozed blood. "Sweetheart, you're hurt."

I grabbed a couple of tissues and reached over to staunch the blood. She took them and pressed them against her forehead. "We don't have time for this," she said. "Just tell me what to do. We've got to get to the train. We've got to."

"I'm going to put it into four-wheel drive. If you get out and rock it a bit, I think we can get back on the road. On second thought, why don't you get behind the wheel? I'll push."

She shook her head, got out, and hurried around to the front of the Rover where it rested against the tree. After half a dozen tries and much spinning of wheels I was able to regain the canal road.

A few miles further on, we turned north on the Karachi-Lahore highway. Although paved, it was scarcely smoother than the canal road. At least it roughly paralleled the railway tracks. We made good time until we caught up to a row of slow moving trucks piled high with sugarcane. Trucks coming the other way kept us from passing. My fingers played an angry rhythm on the steering wheel as we ground along in second gear.

Stephanie had found a Band-Aid to cover the cut on her forehead, but the blow she'd received must have given her a headache. I pointed to the glove compartment. "There's probably some aspirin in the first aid kit."

"I'm okay." Her voice broke and her eyes leaked tears. "Can't think of anything but Jan."

"They're not going to hurt Jan. She's a foreigner. They don't want a special forces unit breathing down their throats."

Stephanie massaged her forehead. "What about that U.S. reporter? They cut off his head."

My fingers trembled on the gearshift. I felt leaden with dread. "You mean Pearl? That was completely different. Political. Janice is a young woman and a tourist. Muslims have a code about treating women with respect. Plus rigid customs about hospitality to foreigners."

"They didn't treat that tribal girl with respect. People who would stop a train—kill people—don't care about customs and respect. Who would do this, anyway?"

"*Dakoos*—bandits. This area has lots of bandits. We're not far from either the Indus River or the Thar Desert. For centuries, islands in the river have provided hideouts for outlaws. And the frontier with India is desolate and wild—uncontrollable."

"That's not very comforting, Josh."

A lumbering truck veered into the passing lane just as I was about to pass. I blew a long blast on the horn and pounded the steering wheel. "These stupid truckers."

I bit my lip in frustration. "Can you get us some water from the cooler?"

Even with the cooler weather, we always traveled with bottles of water and ice in a picnic cooler. Stephanie reached behind her and retrieved a bottle. She unscrewed the cap and handed it to me. I took a deep draft, then passed it to her.

Finally, seeing a break in oncoming traffic, I pulled out and accelerated past the line of trucks. Stephanie rearranged her *dupatta* to hide her face from the truck drivers. With them behind us, I raced down the narrow ribbon of highway trying to avoid potholes. Even so, throughout the ride both of us barely avoided banging our heads against the roof again and again.

On a more level stretch, Stephanie turned to me and sighed. "Could your nightmares have been a warning from God?"

"But why, Jan? Why didn't something happen to me?"

"Maybe you were meant to warn us not to come."

"Yeah, why didn't I?"

"I wish you'd warned us about the danger of kidnapping."

"I told you about the tribal girl, but I thought that was an isolated incident. And I didn't want to worry you." Stephanie fell silent so I rushed on. "Sweetheart, I so wanted you to experience the good side of the Pakistan I remembered: the food, the hospitality, the history..."

Stephanie interrupted. "Instead we get violence and poverty, dust, dirt, disease, and kidnapping."

I cringed.

She buried her head in her hands. "I'm sorry Josh, that's not fair. I'm not thinking clearly."

"I'm not either. If only..."

Stephanie lifted her head. "Josh, I don't blame you. I wanted to come. Janice was wild with excitement about this trip." She wiped her eyes with a tissue. "There has always been a side of your personality I never understood, but loved. You're... more tuned into other cultures, the world, than most of us—more sympathetic." Her voice broke again. "We've got to get Jan back."

I reached over and gripped her hand. She entwined her fingers in mine. "We can't be far now," I said. "The railway parallels the highway. The train should be off there to the left somewhere."

In the distance, I caught sight of a blue dome, the Baba Farid shrine. On the near side of the village that surrounded the shrine, I made out the line of trees marking the main feeder canal that Janice had mentioned. The train should be on the tracks somewhere before the village, or possibly beyond it.

"I see it." Stephanie pointed.

The Khyber Mail stood on the tracks about a mile west of us across a series of farmer's fields. I pulled over to the side of the road, engaged the four-wheel drive, and scanned the fields for some way across them to the railway right-of-way. "Hold on."

I roared along the shoulder, negotiated the ditch, and turned down a dirt track. We bounced along the rutted lane kicking up a cloud of dust. At the end of the lane, I powered through a row of bushes onto the railway right-of-way, where we came upon a scene of chaos.

CHAPTER SIXTEEN
Terror on the Train

We had approached the rail line along a rough farm track. The engine stood silent and idle, like a prehistoric animal felled during flight. I dimly made out something hanging out the window of the cab. Must have been one of the engineers—dead. A dump truck blocked the line.

We intersected the train about two-thirds of the way back in the second and third class section. I manoeuvred the vehicle through the scrub parallel to the tracks. We passed clusters of passengers—eyes wide with shock—who crouched beside their carriages or in the scanty shade of stunted bushes. A few stared from the windows. No police were present.

Ululating wails of grief drew our attention forward toward the carriages nearest the engine. When I could drive no further, we leaped out and picked our way through a scene from hell.

Bullet holes pocked the three foremost carriages. Many of the windows had been shot out. At irregular intervals, bodies, most covered with sheets or blankets, lay beside the tracks. A few looked to be children. Near us, a keening woman rocked back and forth beside the body of a man whose face had been almost shot away. Gore clung to her hands and blood stained her face where jewellery had been torn from her ears and nose. Beyond her, a woman pulled at her hair and screamed as she knelt beside a man who rocked the bodies of two young children in his arms. The man, probably her husband, stared into the distance.

Stephanie ran toward the first class carriages shouting, "Jan. Jan!"

I ran after her, asking anyone not prostrate with grief if they had seen a foreign girl. All shook their heads. When we came to Jan's carriage, we saw that the window she had waved from was gone. The bodies of two conductors lay sprawled beside the track. Blood stained the steps leading inside.

I held out my hand to restrain Stephanie, who was about to climb into the car. "Let me go first."

Upper class carriages like Jan's had self-contained compartments accessible by a narrow corridor down one side of the car. Splotches of blood smeared the corridor. The doors to all the compartments had been either ripped off their hinges or shot open. Partway down lay the bodies of two men. My heart pounded as I stepped over them and looked into Jan's compartment. Just inside the door, the man who had been shouldered aside by the coolie at the Nowshera station lay sprawled on his back with his hands flung out. Holes stitched across his chest oozed blood. It was as if he'd tried to bar entry. His wife lay in a crumpled heap half-on and half-off the seat to the right. The stubs of two fingers, ring fingers, oozed blood. Clothing was strewn everywhere. Jan's suitcase lay open on the floor.

A sob from the bathroom made me jerk. "Jan, is that you, honey?"

A wail rose from within. I jerked open the door, but instead of Janice a young Pakistani woman stared at me, her face twisted in an expression of terror. She was squeezed into the tiny space between the commode and the sink.

I held empty hands toward her. "*Teak hai, teak hai*—okay, okay. The *dakoo* are gone."

With a whimper, she fainted. I ran to the window and signalled for Stephanie to come. She shouted, "Jan?" but I didn't answer her.

When Stephanie entered the compartment, her face was pale and she gnawed on her lips. Her eyes sought mine in a silent question. I put my arms around her and sat her down on the seat opposite the dead woman. Kneeling in front of her, I held her face in both my hands. "Steph, Jan is not here. That means she is not dead."

She reached over, clung to me, and gasped, "Some things are worse than death."

I whispered in her ear, "There is a young woman in the bathroom. She's alive, but she fainted when she saw me. She may be able to tell us what happened. Can you help her?"

Stephanie let me go, took a deep breath, and stood up. She pointed toward the two bodies. "Cover them with a couple of sheets from the upper bunk. Seeing them like this will be too much of a shock for her."

She walked over to the bathroom door and paused. Then she turned toward me. "Has she been shot?"

"I don't think so."

I watched Stephanie as she opened the door and went in. She moistened a towel in the sink and began to wipe the girl's face. With a shudder, her eyelids fluttered open and she screamed something unintelligible.

"Hush, hush," Stephanie said as she knelt to embrace her. "You're safe. What is your name, sweetheart?"

"Mee... na. Y—you, Miss Jan's *ammi*." Her *dupatta* lay on the floor. Tears streamed down her face. "Saw you... station."

While Stephanie tried to console Meena, I lifted her father off the floor and laid him out on the seat beside his wife. I covered both of them with sheets, then collapsed on the opposite seat with my head in my hands. My chest felt constricted by a steel band of terror. *Jan. Oh, Jan. Sweetheart.*

After a few minutes, Stephanie led Meena to a seat, but stood blocking her view of her parents' bodies. She peered around Stephanie and pointed across the compartment. *"Ammi? Abba?"*

Stephanie put her arms around her. "I'm very, very sorry."

Meena began to wail and beat her head with both hands. Stephanie motioned for me to get a blanket from the upper bunk. I threw it to her and watched as she wrapped Meena in its folds. Would shock or hysteria prevent us from getting any information?

I turned to the window at the sound of sirens. Across the fields, I could make out five or six jeeps and a truck loaded with police speeding down the highway toward the road to the shrine which would intersect the rail line ahead of the engine. A couple of ambulances followed them.

The sound seemed to snap Meena out of her hysteria. She gasped a couple of times.

Stephanie looked into her eyes. "Janice, my daughter... did you see what happened?"

"Gunshots. I hid. Took her. Your *beti*. Heard men talk. *Khubsoorut aurat. Zareen bal. Bahut rupeah.* Very bad men."

I didn't translate for Stephanie the ominous words that described Janice's beauty, her golden hair, and the price she'd bring.

Sensing the meaning anyway, Stephanie collapsed onto the seat beside Meena and put her head in her hands. In a stifled voice, she repeated over and over, "Jan. Janice, honey. Oh, sweetheart."

I paced up and down from the window to the compartment door. *Why? Why didn't I stop her? Why did I come to Pakistan anyway? Get a grip, Josh. Think.* Out of the corner of my eye, I saw Meena watching me, so I asked her, "You talked with Janice?"

She wiped her eyes with the corner of her *qamiz*. "Yes... in just a few minutes... became friends. I promised to show her the Anarkali Bazaar."

I glanced out the window, then back to Meena. "Can you think of anything about the men, the vehicles they drove, anything?"

"Wore gray *shalwar-qamizes* and gray turbans. They used cloth from their turbans to cover their faces. All I saw. *Abba* told me to go hide in the latrine." She stared at the sheet covering her father and began to wail.

Stephanie put her arm around her again. I stuck my head out the window. A police officer shouted instructions and men with automatic weapons scattered to positions along the length of the train. *Great, lock the bank vault after the looting is over.* The two ambulances screeched to a stop and several male orderlies jumped out.

I turned back to Stephanie and with an uplifted eyebrow asked the unspoken question: what were we going to do with her? We had our own tragedy, but we could hardly leave her to deal with the bodies of her two dead parents. "Do you have relatives in Nowshera?"

"*Dada. Dadi.*"

"Your grandparents. Good. Phone number?"

She shook her head.

I touched Stephanie on the knee. "We've got to go. If we stay any longer, we'll be caught up in a bureaucratic nightmare. The police will take hours getting statements from everyone. Meanwhile the bandits are getting farther away by the minute. Can you gather Jan's things into her suitcase?"

"And her?"

"We'll take her with us. Drop her at her grandparents' place. They can send someone back for her parents." I turned to Meena. "Miss Sahiba, did you understand?"

She nodded.

I gestured toward her luggage. "Do you want to pack anything?"

She held up her purse, which she had been clutching, and shook her head.

Clutching Janice's suitcase, I shepherded them down to the opposite end of the carriage, then helped them down. We hurried toward our vehicle, but before we'd gone far, a shout followed by a pistol shot froze us in place.

Looking back, I saw a police officer striding toward us, waving his smoking revolver. As he got closer, I recognized him as the Superintendent of Police.

"*Roko. Roko. Kya karte? Loot-ra-he-hain?*" he shouted.

I whispered to Stephanie, "He thinks we're looters."

I set the suitcase down and held up my hands to show they were empty. Then, unable to contain myself any longer, I shouted, "Our daughter was on that train. She's gone. Where were you then?"

Stephanie poked me in the side to calm me down. Behind me, Meena began to weep.

The SP frowned as he holstered his pistol. "Mister Radley. You say your daughter is gone, kidnapped? Tragic. Very tragic." He pointed at Meena. "And who is this?"

Through her tears, Meena whispered, "*Chacha*—uncle."

The SP's mouth fell open. "Meena! What are you doing here? Your father said you were travelling tomorrow."

Like many, Meena and the SP switched easily between English and Urdu. Meena dried her eyes with her *dupatta*. "*Abba* get earlier reservation."

He pointed toward the train and grasped her arm. "Your *abba*? Your *ammi*?"

Meena whispered, "Dead. Murdered."

He dropped her arm and let loose a string of Punjabi curses. "How terrible. We will hunt down the perpetrators. We will..."

He began to pace up and down. Stephanie frowned at me. I could guess what she was thinking. The Superintendent of Police was Meena's uncle? And why would he be shocked by her parents' change in traveling plans, unless he had known something was going to happen on today's Khyber Mail? Why would he use the word kidnapped for Janice when I hadn't?

The SP barked a series of commands to a couple of officers nearby, then turned back to Meena. "I'm filled with grief for your parents. Be assured that we will apprehend the miscreants. We will leave no stone unturned. We will..." He fingered his moustache as if he wasn't sure what else to say. "But we must take care of you. These officers will collect your luggage and drive you to your grandfather's place. I'll phone them. We'll arrange everything." He waved back toward the carriage. "Which compartment?"

Meena pointed to the carriage we'd just left. "Number three... but *chacha ji*? Mr. and Mrs. Radley take me home. Very kind."

His eyes glinted and his hand rested on his holster as he looked from her to us and back again. In Urdu, he said, "But Meena, they're infidels, strangers. You should let your relatives care for you."

Meena gripped Stephanie's arm. "*Chacha ji,* I trust them. Please."

He stood silent a few moments, then nodded.

"Their daughter—Janice?" she said. "You will find her?"

"Yes, yes, we will be bringing the full resources of the police department to bear in tracking down these gangsters." He turned to me. "Do you have a picture?"

I fumbled through my wallet until I found a dog-eared picture, stared at it a minute, took a deep breath, and handed it to him.

"Most distressing," he said. "But do not give up hope. We will find her. Oh, and Mr. Radley, we will need you to come into the police station this afternoon to file a report."

With Stephanie gripping Meena's arm, we hurried away before the SP could change his mind. Stephanie got into the back of our Land Rover with Meena and immediately began whispering words of comfort. I recognized several Scriptures, including the Twenty-Third Psalm. What a trooper. I knew she had to be in anguish over Janice's abduction, but even in this state she was trying to comfort a young woman we hadn't even met before. I sensed Meena felt uneasy around her uncle—but it could just have been my imagination, which was out of control. My emotions gyrated between blazing anger at the brutality of the attack on the train and stark terror as images of Janice's plight flashed before me. Chained in the back of some van. Beaten. Raped. Forced into prostitution in some Middle Eastern brothel. I shook my head and focused on getting back to the main road.

At the Karachi-Lahore highway, a convoy of trucks ambled past. As I sat waiting for a break in the traffic, I pondered what to do. We had no idea where they'd taken their victims. North? South? East across the desert?

Turning to Meena, I said, "Miss Sahiba, do you remember anything more about the vehicles?"

She stared out the side window of the Land Rover, then pointed north. "There, under that big tree near the highway. A jeep like yours stopped. The big vans drove right up to the train."

"A jeep like ours?" I asked. "Are you sure it was a jeep?"

"Same colour and with picture on side." She shook her head. "Toyota, Jeep—confusing. This is a Land Rover? Maybe was a Land Rover."

"Picture on the side?"

"I just see quickly before hide... but much same."

What would an expedition vehicle be doing at the scene of such mayhem?

CHAPTER SEVENTEEN
Nadia

Before Stephanie and I drove Meena back to Nowshera from the scene of our daughter's kidnapping, I decided to check out the area around the tree where Meena had seen the vehicle. All the archaeological expedition's vehicles were the same, painted a sand colour with a stylized icon of the Pattan Minara tower on the door. What would one of ours be doing at the scene?

Attracted by all the police activity around the train, a crowd had begun to gather where the Lahore highway intersected the road to the shrine, the road used by the mobsters. A couple of police officers kept spectators distant from the train itself. I parked on the shoulder of the highway behind six or seven trucks that had pulled over.

"Stay in the vehicle," I said. "I'm going to check out the ground under that tree."

As I strode past the trucks, several drivers shouted, "*Kya ho ra ha ji?*" wanting to find out what was happening.

"Attack on the train," I flung over my shoulder.

Beneath the tree, all I saw were the tire tracks of police vehicles and the footprints of the curious until I noticed a cigarette butt ground into the dirt. Something unusual led me to crouch to get a better look. Only half-smoked and foreign. Using a twig, I turned it over. A Marlboro. Strange. Who would smoke an American cigarette out here? I scanned the ground around the tree and found another of the same brand, but this one smoked down to the filter. I picked it up, blew off the dirt, and put it into my pocket. Back at the car, I slipped it into a plastic bag and set it aside.

On the way back to Nowshera, I watched for vehicle tracks in the dust of smaller roads turning east or west off the Grand Trunk Road. A couple of miles from Baba Farid, I pulled over at the junction of what looked like a seldom-used lane heading east. I could clearly see the imprint of three or four vehicles turning off the main road onto this track. The tire marks were recent, superimposed over the prints of what might have been goats or sheep.

I mused about my discovery as I continued to drive toward Nowshera. Maybe it was nothing. Or it could have been a wedding party going to a farm, or a landlord visiting his holdings. But the tire marks did resemble those I'd seen at the scene.

I gritted my teeth and blew my horn at a truck barrelling down the center of the road straight for me. At the last minute, I shook my fist out the window and swerved onto the shoulder. As I fought the wheel to regain the road surface, I took several deep breaths to try and rein in my rage. I'd need to keep my emotions under control if I was going to be of any use in finding Janice. Better a cold, implacable anger in the grip of reason than a wildfire of rage. And I needed all the information I could gather.

I turned toward the back seat and asked Meena, "Is the Superintendent of Police your father's brother?"

"Yes, Sahib, *wuh chacha hai.*"

"Do you know him well?"

"Not well. My father have five brothers." She paused and then blurted out, "He very powerful but my father not like. I not like." Her voice trembled. "One of his police officers... tried to touch me. I told him but he did nothing. I thank you very much for taking me to my grandparents." She shuddered. "Not want to go with his police officers."

Meena stared out the window, occasionally wiping her eyes with her *dupatta*. She had answered my question about whether her uncle and Chaudri Gujar were friends by shaking her head. Did that mean, "No," or "I'm not sure"? I left her with her grief while I nursed mine with vows about what I'd do to Janice's kidnappers.

Stephanie held her head in both hands and stared at the floor. The movement of her lips told me she was praying. We could use divine help. Evil seemed to be winning some foul decathlon.

After we dropped Meena at her grandparents' place, I drove out of town to a quiet spot on the canal. For a few minutes, Stephanie and I clung to each other and said nothing. I watched the dirty water glide past.

"Oh, Josh, what are we going to do?"

Through the moisture clouding my eyes, I tried to focus on two parrots cavorting in the shesham trees. "I don't know."

"We've got to do something."

I hit the dashboard with my fist. "The police aren't going to help—probably implicated. We've got to inform the consulate, but they have a history of doing nothing. We need someone local, someone with clout."

Stephanie gripped my arm. "Nadia! Her name came to me again while I was praying."

"She's in Canada," I said. "How can she help us?"

"She knows the country—has powerful friends. Doesn't she even have contacts in the Pakistan security bureau, whatever it's called?"

I massaged my forehead to try and forestall the headache that was building. "You mean the ISI, the Directorate for Inter-Services Intelligence. They're a scary bunch—supposed to be shot through with Taliban sympathizers."

"All the more reason to call her. She'll know what to do."

"True. Maybe she can shake the tree a little. Get some of her powerful friends to apply pressure."

I started the engine and headed back into town. "Let's call her right now. Do you have your address book?"

"I think so." Stephanie grabbed her purse from the back seat and began sifting through the contents. "How are you going to call her?"

"We'll use one of those internet cafés."

While I threaded my way through the bazaar traffic, I thought back to the year before Steph and Nadia became good friends. I had met Nadia on the train and been smitten by her personality as much as her looks. Her honey-coloured skin, raven hair, and heart-shaped face had reminded me of Shamim, my high school sweetheart. And behind Nadia's dark eyes lurked a first rate intelligence that shone through in conversation.

Stephanie and I had been going through a bad patch. Our communication seemed to consist of either bitter arguments or long periods of silence. By contrast, a few minutes after I'd met Nadia, she and I were chattering away like old friends about favourite restaurants, historic sites, religion, even cricket.

We'd met a few times for dinner and arranged to travel on the same train. She had signalled her openness to embrace something more intimate. Since I had been lonely and hurt by what I perceived as Stephanie's spitefulness, I was tempted to take the irrevocable step and plunge into an affair. Fortunately, before I could do so, I began to see a few flaws in Nadia—she didn't care for children, for one thing. How could she not love kids? I couldn't imagine life without our kids, Jonathan and Janice. *Oh, Janice, wherever you are, we'll find you. We must.*

I glanced sideways at Stephanie and found my eyes watering. Just when I'd been on the verge of marital suicide, I began to remember the good times we'd had. The chaos surrounding the terrorist plot had driven us back into each other's arms. We still had our arguments, although they were fewer. We'd come a long way in a year. Our love was deeper, more realistic, more forgiving, kinder. We talked more and the sex wasn't bad, either. Why are men like me tempted to throw away a lifetime of companionship for a night or a month of passion? Especially when we had kids as wonderful as Janice and Jonathan?

The age-old questions. *Why did Adam and Eve throw away paradise for one taste of the forbidden fruit? And why do men seek out prostitutes? Why do they kidnap women and children? Why do they drown in pornography? How can they live with themselves?* I shuddered. *Oh, Janice. Sweetheart. My beautiful, grown-up little girl. So independent, so smart, so...*

"I found it," Stephanie said. "Nadia's home number."

I pointed toward a teashop advertising, *Fastest, Best, A-1 Internet Connections.* "Can you hop out and buy us some time on Skype? I'll find somewhere to park."

Stephanie wound her *dupatta* tightly around her head and jumped out. It took me ten minutes to bully my way into a spot between a sweet shop and a bakery. I hired the merchant running the bakery to watch the Land Rover and ran back to the teashop.

To the left side of the café, a chipped Formica counter was used to serve tea, tiny cakes, and biscuits, what we called cookies in North America. On the right, six or seven round tables were covered with faded and spotted tablecloths in a checkered pattern. A family with three children drank pop and munched biscuits at one table. At another, a couple of Punjabi farmers sipped tea from the saucers of their cups. Three college students sat at another, their fingers tapping away on their cell phones. Everyone in the shop stared toward the back. I guess Stephanie's arrival had created what passed for a sensation in this sleepy town.

I hastened toward the series of booths housing a motley array of computers. Three giggling girls occupied one booth. In another, a middle-aged man stared at what could only be porn from what I glimpsed over his shoulder. I found Stephanie in a booth at the back. As I pulled up a chair beside her, I saw that she already had the number logged in, ready to call.

She turned to me. "What time is it in Ontario?"

"About four in the morning."

"Too early?"

"This is a desperate situation. She'll understand."

"Let's do it then." Stephanie hit the dial key and we waited.

The phone rang once, twice, three times. "You do the talking, okay?" I said.

After a click, we heard, "H—hello?"

"Nadia?" Stephanie said.

"Whoever you are," we heard a yawn, "do you realize what time it is?"

"Nadia, this is Steph and Josh Radley. We're really sorry—"

Nadia interrupted. "Stephanie? Where are you calling from?"

"Pakistan. We have a terrible emergency."

"What? Pakistan?" Nadia sounded suddenly alert. "What happened?"

"Our daughter's been kidnapped." Stephanie gulped as tears began to stream down her face.

"Nadia, this is Josh. We don't know what to do. So we called you."

"Janice, your daughter, kidnapped? How?"

Stephanie dried her eyes with her *dupatta*. "Her train held up. Many dead. Women kidnapped—Janice—terrible. Blood everywhere."

"Oh, Stephanie, I'm so sorry."

I glanced around. Several people continued to stare in our direction. I leaned over the mike and, as softly as I could, tried to describe what had happened without choking up.

"Slow down a little. Our connection is not very good. Where did this happen?"

"About thirty miles north of Nowshera near the shrine of Baba Farid."

"I know the place."

Stephanie broke in. "Nadia, we need help, but don't know who to turn to."

"I'll make some calls. Get the CID involved. What about the local police?"

I turned down the speaker volume and whispered into the built-in mike. "We're in an internet café. Quite public and we don't yet have earphones. We can't tell you all the details over this phone, but there seems to be more going on than a simple train robbery. The police don't appear to be surprised... and this is not the only kidnapping. Something is going on here that may involve the most powerful landlord in the district."

"I bet that's Chaudri Gujar Mohammed."

"How do you know him?"

"Been rumours about him for years. He runs the Nowshera District like his own kingdom. Can you get to a safe phone and tell me the details?"

"There's a satellite phone at the archaeological site. We could call you from that in an hour."

"Give me the number and I'll ring you. Meanwhile, I'll contact some of my friends in Islamabad. They owe me big-time. If only things in Pakistan weren't in such chaos right now."

"Nadia," Stephanie said. "Thank you."

"Hey, that's what friends are for. If necessary, I'll come myself. *Insh 'allah*, we'll find Janice. *Fikr nah karen. Agar apka khuda dua soonta hai, jaisa ap mante hain.* We'll rescue Janice. You can get Josh to translate what I said."

After we broke off, Stephanie turned to me. "What did she say?"

I gripped her hand. "She was telling us not to worry, that, God willing, Janice will be rescued." I sighed. "We've got to believe that."

"Is that all she said?"

"She must be impressed by your faith. She said something about, 'If your God answers prayer as you believe, we'll find her.'"

Stephanie nodded. "Prayer. Strange that she would remind us about prayer."

CHAPTER EIGHTEEN
The Mysterious Missing Vehicle

We reached the dig with fifteen minutes to spare before Nadia's call. But instead of us breezing right through the gate, two of Luke's new Chinese guards waved us to a stop. One stood on either side of our vehicle with their fingers caressing Chinese submachine guns that hung from straps over their shoulders. Stockier than typical Chinese, I placed them as possibly Mongolian. Holstered pistols, walkie-talkies, and a canister of some kind hung from their belts.

The one on my side demanded in fractured English to know why we didn't have our identification passes hung around our necks.

"We're Mr. and Mrs. Josh Radley. We come everyday."

The guard raised his automatic. "No exceptions. You show."

I fumbled in the glove compartment, found our badges, and passed them over. He ran his finger down a list on a clipboard, shook his head, then spoke into his walkie-talkie.

My fingers drummed on the door. "This is urgent. We have to hurry."

He stared at me, then returned our passes, had me sign in, and signalled for us to proceed. I sped across the dry riverbed, climbed the bank, and braked to a stop in front of Luke Wu. He stood by the door to the brick shed where he had his office and stored the most important discoveries. As the cloud of dust kicked up by our vehicle enveloped him, he covered his nose with his handkerchief and turned away.

I jumped out of the Rover. "Sorry about the dust."

He sneezed. "I see you've met our new security. But what are you doing here? I didn't expect you on a Sunday, so your names weren't on the list."

"Daughter's been kidnapped. We need to use your satellite phone."

"What! Kidnapped? When?"

I took a deep breath. "The Khyber Mail was held up. People killed. A number of women kidnapped, including Janice."

"No."

"We're expecting a call back any moment from someone who may be able to help."

Stephanie came around the front of the vehicle. Her eyes were red and puffy, her cheeks streaked with makeup. "Please Mr. Wu."

"Yes, yes of course."

Luke returned with the satellite phone. "Mrs. Radley, I'm so sorry. Your daughter was—*is*—a wonderful young woman. Anything we can do. Just tell me."

We sat on a bench in the shade to wait for Nadia's call.

Precisely on time, the phone chimed. Nadia's voice came through as clear as if we were in the same room. "Josh, I'm devastated at the thought of Janice being kidnapped."

I put the phone on speaker and mumbled, "Thanks, Nadia."

"Don't lose hope. I've already lit a fire under Faqir Moham-med with the Foreign Service. He's dispatching a squad and posting a large reward. The attack is all over the news and it's not the kind of publicity Pakistan needs right now."

"Nadia, Stephanie here. We appreciate anything you can do."

I scowled. "They're worried about bad publicity? We have a daughter missing!"

"I know, Josh. It sounds callous, but the government is worried that pictures of this attack on BBC will scare away businessmen and tourists. So they're highly motivated to find the perpetrators, fast. The promise of a reward will have stool pigeons coming out of every bush. One of them will give us the lead we need."

Stephanie leaned over and whispered into the phone. "The pressure might make them crazy enough to kill her!"

"They won't kill her. The death of a foreign woman would bring a hurricane down on their heads. They may just be holding her for ransom. Kidnapping for ransom is a growth industry over there."

"Ransom," I said. "We don't have enough to ransom a mouse but—"

"Don't worry, the Pakistan government will cough up what's necessary. I'll see to that." Her voice faded. "—plane."

"Would you repeat that?" Stephanie said.

"I was saying that I'm coming out to help you and I'll be on the first available plane. My travel agent is searching for space on today's flight. I may get confirmation before I'm off the phone."

Stephanie sighed. "Oh, Nadia, you can't know how relieved that makes me feel."

"Can you do that?" I said. "Just take off?"

"Work be damned. I'm coming. You can rely on it. Now, Josh, fill me in on whatever I need to know to set the wheels in motion."

I described the kidnapping of Raju Moro's daughter, the bulldozing of their village, and Padri Fazal's indictment of Chaudri Gujar Mohammed's corruption.

Nadia broke in with some Urdu curse that I didn't catch. "Chaudri Gujar Mohammed—the snake. Your Padri friend is right about him. Been rumours for years. He's more powerful in Nowshera District than the Prime Minister."

A gust of wind blew fine grit into our faces. Stephanie covered her nose with her *dupatta*. I fumbled for the handkerchief I'd taken to carrying and wiped my face. Turning to Stephanie, I whispered, "Can you get us a bottle of water from the ice chest?"

I continued to fill Nadia in on everything I could remember that might have relevance: Chaudri's mention of drugs, the two loaded trucks from the Frontier Province, and Stephanie's instant dislike of Chaudri based on the way he leered at Janice.

Nadia broke in again. "Keep away from that guy—and his sons. They're bad news."

"Yeah, we know that now. Janice saw a woman with black eyes and a huge bruise on the side of her face. She had what looked like an iron ring around one wrist—the kind you can attach a chain to."

"Did you see the woman?"

"No, only Janice."

"Too bad, we could use a witness. Anyway, we'll get a subpoena. Anything else?"

"I visited the SP's office to ask for his help in finding the tribal girl, but left with nothing but a veiled threat to mind my own business or else."

A fax machine whirred in the background as Nadia responded. "The SP is probably in Chaudri's pocket. Everything you've told me is circumstantial, but taken together gives us enough to investigate further. Unfortunately, you seem to have arrived just when Chaudri, or whoever is behind this, feels he can take advantage of the deteriorating law and order situation in the country. The government is newly elected and already in trouble. The army is preoccupied with incursions by Al Qaeda along its western frontiers. Baluchistan is restive... Just a minute."

I took a long draft of the water Stephanie offered.

Stephanie pointed to the phone. "Is she still on the line?"

"I think so. You want to talk to her?"

Stephanie took the phone. "Nadia, are you still there?"

"I'm here... Give me a minute... Oh, good, I've got a reservation for a flight from Toronto to Karachi, leaving in a few hours. *Insh 'allah*, I'll see you tomorrow evening."

"Nadia, I'm so relieved." Stephanie pushed a stray lock of hair behind her ear and passed the phone back to me. "Did you hear that? She'll be here by tomorrow evening!"

"Don't do anything until I get there," Nadia said. "Remember, don't go near Chaudri. He's poison. Colonel Yaqub Nasri, a friend from Islamabad, will contact you later today. You can trust him. Look, I've got to dash if I'm going to make that plane."

We both replied, "Thanks, Nadia."

"And keep your hopes up. We'll find Janice."

When I returned the phone to Luke, he gripped my shoulders and looked me in the eye. "Josh, I can't believe this is happening. Whatever you need, just ask. It's yours."

"Thanks, Luke." I ran my hands through my hair. "I do have a question. Are any of the expedition vehicles out?"

"Vehicles? Why do you need to know that?'

"I'll explain later."

"Mine and yours are here. The students have one. It's parked beside mine. That makes three. Ali, our head of security, also has one." Luke pointed toward the mud-walled farm compound encroaching on the south end of the tell. "He parks it in his compound so it's convenient at night when he needs it to check on security around the perimeter. He usually sleeps during the day."

Luke walked with us over to our Land Rover.

"Are they all painted like this?"

"Exactly the same."

Instead of taking the road to our canal bungalow, I turned left along the fence toward the farm compound Luke had mentioned.

"Where are you going?" Stephanie asked.

"Checking on the fourth vehicle. A Land Rover painted like ours was seen at the train hold-up. Three of the expedition vehicles are accounted for. That leaves only one. This security guy's. If he's there, I'll ask him a few questions."

"Shouldn't we wait for Nadia, or the man she's sending?"

"This can't wait. The trail will go cold."

"Okay, I'm with you." She took a swig of water and passed the bottle to me. "Doing something is better than sitting... waiting..."

I braked in front of a reinforced timber gate set into the high mud brick wall that surrounded the compound. Broken glass studded the top of the wall. I could make out the flat roofs of several substantial brick buildings. To the right of the gate, under the meagre shade of a *kikar* tree, lounged a couple of water buffaloes chained to stakes. Except for the animals, it didn't look like the typical Punjabi farm. More like a fortress.

I walked over to a small door set into the gate and pulled the bell rope. From somewhere inside came the tinkle of brass bells. I stared back at Stephanie as I waited. Nothing. I gave it another tug. With a rasp, the door opened and a man with a pockmarked face and bristly gray hair peered at me through coke bottle glasses.

"*Kya chahe-e?*"

I pointed toward the archaeological site. "I'm with the expedition. I wanted to see Ali Sahib about something. Is he home?"

I peered over the man's shoulder as he explained that Ali was away, but would be back that evening. On the north side of the courtyard, near what looked like a barn for animals, rested a huge mound of burlap-wrapped bundles. A red tractor stood in front of the barn. A rather attractive whitewashed bungalow with a flower garden across the front took up the whole east side of the compound. No vehicle was in sight.

I thanked the man without giving my name and strode back to our Rover.

"So what did you find out?" Stephanie asked.

"He's not there." I accelerated back the way we had come.

"I'm getting bad vibes about this guy. Why don't you ask Luke about the cigarette butt you picked up?"

"Good idea."

By the time we'd passed through security again and pulled up to the shed where Luke had his office, it was padlocked. I jumped out and scanned the site for his diminutive figure. I saw that they'd cut a new trench farther north. From it, a stream of labourers—both men and women—trotted back and forth to empty their baskets on the growing pile of debris in the dry riverbed. Three of the trenches dug earlier looked abandoned. Canvas awnings over two others indicated where active excavation continued. But there was no sign of Luke.

My eyes traveled south across the tell toward the Hindu tower where the largest group of labourers gathered. Work on the tunnel under the tower must have been progressing well. I climbed the mound and strode toward them.

Luke detached himself from those gathered below the tower to hasten toward me. "I thought you were on your way to Nowshera."

"I went to check on your security chief. He's not home."

He cocked his head to one side and stared at me. "I didn't know you wanted to talk to him. I sent Ali to the airport to pick up a shipment of equipment. So, of course, he wouldn't be home. But why is that important?"

"I may be paranoid... but I'm pretty desperate. Following up any lead. What looked like an expedition vehicle was seen at the site of the train robbery."

Luke frowned. "Must have been a mistake."

I kicked at a broken piece of brick. "Probably. The person who identified it was very traumatized."

"You know how confused people get when they're under stress."

I nodded. "A mistake. You're probably right. By the way, does your security chief smoke?"

"Smoke?"

"Yeah, does he smoke *bidis* or one of those local brands, like K2?"

Luke extracted a tissue from his pocket and cleaned his sunglasses before returning them to their perch on his forehead. "Josh, what's going on? Why are you so interested in my security chief? Should I be worried?"

"No, it's probably irrelevant. Like I said, Jan's kidnapping has me paranoid." With my toe, I turned over a fragment of broken pottery and sighed. "Being nosey, asking a million questions... It's part of being a reporter."

Luke reached over and gripped my shoulders with both hands. "I understand. In your place, I'd be a basket case."

He dropped his hands and made to turn away. Then he stopped. "Ali smokes some kind of expensive foreign brand. American, I think. Filter-tipped. I keep warning him not to smoke inside our storage sheds."

CHAPTER NINETEEN
Grief

Stephanie and I sat silently on the veranda of the canal bungalow, numb. Neither of us commented on the fragrance of the oleander that had charmed us the day before, nor the bobbing dance of a hoopoe on the lawn.

When we'd told Musa and Mohammed of Janice's kidnapping, their faces had registered shock and disbelief. I thought about how different our approach to grief was from theirs. They assumed we'd want to be surrounded with people who could share our anguish. As a result, they had brought their families to offer *afsos*.

I wasn't sure if I had offended them or not—and I really didn't care—but I finally made Musa understand our desire to be alone. He urged us to eat at least some of the meal he'd prepared with such care. We couldn't. Finally, to give him something to do, we had him make us some tea, which sat cold and almost untouched in front of us. To get rid of Mohammed, I sent him off on his cycle to tell Pastor Fazal what had happened.

I rubbed my throbbing forehead. They both meant well, but neither of us felt like rehashing events for the curious, or engaging in polite chitchat.

My weary mind couldn't stop thinking about Jan. I could see her taking her first steps, bouncing on my knee, falling asleep in my lap, marching off to grade school with her tiny red backpack, chasing butterflies, showing me a skinned knee and asking me to wipe away the tears.

I hadn't been home much during her high school years, but Stephanie had kept me up on her scholastic triumphs and the boys that buzzed around her like bees. How deftly she had fended them off. I hadn't been there much to watch her play basketball or take part in school plays. And I'd been around even less when she went to college.

I sighed. "I've been a lousy father."

"I wouldn't say lousy." Stephanie pushed a lock of hair behind her ear. "Haven't been around much lately... but she knew you loved her."

"I just wish..." I gnawed on my lower lip. "I've got so many regrets. I thought this time in Pakistan would bring us closer. And now—"

"Don't say it. We'll find her." Stephanie reached over and turned my face toward her. "She loves you very much."

Moisture gathered in the corners of my eyes. "She's such a sweetheart."

"She's very proud of you, you know? She keeps a scrapbook of your articles to show her friends."

"You're kidding. I didn't know that."

"I think there are depths to her personality that neither of us understand. And I wouldn't be surprised if her faith is stronger than both of ours combined."

I sighed again. "Faith? But why would God allow this to happen?"

Stephanie dropped her hands and balled them into fists. "I don't know the answer to that question, but I do know that God is angry—angrier than we are. And when we find Janice, and we will, we're going to make those degenerates pay."

Startled, I turned to look at Stephanie. Her lips were set in a thin hard line and sparks like those from a welder's torch seemed to fly from her eyes. I'd seldom seen her filled with fury. Usually, she projected a gentle competence. Seeing her like this caused me to feel better. One thing I knew was that her faith was no pretend faith, no mere convenience. It took her down into the mud and mire of our murky world, but left her unsullied. If she'd been a man, I'd have called her faith muscular.

I stared down at a line of ants carrying miniscule bits of organic matter across the concrete floor of the veranda. Was God angry? Did God sense our agony? Of course, he felt something but... Perhaps that was the difference between us. Her faith reflected how intertwined her life was with God and this gave her more of a sense of how God felt about things. My faith was more in my own ability to get out of a jam than in God. Well, that wasn't entirely true—I did believe in God's help, but I wasn't sure I deserved it. Steph would have chided me for not believing in God's unconditional love.

She turned toward me. Her lips had relaxed into a soft line and her eyelids were arched as if she couldn't believe she'd been so forceful.

"You really believe we'll find Janice?" I asked.

She nodded. "I do. Ever since this happened, I've been praying. I believe God has given me assurance we'll get her back."

"I've been praying too, but I'm afraid I don't have your confidence. Bad things often happen to God's people."

"Often. And I could be wrong, but in this case, I get a sense that God will rescue Jan and expose whoever is behind this evil."

If Steph believed we'd get Janice back, then we probably would.

"Besides," she said, "we can't give up hope."

I reached over to grasp her hand. "We've got an hour or so before we're supposed to see the SP. I'm going inside to lie down, see if I can get rid of this headache."

"I'll join you."

We shut the door of our bedroom and lay holding each other tightly. I listened to the drone of flies on the screen and the sound of an occasional vehicle going by on the canal road. My eyes followed a *chipkilli* run across the ceiling. I wondered if there'd be *chipkillis* where she was being held. *Lord, please protect her and remind her how much we love her.*

We must have drifted off, because I don't remember anything else until we heard a loud knocking.

"Sahib," Musa said. "You have guests."

I stepped out onto the veranda, leaving Stephanie to wake slowly. Chaudri Gujar and Padri Fazal sat on the veranda at some distance from each other as if they'd catch some bug if they got too close. I nodded to Chaudri, then turned toward Padri Fazal.

He strode over and gave me a bear hug. "Joshua Sahib, *muje bahut afsos hai.*"

Chaudri rose. "I'm shocked and saddened by this terrible news. Horrible. Horrible."

I waved them back to their seats as I positioned a chair for myself between them. I could see that Musa had already brought them cups of the ubiquitous tea. Chaudri's cup was one of the two China cups from the cupboard. Fazal's was a chipped blue Multani mug—from the everyday set. I'd have to chide Musa about this subtle form of discrimination.

"I'm outraged," Chaudri said. "In broad daylight. These *dakoos* must be apprehended and Miss Janice rescued."

Padri Fazal watched Chaudri through narrowed eyes, but said nothing.

Chaudri waved his hands in the air. "I'll put my men at the disposal of the police force. And I'll offer a reward. Forty thousand rupees."

"I appreciate your concern, Chaudri Sahib. And it's very generous of you to offer a reward."

"Yes," Padri Fazal said. "We must do everything we can. I'll mobilize a nation-wide prayer chain for Miss Janice's return."

Chaudri quickly covered the trace of a smirk with his hand. "Hmm, prayer, yes, of course, prayer. Joshua Sahib, can you tell us what happened? Perhaps there is some clue we can follow-up."

With the spectre of Janice's abduction intruding on every thought, I didn't want to go over it again—the hurt only cut deeper. But I gave them an abbreviated version of events. I left out the matter of the expedition vehicle and the cigarette stub. After sufficient time had elapsed to fulfill the most meagre social requirement, I stood up. "Mrs. Radley and I have to go into Nowshera to report to the SP. So if you'll please excuse me, I need to check on her to see if she's ready."

Chaudri pointed toward his Mercedes. "Why don't I drive you in? I know the SP well."

I glanced toward his chauffeur, who stood beside his car. It was Chaudri's bodyguard, the giant with the black beard and white skullcap who had so intimidated me on the day of my arrival. I bowed toward Chaudri. "Your offer is most appreciated, but *Memsahib* and I need to do this ourselves."

After reiterating his offer to help in any way he could, Chaudri gripped my shoulder, repeated his condolences, and strode toward his car.

When Chaudri's car had disappeared down the canal road, Padri Fazal came over to give me a parting hug, but first he stood back and looked me in the eye. "Joshua Sahib, you said you wanted to be alone, but I wonder if that is wise? I've dealt with tragedy and grief for many years. People think they are very strong, but sometimes they unexpectedly break down and become inconsolable. It's not wrong to accept help—help from those you trust. Let me go with you to see the SP."

His earthy brown eyes radiated a warmth I remembered as a child sitting in his lap. I nodded. "We would feel better with you along."

The crowds of petitioners I'd seen the first time I visited the SP's office were absent when I drove up to the rambling colonial-era bungalow. The jacarandas and *gul mohars*, however, as if ignoring the rift in the universe caused by Janice's abduction, bloomed as brilliantly as ever. We parked behind a Bedford truck and two jeeps. A group of *sipahis* clutching ancient Enfield rifles stared at us as we passed. We must have looked like a strange trio: Stephanie with her hair carefully hidden by her *dupatta*, me wearing a Blue Jays baseball cap, jeans, and a long-sleeved blue shirt, and Padri Fazal with his thatch of snow-white hair.

A police officer brandishing a *latti* held the door for us. Inside, the SP's *babu*, the one with the smallpox scars and the wild wings of greying hair, peered at us over a pile of dog-eared files. Three officers with brass on their epaulets stood before a large map of the district.

The *babu* had obviously been expecting us, for he said, "Please be seated. I will inform the SP that you are here."

I was as surprised this time by his good English as I had been the first time. It just didn't seem in character for an arch-typical Asian *babu* to speak without butchering the King's English.

The officers glanced at us briefly before returning to their study of the map. We gingerly sat down on a rickety bench and waited. How the *babu* had communicated our arrival was a mystery. He hadn't spoken into any intercom or left his desk to tell the SP in person. Perhaps the SP hadn't arrived yet. Or had the *babu* sent him a text message? The juxtaposition of modern technology alongside archaic practices frequently astonished me.

Fifteen minutes went by. The police officers who had been studying the map disappeared into a side office. I glanced at the flyspecked monitor on the *babu*'s desk and tried to catch his eye. He ignored us. I studied the dusty shelves, stuffed with files that lined the whole wall, and willed them to fall on his head. To no avail.

When my frustration began to show in my tight lips and clenched hands, Fazal reached over and touched me on the arm. "*Subar, ji.* It is standard practice to test us. People in authority demonstrate their power over those below them by making them wait. There is nothing we can do but show that we have superior patience."

I looked over at Stephanie. She sat with her head down as if she were praying.

Twenty-five more minutes went by. Suddenly, we heard shrieks from the veranda. The door swung open and two police officers came in dragging a young woman in chains—her *dupatta* askew, her *qamiz* torn, and her white *shalwar* streaked with dirt. Tears guttered her dirty face. My mouth dropped open in outrage at the sight of the heavy chains that bound iron manacles at her wrists to those at her ankles.

The officer in front of her pulled on the chain to drag her forward while the one behind cuffed her repeatedly on the head. An officer from inside the cellblock opened the door for them and they disappeared inside. Her screams reverberated throughout the building until they were suddenly cut off.

Fazal whispered. "That's Akhtar Bibi from Village 11. I know her family well."

"What's she done?" Stephanie asked.

"Nothing. She's the victim. Two sons of the *numberdar*—the village head—raped her."

Stephanie stared at Padri Fazal with her mouth open. "What?"

I gripped Fazal's arm. "Why aren't they here? Are they in another jail?"

"No, they're scot-free. She's the one charged." Fazal spit out the words. "In a case like this, it's often the woman who is thought to have brought dishonour to the village. So they charge her with *zina*—immorality."

Stephanie and I sat silently, trying to comprehend the unspeakable cruelty we'd witnessed.

CHAPTER TWENTY
Incarceration of an Innocent

The SP's *babu* continued to ignore us as we sat waiting to make our report.

Stephanie screwed up her face in anger as she pointed toward the door leading to the holding cells. "How can they do that; arrest the victim and let the rapists go free? Where's the justice?"

Padri Fazal snorted. "Justice, pah! Justice is whatever the rich and powerful think it is. They dispense justice in order to get richer and more powerful. The poor and illiterate receive the lash of justice on their backs and eat dirt."

I frowned at Fazal. "So Akhtar Bibi's family is poor?"

"Very poor. Her father is a small tenant farmer who owes money to the village *numberdar*."

"What's a *numberdar*?" Stephanie asked.

"He's the village headman. In the case of Akhtar Bibi's village, the *numberdar* owns the land and has half a dozen sharecroppers who farm it. It's a feudal system from which there is no escape.

The tenant farmers share a percentage of the harvest, but it's not enough. They borrow from the landowner to buy seed, to replace oxen if they die, for fertilizer—everything. They never get out of debt."

Stephanie clenched her fists. "So if they oppose the *number-dar*—?"

"They'll get thrown off the land, and their neighbours may suffer as well." Fazal gnawed on his lip. "When Akhtar Bibi's father threatened go to the police, a delegation of other tenant farmers pleaded with him to drop the matter."

I leaned toward him. "The *numberdar* threatened to kick them all off the land?"

"Exactly." Fazal massaged his right knee. "And land is everything. Someone has said, 'That's what feudal power is. It begins with land, and ends with rape.'"[2]

"No wonder Bhutto's promise of land distribution was so revolutionary it got him hung."

Stephanie flung the tail of her *dupatta* over her shoulder and tightened it around her head. She leaned forward so she could see Fazal at the end of the bench, pursed her lips, and spat, "Land, hah! Everyone knows that a woman doesn't rape herself! There must be some court she can appeal to."

"Yeah," I said. "Don't they have village councils to settle these things?"

Fazal glanced at the *babu*, who, attracted by Stephanie's raised voice, glared in our direction. Fazal turned toward Stephanie and replied in a low voice. "In her case, they held a *jirga*. But the *numberdar* chaired the council. The *jirga* declared the boys innocent and the girl guilty of seductive behaviour."

Stephanie threw up her hands and walked out as if she needed fresh air. I followed her out into the garden where we paced up and down.

---

[2] Mukhtar Mai with Marie Therese Cuny, *In the Name of Honor – A Memoir*, New York: Atria Books, 2006, p. 38

"Josh, we should never have brought Janice to this place."

"We'll get her back, honey."

"But in what condition? Will she be raped, too?"

I shook my head, but couldn't speak as I took her in my arms. Damn. Damn. Damn. Why hadn't I listened to my gut and refused to return to Pakistan, or at least refused to let Jan take the train to Lahore?

Over Steph's shoulder, I saw Padri Fazal motioning for us to return.

Stephanie fumbled for a tissue and blew her nose loudly. "Okay, let's go back in."

The SP had kept us waiting an hour, but when we entered his office he was the model of civility and concern.

He stood up from behind his desk to receive us. "Mr. Radley, Mrs. Radley. Please have a seat. I've sent for tea."

"We don't need—"

He cut me off. "Please accept my small gesture of hospitality. This is a terrible business, but I don't want to make it more painful than it is. First of all, I apologize for the delay in seeing you, but as you can imagine this dastardly deed has affected not only yourselves, but also many others. We've had to mobilize extra resources."

He opened a folder on his desk. "Now, were you able to find a more recent photograph?"

Stephanie extracted a photo from her purse and passed it to him.

He stroked his fastidiously trimmed beard as he gazed at the picture. "Such a charming young woman. We will do everything in our power to find her. Can you describe what she wore?"

Stephanie leaned forward. "She wore a light blue *qamiz* with a pattern of small, darker blue flowers. Her *shalwar* was also light blue. Her *dupatta* was white."

The *babu* arrived with three cups of Pakistani tea, which he passed around. The SP motioned for us to drink our tea while he continued to write down details in the folder open on the desk. "What about jewellery? That kind of thing."

Stephanie touched her left ear. "A simple gold loop in each ear."

"And a Bulova watch," I said, thinking about the watch I'd given her for graduation. "A gold watch with a blue dial."

I sipped my tea as he continued to query Steph about anything distinctive about her dress or the contents of her purse. I stared idly at the portraits on the wall behind the SP and wondered if Pakistan would have developed in a more democratic direction if its founder, Mohammed Ali Jinnah, had lived. Probably not.

I turned slightly to stare out the window at the SP's rose garden. Where was Jan right now? How was she feeling? I bit my lip in frustration.

Stephanie touched my arm. I'd missed the SP's question. "I'm sorry, I was thinking about my daughter."

He nodded. "I was asking how you came to be at the scene?"

The SP looked at us over his cup while Stephanie and I explained about Jan's phone call and our race to the train. His forehead was furrowed as if he was trying very hard to project sympathy. The apparent warmth of his concern did not reach his eyes, which looked as dark and cold as anthracite.

With our report complete, he stood, came around the desk, and led us toward the door. "You've been very helpful. Now if you'll leave it with me, I'll do what I can. I've already cancelled all leaves and called for an extra squad of men. The police in Bahawalpur to the north and Sukkur to the south have established roadblocks to examine all traffic, but signs indicate the *dakoo* went west, toward the river. We've called in the river patrol to search for them."

He held the door open. "Please accept my sympathy, and be assured that this kidnapping will be short-lived. We will find the miscreants and deal with them severely. *Insh 'allah.*"

As we exited the office, Padri Fazal came forward and addressed the SP. "*Janab-e-ali.* May I take but one moment of your time?"

The SP glared at Fazal. "Ah, Padri Fazal." His voice rose. "And how is my thorn today?"

Padri Fazal bowed with his hands folded together in front of him in supplication. "Thank God, my health is good, but sadly, my soul is sorrowful."

The SP turned back toward his office with his hand on the door. "Yes, well, we are all sad about the events of this day." His voice took on an edge of anger. "Now, leave me to get on with finding these criminals."

Before he could close the door, Fazal said. "Sir, I just wanted to ask if the Pakistan Women's Benevolent Society has been informed yet about Akhtar Bibi's situation." He bowed again. "If not, I can inform them so they can send a lawyer to represent her interests."

The SP took a step forward and shook his finger in Padri Fazal's face. "Are you interfering again in a police matter? You should go back to your pathetic flock and do your preaching there. Leave matters of justice to us and to the courts."

With that, he turned and walked into his office, slamming the door behind him.

As we drove away, I glanced over my shoulder at Padri Fazal in the back seat. "What was that about?"

"*Muaf kijie*—I'm sorry," he said. "I hope I didn't prejudice him against you. In the last three or four years, I've tried to get him to drop cases against a number of innocent people. Then just last week, I came with Raju Moro to plead his case. This time I should have been quiet and come back some other time. I'm sorry."

"You can't be sorry for doing what's right." Stephanie batted again at the errant lock of hair that kept curling over her eye. "What is this women's benevolent society?"

"The Pakistan Women's Benevolent Society is one of the groups that fights for the rights of women. They publicize women's issues and arrange for lawyers to represent those who can't afford counsel."

"The court won't appoint a lawyer for Akhtar Bibi?" Stephanie asked.

"If they do, it will be some establishment lawyer who knows his duty to the rich and powerful."

I listened to their conversation, but concentrated on avoiding the taxis, horse carts, trucks, and cyclists who all seemed bent on asserting their divine right to the roadway.

"Akhtar Bibi can't afford a lawyer?"

"She probably doesn't even know she has a right to a lawyer. Like many, she's illiterate." Fazal's speech accelerated and his voice took on an edge as if a fountain of deep-seated anger had been breached. "That's the way most of the men want to keep them. Ignorant. Compliant. Shut away behind walls, behind *burquas*. Silent. Invisible. There to serve men. To be used like cattle and then discarded. If a man gets tired of his wife, he can divorce her with a word, or get a younger wife."

He took a deep breath and leaned back against the seat as if his energy was spent. We drove along silently for a few minutes until we cleared the congested bazaar area.

Fazal broke the silence, speaking slowly, quietly. "You may wonder why I feel so strongly. According to confirmed reports by a women's watch group, eighteen women were raped by fifty-one men last month! Three women died. One was murdered by her attackers. Another killed herself. Still another was burned alive by her brothers-in-law who accused her of adultery. Akhtar Bibi is not even mentioned on that list. She represents thousands who go unreported.

"Our school lost three of the brightest girls—even before the term was finished. One was married off to an older man from Karachi, his second wife. The other two had to drop out of school to help on their parents' farm.

"Without proper education, our women will continue to be abused. Did you know that some studies claim that half the women in Pakistan are the victims of violence? But I shouldn't be burdening you with this. You have enough on your minds."

We said little during the rest of the trip back to the canal bungalow. What was there to say? All I could do was think of Jan.

Before he drove off on his motorcycle, Padri Fazal put his hand on Stephanie's head to bless her and then gave me a crushing hug. "Let me know," he said, "if there is anything else I can do besides pray for the safe return of Miss Janice."

In a thoughtful attempt to comfort us, Musa had prepared an English style dinner of mashed potatoes, peas, and roast beef. We tried to eat, but felt too filled with grief to do more than push the food around on our plates.

I finally followed Steph's lead and set down my spoon after only a few mouthfuls. Musa brought us coffee, then stood there a minute, looking from one to the other as if he didn't know what to say. I thanked him for a tasty dinner and explained that we just didn't feel hungry.

"*Bahut afsos, Sahib.*" Musa shook his head as he expressed his sorrow. Then he quietly left us.

Stephanie poured cream into her coffee. "I don't trust the Superintendent of Police."

"I don't either. He's too polished to be sincere. Did you notice that he didn't mention the possibility that the bandits escaped by going east, into the desert?"

Stephanie frowned. "Isn't the desert impassable?"

I ladled sugar into my coffee. "Not really. For millennia, the tribes have traveled back and forth across the desert along the India-Pakistan border. There's a whole series of old forts out there. Besides, I'm sure the tracks I saw turning off the Grand Trunk Road near Baba Farid led east toward the desert not west toward the river."

"I'm glad we called Nadia."

"Yeah, it doesn't look like we can expect much help from the local police."

Stephanie shivered. "I can't get the image out of my head of that woman being dragged into the police station."

I looked down at my coffee cup. Without thinking, I'd been stirring it for the last few minutes. "Best not to think about her. Let Padri Fazal get that women's organization to arrange a lawyer."

"I see her and—" She set down her cup with a clink that sloshed coffee into the saucer.

She dropped her head into her hands and began to sob. I knelt beside her and put my arms around her. Convulsive moans shook her. Then, slowly, her shudders eased. She stood up, wiped her eyes, and began to pace back and forth. "Blubbering is not going to help Jan. There must be something more we can do."

"I've been racking my brain to come up with something and I keep coming back to Chaudri's farm. You remember what Jan said about the woman she saw cleaning his stable?"

"The one who had a bruise on the side of her face—one eye black and blue?"

"And one of her wrists in an iron manacle, the other rubbed raw."

Musa came in to clear the dishes, so we went out into the garden.

I leaned against the trunk of a shesham tree. "Whatever is going on, I bet Chaudri Gujar is in the middle of it."

"Nadia knew immediately who we were talking about. I've had a bad feeling about that man ever since we first saw him."

I kicked at the dirt. "The trucks from the frontier that I saw in his yard could easily have contained drugs smuggled in from Afghanistan."

"Drugs?" Stephanie twirled a frangipani blossom in her fingers. "Our concern right now is finding Jan."

"But what if kidnapping and drugs are connected? Raju Moro's son identified the vehicle used to kidnap his sister as belonging to Chaudri. Children and young women have gone missing for years. Plus, Padri Fazal told me that people suspect Chaudri is corrupt despite that they can't prove anything. An officer who came from Islamabad to investigate disappeared."

Stephanie crushed the blossom she'd been twirling and threw it down. "If he's involved, he will be ruthless unless the fact that we're foreigners moves him to caution. Perhaps if we appeal to him..."

I swatted a mosquito. "No use. We need some kind of evidence."

CHAPTER TWENTY-ONE
Midnight Search

Stephanie and I continued to wander around the garden until the mosquitoes became so bloodthirsty that we had to flee inside. I picked up a mystery book and tried to lose myself in New Orleans. Stephanie went into the bathroom and took a shower.

She came out in her pyjamas with a towel around her head. "Josh, we need to let Jonathan know about Jan. It would be terrible if he heard about her kidnapping through the media."

I threw down the book I'd been trying to read. "You're right."

I booted my laptop and opened my e-mail server. Stephanie towelled her hair dry, sat down beside me, and we composed a message to our son. We discarded half a dozen attempts before coming up with the right words to convey both the facts and our grief. We asked him to tell our parents and the church. We also told him of Nadia's coming, but mentioned nothing of what we suspected.

After my shower, I joined Stephanie in bed. We prayed together for Jan's release, turned off the light, and tried to sleep. I lay there staring at the ceiling tiles in the faint starlight that poured in through the *roshandans,* the small windows near the ceiling built for air circulation. Incredible how brilliant the stars were this close to the desert. Could Jan see the stars? Was the God who made the stars watching over her? Of course he was—wasn't he?

I turned onto one side, then the other. Sleep would not come. I whispered, "You awake?"

"Wide awake."

"Steph, I can't get rid of the feeling that there is evidence in Chaudri's barns. I'm going to drive over there and see what I can find."

"What?"

"It's midnight. Everyone will be asleep. I'll park the car at a distance and walk the last mile."

"He'll have a night watchman patrolling the grounds."

"He might, but even burglars would be so afraid of Chaudri that I doubt a *chaukidar* has much to do. Probably asleep."

Stephanie sat up in bed. "If you're going, I'm going with you."

We drove the last few miles to Chaudri's farm, slowly and with the lights off. I turned down a track beside a narrow feeder canal that watered his fields. After parking in a grove of trees, we waited a few minutes to let our eyes adjust to the darkness.

We wore dark clothes—blue jeans, black turtlenecks, and dark blue jackets. Each of us carried a flashlight. I had a digital camera slung around my neck and some plastic bags in my pocket in case I found some evidence.

I shivered as much from the thought of what we were about to do as the chilly night air. As our eyes adjusted to the starlight, we could clearly make out the shadows of trees and buildings across the field. Except for a light high on a pole in front of Chaudri's house, everything stood dark and silent.

I pointed to our right. "See that laneway?"

"Yeah."

"We'll approach the barns along that lane. Fortunately, the house is on the other side. You act as lookout while I check what's in the buildings."

"I don't have a good feeling about this," Stephanie whispered.

"It's a bit late for me to turn back—but you could stay with the car—be ready to pick me up if I run into trouble."

"No way. I'm not staying here."

"It'll be okay. There's not a sound, not a movement."

Stephanie sucked in her breath. "Let's get this over with."

I pointed across the field again. "The first building is a stable for the horses. We can leave that for the end. From what I re-member, the next holds his prize herd of Brahmas. We can leave that one, too."

"So it's the third and fourth we want to check out?"

"Yeah. Let's go. Watch your feet. There may be snakes along this channel."

Stephanie stepped back. "What! Now you tell me."

I motioned for us to get going. We hurried along the roadway. Stephanie kept her eyes on the ground as she followed.

In the bushes along the canal, we heard a faint rustling.

"What was that?"

"Just mice or something."

Suddenly, a sound like a score of babies in mortal agony erupted all around us. Stephanie screamed and flung her arms around me, knocking me off balance. We tumbled into a heap in the dirt. I clamped my hand over her mouth and whispered. "Shh!"

A file of dark, screaming shapes burst from the bushes and loped off down the roadway. We lay there until their yipping shrieks gradually died out.

"Jackals."

Stephanie sat up with her hand over her heart, taking deep gasping breaths. "Scared me to death."

I could feel my own heart thudding in my chest. "Must have been feeding on carrion." I sat up and peered toward the barns. "Not going to arouse anyone. They hear those critters almost every night."

We stood up, brushed the dirt off our clothes, and set off again. Stephanie glanced back at the bushes as we turned down the lane toward the barns.

We passed dark shapes in the field to our right. Cattle. At the end of the lane, we paused to listen. Nothing but the occasional stamp of a hoof or creak of a board in the first barn.

The pungent smell of cattle assailed our nostrils as we slipped past the second building. We stopped at the door to the third barn. I pointed toward a couple of barrels off to one side. I whispered in Stephanie's ear, "You stay behind those barrels. If you hear the *chaukidar* coming, flash your light through the door, then hide. I'm going in."

I grasped the handle, then let it go. I walked back to Stephanie, leaned toward her, and gave her a kiss full on the mouth. I could feel her trembling as she put her arms around me and whispered, "Hurry, Josh."

The door creaked slightly when I eased it open and slipped inside. I stood there motionless, trying to identify the dark shapes before me. The overpowering stink of grease and spilled diesel hung in the air. The shed was full of farm equipment. I could make out a couple of tractors, a combine, and some hay wagons.

Shielding my flashlight, I began to circle the building looking for anything unusual. A workbench with a full range of tools. A pile of rusted parts in one corner. A row of ploughs. Racks of shovels and scythes. Barrels. Could they hide drugs? I went over to the nearest one and tapped it lightly. Full. Looking around, I found a wrench I could wedge into the bung. I was about to ease it open when I heard the *tap, tap* of the *chaukidar's* stick.

Pocketing the wrench, I flung myself under the nearest hay wagon. With a squeal, the door on the other side of the building flew open. Light flooded in as the *chaukidar* switched on the lights. I lay there holding my breath. I'd been fortunate that Pakistani night watchmen routinely made a noise as they went about their rounds—sometimes hitting their nightstick on the ground, sometimes calling out the hours. *They must be as scared of surprising a thief as I am of being caught.*

With his nightstick beating a cadence on the concrete floor, the *chaukidar* came down the aisle toward where I lay. My heart began to pound so loudly that, when he stopped near where I was hiding, I was sure he heard it. I held my breath and stared at his scuffed, leather boots as he swivelled around. Had I moved anything that he would notice? Had he caught a glint of light from my flashlight?

Finally, he walked back the way he had come, flipped off the lights, and slammed the door shut. I waited five minutes or so before I slid out of my hiding place. *Stephanie will be having a cow, but I have to check those barrels.*

After a couple of tries, I eased open the bung and stuck my finger inside. Oil. I replaced the bung and decided to leave the other barrels. They probably held what the labels indicated.

When I exited the shed, Stephanie glided to my side and whispered, "What happened? I thought you'd been discovered."

With more nonchalance than I felt, I replied, "Just the *chaukidar* on his rounds. I hid under a hay wagon."

"Find anything?"

"Nah. Just farm equipment. Tractors, wagons, that kind of thing."

"I hate to keep saying this, but let's hurry."

"Did you see where the *chaukidar* went?"

Stephanie pointed to the next shed. "There. Turned on the lights for a few minutes, then left."

"Okay, let's go."

I stopped at the door to the fourth barn and looked around before trying the handle. A tractor hooked up to a hay wagon stood parked against the nearest wall, between the third and fourth sheds. "Steph, you wait by that tractor. It'll give you cover."

I tried the door. It was locked. I fished my Swiss knife from my pocket and worked it back and forth until it came in contact with the latch. Nothing.

"Pst." I motioned for Stephanie to rejoin me. "Can you give me a little light here so I can use both hands? And shield the light."

After a few minutes, I heard a click and the door eased open a crack. I waved Stephanie back to her position and crept inside. The interior was inky black. No glimmer of starlight filtered in. A sickening stench greeted my nostrils, the smell of sweat and something rotten and something else I couldn't place.

I swung my light to the wall nearest me. No windows. Becoming bolder, I moved my light back and forth. No windows anywhere. Double doors at the far end. Solid brick construction all the way around. Bales of hay were stacked to the ceiling on the side of the building to my right, except at the corner nearest me. In that corner, I could make out a pile of burlap-wrapped bundles like those I'd seen on the trucks from the North-West Frontier. Bingo!

I ran over to them and, taking out my knife, cut a tiny slit near the back of one of the bales. Inserting my knife, I brought out a tiny mound of powder. Coke. I put a sample in one of the plastic bags I carried and turned on my digital camera. Looking around to make doubly sure no light could escape, I took a couple of flash pictures of the pile of bales. I had to hurry.

Turning to the hay bales, I flashed my light through the cracks between them to see if anything further had been hidden behind them. Nothing. By the time I got to the far end of the building, the stench had become almost unbearable. I took out a handkerchief and covered my nose as I flashed the light into a series of bins built along that wall. Something scurried away. Just a rat after the grain they contained.

This had taken too long. Time to leave. I hurried back toward the door where I'd entered, then abruptly stopped. My flashlight had picked out a chain lying on the floor. With my light, I traced its length to where it was connected to a steel ring fastened to the wall. The chain lay on a dirty piece of cloth. Flashing my light further, I could make out a series of iron rings cemented into the wall. Chains and shackles lay about. I followed the chains toward the door and took a series of pictures.

Suddenly I stopped to look more closely at a pile of rags on the floor. As I approached, a swarm of flies flew up. I gagged. Staring at me with her sightless eyes lay a young girl, her arm still bound by a chain to the wall. Dead.

Fighting down the urge to throw up, I quickly took pictures and hastened toward the door.

Before I reached it, the door cracked open and Stephanie flashed her light once, twice. "Hurry," she hissed. "Trucks on the main road. I think they're coming here."

I ran to the door, slipped through, made sure it was locked, and followed Steph toward the lane leading away from the barns. We'd reached the lane and started to follow it to the feeder canal where we'd left the car when I heard shouts from the direction of the house. Glancing over my shoulder, I saw lights come on all over the barnyard.

"Get down," I whispered.

CHAPTER TWENTY-TWO
Nightmare

W
e lay there in the dust, expecting at any instant to be discovered. After a few moments, I raised my head to peer back toward the farm. With a great grinding of gears, a couple of trucks lumbered up the driveway leading to the barns. I could make out a couple of figures standing in a cluster under a floodlight set high on a pole. No one seemed to be looking in our direction.

I whispered to Stephanie. "Let's go, but keep down low."

Bent over, we stumbled along the laneway toward the feeder canal.

When we gained the clump of bushes where we'd hidden the Land Rover, we paused to catch our breath. "That was close," I said.

"We're not home yet." Stephanie brushed the grass and dirt off her jeans and jacket. "As soon as we open the door, the light will come on."

"You're right! These bushes aren't dense enough to hide it."

"Why don't we use our jackets to cover the side windows. I'll cover the driver's side window, get in first, and climb over to my side. As soon as I'm in, I'll cover the dome light with a rag or something."

"Brilliant." I passed her the kerchief I'd taken to carrying. "Let's do it. Fast."

When we were inside, I grimaced as I turned the key, nervous about the noise starting the Land Rover would create. "I hope the sound of those trucks covers us."

As gently as I could, I engaged the gearshift, backed over a couple of bushes to turn around, and slowly drove toward the main road.

"Any sign we've been spotted?"

"Nothing. The trucks seem to have stopped in front of the fourth barn. Lots of activity there."

With a great sigh, I turned onto the main road.

Stephanie tore open one of the packets of moist towelettes we kept in the car and began to wipe her face. "Where are you going? Isn't the canal bungalow the other way?"

"We can't afford to go directly home—especially not on the road that passes Chaudri's farm. No telling what would happen if someone spotted us."

When we'd put a few miles behind us, I turned on the lights.

Stephanie passed me a bottle of water. "Did you find anything in that last barn?"

"Did I ever." I took a slug of water. *How much should I tell her?* "A pile of bundles that must contain opium." I fished in my pocket and brought out the plastic bag with the sample. "Can you hide that somewhere?"

Stephanie turned in her seat to look for a hiding place. "How about in the crack between the back cushions."

"Perfect. If we get stopped and searched, we can always say it must have fallen out of some passenger's pocket."

"Why would we get searched?"

"We won't, but I'm kinda paranoid."

"Did you get pictures?"

"Sure did. In full, incriminating colour." I flexed my shoulder muscles trying to ease the tension that had them in knots. "The shed is solid brick, no windows, hardly the kind of construction one would expect in a hot climate. Along one wall are a series of iron rings cemented into the wall."

"For animals?"

"For human beings!" I paused a moment, then decided I should tell her what I had seen. "A bunch of chains with shackles were lying around. The kind that would fit over the ankle or wrist of a person. Dirty pallets lay on the floor and on one of them sprawled a girl. Dead, but still chained to the wall. By the smell, she'd been dead for a day or two."

"No!"

Stephanie rolled down the window, stuck her head out, and retched.

I pulled to the side of the road. Stephanie jumped out and began walking up and down. When she stopped, I got out, went to her side, and passed her the bottle of water and a fresh towelette.

She took a gulp of water, rinsed her mouth, and spit it out. "Jan... can't... get Jan... out of my mind."

I put my arms around her. "It's in their interest to take good care of Jan." I wasn't sure I believed that, but for Stephanie's sake... "At least now we have concrete evidence tying Chaudri to criminal activity."

"I'm okay now. Let's go."

I reached into the car, grabbed the camera, and extracted the digital card. "We need to hide this card. Without it, we have nothing."

"Pass me one of those plastic baggies you brought."

I searched the pockets of my jacket until I found one. "What are you going to do?"

She rummaged in her purse for a safety pin, put the chip into the baggie, folded it small, and lifting her shirt pinned it to the inside of her bra.

"Perfect."

We got back into the Land Rover and drove to Nowshera. I pulled into the parking lot of an all-night truck stop on the main Karachi-Lahore highway. "Why don't we get a couple of cups of tea? It'll rinse the bad taste out of your mouth."

Stephanie nodded. "And settle our nerves."

I returned with our travel mugs full of steaming, Pakistani *chai*. I didn't tell Stephanie that the waiter had wiped the inside of our clean mugs with the dirty towel he had wrapped around his waist. Some things were best ignored—especially when there was nothing you could do about it.

We sat blowing on our tea, taking cautious sips. Here and there, drivers and their *cleaners*—helpers—lay sleeping on string beds beside their trucks. In Pakistan, truckers carried their beds with them. I idly wondered if that solved the problem of bedbugs.

Out on the highway, heavy-laden trucks lumbered by on their way to Karachi in one direction or Lahore in the other. In spite of the fact that a few hours earlier a brazen and bloody train robbery had stopped our world from turning, nothing seemed to halt the wheels of commerce. Chinese imports. Sugarcane for the Dharki refinery. Soy for the Lever Brothers plant. Cotton for the mills. Televisions and computers for the burgeoning middle class.

With our tea finished, I turned north on the main highway, then took a country road east. It took us almost an hour by a circuitous route, but we finally arrived back at the canal bungalow around three in the morning.

I was quite sure no one had seen us on any of the roads leading up to our bungalow. However, when we pulled into our driveway, we found Mohammed, our *chaukidar*, standing by the veranda.

"Uh-oh," I whispered. "What story do we tell him?"

We got out, smiled at him, and started up the steps to the veranda.

He frowned. "Sahib and Memsahib drive somewhere?"

Stephanie joined her hands together and lay her head on them, miming sleep, then shook her head and pointed to her eyes, indicating tears. She was becoming quite adept at sign language. Catching her drift, I explained in Urdu that we hadn't been able to sleep because of our anguish over Janice's kidnapping.

In our room, Stephanie turned to me. "Do you think he bought it?"

"Probably. They think foreigners are crazy anyway, crazy enough to wander around at night."

"At least we didn't have to lie."

"That was fast thinking."

I'd always admired Steph's honesty. However, I wondered if a few white lies weren't in order when the alternative was worse. After all, in the Bible, David had told a few fibs to escape King Saul's murderous rage. "I just hope Mohammed doesn't mention this to Chaudri. I think he may spy for Chaudri."

"We did get tea in Nowshera. Someone there can probably vouch for us."

"We'll worry about it later. Why don't you try and get some sleep?"

Stephanie headed off to bed. Before I joined her, I used my laptop to copy the pictures from the digital chip onto a CD. I taped the CD to the back of the picture of Mohammed Ali Jinnah, Pakistan's founder. Surely, out of reverence for this noble figure, no one would look there. I buried the picture chip in an envelope among my correspondence.

That done, I crawled into bed and tried to sleep. Both of us were restless. We turned first one way, then the other. Finally, clasping each other in a snug embrace, we drifted off.

I fell into darkness—darkness punctuated by screams. The screams became the howls of jackals. The howls became the rattling of chains. The chains bound shadowy figures to a wall. The wall and the chained figures stretched infinitely toward the horizon. Suddenly one of the figures sat up, stared at me with eyes dripping gore, and slowly lifted a putrid hand toward me. No, it couldn't be! I tried to flee but my feet remained rooted to the spot. I opened my mouth to scream, but no sound came out except a moan. I tried again to run, but every time I tried to take a step, my feet sank deeper into the sand of a trackless desert. Fear coursed through my veins.

I sat up, rubbed my eyes, and tried to still my racing pulse. After a few moments, I lay back down and turned on my side. I must have drifted off to sleep because the next thing I remembered was a dream of kicking a soccer ball back and forth on a dusty village street.

I was a boy of seven or eight wearing a yellow t-shirt and white shorts with a yellow stripe down the side. The boy I played with wore short pants and a t-shirt that was dingy and torn. We laughed and bantered as we played. It felt good. As long as we avoided the black shapes along the road.

Then I saw that everywhere up and down the dusty street, hundreds of black water buffaloes sprawled in the shade of scrawny trees. They bared their teeth at us. We dodged back and forth as we played, straining to avoid the water buffaloes.

The street closed in on us. The shallow ditch full of putrid water running alongside the road became a pond, green with scum and floating bits of refuse. I tried to shout a warning as the ball bounced toward the stagnant pond—but I couldn't get the words out.

The other boy raced down the street to rescue the ball. I tried to shout again, but my tongue was frozen. Suddenly, a black van roared into the lane trailing a cloud of dust. Paralyzed, I watched the boy sprint into its path. Just when I thought he would be hit, the car swerved and stopped. A robed figure grabbed the boy and threw him inside.

I screamed and screamed.

"Josh, Josh, wake up."

I sat up in a cold sweat. My pyjamas were damp with perspiration. The clock radio read 6:07.

"Did you have the same kind of nightmare you've had before?"

I took a couple of shuddering breaths as I nodded. "But clearer... vivid."

Stephanie clicked on a bedside lamp and then put her arms around me.

I clung to her. "It was me, as a boy... I remember that yellow t-shirt. Grandma gave it to me for my birthday."

Stephanie massaged my back. "It's okay, honey."

I shivered. "Daniel... Playing soccer with Daniel... His village... Steph, it was horrible."

"What was horrible, sweetheart?"

"Soccer ball... pond... I kicked it."

I put my head in my hands as tears began to trickle down my face.

Stephanie's fingers began to loosen the knots in my shoulders. "Whatever happened, it was long ago."

I wiped my eyes with the back of my hands. "Daniel... my fault."

"Why don't you tell me about it? You'll feel better."

I propped up a couple of pillows and leaned against them. "It's all coming back. When I was a boy, Daniel was my best friend. He lived in a *basti* near our house in Nowshera. We'd often play soccer on the streets of the *basti*, sometimes with a group of village boys, sometimes just the two of us.

"We were kicking around a new soccer ball I'd been given on my birthday. Daniel warned me not to kick it near the stagnant pond. We played up and down the street. One of our shots hit a water buffalo. Finally, I kicked a long arching shot that headed toward the pond." I frowned as I concentrated. "Daniel raced down the street to keep it from going in the water. Suddenly, a jeep—or a truck—no, a van turned down the street and drove toward us."

I shook my head.

"What happened, honey?"

"A man grabbed Daniel and threw him into the van. Drove away. Never saw him again."

I clenched and unclenched my fists. "My fault. If I hadn't kicked the ball toward the pond, Daniel wouldn't have been taken."

Stephanie reached over and turned my face toward her. "Josh, that's not true. You were a boy. It wasn't your fault."

"I didn't remember all this until just now." I shuddered. "Daniel... I remember his mother looking at me, screaming his name. I remember my dad demanding to know why I'd been playing soccer in the street. He was angry. Blamed me. We never saw his parents again."

"Oh, Josh, Josh, that's too much guilt for a little boy to bear. No wonder you have nightmares."

I lay there with Steph's arms around me, staring at the ceiling fan. It needed dusting before the hot weather arrived again. Should mention that to Musa. After a few minutes, I turned to Steph and kissed her. "Thanks, honey."

I got up and went into the bathroom, washed my face, and combed my hair. I stood there staring at myself in the mirror, thinking, *Thirty-one years of nightmares. Could this be why?*

Back in the bedroom, I rejoined Stephanie in bed. It was 6:16, still too early to get up. "Steph, I've had nightmares for years, but never one like this. It was too real."

"Sounds like it was based on what happened to you as a boy, the trauma of losing your friend. You suppressed the memory so you could cope."

"Coming here has brought back the memory. Probably why I dreaded returning."

"Oh, Josh—Jan's kidnapping."

I nodded my head. "And Raju's daughter... and now I have Jan's kidnapping on my conscience, too. I should never have let her take the train. I should never have let you both come to visit."

Stephanie leaned against me. "I don't blame you, Josh. I wanted to come. Jan wanted to come even more. This is not about blame, it's about finding her."

"I wish... I wish... No, you're right. I wonder if blaming oneself is a kind of self-pity, a form of escapism?"

We were interrupted by a loud knock on the door.

"Sahib? Sahib?"

"*Kya bat hai?* What is it?"

"Most sorry, sir, but army officer arrive and insists I wake you. Says is most urgent."

"*Teak hai, ji.* Gimme a few minutes."

CHAPTER TWENTY-THREE
Colonel Nasri

I t was cold in the house. I stumbled into the bathroom, took a
quick hot shower. Unshaven, I pulled on jeans, a shirt, a
sweater, and tried to forget my nightmare.

The man who rose to meet me when I entered the living room
looked like an English gentleman. He wore tan trousers, a classic
blue button-down shirt with an Oxford tie, and a fawn sport
jacket. His erect bearing indicated a military background and his
piercing gray eyes bespoke someone used to having his commands obeyed instantly.

He took my hand in a firm grip. "Mr. Radley, my name is
Yaqub Nasri. I apologize for disturbing you so early, but I came as
soon as I got the call from Ms. Nadia Khan."

"She spoke very highly of you, sir." I indicated a sofa. "Please."

I turned on the gas heater to warm up the room, then sat
down opposite my visitor.

He leaned toward me. "I'm absolutely appalled by the kidnapping of your daughter. I have a daughter of the same age, so I feel

for you. Every right-minded Pakistani grieves with you, and with the other victims of this brutal attack."

I bit my lower lip and stared at the floor as memories of the previous day flooded back.

"Do not worry, Mr. Radley. We will find your daughter. I drove all night from Multan so I could coordinate the search." He took out a small notebook. "Now, if you could, fill me in on what you know."

Could I trust him? I gazed out the window before answering. A military officer in khakis stood beside a dust-covered Mercedes.

"Ah, you are quite right to be cautious." He reached into the inside pocket of his jacket and passed over a passport-sized leather folder. "Please."

"I'm sorry, I—"

"Don't apologize. You are wise to be careful."

I opened the folder and saw that Yaqub Nasri was a colonel in the Pakistan Army assigned to military intelligence and a liaison officer with American Forces in Afghanistan.

I passed back his ID. "Please forget," he said, "what you've just read. Forget who I am. I showed it to you only because of the trauma you've gone through and my confidence in your discretion. Now tell me what you know."

I leaned back in my chair and began to describe what I'd found at the scene of the attack. I told him everything I could remember, including the eyewitness account of a jeep like those owned by the expedition and my discovery of the American cigarette butt. I was about to describe what we'd found at Chaudri's compound when Musa arrived with cups of tea.

After he'd gone, Colonel Nasri said, "Were you able to confirm the identity of the jeep?"

"The only jeep not at the site yesterday, except the one I use, was one driven by the head of security for the dig. And he smokes some foreign brand of cigarette. I haven't been able to pin down the actual make yet."

The colonel made some notes, then looked up. "Ms. Khan mentioned another kidnapping."

"A young girl, the daughter of a Marwari, named Raju Moro, was kidnapped in broad daylight from a village not far from here." I set my tea aside. What I needed was a strong cup of coffee. "The girl's brother says that the vehicle used was owned by Chaudri Gujar Mohammed."

Colonel Nasri nodded. "Ah, the infamous Chaudri Sahib. How did the boy identify the vehicle?"

I massaged my forehead. "As far as I remember, it was by a dent on the back bumper. A couple of days later, the whole village was evicted and bulldozed. I believe because Raju Moro registered a charge with the District Commissioner."

"Scoundrels!" The colonel set down his notebook and took a sip of tea. "What about Chaudri Gujar Mohammed? Nadia said you had suspicions."

I took a deep breath, then plunged into a description of the abused woman Janice had seen cleaning Chaudri's stable, the trucks I'd seen arriving on my first day in Pakistan, and the suspicions I'd heard from local Pakistanis. I thought it wise not to mention Padri Fazal. I was about to describe what we'd found during the night when I saw the colonel scowling at the tea.

"Would you like me to get you some coffee? I'd like a cup myself."

"If possible. I don't share my compatriots' enjoyment of *deci chai*. Studying in England spoiled me."

"I'm afraid it will be powdered coffee. I haven't found any ground coffee yet." I stood up. "While I'm getting the cook to make that, please let me have him prepare breakfast."

He pinched the bridge of his nose. "Wonderful. It's been a long night."

In the kitchen, I gave Musa instructions, before heading along the veranda to our bedroom to see if Stephanie was up. I found her dressed, hair brushed, and about to join us.

"So what's happening?" she asked.

"The man Nadia mentioned, Colonel Yaqub Nasri, drove all night to get here. I'm having Musa make some breakfast."

"What's he like?"

"Spit and polish—impressive."

"Are you going to show him the pictures you took?"

I frowned. "Will we get into trouble for breaking into Chaudri's compound?"

"The pictures are so damning, I doubt you'll be blamed."

"We've got to trust somebody."

I walked over to the mirror, where I was shocked by what I saw. Unshaven. Dark circles under my eyes. One shirttail hanging out. I went into the bathroom, washed my face, combed my hair, and tucked in my shirt. Then I grabbed my camera, beckoned to Stephanie, and returned to the living room.

We found Colonel Nasri drinking the coffee Musa had brought. He stood and inclined his head toward Stephanie. "Mrs. Radley, I'm deeply grieved by the kidnapping of your daughter. I will do everything in my power to return her to your side."

"Thank you, Colonel. We're very appreciative of your help."

When we had helped ourselves to coffee and were seated, the colonel asked, "Mr. Radley, what else can you tell me?"

I turned on our digital camera and passed it to him. "Last night, we visited two of Chaudri Gujar's barns. We were shocked by what we found. These pictures prove his involvement in criminal activity—including kidnapping."

The colonel's eyes narrowed. "You visited his barns? Was this a social visit?"

I glanced at Stephanie, who was looking down at the floor. "Well... uh, not exactly. We went in the middle of the night... but, if you'll just look at the pictures you'll see—"

He shook his head. "Very dangerous thing to do, and very foolish. No official warrant, nothing—" He took a deep breath.

"But it's done. Let me see what you found." He clicked through the first few pictures." What are these bundles?"

"Drugs. I'm sure they're drugs. I took a sample."

He held out his hand. "Can I see?"

"Just a minute."

I jumped up, grabbed the keys to the Land Rover, ran outside, and retrieved the plastic bag Stephanie had stashed between the cushions of the back seat. Back inside, I passed the bag of powder to Colonel Yaqub.

He dipped his finger into the powder and tasted it with his tongue. "Heroin."

"Sir, I'm sure he's smuggling drugs from Afghanistan. The day I arrived, I saw two trucks from the frontier at his compound loaded with bundles like these. Then last night, several more trucks arrived. That barn has got to be where he stores the drugs for transhipment."

Colonel Nasri set the camera down beside him. "I'm not overly surprised. Sadly, many are involved in this illegal trade and get off scot-free by bribing the police."

Stephanie's eyes glinted with tears. "Sir, this animal is not only trafficking in drugs, but human beings. Please look at the rest of the pictures."

The colonel picked up the camera again and began clicking through the remaining photos. His lips tightened and his eyes narrowed as he went from one picture to the next. Finally, he put the camera down and leaned back to stare at us. "Dead? The young woman is dead?"

"Yes," I said.

"Excuse me." He stood up, took out a cell phone, and went out onto the veranda where I saw him walking up and down, gesturing with his free arm as he talked into his phone.

When he returned, he was still animated, using his hands to punctuate his sentences. "We won't let the bastard—excuse me, ma'am—the miscreant get away with this. I've put in a call to organize a raid on his farm."

"Today?" I asked.

"This afternoon at the latest."

"There is one other thing," I said.

"Further evidence?"

"Not exactly. I left my Swiss knife behind. It had my initials on it."

Stephanie touched my arm. "Oh, Josh."

Colonel Nasri shrugged his shoulders. "We'll just hope he doesn't find it, but even if he does, I doubt he'll connect it to you. Don't worry about it. Can I take this digital chip? I'll need to make copies of the pictures."

"Sure."

Musa came to the doorway. "Excuse me, Sahib, but breakfast is ready."

"Thank you, Musa. Could you see that the Colonel's driver gets breakfast as well."

"Very good, sir."

Over breakfast, Colonel Nasri steered the conversation away from the events that preoccupied our minds. He told us about his family and asked if we had ever visited London where he had spent four years. He described a mountaineering expedition he had accompanied to K2. He inquired about how I had learned Urdu. We knew what he was doing and appreciated it, but I doubted if either Stephanie or I could smother for long the fears for Jan's safety that gripped us.

Before he left, he gave us both his cell phone number and the number of the hotel where he would be staying in Nowshera. He urged us to do nothing further, to let him handle things from here. He promised to contact us as soon as Nadia arrived.

When he left, we took mugs of coffee into the bedroom and crawled back into bed fully clothed. We sat propped up with blankets pulled up to our necks. Pakistani bungalows never seemed to warm up in the winter, constructed as they were completely of masonry and concrete. During this season, Pakistani farmers often started the day by wrapping themselves in thick blankets woven from raw cotton and sitting out in the sun, their hands cupped around a steaming bowl of *chai*. We could hardly follow their lead as the sun had barely risen. Besides, we wanted to be alone.

Stephanie rubbed her hands together to generate some warmth. "I feel more hopeful with Colonel Nasri involved."

I nodded. "The SP certainly didn't inspire confidence."

"Do you think Chaudri will find your knife?"

"More likely one of his workers will pocket it."

"I hope so. Oh, Josh, I don't know how I'm going to sit here all day, waiting for something to happen."

"Not much else to do. At least we did something last night."

With a great sigh, Stephanie opened her Bible and got out her journal, something she did every morning.

I sat there thinking about my recurring nightmares, the feelings of dread that would sweep over me at odd times. I had always wondered if they were the result of a propensity to depression, something in my DNA. Now it seemed more likely they were due to feelings of guilt and the memories I'd suppressed. Memories of Daniel, my childhood friend. We'd had such fun together. Soccer, kites, chewing sugarcane. Then...

Logically, Stephanie was right. I was not to blame, and yet.... *No, I won't go back there. Finding Janice is my priority, not feeling sorry for myself.*

I picked up my Bible, turned to the Twenty-Third Psalm, and tried to absorb the ancient words. How many millions had turned to this psalm in times of trouble? Jan had memorized it as a child. Wherever she was, would Jan be crying out to the Good Shepherd? Her faith was certainly strong, but in these circumstances? She was hardly being led into green pastures or beside the still waters. Would God protect her in the presence of her enemies?

Would he lead her—would he lead us—through the valley of the shadow of death?

Oh, Lord, why so much evil in the world? Why couldn't kindness and compassion triumph instead of cruelty and greed? Lord, I don't ask for our cup to run over, but please bring Jan back.

I must have drifted off, for I jerked awake when Stephanie shifted in the bed beside me. "Josh, it looks warmer outside. Can we go for a walk?"

I yawned as I got out of bed. "Let's go."

We meandered along the canal road, feeling the sun warm our faces. We paused for a few moments to watch a man and woman cut fodder with practiced strokes of their small sickles. We passed a goatherd illegally cutting branches from one of the shesham trees on the canal bank. He stopped what he was doing to stare at us. Stephanie pulled her *dupatta* lower over her forehead.

At the crossroads, we stood for a while to observe a group of children and a couple of men work at emptying the brick kiln of fired bricks. Then we turned back the way we'd come.

We didn't talk much as we walked along. It was enough to be moving rather than just sitting. But there might have been news, so we returned to the bungalow.

Stephanie set up the sewing machine she'd borrowed and began to stitch the seams of a *qamiz*.

I tried to concentrate on organizing my notes about the dig. Fortunately, I'd finished the first article before our lives fell apart. I idly wondered why Luke hadn't yet organized an extensive exploration of the ruins discovered by the cave-in below the tower. That would make a blockbuster story.

But was that really important—in light of the exploitation of human beings and Janice's kidnapping? I found myself unable to even think of writing about archaeology.

CHAPTER TWENTY-FOUR
The Missing Knife

In the early afternoon, I was wandering around the garden trying to pass the time when the colonel's Mercedes pulled into the yard.

Hearing the car, Stephanie came out onto the veranda.

Colonel Nasri greeted us. "*Salaam alay kum.*"

"*Waalay kum as salaam,*" I replied. "Any news?"

"Bad, I'm afraid."

Stephanie caught her breath. I gestured toward the chairs on the veranda.

When we were seated, the colonel said, "We raided Chaudri's barns and found nothing that shouldn't be there. Not a thing."

Stephanie gasped.

"But," I said, "the pictures?"

He drummed his fingers on the arm of the chair. "We showed him the pictures. He called them fakes, fabrications. Somebody must have warned him before we got there."

"No drugs... no chains...?"

"Nothing but a couple of holes in the wall where chains could have been anchored. The floor was swept clean. Even smelled clean—too clean. Where you took the pictures of bundles of drugs were nothing but bales of hay. We moved every bale and found nothing. We searched every building—nothing but farm implements and supplies."

I put my head in my hands.

The colonel's face twisted into a grim smile. "He was furious. Threatened to bring in the DC, the Prime Minister, and my superior officer. Have me digging trenches on the line of control in Kashmir. Oh, we really stirred up a hornets nest."

Stephanie's finger's grew white from gripping the arms of her chair. "That evil man! He sanitized the whole place."

Colonel Nasri's eyes glinted. "Don't worry. This is just the first skirmish. We've served notice; Chaudri Gujar Mohammed will be running scared. He'll make mistakes, and then we'll nab him."

Stephanie's voice rose. "But what if he harms Janice—or others—to get rid of the evidence?"

Colonel Nasri leaned toward her. "*Memsahib*, that won't happen. For one thing, you're assuming that he directed the attack on the train. He may have, or he may be just one of a number of criminals operating in the area. This whole area on the border between the Punjab and Sindh provinces, particularly along the Indus, has harboured bandits for centuries."

I frowned. "I guess we assumed—"

The colonel gripped my shoulder. "And you may be right, but we must meticulously follow up all leads. So we're quietly questioning people who witnessed the attack on the train, as well as following clues that might prove Chaudri's criminal activity."

"The police?" I asked.

He grimaced. "Not the local police. I've only been here a few hours and I can already smell something rotten in the SP's office. I had to use local police for this raid, but I won't do that again. I'll call in men from the special investigations unit I supervise."

"Is Nadia Khan—?"

He interrupted me. "Not something you need to know. Forget what I said. But to ease your mind a little, let me explain some of our actions. There are tire tracks in the ground beside Chaudri Gujar's barns. Trucks can't go east through the desert and they can't go west across the Indus River unless they tranship to boats. We've set up roadblocks north and south on the Lahore-Karachi Highway for a hundred and fifty miles. And we've also got every river crossing manned, just in case."

The colonel's car had barely disappeared when a jeep from the archaeological dig roared into the yard trailing a great cloud of dust. Luke Wu leapt out and strode toward where we sat on the veranda.

I stood to meet him. "What is it Luke?"

He plopped into a chair. "Catastrophe!" His legs fidgeted and he kept running his hands through his hair, but said nothing further.

"Another accident?" Stephanie said. "Tunnel collapse... what?"

"I'm sorry." He massaged his forehead. "You have enough troubles. Any news of your daughter?"

I glanced at Stephanie. "Not yet. But we're hopeful."

"Good... I'm sure you'll get her back, unharmed."

"What happened, Luke?" I asked.

I hadn't seen Luke in such a state of agitation before. He'd always been highly strung, but never like this. He put both hands on his knees, apparently to stop them from twitching, and took a deep breath. "Chaudri threatens to have the dig closed down! Just when we're on the brink of cracking the Indus language. Just when we're about to start exploring the complex exposed by the cave-in. It's a catastrophe!"

"Why would he do that?" I said.

Luke leaped up and began pacing back and forth across the veranda. "Who knows why? He came out to the dig ranting and raving. He started ordering my men to go home. Can you believe it? Barged into my office. Threatened me. Shouted at Scott. Knocked over a tray of artefacts. I pleaded with him to please sit down, have a cup of tea, and tell me what was wrong."

"I don't understand," I said. "I thought he was a hundred percent behind the excavation."

Luke stopped pacing and sat back down. "He was. But today he shouted about some conspiracy directed against him—somehow connected to the dig. How we're implicated, he didn't say. He just raged about foreigners upsetting local customs, about people sticking their noses into local affairs."

I glanced again at Stephanie. "Did he mention any names?"

Luke frowned. "No, but he said he'd find out who they were. Any ideas?"

"Not really," I said. "I did hear that the police raided his farm this morning. That probably made him crazy. From what I gather, he's the most powerful man in the district—not used to being questioned, let alone raided."

Luke stared at me with lowered brows. "Police raid? Where did you hear that?"

Stephanie stood up. "Can I get you some tea, Mr. Wu?"

"Tea? Why yes, please."

Stephanie's interruption gave me time to think about how much I should reveal to Luke. Did Chaudri suspect us? Best to keep Luke in the dark.

"I heard about the raid," I said, "from an officer assigned to find Janice's kidnappers."

"Oh... but why would the police raid Chaudri's farm? And how could there be any connection to what we're doing at Pattan Minara?"

"A mystery," I said. "Sometimes when people are attacked, they lash out at anyone available."

"But it's so unfair."

Stephanie brought in a tea tray. We sat there a few minutes sipping our tea, not saying anything. Finally, I asked, "What are you going to do?"

Luke set down his cup. "What can I do? Chaudri's threats have scared the labourers. Some have already left. I'll have to give them a couple of days' holiday until Chaudri changes his mind. We're getting farther and farther behind and the dig is so promising."

We fell silent again. With Janice uppermost in my mind, I didn't feel like making polite conversation.

When he finished his tea, Luke stood up. "I don't suppose you've been able to finish the first article about the site?"

"Actually, I have a draft ready. Finished before... before all this happened. I'll e-mail it to you."

"Well that's good news. With Chaudri acting the way he has, we need to generate some international interest."

After Luke drove away, I rejoined Stephanie on the veranda.

She pushed a tendril of hair behind her ear. "You think Chaudri suspects us?"

"I don't see how he could."

"Maybe someone saw the Land Rover—or identified your knife."

"Unlikely." I didn't want to let on to Stephanie how worried I was. If Chaudri was the brain behind a criminal outfit dealing in drugs and human slaves, he was very dangerous.

"Not many foreigners here to accuse of sticking their nose into local affairs."

I rubbed my jaw. "Yeah, just Luke Wu, the two students from Penn State, you and me. And I was the dumb foreigner who pushed him to help find Raju's daughter."

"Josh, I'm worried. If Chaudri is powerful enough to shut down the dig, there's no telling what he will do."

I reached over and took her hand. "Don't forget, we've got Colonel Nasri and Nadia on our side. They must carry a lot of clout."

"We can't leave God out. I've been praying that he would send angels to surround and guard Jan."

"Amen to that."

Stephanie returned to her sewing. I edited the article I'd prepared on Pattan Minara and sent it off by e-mail to Luke. A score of personal e-mails had arrived, most from family and friends expressing their concern and promising to pray for Janice's rescue. I beckoned for Stephanie to join me, and together we answered them as briefly as we could.

We sent a more detailed reply to our son Jonathan, who offered to come out on the next plane. My dad wanted to join us also, in spite of his failing health. Instead of accepting their offers, we suggested they mobilize help through the consulate and media.

Late in the afternoon, Mohammed knocked on the door.

In Punjabi, he asked, "Sahib, could I look more closely at your knife? You know, the red one? I want to order one from Karachi for my son's graduation."

I paused, then stepped out on the veranda where I went over to the railing. "I'm sorry, Mohammed. I lost it a few days ago."

He shook his head. *"Afsos ki bat."*

My mind raced as I tried to come up with a plausible explanation. "I'm not sure where I lost it, but can you pass the word around. I'll give a two hundred rupee reward to anyone who finds it."

"Very good, sir." He saluted and turned away.

Back in our room, I stared at Stephanie. "What was that about?" she asked.

"My lost knife."

"How did he know you'd lost it?"

I walked over to an armchair and sat down. "He didn't. Said he wanted to borrow it so he could order one like it for his son."

"You did use it to peel oranges a couple of times this week. Must have impressed him."

"But why ask today? Someone—Chaudri, no doubt—put him up to it to find out for sure that mine was lost. I've wondered from early on if Chaudri employed Mohammed to report on us."

Stephanie's eyes widened. "Chaudri must suspect us."

"Me. Not you. Anyway, we have to assume he does. Let's get our stories straight. I had to tell Mohammed I'd lost my knife a few days ago and offer a big reward."

"Did you have to tell a lie? I'm not very good at pretending something is true when it's not."

"We don't have much choice. A little lie is small potatoes compared to kidnapping, murder, smuggling, and who knows what else."

At that moment our cell phone rang. Colonel Nasri came on the line to tell me that Nadia Khan had arrived and was on her way to see us.

CHAPTER TWENTY-FIVE
Major Nadia Khan's Arrival

We were waiting at the bottom of the veranda steps when Colonel Nasri's car arrived for the third time that day. As soon as the car stopped, the back door flew open. Nadia ran over to Stephanie and hugged her. They'd been close ever since the Lightning File affair.

"I'm so sorry," she said to Stephanie. With one arm still around her, she extended her hand toward me. "Josh, what can I say?"

I gripped her hand. "Nadia, we're grateful you've come."

The only change I saw in Nadia was her dress. Instead of the tailored business suit I'd grown used to seeing, she wore a tan *shalwar* and an intricately embroidered coffee-coloured *qamiz* with a matching *dupatta*. If anything, the woman I had been drawn to during my separation from Stephanie had grown more attractive. Her dark, brown eyes seemed alive with feeling. Her honey-coloured skin more perfect. Was that a tiny tremor of excitement her touch generated? No.

I dropped her hand and turned to Colonel Nasri. "Any news?"

He signalled by the inclination of his head the need to talk in private. Both Mohammed and Musa had come around the corner of the bungalow to meet the car.

I walked over to them. "Musa, can you set two extra plates for supper?"

"No problem, Sahib." He hurried toward the kitchen.

I turned to our *chaukidar*. "Mohammed, the driver must be very tired. Please bring him a *charpai* to rest on—and some tea or a coke. Whatever he wants."

Mohammed saluted as he left.

I turned to Colonel Nasri and Nadia. "Why don't we go inside?"

In the living room, Nadia sat beside Stephanie on a settee. The colonel and I sat opposite them on armchairs.

Nadia gripped Steph's hands in both of hers and asked, "How are you two coping?"

Stephanie bit her lower lip. "Not well."

"I guess we're still in shock," I said.

"We've prayed a lot," Stephanie said.

"The Colonel told me you did more than that—broke into Chaudri Gujar's barns in the middle of the night." Nadia frowned as she looked from Stephanie to me and then back to Stephanie. "Dangerous. Oh, I'll admit you found concrete evidence, but you took unnecessary risks. From now on, you concentrate on prayer and let Colonel Nasri and I find your daughter."

"We can't just sit back and wait," I sputtered. "Janice is our daughter. We've got to do something." Seeing the colonel's puckered brow, I changed tack. "Not that we don't appreciate... I mean, we do, but..."

Nadia joined her hands in appeal. "Josh, we understand your concern, but it'd be best if you left this to us. This is the kind of thing we do. We speak the language. We have the contacts."

"I'd be blundering around," I said, "causing problems?"

"I didn't mean that," Nadia said.

Colonel Nasri drummed his fingers on the arm of his chair. "Mr. Radley, I empathize with you, but having a foreign national involved—"

I interrupted. "But surely Pakistanis can understand the grief and concern of a father for his kidnapped daughter."

"And a mother's concern," Stephanie said.

Nadia leaned back and caught Colonel Nasri's eye.

"Josh did get us the pictures from Chaudri's barn," Nadia said. "He seems to have a knack for this kind of thing. Last year, he helped catch a group of terrorists in Toronto."

"I didn't just help," I said. "I found the file that identified them."

Nadia cocked her head to one side. "Okay, you were a *big* help." She turned toward the colonel. "What do you think, Colonel Sahib?"

"I'm not happy about either of them being involved. Especially Memsahib Radley. It's too dangerous. We could allow Mr. Radley some access, as long as he agrees to stay in the background."

"That's all I ask," I said. "To be there when you rescue Janice."

Stephanie fidgeted in her seat. "I don't like the idea of sitting here doing nothing. At least you'll keep me informed?"

"Absolutely," Nadia said.

"So what's next?" I said.

Colonel Nasri frowned. "Wait for a break. I have a couple of men interviewing witnesses to the train hold-up and a man at each of the roadblocks."

"Since we have questions about the reliability of the local police," Nadia said, "the colonel has called in men from his own unit."

Colonel Nasri jabbed the air. "Someone from the SP's office must have leaked information to Chaudri Gujar. So we assume they can't be trusted."

"Seem to be leaks everywhere." I raised my eyebrows. "My *chaukidar*?"

Nadia's eyes narrowed. "Why him?"

"Just a feeling I've had. Then, today, he came and asked to borrow my Swiss knife. I don't have it. I must have lost it in one of Chaudri's barns. I'm guessing Chaudri found it, saw the initials *JR*, and had Mohammed ask about it."

"Spilt milk," Colonel Nasri said.

Nadia tossed her *dupatta* over the back of her chair. It looked like she was having as much trouble as Stephanie keeping it in place. "Any other leads, Josh?"

"Two," I said. "On our way back from the train hold-up, I noticed vehicle tracks turning off the road onto a narrow lane heading east. I couldn't be sure, but the tire tracks resembled those at the scene of the hold-up and were too numerous to have been made by a farmer. The bandits could have headed east, into the desert—where they transferred to four-wheel drive vehicles. Could they have stashed their captives in one of the old desert forts? Maybe even smuggled them across the border into India?"

Colonel Nasri had taken out his notebook and was flipping pages. "You didn't mention this before."

"No, I forgot."

The colonel rose. "Excuse me a minute." He walked over to the corner of the room and punched some numbers into his cell phone. After barking orders into the phone, he returned to his seat. "You mentioned two clues."

"Yes," I said. "In spite of heavy security and a high fence, valuable artefacts are being stolen from the Pattan Minara excavation. I have a strong hunch about the man in charge of security there. Before the expedition arrived, he was ostensibly a tenant farmer. Yet he lived on the large compound built right into the south end of the mound. His compound is much more substantial than the usual farm compound. I believe a check will find that Chaudri Gujar owns this farm."

Colonel Nasri stabbed the air with his pen. "Chaudri stealing artefacts? Hardly fits. Besides, he is the largest landowner in the district. We can hardly raid every one of his farms."

I sighed as I leaned back. "You may be right. I'm getting quite paranoid."

"I don't think Josh is paranoid." Stephanie began counting on her fingers. "One, the head of security at Pattan Minara, and his jeep, were away during the time of the hold-up. Two, that jeep or its twin were seen at the hold-up. Three, his jeep is the only one unaccounted for. Four, he smokes some brand of foreign cigarette. Josh picked up a Marlboro butt at the scene."

Stephanie leaned back and looked from Nadia to Colonel Nasri. Nadia tilted her head to one side as she looked across at the colonel. He smiled. "You make some good points."

"Something is going on in that compound," I said. "I can feel it."

"We can set up surveillance," Nasri said. "Maybe even bring the guy in for questioning. But let's not forget those Marwaris."

I nodded. "The kidnapped girl's brother identified the vehicle."

"And just when we need him as a witness, the whole clan has disappeared." Nasri tapped his pen on knee. "We need to find them. Look into who ordered the eviction of the village."

Musa appeared in the doorway. "*Khana tayar hai, Sahib.*"

We adjourned to the dining room. Stephanie and I picked at our food. Nadia and Colonel Nasri ate heartily. For desert, Musa had prepared bread pudding laced with raisins and coconut. I couldn't stand bread pudding—some memory from childhood. Nasri was taking a second helping and commenting on Musa's culinary skill when his phone chimed. He excused himself and went out onto the veranda.

A few minutes later, he signalled to Nadia from the doorway. "We've got to go."

Nadia stood up. "Some new development?"

"Could be the break we need," he said.

I looked from one to the other. "So?"

He stepped into the room. "I guess you both deserve to be kept informed. Our men stopped a truck at a roadblock on the Karachi Highway. In a compartment behind bales of cotton, they found women and children. Apparently drugged."

Stephanie gasped. "My daughter?"

He shook his head. "No one of her description. But they may give us leads to who is behind this... and to other victims."

I swallowed a lump in my throat.

Nadia gave Stephanie a hug, retrieved the *dupatta* which she'd draped over the back of her chair, and went to join Colonel Nasri.

"Why don't you take us along?" I asked. "We won't get in the way."

Colonel Nasri frowned. "We can't do that."

Stephanie strode over to Nadia and gripped her arm. "These women and children will be traumatized. They need a woman's touch." She looked from Nadia to the colonel. "Do you have any other women officers besides Nadia?"

The colonel scowled. "No, but—"

Nadia put both her hands on Stephanie's shoulders and looked into her eyes. "This is police work. Leave it with us."

"My wife makes a good point," I said. "Those poor women will need the gentle touch of a woman—they may even open up to a woman where they'd say nothing to a man—especially a policeman."

"That's where I come in," Nadia said.

"Yeah, but two is better," Stephanie said. "Besides, with Josh's help I can describe my daughter. Perhaps they'll recognize her... give us some information."

The colonel shook his head. "We can't have civilians involved. Just not done."

"Please, Colonel," Stephanie said. "You don't know how terrible it is to be sitting here... doing nothing... waiting."

He looked from Stephanie to me. His face bore a puzzled expression as if he wasn't used to having his orders questioned by a woman and didn't quite know how to deal with the situation.

Nadia's hands dropped from Stephanie's shoulders and she turned toward him. "Colonel, it can't do any harm to have them along. They're right about the victims. They will be terrified. We could use the help of another woman."

Colonel Nasri rubbed his forehead as he strode back and forth. Finally, he stopped in front of me. "Okay. But we leave in five minutes—or less."

CHAPTER TWENTY-SIX
Roadblock

Colonel Nasri's driver drove us to the Shalimar Hotel in Nowshera. Stephanie and I waited in the lobby while Nadia ran up to her room to change and the colonel went off to commandeer some military transport. Nadia returned, dressed in an anonymous khaki uniform. The khaki cap on her head bore an insignia that I couldn't place. The colonel returned with military jeeps. He had changed into a khaki uniform of his own with a couple of rows of combat ribbons on his left breast.

Nadia, Stephanie, and I rode in one of the jeeps driven by an army officer. The colonel rode in the other along with his driver and two heavily armed military men—probably special forces.

We approached the roadblock about an hour after sundown. Arc lights illuminated a long line of trucks waiting to be checked. At the head of the line, we found a cluster of security personnel, dressed in camouflage uniforms and wielding AK-47s, guarding the barricade. In an attempt to ward of the chill, a small bonfire had been lit on the shoulder of the road.

We stopped in front of a uniformed officer and got out. The officer saluted Colonel Nasri, who motioned him to one side with a nod of his head. He beckoned for Nadia to join him. While they were talking, I took in the scene.

Off the road on the shoulder stood a truck being guarded by two soldiers. The back yawned open and dark. Five or six huge bundles of cotton lay tumbled on the shoulder of the highway. Three men sat on the gravel behind the truck, their arms bound behind them. The face of the stockiest of the three was smeared with blood from a gash over his swollen right eye. His full, black beard looked to be matted with blood. His face was set in a fierce scowl. The two others cowering beside him appeared to be scarcely out of their teens—probably the *cleaners* that truck drivers employed at a pittance to fetch and carry.

A fourth man hung limp and unconscious from a rope tying his hands above his head to the left side of the truck. Welts oozed blood from a crisscross of gashes on his chest where his *qamiz* had been torn open.

Brutal, I thought as I grasped Stephanie's hand. She pointed to our right. I followed her gaze to a tent set up in the field beside the road. Although three sides had been closed in, the side facing the road was open next to a bonfire made from cotton stems. A group of women and children huddled in the shadowy interior as far back in the tent as they could go. Several lay prostrate on the canvas floor. The children seemed to be between six and fourteen or so. Many were whimpering.

Stephanie dropped my hand and ran over to kneel before them. I stopped at a modest distance when I saw the tattered nature of most of their clothing. There were about a dozen women and eight children. All the women seemed to be in their late teens or early twenties. Several of them covered their chests with their arms to hide the tears in their clothing. Few had *dupattas*. Some wept softly. Others slumped as if drugged. The children huddled in a group behind the women. Most of the released captives still had plastic or metal shackles on their wrists.

Suddenly, I heard the loud voice of the colonel behind me. "Son of a pig!"

I turned toward him. He was waving his swagger stick in the face of the officer he'd been talking to, and then pointing toward the women in the tent.

"Why haven't you given them some privacy?"

"Well, sir—"

"Have they had any tea? Any food?"

"Very busy, sir... happened so suddenly, sir..."

"I guess you were more interested in torturing the driver than protecting the modesty of these women?"

"N—no, sir."

"See to it. Now. *Ek dum.*"

"Right away, sir."

The officer shouted instructions for a couple of soldiers to bring blankets.

"And have a *deg* of tea brought up from that tea shop a mile back—and *prata.*" Colonel Nasri paced up and down, punctuating his sentences with thrusts of his swagger stick. "And when you've done that, go into Dherki, wake up whoever owns the ready-made shop in town and buy enough outfits for the women. Don't forget *dupattas.*"

"But sir, how do we pay—?"

"Just do it. Tell the owner the army will make good." He paused. "Do you have any bolt cutters?"

"Why, yes, sir. Two or three pair."

"Good. Get Major Nadia Khan a pair. She'll cut off those shackles."

So Nadia was a major in the Pakistan military. I wondered what else about her we didn't know.

"Major Khan, please reassure the women of their safety. And find out what you can."

Nadia saluted and went to kneel with Stephanie in front of the women. In a soft voice, she began to assure the group of their safety. Since the women might be from any area of Pakistan, she alternated between Urdu and dialects of Pashto, Punjabi, and Sindhi. How many of Pakistan's main languages did she speak?

Two soldiers ran up with a rope and blankets to rig a privacy screen across the front of the tent. About time. I didn't like the glances men from the security detail had been throwing toward the women.

Before the soldiers hung the last blanket, I noticed a girl dressed in a red outfit crouched by herself in the far corner of the tent.

"Nadia," I called.

Nadia got up and came to my side. "What is it, Josh?"

"There's a young women at the back, left side—a Marwari. Can you find out if her name is Chandi and her father's name, Raju Moro? If so, she's the one who was kidnapped the day I arrived."

I wandered back to the truck and peered inside. Like most four-wheeled Pakistani trucks, the cargo box was framed with hardwood and ornately painted with scenes and calligraphy. The sides rose at least two feet higher than the cab, allowing for the goods compartment to be extended over the roof of the cab. In this case, a false roof had been constructed three feet below the top of the stake sides and extending two-thirds of the distance to the back of the truck. This created a space that could be hidden by goods piled on the roof and at the back of the truck. A bunch of thin, stained mattresses covered the floor of the room thus created. The space reeked of sweat, urine, and fear.

I turned away and sat down on an upturned bale of cotton. Having dismissed the officer in charge to arrange tea and buy clothing, the colonel took his place. He proceeded to go from truck to truck, in each case ordering the driver and his helpers to step down onto the roadway and throw open the back of their truck. While his AK-47-wielding troopers probed the cargo, he slapped his swagger stick on his leg and stared at them silently. After a few moments of intimidating silence, he'd wave them back to their truck and order them to get underway. Here was a man used to making quick assessments of character. In short order, he had the line of trucks cut in half.

Leaving a couple of sergeants in charge of questioning the truck drivers who remained, Colonel Nasri strode over to the handcuffed men. He stared at them for a few moments, then without saying a word he began to slowly pace back and forth in front of them. Their eyes followed him. The bearded one spat on his highly polished boots. The colonel walked up to him, grasped his *qamiz*, tore it down the front, and resting his boots one at time on one of the man's outstretched legs he used the torn *qamiz* to wipe his boots clean. As he turned away, he lashed out with his swagger stick, cutting the man's cheek open.

He turned to one of the soldiers guarding the truck and, pointing toward the unconscious man strung up by his hands against the side of the truck, he said, "Bring a bucket of water and douse that felon."

"Yes, sir."

I shivered when the soldier returned with a bucket and threw it in the man's face. The man groaned as he regained consciousness.

Colonel Nasri stood in front of him. With his swagger stick, he lifted his head so he could look him in the eye. A trickle of blood dribbled from his mouth. "I want you to tell me exactly what I ask. You understand?"

The man nodded, then grimaced.

"Where did you pick up your cargo?"

His speech was slurred as he answered. "Cot... ton... gin... Now... shera."

"Name of the gin?"

"Rah... mat Ginning."

"Were there other trucks picking up loads?"

He licked his lips. "Two. No, three... left before me."

"Describe them."

"Sahib, please... I am only driver..."

The colonel waved his swagger stick in front of the man's face.

"*Accha, ji,* old Bedford, painted red... gold writing..." He coughed. "Volvo, very new... blue, pictures of mountains, and... and a black Fiat... picture of, of Younis Khan, cricketer."

"What was your destination?

"Karachi." He tried to shake his head, then stopped with a gasp of pain. "Not know where." He took a breath. "On manifest."

"Have you picked up cargo at Rahmat Ginning before?"

He strained to take the weight off his hands. "Ahh... no, sir. Never. I hired first time to drive this truck."

"Never driven it before?"

"No. I sick. Lost job... Just hired."

"Have you ever seen the bearded one before?"

"Never... he in charge of loading." He gagged, then spit out blood. "*Dardi wala* sent me away. Gave me money for meal."

He beckoned to a sergeant. "Sergeant, contact our units and the police in Rohri, Sukkur, and Khairpur to be on the lookout for three trucks. A red Bedford with gold calligraphy, a newish blue Volvo with pictures of mountains and a black Fiat with a picture of Younis Khan, the cricketer. Have them stopped and searched. Let us know what they find."

The colonel then turned to the nearest soldier. "Cut this man down and give him a blanket." He pointed toward the bearded man. "And two of you take that man up the road a hundred yards and tie him to a tree."

The colonel came over and stood in front of me. "I'm sorry you have to witness such brutality. Sometimes it is the only way. And time is short."

I didn't answer, just nodded. Anything to find Jan. I sighed. Had my qualms about torture been overcome so easily? I felt my eyes begin to water. *Oh, Jan, honey, where are you? Don't give up. We're going to find you. But torture? Violence to stop violence?* I shook my head. There had to be a better way. So confusing.

I looked up to see Nadia and Stephanie coming toward me. I wiped my eyes on my sleeve. Stephanie's face was set in a grimace.

They sat on either side of me on bales of cotton. In spite of the presence of men, Stephanie reached out and gripped my right hand. I turned to look into her eyes. They looked haunted. I squeezed her hand.

"It's awful, Josh. These women have suffered terribly. And the children..." She shuddered.

I turned to Nadia. "Find out anything?"

"Three of the women are from the train robbery. They remember a blonde, blue-eyed American—they call all westerners American. She, along with several other women from the train, were separated and taken away, probably in a jeep or Land Rover."

"Where did they go?"

"The women aren't sure. They think the jeep may have headed east off the national highway into farming country."

I rubbed my forehead. "The tracks I saw... So we're back to square one?"

Nadia scuffed the dirt. "Not exactly. We're getting the picture of a widespread criminal organization. The women come from scattered locations throughout the Punjab. Most are poor and illiterate and come from rural villages. Some have been held for weeks."

"Do you think they smuggle them out of Pakistan through Karachi?"

"Probably—or through Quetta into Afghanistan and Iran. We don't know yet."

"Then why would a jeep head east, toward India?"

"They could be smuggling some across the border into India, but I doubt it. More likely they took them to someplace where they're held until transport can be arranged. Most of these women were held in windowless buildings or warehouses for anywhere from a few days to a few weeks. Sort of like slave depots... sorry, I shouldn't have used that word."

I gripped Stephanie's hand tighter. "Were the women mistreated—raped?"

"It's too early to say, but I get the impression that some were... while the younger, more attractive ones were not."

Suddenly a long drawn-out scream erupted. Involuntarily, I stared down the road toward where they'd taken the bearded man.

"Nasty business," Nadia said. "You probably shouldn't have come."

Instead of responding, I nodded toward the tent. "The Marwari girl?"

"Yes, she is the Chandi you mentioned."

"A bit of good news. But her father—the whole clan has disappeared."

Nadia stood up. "We'll find them. Now, I must get back to the women. Steph's helping me get those shackles off their wrists. Then we have to list each one, summarize their stories, and find out where they are from."

I let go of Stephanie's hand and nodded. From down the road, a torrent of cursing was quickly cut off by a shriek of pain. I covered my ears.

CHAPTER TWENTY-SEVEN
Kidnap Victims

There was a chill in the night air. I sat on a bale of cotton in front of a small fire and tried to warm my hands. Stephanie was busy helping Nadia comfort the women and cut off their shackles. Colonel Nasri had gone down the road to supervise the interrogation. I had nothing to do but watch the security personnel question truckers, try to ignore the screams of the bearded man, and think.

One part of me cheered at every shriek of pain; any one who treated women and children to this kind of abuse should endure endless agony. But the other side of me—and I hoped it was still the dominant feature—cringed at every cry.

Am I becoming vengeful? Inured to trampling on the rights of criminals? Aren't human rights the bedrock of civilized societies? Something was changing inside me. Jan's kidnapping had suddenly rendered ivory tower musings about morality irrelevant. Platitudes about compassion and respect for human life seemed to lose their significance out here in the darkness on Pakistan's national highway.

Perhaps the pundits were right who called for brutality to be met by brutality. How else to fight the merchants of addiction and misery and terror? Couldn't good ends be secured through questionable means? What right had the self-proclaimed guardians of morality to question those who struggled daily to stem the tide of bestiality?

No, Josh, don't go there! There have to be standards. Otherwise the jungle prevails and we have Stalin and Hitler and Guantanamo instead of Churchill and MacArthur and Desmond Tutu. What of decency and civility and due process? What of justice tempered by mercy? What of Jesus of Nazareth? Lord, please protect Janice.

The arrival of a jeep interrupted my thoughts. Two men got out, opened the back, and using a couple of thick sticks began manhandling a huge *deg* of *chai* from the jeep to the tent. I ran to help them carry cups and a stack of *chapaties* to the women.

With that small task complete, I zipped my windbreaker tight around my neck and began walking down the line of trucks, trying to get warm... and distance myself from the moans and occasional curses of the bearded man. I walked beyond the reach of the arc lights set up at the roadblock, past the last of the idling trucks, out into the darkness where the stars ruled the night.

It was a beautiful night. How ironic, I thought, as I gazed heavenward. *Every prospect pleases and only man is vile.*

When I returned to the roadblock, I found Colonel Nasri and Nadia sitting on cotton bales, deep in conversation. A map was spread out between them. They looked up as I approached. "We wondered where you were," Nadia said. "Colonel Nasri wants me to go back with you and Steph to Nowshera."

Colonel Nasri inclined his head toward me. "I must admit, in spite of my misgivings, allowing you and your wife to come with us has been helpful. Major Khan has told me about Mrs. Radley's rapport with the women and children. Comforting them is not something my men are capable of, even if the culture allowed it."

"A bus will be arriving any moment," Nadia said, "to take them to Nowshera where we'll begin to arrange for their return to their families."

Colonel Nasri stood up. "Tell your wife how appreciative I am for her help and assure her that we'll move heaven and earth to find your daughter." He turned and strode away.

One of the privacy blankets parted and Stephanie slipped out of the tent and came to stand in front of us. She stood there flexing her shoulders and turning her head from side to side. "Some of the children have fallen asleep—poor lambs. The women seem to be feeling safer. Hot tea and new clothes—thoughtful of the colonel."

She plopped down on a bale and slumped over with her elbows on her knees and her head in her hands, as if she could hardly keep her head up otherwise.

Nadia reached over and laid her hand on her shoulder. "Great job, Steph. Hang in there. The bus will be arriving any minute with a woman doctor and some female officers. Our work is finished. Let's find our driver and get back to Nowshera."

As soon as we were in the jeep headed back the way we'd come, Stephanie laid her head on my shoulder and began to sob. I put my arms around her and held her close. I felt like crying myself and I hadn't been involved with cutting shackles off the women or comforting them. The driver, an army officer, glanced in the mirror and said. "Memsahib, all of Pakistan grieves with you. We will find your daughter and stop this great evil."

Stephanie sat up, fished in her purse for a tissue, wiped her eyes, and blew her nose. "Thank you, sir."

Silence fell for the next few miles. Around Dherki we passed an empty bus going the other way. Nadia finally broke the silence. "I don't think you should go back to your bungalow tonight. You can stay both in one of the extra rooms we reserved in the Shalimar Hotel."

"Thanks, Nadia," Stephanie said.

"So what will happen to the women and children?" I asked.

"We'll put them in one wing of the hospital. Fortunately, the hospital's patron, the sheikh, is not in town and has given his permission to use his reserved suite of rooms. Any who are injured will be treated. Attorneys will take their statements. Then we'll arrange chaperoned travel to their homes. They've been through so much trauma, we'll make it as easy on them as possible."

"No press, I hope," Stephanie said.

"No... although it may be hard to keep them away."

"Aren't women like these," I said, "often abandoned by their families?"

Stephanie's voice rose. "They're victims. Why would they be abandoned?"

"*Beiziti*," I said.

"Dishonour," Nadia nodded. "Unfortunately, Josh is right. They may be treated as an embarrassment, as if they're guilty of bringing dishonour to their families."

"That's ridiculous," Stephanie said. "They ought to be comforted and loved."

"It may be ridiculous, but it's a sad fact." Nadia took off her khaki cap and shook her raven hair into place. "Most families consider *izat*, honour, their most valuable possession. When a girl loses her virginity, or is even suspected of having lost it, she becomes a liability. She forfeits all prospects of marriage. Her family has to give up all hope of rising in status."

She continued, "A few are actually killed by their families. They call it an honour killing. Some families expect, indeed encourage, a shamed girl to commit suicide. Many just live out their lives as unmarried servants in their own home."

"Surely... something can be done to change all that," Stephanie sputtered. "It's so barbaric—so medieval."

"So Islamic," Nadia said softly, glancing at the driver. "Don't get me wrong, I'm a Muslim, though perhaps not a very good one. But Islam has been hijacked by misogynists. There's nothing wrong with Islam that a return to basic principles wouldn't solve."

I leaned across Stephanie. "With all due respect, Nadia, I can't agree. Surely, one shouldn't be surprised that a religion founded by a man who had multiple wives treats women as inferior and lets men get off scot-free."

In the dim light, I could see Nadia smile. From the time I'd spent with her working in Toronto, I knew how much she enjoyed a good argument, so I wasn't surprised when she replied, "You don't agree with the explanation that Mohammed, peace be upon him, married multiple wives to show compassion on them?"

"No, I don't."

"I don't either. But it's hardly fair to blame only one religion for mistreating women. Christianity doesn't have a great track record. After all, the West has the greatest appetite for pornography—and prostitutes. If there wasn't a market for the women we just freed, I doubt if this vicious trade would be as profitable."

"You make a good point," I said. "But I can't agree that Christianity is to blame. Jesus' treatment of women was revolutionary in his day. At least it hasn't institutionalized polygamy, nor smothered women in *burquas*."

Nadia rubbed her eyes. "Josh, this is no place for an argument. I admit that in Muslim countries women have a long way to go toward achieving equality. But they are making strides."

I lowered my voice when I noticed the driver had his head cocked to one side as if he was listening. "The whole system of *burquas* and *purdah*—seclusion—is based on the assumption that women are the source of temptation. Keep them hidden away from male eyes, lest the powerful allure they project cause innocent men to stumble. As if immorality is caused by women."

Stephanie tapped my knee. "Innocent men. Ha!"

Suddenly, the driver applied the horn and swerved onto the shoulder to avoid two trucks racing side by side toward us. The jeep bounced wildly before the driver regained control and steered back onto the highway.

I took a deep breath. "That was close."

After we were breathing normally again, Nadia leaned toward me. "Josh, you know I don't agree with *burquas* and *purdah*. Those are pre-Islamic, tribal customs. What we need is a return to pure Islam."

"Good luck," I said. "Tell that to Bin Laden or the Taliban."

Nadia nodded. "Touché."

Stephanie punched me. "Josh, you're too hard on Nadia. She's here to help us, not to argue with."

I grimaced. "Sorry, Nadia, I got carried away."

"Truce?" she said.

"Truce. So, what do you plan to do next?"

"Colonel Nasri will keep the roadblock manned for another day or two. Tomorrow, he's going to raid Rahmat Ginning in Nowshera. He'll also hit a warehouse in Multan mentioned by a couple of the women."

"Any more clues about Jan's whereabouts?"

"We're not sure," Nadia said. "I'm meeting with Colonel Nasri in the morning. We'll go over the statements I've taken from the women and try to connect it to what he's beaten out of the bearded pig."

Steph brushed a lock of hair out of her eye. "Has to be a clue somewhere."

Nadia patted her on the knee. "We'll find her."

Silence fell for the rest of the drive to Nowshera.

●●◆●●

The next morning, we were finishing our breakfast in the hotel restaurant when Nadia and the Colonel came in. Seeing us, they waved.

"Mind if we join you?" Colonel Nasri asked, carrying over a chair.

"Please," I said, getting up to fetch a chair for Nadia.

The waiter brought them menus and topped up our coffee.

Except for a tiny stain on the collar of his khaki uniform, the colonel looked like he'd just stepped off the parade ground. Nadia, however, looked worse than I had ever seen her. Lines creased her forehead and she'd only been partially successful in hiding the dark smudges under her eyes with makeup.

"Did you get any sleep?" Stephanie asked her.

She gave a thin-lipped smile. "Not much. I've been sifting through the women's statements for clues."

"Did you find any?" I said.

She looked around, gauging whether any diners were near enough to overhear. Some were certainly staring our way, openly curious about why two military personnel were having breakfast with a foreign couple.

Nadia idly picked up a piece of toast that Stephanie had left on her side plate untouched. "Not much."

Stephanie passed her some marmalade. "Thanks. I didn't realize how hungry I was. Anyway, we're developing a profile on two or three of the abductors." She spread marmalade on the square of toast and popped it in her mouth.

Colonel Nasri signalled for coffee. "Nothing yet tying the slippery Chaudri Sahib to this nasty business—but we'll get him."

Nadia wiped her lips. "Josh, I know it's a lot to ask under the circumstances, but... we need to find the Marwari girl's family."

"What can I do to help?" I said.

Before Nadia could reply, the waiter arrived with coffee. Colonel Nasri pointed to himself and Nadia. "And two full English breakfasts, *jaldi.*"

As the waiter hastened away, Nadia poured cream into her coffee and stirred in two spoonfuls of sugar. She took a sip and smiled. "Ambrosia... Now where was I? Oh, yeah, Josh, you know that pastor you mentioned? He's friendly with the Marwaris. Can you see if he knows where the girl's family went?"

"Will do."

The colonel's request must have lit a fire under the kitchen staff, because their orders came unusually quickly. We leaned back in our chairs to let them enjoy their breakfasts.

Gradually, the vague awareness of background noise resolved into the distinct sound of chanting and drums punctuated at intervals by shouts. Curious, I joined a couple of other diners at the windows overlooking the main street. At first, we could see nothing, but then a great crowd of people carrying banners and chanting slogans came into view. A group of black clad, heavily bearded men led the procession.

CHAPTER TWENTY-EIGHT
Nowshera Demonstration

DECEMBER 9

Like a hungry monster, the demonstration surged down the road toward us, engulfing everything in its path. Swallowing up cars and swirling around trucks, it blocked all traffic. Shopkeepers ran outside their stores to pull metal shutters over their windows and retrieve outside displays before they could be destroyed. I saw the table of a sidewalk fruit vendor fall before the beast in a cascade of oranges, melons, and guavas that were quickly trampled underfoot.

As it marched past the cinema, just up from the hotel, it paused. Men, who the night before had probably attended the latest epic of love and war, swarmed over the grounds tearing down posters of buxom women and pelting the front of the movie house with stones. To a crescendo of cheers, they tore down the main sign, a two-storey depiction of a tribal woman beseeching a turbaned warrior on a white steed to carry her away.

From the cinema, it surged back onto the street. As it neared the hotel, I could begin to distinguish the wording on the banners and make out its shouts. Two men beating drums marched in front of a group of *maulvis*—Muslim priests—who chanted slogans proclaiming God's greatness, the supremacy of Islam, and the need for Muslim law to be obeyed. The crowd punctuated these mottoes with cries of *"Allah-hu-akhbar."* At frequent intervals, the mob hurled more ominous epithets, many of which were painted on carefully lettered banners: Long Live Islam, Death to America, Death to All Infidels, Pakistan for Muslims, Death to CIA Spies.

Stephanie had slipped up beside me to watch, as had most of the diners, including Colonel Nasri and Nadia. I could feel Stephanie tremble as she pressed against me. The naked hatred visible on the faces of men in the crowd sent a shiver down my spine. Just as I took her hand to lead us away from the window, someone pointed toward us and shouted, *"Amrikan. Kafir. Amrikan murdabad."*

We stepped back from the window just as the crowd surged toward the front of the hotel restaurant. I caught a glimpse of a couple of men picking up bricks and throwing them at us. Fortunately, the window cracked, but didn't break. Several women screamed. We instinctively staggered further back into the dining room. Out of the corner of my eye, I saw Colonel Nasri shouting into his cell phone. Next thing I knew, he had drawn his revolver and run outside.

Four or five shots rang out. Upon sight of a uniformed officer waving a gun, the crowd paused before stampeding back onto the street. They were soon out of sight. The sound of chanting and the beat of drums, however, continued to rattle those of us in the dining room.

Shaken, we returned to our table. Nadia joined us.

"Those bearded rats," she muttered. "Very convenient to stage a protest just when we're gearing up to investigate human smuggling."

"You think?" I asked.

"Yes, I think that pig, Chaudri Gujar Sahib, is behind this. Too much of a coincidence. Just what he needs to distract us. Muddy the waters. Give him time to erase any evidence."

Stephanie narrowed her eyes. "But those Muslim priests at the front?"

Nadia lay her khaki cap on the table and ran her hands through her hair. "They're in his pocket. He subsidizes a couple of their mosques. And did you see those signs? Chaudri probably paid for them. Another thing: most of the men looked young, poorly dressed. I bet every one has a hundred rupee note in his pocket. No, this was not a spontaneous demonstration—of course, few of them are. But usually there's some local cause. Nothing like that here."

I fiddled with a spoon. "So what will happen?"

"Since we think the local police are also in Chaudri's back pocket, the colonel has called in the army. The army will get the demonstration under control. Arrest the instigators."

Stephanie brushed her *dupatta* out of her eyes. "So, Colonel Nasri will have to leave off trying to find Jan?"

Nadia shook her head. "Someone from the local command will take over. Colonel Nasri is committed to finding your daughter. But right now we need to get you two back to your bungalow."

I scowled.

"No argument. The city is in an uproar. And with those *maulvis* stirring up anti-foreign feelings, you're not safe here."

"But I feel safer in the hotel," Stephanie said, "than out of town in an isolated bungalow."

"Look, I'll have a soldier bivouac on the bungalow grounds. We'll be in constant contact and you'll be out of sight."

Memories of riots from my childhood came back. "I think she's right, Steph. Things could get ugly."

We left town in an army jeep with the driver and a heavily armed trooper in the front. At my request, I'd had Nadia instruct them to stop at Padri Fazal's village on the way to our canal bungalow.

When we pulled up in front of Padri Fazal's compound, we found his son Caleb dabbing whitewash over another slogan scrawled on their wall. I could make out *murdabad*—death to— but the rest had already been covered up. When he saw the military jeep pull up, Caleb turned from the wall to stare at us nervously.

I jumped out. "*Salaam*, Caleb. Is your father in?"

He smiled. "Mr. Radley. Yes, *abba ji* is home. Please come in."

I followed him into the courtyard, where we found Padri Fazal squatting on a string bed with his Bible open before him. When he saw me, he stood up stiffly and beckoned with his hand. "*Salaam*, Joshua, please have a seat. We have been praying for your daughter. Any news?"

I shook my head as I sat down on another string bed beside his. "Not really. Someone saw her being taken, but we don't know anything more."

He signalled for his daughter-in-law Rahima to make tea. "Someone on the train saw her?"

"No, afterwards somewhere. We're not sure where. Let me explain."

After urging him not to make tea, I went on to describe Colonel Nasri and Major Khan's arrival, the roadblock, the discovery of the truck smuggling women and children, and finding Chandi, Raju Moro's daughter, among them.

His face brightened at the mention of Chandi. "That's good news. Raju and his wife will be overjoyed."

"That's the problem. Her family has disappeared. The colonel thought you might be able to help."

Fazal scratched his forehead. "Me? Help?" Then he nodded. "Oh, I see. I can ask the Marwaris who go to our church where Raju's people went."

"Exactly."

Fazal stood up. "Raju has relatives in Chak 36. I'll go over there right now and find out." He shouted for Caleb to bring his motorcycle.

I got up and walked toward the gate, then turned back. "Padri Sahib. One more thing. There's a demonstration, a riot really, going on right now in Nowshera... against foreigners and Christians. You better not go near the town."

He waved his right arm as if he was swatting a fly. "*Bevakoof.* Idiots. They won't touch me."

I pointed toward the courtyard wall. "Another slogan?"

"Pah, don't worry about it. I'll contact you as soon as I get any news about Raju's people. *Khudavand zinda hai.*"

As we drove away, I thought about Fazal's untraditional farewell—the Lord is alive. He obviously took his faith seriously. So did Stephanie. And, as I had begun to realize, so did I.

Mohammed and Musa appeared as soon as the jeep pulled in front of the canal bungalow.

"Welcome home, Sahib, Memsahib," Musa said. "We very worried."

Mohammed eyed the heavily armed trooper who had accompanied us with a frown.

I nodded. "Thank you, Musa, Mohammed. We appreciate your concern. We've been trying to help find our daughter."

"Any news?" Musa said.

I shook my head.

"Breakfast, let me fix you some breakfast."

I gave Musa a thin-lipped smile. "Thank you, but we've already eaten."

Musa looked crestfallen. "Tea? Coffee? Orange juice?"

Stephanie stepped forward. "Musa, would you please make tea for the officers? We've had a lot of coffee this morning."

I turned toward the trooper and the driver, forgetting that I didn't even know their names. "Ah, yes, this is, uh..."

"Corporal Ijaz, sir."

"And I'm Private Nawaz," the driver said.

"Uh, yes, Corporal Ijaz will be staying here with us... to... uh, to communicate with the colonel you met yesterday. Private Nawaz will be returning the jeep to Nowshera."

"Very good, Sahib," Mohammed said. "Shall I arrange accommodation in the servants' quarters?"

Corporal Ijaz stepped forward. "That won't necessary, sir. With your permission, I'll bivouac right over there." He pointed to a spot in the garden. "But I would appreciate the occasional meal." He smiled. "Army rations can get tiresome."

"Very good, Corporal," I said. "Let us know if there is anything you need."

"I will, sir."

We left Corporal Ijaz and Private Nawaz setting up a small tent between a couple of orange trees.

Inside our bedroom, we plopped down on armchairs and stared at each other. "What now?" Stephanie asked.

"Wait, I guess."

She put her head in her hands. "Wait and pray. Hard to believe just forty-eight hours have gone by since Jan was taken. Seems like a lifetime."

I gnawed on my lip. "This is worse than any nightmare... and yet it seems surreal. As if it can't be happening."

Stephanie sighed.

"Why don't we go out to the dig?" I asked. "See what's happening."

"I don't feel much like looking at broken pottery."

"Better than doing nothing."

She nodded. "Okay, but first we should send a couple of e-mails."

"Yeah, the family will be frantic."

"Honey, do you mind doing that while I freshen up? I feel absolutely grubby."

"You got it."

We had nineteen personal e-mails. Our son Jonathan had sent three, liberally dotted with exclamation and question marks, and laying out the reasons why he should come and help find his sister.

My parents told us about the prayer group they'd activated in their church and the pressure they were putting on their Member of Parliament to get involved.

Stephanie's parents had demanded that their Representative get the State Department to send in Marines. They didn't seem to see any conflict in sending U.S. Marines to rescue a Canadian citizen. After all, she was their granddaughter.

The pastor of our church wrote to say that he had mobilized a twenty-four hour prayer chain for Janice's rescue.

Three other e-mails really surprised me. One was from Jack, the computer whiz I'd come to depend on when researching stories. Another was from Rose Tonelli, my former colleague at the *Toronto Times*. Then there was one from Red Farman, who'd been my boss at the *Times* when I got sacked—not that he'd been the cause. Evidently, the story of Janice's kidnapping and the train hold-up was occupying the front page of most newspapers.

The rest contained expressions of concern and promises of prayer from various friends.

It took me ten minutes or so to compose a general e-mail that gave a few of the facts and conveyed urgency without sounding hopeless or inviting trouble from the Pakistani spooks in the ISI.

While Stephanie read the e-mails, I took her place in the bathroom. Before I could finish, I heard a car pull into the driveway.

A few minutes later, Stephanie peeked in. "Chaudri Mohammed. He's asking for you."

I finished shaving and threw on a fresh shirt. Chaudri was the last person I wanted to see. I took a deep breath in an attempt to control my rage and walked out onto the veranda with as bland an expression on my face as I could muster. He stood by the open rear door of his dusty black Mercedes.

"Chaudri Sahib," I said as I descended the veranda steps. "*Salaam alay kum.*"

He nodded to me. "*Waalay kum as salaam*, Mr. Radley."

I didn't offer my hand. I couldn't bear to touch him. Instead, I stood at the bottom of the steps about ten feet away and waved over my shoulder toward the veranda. "Please, have a seat. Can I get you some tea? A Coke?"

"No, thank you. I won't be long. I have a very busy day ahead." He put his left hand into the pocket of his tan jacket.

I looked beyond him toward a gray Indian jay hopping around on the lawn. Busy doing what? Hiding evidence? Kidnapping more women? My pause in responding seemed to stretch the invisible tension in the air to the breaking point.

He broke the silence. "Any news of your daughter?"

I shook my head, "No."

"I'm sorry. Such a delightful young woman."

Unable to control my emotions any longer, I sat down on one of the veranda steps and stared at the ground.

"I apologize for intruding on your grief. I just wanted to return something I believe you lost."

I looked up. He came toward me holding out a Swiss knife.

He stopped in front of me. "Is this yours?"

"I—I'm not sure. Could be."

He handed it to me, pointing out the gold initials on the side. "JF, your initials."

I turned the knife over in my hand as I stood up. "Must be mine. I lost it last week sometime. But how...?"

He stared at me. "I found it in one of my barns. A barn that was broken into."

I could feel a flush beginning to rise on my neck. I flicked open the blade and walked over to a nearby bush where I cut off a twig. "Doesn't seem damaged. Thank you for returning the knife."

I could see the flecks of gray in his obsidian eyes as he engaged mine. I held my breath and strained to hold his gaze. Finally, he broke off and gestured toward the trooper who stood off to one side. "Army got involved? Very good, but you may need more than one soldier. Can be a dangerous area. Unfortunately, bad things happen."

With a wave, he turned and walked back to his car.

As I watched him drive away, I struggled to get my breathing back under control.

CHAPTER TWENTY-NINE
Subterranean Discovery

Stephanie came down the steps of the veranda to stand beside me as I watched Chaudri Gujar Mohammed drive away.

"What was that all about?"

I showed her the Swiss knife. "Returned my lost knife."

"How did he know it was yours?"

"My initials on it. Our *chaukidar* probably told him I'd lost it."

"You think he suspects?"

I nodded. "He knows. The rat threatened me. You could have cut the tension between us with a chainsaw."

Stephanie sat down on the veranda steps. "Threatened?"

I joined her. "Nothing overt. Very subtle. As... as subtle as a cobra sunning itself on a rock."

"I hate that man."

"He inquired about Jan, called her a delightful young woman, then warned me about bad things happening. Said a single soldier wasn't much protection."

Stephanie spit on the ground. "Hell is too good for people like him."

I squinted at her. This was a side of her I hadn't seen much before. Quite a contrast from the image I had of her kneeling before a senior in a wheelchair whispering words of comfort. But she certainly captured my sentiments.

I jumped up. "Let's go out to the dig. It'll give us something to do while Nadia follows up leads."

I fetched my camera, notebook, and the keys to the Land Rover while Stephanie got a couple of bottles of water and our cell phone. We were about to drive away when Corporal Ijaz hurried over. He looked quite agitated.

"Sahib, please to inform me where you be going?"

"Out to Pattan Minara, Corporal. Anything wrong?"

"Colonel Nasri give orders. I must stay with you at all times."

"But Corporal, we'll be okay. They have guards at the site."

He shook his head. "Please. If I not go. Get into much trouble."

I looked at Stephanie. She nodded, so I said, "Can you drive a Land Rover?"

"Of course, sir."

"Okay, why don't you become our driver?"

"Very good. One moment, sir."

He fetched his MP5 machine pistol and slid into the driver's seat. Stephanie switched to the back seat and I took her place in front. I liked to be behind the wheel, but Corporal Ijaz's presence did make me feel safer.

At the entrance to the site, the Chinese guard nodded at our passes, but wouldn't let the corporal in without calling Luke.

Having finally secured authorization, he waved us through. As we drove to Luke's field office, I glanced over the site. It was eerily empty, silent. Chaudri's threats had been effective.

I directed Ijaz to park beside Luke's Land Rover. Luke came out of his office and stared at us quizzically. "What's going on? Why the guard?"

I frowned as I thought about where to begin and how much to tell him. "Some vague threats—that kind of thing."

"A rather nasty demonstration in Nowshera," Stephanie added. "Anti-American, anti-Christian.

He nodded, then pointed toward a couple of picnic tables set up under a shelter he'd had made from branches and palm fronds. Corporal Ijaz remained in the vehicle while Stephanie and I joined Luke at one of the tables. I tried to describe recent events without going into too much detail. Partway through my explanation about the involvement of Colonel Nasri and Major Nadia Khan, the three student archaeologists came out of Luke's office to join us. I paused to acknowledge them.

Parveen, the student from Oxford, came over and sat beside Stephanie. "Any news of Janice? I can't sleep for thinking of her."

"A sighting, but not much else... yet," Stephanie said.

"The police," I said. "Well, really the army, they stopped a truck at a roadblock south of Nowshera."

Stephanie struggled to keep from tears as she described the discovery of drugged women and children hidden behind bales of cotton.

Scott, one of the students from Penn State, frowned. "That's barbaric."

I found myself unconsciously clenching my fists. "Not too barbaric for supposedly civilized people in the West to bankroll."

Luke ran a hand through his wiry, black hair. "Sadly, Asia is also involved. India. The Philippines. Thailand. Even China. No one knows how much of this vile trade goes through Hong Kong... But now, with the army involved?"

I nodded. "It's more hopeful. They've already found information on two transit warehouses in Multan and Nowshera. And they're following up a number of leads."

Stephanie wiped her eyes with her *dupatta*. "We came out here to have something to do while we wait for word."

I gestured over my shoulder toward the mound. "Chaudri's tantrum scared off the workers?"

Luke glanced from Stephanie to me, obviously catching my unspoken request to change the subject. He gritted his teeth. "I had to give them a day off—but they'll be back. Pay's too good and food prices in the bazaar have skyrocketed."

"Mr. Wu," Parveen began, "why don't we use this opportunity to explore the room below the tower? Josh and Stephanie can help."

Darren, the other student from Penn State, nodded. "Great idea. And we can keep anything we discover quiet."

Luke raised his eyebrows as he looked from Darren to Parveen. "Eager, are we? Well, why not? Let's do it... Oh, by the way, Josh, that article was great. Exactly what we wanted. I've already sent it off to Asian Archaeology."

I acknowledged his praise with a nod that turned into a frown as the four of them went off to get their gear. I thought of my commitment to write a whole series. How could I do even one more? The real story was about enslaving living people, not digging up ancient skeletons.

While Steph and I waited, one of the expedition jeeps drove up. A tall, bearded man wearing a Sindhi skull cap embroidered with scores of tiny mirrors got out, nodded to us, and then sauntered over to another of the picnic tables and sat down. The vest he wore over his gray *qamiz*, like his cap, was intricately embroidered in the Sindhi style. He reached into a pocket of his *qamiz* and took out a pack of cigarettes. Extracting one, he lit up and inhaled deeply. I tried not to stare, but the growth of hair sprouting from each of his ears was quite astounding, like a bush growing out of each side of his head. Why did that ring a bell? I was wondering if his religion provided instructions regarding the frequency and type of haircuts when I glanced again at his cigarette.

It looked American, as had the packet he drew from his pocket. With American markets closing, U.S. companies were no doubt cultivating more lucrative markets. Maybe everyone with a decent job smoked American brands. But no, I'd seen only local brands in town and among the workers.

When Luke returned, he went over to the bearded man. "Ali, I need you to start up the generator at the tower and make sure it keeps going while we're inside the tunnel."

"Very good, sir," he said as he ground out his cigarette and tossed it away.

Ali, who I gathered was the head security guard, got in his jeep and drove across the mound to the old tower. Luke and the students threw backpacks into another jeep.

"Josh, you can follow us in your Land Rover," he said.

"I think we'll walk. It's not far."

As soon as they drove away, I grabbed a Ziploc bag from the glove compartment and bagged Ali's butt. Corporal Ijaz, who had remained in the Land Rover while we talked with Luke and the students, looked at me strangely when I returned to stash the bag. I didn't explain, just shrugged, grabbed my hat, camera, and a couple of bottles of water and hastened to catch up with Stephanie.

"Sahib," he shouted, "where you go?"

I stopped and pointed. "We're going to explore a tunnel beneath Pattan Minara, that old tower."

"I go with you."

I nodded. "*Teak hai, ji.*" It wouldn't hurt to have him around. I didn't trust that Ali character.

Ijaz retrieved his MP5, locked the vehicle, and followed me across the debris field. Fifty yards or so from the tower, we passed a shed from which came the chug of a generator. Ali lounged in the doorway. A few yards beyond that, we began descending the sloping trench dug into the mound to give access to the tunnel beneath Pattan Minara. By the time we arrived at the entrance,

Luke had unlocked the steel gate and disarmed what appeared to be motion sensors. Clearly Luke was taking no chances.

I glanced up at the weathered *minara* above us before I followed the others into the tunnel. The tower didn't look stable, but I told myself that if it had withstood centuries of sandstorms I was foolish to worry about its collapse.

This time, instead of plunging into choking dust and thick darkness, electric lights lit our way along the timbered passageway. A fat, flexible plastic pipe strung along the floor pumped in fresh air. Still, nothing could disguise the dank stench of mould and ancient dust that issued from the yawning hole where the tunnel floor had collapsed into the structure below. Nor could anything silence the occasional creak of a stressed timber in the roof. I eyed the roof supports nervously.

Luke plugged a dangling cable into a receptacle and floodlights suddenly illuminated the room below. We gathered at the edge of the hole to stare into a space that must have been hidden from human eyes for centuries, possibly millennia.

Scott climbed onto a bamboo ladder that descended into the hole. "What are we waiting for? Let's go."

Corporal Ijaz stayed in the tunnel while the rest of us descended the ladder into the mysterious room. Our movements immediately stirred up a cloud of choking dust that obscured our vision and had us all coughing.

"Everyone stand still a minute," Luke said, wetting a kerchief and tying it over his nose and mouth. "Let the dust settle. Just look around."

Following his example, I covered my mouth and nose, then began to gaze around. The opposite wall appeared to be very uneven, as if poorly constructed. To the left, partway along the wall, I could make out a debris-choked, arched doorway. The intersecting wall on that side—I assumed there had to be one—was beyond the reach of the floodlights.

Luke took a water bottle from the pack he'd brought and began to carefully sprinkle the dust in front of him. All of us followed his lead until we had cleared a large area around the ladder where we could step without stirring up the ancient dust.

Parveen suddenly pointed across the room. "Someone has been here recently. See the way the dust is disturbed over there?"

"The women who fell through would have done that," Luke reminded her.

Parveen tilted her head to one side and continued to stare at the opposite wall. "I don't think so. See that hollow in the wall—how clean it is of dust?"

She was right. The wall was not rough, but had what appeared to be niches or alcoves built into its surface. One of them seemed swept free of grit. I looked closer and noted another empty niche. In fact, there seemed to be three. Each showed signs of disturbance and each stood eerily empty.

"I see what you mean," Luke said. "The dust is disturbed all along that wall and in several of the alcoves."

He flicked on a flashlight and shone it to our right. An intersecting wall with an arched doorway appeared from the shadows. "Whoever has been here came and went through that arch."

Darren hurried toward the opposite wall, stirring up a great cloud of dust.

"Darren, slowly!" Luke shouted, then turned to the rest of us. "Follow Darren, but very slowly, very carefully. Step in his footprints. Parveen and Scott, join Darren in brushing off a section of that wall. I think there are figures sculpted into it."

Luke took a brush from his backpack and joined his students. Stephanie and I gingerly followed them, but stood back to see what they uncovered. Gradually, an incredible array of carved figures appeared: gods, goddesses, animals, birds, plants.

"What a disappointment," Luke said. "Hindu sculpture—must be from the second or third century BC."

"Disappointment?" I said. "This is astonishing."

Luke turned toward me and nodded. "Yes, quite a find, but I had hoped for an intact Indus temple. This is much later, probably connected to the *minara* above us, which means the Hindu builders constructed their temple over an Indus site."

Luke turned back to the wall where a typical Hindu frieze was beginning to appear from the dust and grit of centuries. I took several pictures with my digital camera and then stood watching them work.

After a few minutes, my curiosity got the better of me. I borrowed a flashlight from Scott and shone it to the left, toward the intersecting wall hidden in shadow. It too looked irregular. Carefully, one step at a time, I made my way past the debris-choked archway to the corner where the two walls intersected. I stopped in front of what appeared to be a pile of rubble that had fallen from the wall. Idly, I probed the pile with my shoe. Smoother than brick fragments.

I stooped to brush off an irregular object and a gild arm appeared. It shone dully in the light from the flashlight. "Guys," I shouted. "There's something here."

Luke came over and began brushing off the object. A golden image about three feet high appeared. He reached down to pick it up, but only succeeded in flipping it over. "Very heavy."

He continued to clear away the sand and grit that clung to the face of the image. Gradually a mouth, nose, and then two eyes appeared. One eye socket stared at us blankly, but the other blinked ruby fire. "Krishna. Must have come from one of the wall niches."

He was in the process of cleaning away grit from the elaborate headdress when the lights dimmed, flickered, and then went out.

CHAPTER THIRTY
Sabotage

From the sudden darkness of the room below the tower, Luke shouted, "Hey! What happened to that generator?"

For a few moments, no one said anything, just fumbled in their packs for flashlights to add to the dim light from mine.

"Sahib," Corporal Ijaz shouted, "*teak hain?*"

I flashed my light toward the ladder. "We're okay, Corporal. Do you have a flashlight?"

"No, sir."

I shouted back. "Just a minute. We'll bring one up to you."

"Darren," Luke said, "can you and the corporal find out what happened to the generator? Walk slowly to the ladder. Don't stir up any more dust than you can help."

"Will do."

Luke flashed his light toward the statue. It shone dully. "We can't leave that here." He took off his backpack. "Parveen, let me dump my stuff in your backpack. Then we can use mine to carry it."

When his pack was empty, Luke knelt beside the stature and tried, but failed to lift it. Scott joined him and together they succeeded in getting it into the backpack.

"Scott, I'm not going to be able to carry it. You're the strongest. Can you...?"

"No problem."

"Let's wait a few minutes," Luke said. "See if Darren gets the generator running."

Parveen knelt down and began to carefully dust the pile of rubble where the statue had been lying. Fragments of brick and the odd pottery shard came to light. "Nothing much so far, but I'm getting the impression that this structure merits serious exploration."

"You're right about that," Luke said. "But it's not in our mandate. We may have to mount another expedition next year."

Scott flashed his light along the base of the wall where we'd seen signs of an intruder. "We can't just leave it like this. Somebody's obviously determined to plunder everything of value."

Luke coughed. "We'll have to deal with that later. The air is already getting stale and there's no sign of the generator coming back on. Let's head out."

Luke and I lifted the knapsack onto Scott's shoulders and we slowly made our way to the ladder. Stephanie and I held the ladder steady while the rest climbed out. I could see the bamboo rungs bend under Scott's weight as he ascended. A dozen scenarios played on the screen of my mind as I watched him climb up. The ladder breaking. Scott falling. Us being entombed down here with the tower collapsing above us. No light. No fresh air.

Like most of my fears, this one was a figment of my imagination. When he heard us coming, Darren poked his grease-streaked face out of the doorway of the generator shed. "Not going to start any time soon."

The corporal came out with his sleeves rolled up. "Sabotaged."

Luke threw up his hands. "How could it be sabotaged?"

Darren wiped his hands on a rag. "Someone smashed something and cut the fuel line. There's diesel all over the ground."

Luke began to swear in what had to be Chinese, then strode over to his Land Rover. "Get in."

As everyone was piling in, Luke hit the starter switch, but all we heard in response was the sound of clicks and a whir. Luke jumped out, lifted the hood, and again began to curse. "Someone—must be Ali—took a wrench to the carburetor."

Luke pointed across the mound. "We better check out the office and storeroom. Fast."

I took out my cell phone and dialled the number Nadia had given us. After a couple of rings, she answered. "Major Khan here."

"Nadia, this is Josh."

"Oh, hi Josh. Not much to report I'm afraid."

I hurried after the others. "We've got a major problem at the archaeological site. Sabotage that may be related to what's going on."

"Related? How could it be?"

"When you debriefed the women, did any of them mention a man with a large handlebar moustache and hair growing out of his ears?"

"Let me check my notes."

After a few moments, she came back on. "Yeah, two of them mentioned a character like that."

"Ali."

"Who is Ali?"

"The head of security here at the site. You remember me mentioning the American cigarette butt I picked up at the site of the train hold-up? Well, this guy smokes them. I picked up another butt out here. DNA should match."

"Evidence sounds flimsy. And we've got no way to check DNA. You mentioned sabotage?"

I described what had happened to us and then rushed on. "He's taken off in the expedition vehicle he uses, the very one identified by several on the train as being at the hold-up. Valuable stuff is being stolen here... his compound is very suspicious. Can you put out an APB on his vehicle and raid his compound?"

"Whoa, not so fast."

"Nadia, this guy is obviously connected to the abduction of the women and now he's spooked." My voice rose as I thought of the implications. "He'll warn the gang. They'll hide their tracks, destroy evidence." Stephanie caught me as I stumbled on some pottery shards. "What if they kill Janice?"

"That's not going to happen. Look, Josh, we're making progress. This morning's raid on Fatah Ginning uncovered more evidence. And Colonel Nasri is interviewing witnesses of the train hold-up."

"But Ali..."

Nadia broke in. "Okay, give me a description of his vehicle. We'll send out a bulletin."

By this time, we'd arrived back at Luke's office-storeroom, so I passed the phone to him. "Luke, can you give Major Khan a description of Ali's vehicle?"

While Luke talked to Nadia, I checked on our Land Rover. Fortunately, it was okay. Scott tried the jeep assigned to them and found it in working order as well.

Luke passed the phone back.

Nadia answered. "Josh, I'll send out a description of Ali's vehicle. And I know this sounds like a cliché, but try to be patient. Our leads are quite promising. The colonel is skilled in this kind of thing. I doubt if sending a team out there to the dig will help us, especially if this Ali character has already fled. Our priority is finding Janice."

"Okay, Nadia, I'll try to be patient."

"The gang we've uncovered probably traffics in arms and drugs as well as humans. Anything for money. The thefts at the dig could be a minor sideline to their main operation—or completely unconnected. It could be another gang."

"Anything tying Chaudri to this?

"Nothing yet. But if it's there, we'll find it."

"Thanks, Nadia."

I clicked off, turned to the group, and explained what Nadia had said about the thefts being unconnected."

Luke beckoned to one of the Chinese guards who had come over while we were talking. "Doesn't mean we should ignore what's happening here."

After talking to the guard in Chinese for a few minutes, the guard ran off.

Luke unlocked the padlock on the door to his office-storeroom, locked away the statue, and came out with two heavy-duty flashlights and a couple of pistols. He tossed one of the pistols to Scott. "Scott, you and Parveen stay here with the Radleys. See that no one tries to break into our storeroom. Darren, you come with me. We'll take a couple of Chinese guards and see what we can find at Ali's compound."

I touched his arm. "I should go with you... along with the corporal. He's well armed."

"Josh, with all due respect, what Major Khan said is probably true. This concerns the theft of artefacts. You and the corporal can be more help staying here."

"Wait a minute. It was my lead that pointed the finger at Ali. I know he's involved in more than stealing relics."

Luke looked down and scuffed the sand with his boot. "Okay, but can we use your Land Rover? We need to leave the other one here. That way, all of us can be mobile."

Corporal Ijaz looked from me to Luke with a quizzical expression on his face.

"Corporal," I said, "Please stay here with my wife."

Stephanie frowned. "I'm not sure I want to wait here. You won't be long?"

"No, Mrs. Radley," Luke said. "We just want to check out Ali's compound. We'll feel better if you stay here with the corporal."

●●◆●●

I braked the Land Rover in front of Ali's fortress-like compound. Luke got out and strode over to the massive timber gate where he gave the bell pull a couple of tugs. We could hear the sound of a couple of camel bells tinkling inside, but nothing else. No footsteps. No radio blaring Bollywood tunes. No animals snorting. Silence. Luke pounded on the door with his fist. Still nothing.

Luke beckoned to the two Chinese guards who had accompanied us and pointed at the wall. Like all of his guards, these two were taller than most Chinese; probably Mongolian or Kazakh. Tough-looking characters. One boosted the other up to the top of the wall where he swung over and dropped to the ground.

While they were getting the gate open, I wandered around to the back of the compound. Wheat straw covered the ground in all directions. Strange for it to be strewn around like that, given the value of straw. When I walked over and kicked some aside, I was startled to see shards of broken brick and terracotta pottery. Wherever I scraped the straw away, I found the same result. The ground for hundreds of yards was littered with shards excavated from the mound.

By the time I returned to the front gate, the Chinese guards had it open. I immediately noticed that the mound of burlap-wrapped bundles I'd seen piled near the barn was gone, along with the red tractor. Aside from tire marks and the hoof prints of animals in the dust, the place looked deserted. Shutters covered the windows of the whitewashed bungalow built against the back wall. The flowers in the garden across the front of the bungalow drooped as if they hadn't been watered for a couple of days.

Luke peered through a crack between two of the shutters. "Place looks abandoned."

Darren answered from the barn. "Not a sign of life in here either."

I joined Luke. "Ali must have suspected he was about to be discovered."

Luke looked in my direction with raised his eyebrows. "So you really think he was carrying on some kind of nefarious activity?"

"Why else would he sabotage the generator and take off in his jeep?" I pointed over the back wall. "The ground back there is covered with brick and terracotta shards—hidden by a scattering of straw. Someone from this compound has been excavating in the mound."

Luke slumped. "I think you're right. How else could someone have gotten into that room below the tower and stolen statutes from those niches?"

He pointed to the bungalow's front door and shouted something in Chinese. The two guards ran over and tried the door. When it didn't budge, one of them rammed it with his shoulder. With a splintering of wood, it burst open.

Inside, paper and plastic bags littered the floor. A couple of unwashed pots stood in the kitchen sink. Down the hall in a bedroom, the drawers on a chest stood open. A dirty *shalwar-qamiz* lay discarded in the corner.

Darren shouted at us from the courtyard. "Guys, found something."

When we joined him, he beckoned us to follow him into the barn. Inside the barn, I noted a series of animal stalls along one wall. But an open trapdoor on the other side caught my attention. The trapdoor exposed a stairway. Darren flicked a switch and a dim light illuminated the stairs and room below.

Luke sent one of the guards back to watch the Land Rover. The reek that assailed our nostrils as we descended the stairs had me fumbling in my pocket for my kerchief. The stench combined the smell of the worst football locker room I could imagine with that of a holding cell where torture prevailed: stale sweat, urine, and fear. In the concrete room below the barn, two low wattage bulbs gave just enough light to make out the rusty chains along one wall and the row of dirty bedrolls lying below them. A couple of stinking buckets that must have served as latrines for the wretches imprisoned in this hellhole stood in one corner.

The five of us stopped at the base of the stairs to stare. Darren bit his lip and held his hand to his mouth as he tried to control an onset of the heaves. The guard who accompanied us let out a stream of Chinese. Luke punched a wooden roof support. "Ali won't get away with this."

I tied my kerchief around my nose and walked across the room to a door set in the far wall. I opened the door and flicked on another light switch, illuminating a long timbered tunnel. Bits of brick and terracotta littered the floor. When I looked back into the room, I could see a trail of fragments leading to a square metal box hanging on chains from the ceiling. The chains disappeared through holes in the corners of another trapdoor.

"Slave labour," Luke said. "That's how he beat us to that room below the tower."

Darren pointed to the metal box. "Used that box and chain affair to take out the debris through another trapdoor. Must be some lifting device above and a back exit from the compound."

I nodded. "They could take out the debris without being seen, scatter it on the ground at the back, and hide it with straw. Very convenient the way this compound is built into the back of the mound so close to the tower. Any unusual activity could be easily disguised as farm work."

"Sounds of digging wouldn't be heard either," Darren said.

Luke waved around the concrete room. "But this has been here for years. Long before we started to excavate Pattan Minara and began to discover valuable artefacts."

I scratched my head. "You're right... I bet this was a way station used by a gang to hold kidnapped men and women. Originally, it probably had nothing to do with stealing relics. This site is far from town, at the very edge of farmland, and thought to be haunted. An ideal base for smuggling... anything."

Darren indicated the tunnel. "Are we going to see where this leads?"

"I think we know," Luke said, "but let's check it out." He eyed the ceiling. "We better be careful. That doesn't look very secure."

"Cheap labour," I said. "If it collapsed and they lost a couple of men—no problem."

Although the tunnel was much rougher and more poorly supported than the one Luke had supervised, it was dimly lit by dangling bulbs connected to the same power grid that fed the farm compound. As we'd surmised, it eventually led us into the very room where we'd found the gold statue.

Back in the courtyard, we gathered around Luke.

"So what now?" Darren asked.

Luke shrugged his shoulders. "Head back to my office, I guess. Ali and whoever helped him have obviously gone and they're not coming back. We need to inform the police and arrange for that tunnel to be closed."

Back at the Land Rover, I motioned Luke to one side. "I don't think it's a good idea to tell the police. There's some thought they may be involved. Let me call Major Khan or Colonel Nasri."

"I'm not sure I can believe that." Luke frowned at me. "Okay, give your friends a call."

I walked a few yards away from the vehicle and keyed in Nadia's number. She answered on the fifth ring. "Major Khan, *bol rahi hun.*

"Nadia, we've made a major discovery out at the compound I told you about."

"Josh, I was just going to give you a call. I have some bad news."

CHAPTER THIRTY-ONE
Bad News

I stared at the cell phone. *Bad news? No. Not Jan!*

"Josh. Josh, are you there?" Nadia said.

I bit my lip and answered in a whisper. "You said... bad news?"

"Not Janice. I should have made that clear. It's something else. And we are making progress. Getting a description of the people involved and their vehicles. We're tightening the net. Only a matter of time."

"But you said..."

"You first. Tell me what you found."

I took a deep breath. "The farm compound I told you about. It's got to be one of the places where this gang held their victims."

I brought her up to speed on the evidence we'd discovered of human trafficking, the fact that the compound predated the archaeological excavation, and the recent tunnel they'd dug. "The opportunity to steal artefacts was probably too good to pass up."

"Very lucrative. Smuggling antiquities is number three after drugs and slaves."

"I didn't know that."

"I'm surprised you didn't. Your instincts always amaze me."

"Enough of that. What's the bad news?"

"Colonel Nasri has been ordered to report immediately to Peshawar. There've been heavy Taliban attacks just outside the city."

"Oh no, and he's heading the investigation..."

Nadia cut in. "The threat around Peshawar is real enough, but there's something rotten about his reassignment. He's been ordered to turn over the investigation to a junior officer—someone who's palzy walzy with the local police."

Seeing my frown, Stephanie came over to listen. "But they're implicated," I said.

Nadia's voice rose and took on a bite. "Someone is pulling strings at the highest level. When I find out, I'll..." Her voice quieted. "Who am I kidding? I've been recalled as well."

"What?"

Stephanie whispered. "Josh, what's going on?"

I held up my hand to Steph as I injected a note of appeal into my voice. "But we really need you!"

"I'm sorry, Josh. I've been ordered to Islamabad for a debriefing."

"When?"

"Today. Now. I was just going to call you."

My shoulders slumped. "Nadia, this is devastating. Your coming has given us hope... Now I don't know what to say. It's like they're throwing us to the lions."

"Don't worry. This isn't the end. I've leaked the story to some press contacts. Once the foreign press gets a whiff of a cover-up, there'll be a frenzy. Islamabad will have to do everything in its power to find your daughter—or risk alienating the American public further. Jan's grandfather is American, right?"

"True, but—"

"And I'll be back after I rattle a few skeletons in Islamabad. They'll be happy to send me back. Another thing. That vehicle you mentioned has been spotted by an army patrol about twelve miles east of you. Toward the Indian border. Abandoned."

"But that's desert out there."

"Very strange. Josh, I've got to go. Just be careful with e-mails. Is Steph there?"

I left Stephanie talking to Nadia and walked over to the group who had been staring in our direction.

"What's wrong?" Luke asked.

"We're on our own. The two investigators I told you about have been recalled. Pulled off the case."

Luke squeezed my shoulder. "But the police..."

I frowned. "Yeah, the police—not much help."

"Well, we're not going to dump you. There's obviously a connection between the thefts here at the site and human trafficking. Maybe we can find a lead."

"Thanks, Luke."

I wandered over to the shelter and plopped down. I stared at a dust devil whirling like a dervish across the mound. To the north, a bank of clouds darkened the horizon. Rain?

Stephanie sat down beside me. Her face told the story; anguish, frustration, anger—and possibly fear—were written in the creases of her forehead and the moisture welling up in her brown eyes. The tiny mole on her right cheek seemed to throb. "What are we going to do?" Her voice was low, barely discernible, as it often was when she struggled to control her emotions.

I sighed deeply. "I don't know."

In my mind, I explored options, but came up with nothing. Nothing. A few bars from a Punjabi song broke into the silence. I looked over at Corporal Ijaz, who had taken out his cell phone. After nodding his head a few times, he pocketed the phone and walked over to where we sat.

"Sahib, you please to drive me to bungalow. Jeep meet me there."

I stood up. "But why, Corporal?"

He looked down. "My commanding officer say you not need protection."

"But Corporal, you saw what just happened here. Sabotage."

He made a face. "I know, Sahib, but I receive order. Must obey. But will explain to CO and, *Insh 'allah*, I will return."

I turned to Stephanie. "Checkmate."

Luke had overheard our conversation. "Why don't you take one of our Chinese guards? I don't think you should be left alone at that canal bungalow. It's quite isolated."

"Thanks, Luke, but we won't be alone. We have Musa and Mohammed."

"Not the same. I have a bad feeling about this. I know! Why don't you move out here for a few days? I can easily have another tent set up."

Parveen came over and took Stephanie's hands in both of hers. "That's a great idea. Mrs. Radley, why don't you do that? You'll be safer here. Besides, I could use the company... another woman."

Stephanie squeezed her hands and stood up. "Luke, Parveen, that's a generous offer. Let us think about it and give you a call back."

Stephanie and I sat on the steps leading up to the veranda of the canal bungalow. The jeep that had come to pick up Corporal Ijaz was waiting when we returned, and before long he was gone. With the electricity off again and the weakness of our laptop battery, we couldn't check our e-mails. Musa was preparing lunch. Like most cooks, he seemed to feel that the answer to bad news was a good meal. We'd stressed that we weren't hungry and urged him to prepare something simple. Whether he understood the concept of simplicity would soon become evident; whether I could eat anything was the real question.

I could taste the acid welling up from my stomach as I thought about Jan being somewhere out there. Where? The hope that had flared when Nadia and Colonel Nasri came charging onto the scene now flickered dimly somewhere in my knotted stomach.

Stephanie nodded toward Mohammed's quarters. "Do you really think Mohammed reports our movements to Chaudri?"

I took a gulp of water to wash away the taste of bile in my throat. "How else could Chaudri have known I lost my knife?"

Stephanie shivered. "Chaudri gives me the willies. Do you suppose he's behind the recall of Nadia and Colonel Nasri?"

I studied a bougainvillea blossom I'd plucked from the vine growing beside the steps. "Probably. If he's linked in any way to the gang the colonel is exposing, he must feel threatened. And he's got the clout to get them replaced."

"Surely, there's no doubt about his involvement. Didn't you say a witness saw one of his vehicles abducting that tribal girl?"

I tossed away the blossom. "Yeah. The girl's brother. You're right. There's no doubt. The boy's testimony and what we saw in Chaudri's barn erases any doubt from my mind."

Stephanie pushed a stray lock of hair behind her ear. "Bet he's the mastermind. But what about Ali?"

"Got to be connected. The cellar under his barn is a duplicate of what I saw in Chaudri's place."

"And the train hold-up?"

"That too. Can't be a coincidence."

Stephanie shivered again. I reached for her hand. She leaned against me. "Josh, if he blames us for the raid on his barn, that leaves us vulnerable here."

I squeezed her hand. "Very vulnerable. Do you think we should have taken Luke up on his offer?"

"We'd feel a lot safer," she said, squeezing my hand in return.

Musa suddenly appeared. "Sahib. Memsahib. *Khana taiyar hai.*"

I dropped Stephanie's hand and she leaned away from me—both of us startled that we'd inadvertently breached a cultural taboo by showing affection in public.

"*Teak hai,* Musa," I said.

We sat down to lunch more out of a desire to please Musa than anything else. He'd prepared lentil soup and fresh buns. I crinkled my nose and took a spoonful, then another. I could feel the soup soothing my queasy stomach. I glanced over at Stephanie only to find she was looking at me with raised eyebrows.

The soup was delicious: smooth and delicately flavoured with a few sprigs of coriander floating on top. Before I knew it, I'd polished off the whole bowl and was reaching for more. Along with the soup, Musa had made yeast rolls and opened a jar of mango jam. Early on, he'd noted my craving for jam. Maybe there was something to be said for Musa's way of dealing with trouble.

Stephanie nodded toward the kitchen door. "This guy is a genius."

I opened a roll, watched the steam rise, and then smeared it with jam. "Better than the cooks we've sampled in Little India back in Toronto."

When Musa came in with tea, Stephanie pointed toward the soup. "Number one, Sahib. Very good." She imitated writing, pointed to herself and said, "Write out, recipe. For me."

Musa's mouth opened in such a grin that I could see he was missing a couple of molars. He nodded vigorously. "I write... re-cip-e for you."

After Musa left, I took a sip of tea and turned to Stephanie. "I think we should move out to the site. They have twenty-four hour protection."

Stephanie nodded. "I hate to disappoint, Musa, but I agree."

The light flickered a couple of times and then came back on.

I put down my cup and stood up. "I'll call Luke. Then we better check our e-mail while we have the chance."

In our bedroom, I called Luke to tell him how thankful we were to accept his invitation. Then, I booted the laptop and watched it download e-mails while I pondered what to do.

"Steph, why don't we bombard the media?"

Stephanie looked over my shoulder at the list of e-mails. "Why not? We've been more or less abandoned—even by the embassies. Publicity is about the only weapon we have left."

I got up and gave Stephanie my chair. "Why don't you deal with the e-mails? I see several from your father, one from Jonathan, a couple from the church. I'll rough out a press release. And can you toughen up that e-mail we sent the U.S. Embassy and the Canadian High Commission and resend?"

I grabbed a pad of paper and began to scribble. After twenty minutes, I passed the pad to Stephanie. "See what you think of this."

> *For immediate release:*
>
> *Investigators expose human trafficking ring only to be recalled*
>
> *Nowshera, Pakistan: November 26, 2008*
>
> *On Wednesday, Pakistani authorities pulled Colonel Yaqub Nasri and Major N. Khan off the investigation of a massive human trafficking ring just when they were getting results. Authorities have not explained their actions. Could high level officials or local law enforcement personnel be implicated by the probe?*
>
> *The investigation by Colonel Nasri and Major Khan followed the Sunday attack by a gang of heavily armed men on the Lahore-bound Khyber Mail. During their barbaric assault on several first class coaches, seventeen people were killed and*

scores were injured when they stripped passengers of jewellery and other valuables. Eleven young women and several children were kidnapped. Janice Radley, a 24-year-old Canadian, was among those taken. She is the daughter of Joshua and Stephanie Radley, who were visiting the Pattan Minara archaeological excavation.

In the course of their investigations, Colonel Nasri and Major Khan discovered eighteen kidnapped women and children hidden in a Karachi-bound truck transporting bales of cotton. Three of the women had been kidnapped from the train. Others, including a young tribal woman, had been snatched from their families in widely scattered locations.

Why were Nasri and Khan removed from the investigation? Informed sources tell us that they had begun to piece together the picture of a powerful criminal consortium with tentacles reaching throughout the Punjab and Sindh provinces. They had already discovered three warehouses where women and children were kept in chains until their sale could be arranged. Public figures and law enforcement officers were certain to be implicated.

Repeated requests for diplomatic pressure to be used to ensure the rescue of Janice Radley have received a lukewarm response. Is terrorism the only word that lights a fire under our diplomats?

-30-

Stephanie read through my attempt and then raised her eyebrows. "Public figures and law enforcement personnel implicated? Are you sure you want to say that?"

I frowned, chewed on a fingernail, then answered slowly. "Why not? What have we got to lose?"

Stephanie passed back the pad. "It'll land like a bomb—antagonize the police—and maybe get us expelled. Jan..."

"Chaudri, or whoever is behind this, wants us to back off. That won't help Jan. We've got to bring more pressure to bear."

She nodded. "If you can get their attention, the press will see to that. Just so some new story doesn't distract them. Another terrorist attack and this will get shunted to the back burner."

"That's the thing. We've got to strike before this story gets forgotten. Embarrass Islamabad. Force them to act and maybe reinstate Nadia and the colonel."

Stephanie took a deep breath. "Okay. Do it. I just hope and pray it doesn't make things worse for Jan."

I leaned back in my chair and followed the progress of a *chipkilli* slithering along the wall. "Nadia warned me about e-mail surveillance. If we fire off a flurry of press releases from here, they'll be easily traced to us."

"We could go into town. Send them from an internet café."

I grimaced. "Still not secure. Besides, I'm leery about going into Nowshera right now."

"Can you hide the press release somehow in another e-mail? Surely, those conducting surveillance can't read through everything."

"That's an idea. Do you still have some to send?"

"Six or seven. Hey, why don't you send it to that Jack character you depend on so much for your internet research? He'll know how to hide the source."

"Perfect."

Jack the Hack, as I called him, had been instrumental in helping me gain access to the files of several companies laundering drug money, which led me to the Lightning File, with its encrypted information about terrorists and their targets.

I took Stephanie's spot at the laptop and composed an e-mail to Jack. I copied a bunch of stuff on Pattan Minara, including my first article. At the beginning, I gave him a subtle hint to look for the press release, which I hid in the middle of my message. I also hid some instructions about contacting every media outlet he could think of.

With his message ready to go, I returned the laptop to Stephanie, who sent it amongst a cluster of other e-mails. Our subterfuge wouldn't escape the attention of a sophisticated tracking program, but hopefully the Pakistani censors would be too busy looking for Taliban and Al Qaeda stuff.

With that done, we gathered up what we needed for a couple of days away and dumped it in a suitcase. We were about to leave when we heard a knock on the door.

"Sahib," Musa said. "You have guest."

When I opened the door to inquire who it was, I saw Raju Moro grinning over Musa's shoulder. Out in the garden behind him stood his camel calmly munching on leaves from the lower branches of a shesham tree.

CHAPTER THIRTY-TWO
Raju's Return

Raju bowed with his hands folded in a gesture of respect. A wide grin creased his leathery face

"Raju! I'm delighted to see you."

He doffed his turban and reached down with his hand to touch my shoe in a mark of honour. "Radley, Sahib. Our family is in your debt." I moved back, removing my feet from his reach. "Raju, Sahib, there is no debt, just joy at the rescue of your daughter."

I turned to Musa. "Tea, Musa. *Jaldi, jaldi*. Raju Moro's daughter has been rescued."

"Come." I led Raju into the living room and indicated a seat. He kicked off his hand-embroidered shoes and sat on the couch, lotus style, as I'd seen him do on the plane.

I pointed to him. "We were worried about you when we saw your village."

A cloud passed over his face and he shook his head. "*Badkar* landlord. No justice for poor."

"Where did you go?"

He waved his hands vaguely. "Sindh. To relatives."

"And your daughter... how is she?"

He grimaced. "Much cry, but..." His face broke into a grin again. "*Prebu ka shukr*, she okay. Not... how you say?"

"Abused, raped?"

"*Shukr hai.* No rape. God protected her. Her heart heal soon."

Musa came in with bowls of *chai*, showing his sensitivity to the more general Pakistani custom. Villagers almost invariably drank tea from bowls specially made for the purpose.

After Musa left, I asked, "And the wedding?"

He nodded. "Yes." He pointed to me. "You and Memsahib come to *shadi*."

"Thank you. We'll try if..."

"Your daughter?"

I shook my head and looked away.

He sipped loudly. "Your God will find." He nodded his head several times. "*Prebu Jesu* rescue. You pray, no?"

"Yes."

I poured him some more *chai*. "Raju, do you know Pattan Minara?"

"I know."

"What about the desert between Pattan Minara and the Indian border?"

He looked around as if checking for someone listening. "Know well. Have relatives in India. Sometimes visit."

"Could a jeep be used to cross the desert?"

"Camel best... but the sheikh hunts with jeeps. Smugglers use."

"Is there much smuggling across the border?" I suspected that he and his tribe were not altogether innocent of smuggling goods across the border. Since the partition of India and Pakistan had split their tribe in two, his people drifted back and forth to visit their kin.

He chuckled. "Much." Then he mimicked smoking a *hooka*. "Smuggle *bung, afeem,* very bad stuff... two very old forts out in desert. Bad men with much guns at one fort. With jeeps."

Since childhood, I'd heard about the string of ancient forts that guarded the trade route from Central Asia to the Indian subcontinent. A fort would make a natural headquarters for smugglers.

"You've seen?"

He nodded.

"Could you guide the police?"

He jumped up, retrieved his shoes, and turned toward the door. "No police. Police very bad. Some help smugglers."

I mentally smacked myself for mentioning the police. I stood and folded my hands in a combination of appeal and regret. *"Muaf karna, Raju Sahib.* No police. A good man, Colonel Nasri, rescued your daughter. He's trying to find my daughter. Maybe you could help him?"

Raju turned back toward me and looked at the floor. What struggles were going through his mind, suspicions about everyone in authority, memories of decades of ill-treatment? *"Shaid—* perhaps."

With that, he nodded and left the living room. I followed him out to the veranda and watched while he mounted his camel. At some imperceptible signal, the camel left off stripping the branch he was working on, came over to Raju, and knelt down—bending first his front legs, then his rear legs. Raju mounted, flicked the reins, and clucked some command. With the great blowing, blubbering sound that I'd tried to imitate as a child, the beast lumbered to its feet. As he was turning to go, I shouted, "Raju, Sahib. How do I find you?"

"I you find."

With that, he jerked on the reins and the camel loped away.

By the time we arrived at the site, Luke had a tent already erected for us between Parveen's and his. A couple of men were in the process of fencing off the ground around our tent with the portable cloth siding used for wedding tents. Bamboo inserts in the siding stiffened the material so it could remain erect when tied down with guy wires. The fence would help to give us a bit of privacy and reduce the amount of sand and grit driven by the wind off the desert.

Inside, it was surprisingly roomy and had a canvas floor. Luke had given us two cots, a small table, a kerosene lamp, a couple of chairs, and a portable sink and towel rack. A tin trunk to hold our clothes and valuables sat in one corner. How we could sleep apart would perhaps be a problem. In the past year, we'd revived our habit of snuggling together like two hibernating bears.

The tent couldn't compare with the comfort we'd enjoyed at the canal bungalow, but I was sure Stephanie shared my feeling of safety. We were so relieved that both of us collapsed on our separate cots and fell fast asleep. I guess we hadn't slept well for days.

The next thing I remembered hearing was the *azan*. The reedy voice of the young *maulvi* with his accented Arabic echoed over the encampment. I glanced at my watch. Six-fifteen. I sat up quickly, almost capsizing my cot, rubbed my eyes, and looked around. Stephanie was lying on her side, still dozing, her hair all tousled.

I felt a catch in my throat as a wave to tenderness came over me. I shook my head. How had I become so blasé about our relationship? So dissatisfied that sight of another skirt would set my hormones pinging? Steph. Darling Stephanie. Without her, my life would be a desert more blasted than Cholistan. She truly was a gift from God.

"Josh?"

Startled, I stood up, went over to the tent flap, and peered out.

Luke stood there. "Oh, good, you're up. I didn't want to wake you earlier. You've had a rough few days."

I ran my hand through my unruly hair. "Oh, hi Luke. We slept like logs."

"Chow's on in fifteen minutes... unless you want me to have some sent to you here."

"No, no. We'll be there."

I let the flap fall and turned to arouse Stephanie, but our voices must have woken her. She sat up and yawned. "Fifteen minutes to supper?" She stretched. "We better hustle."

We freshened up and hastened to join Luke and the three students in the staff dining tent. Most of the workers, many of whom had their wives with them, cooked for themselves or ate in the separate communal tent.

We arrived just in time to help ourselves to curried goat and rice. Since it was one of my favourite meals, I took a heaping portion, but Stephanie seemed reluctant to eat much. Probably images of the cute little goats we'd seen gambolling along the canal played around in her head. More likely, grief over Jan curbed her appetite. The thought made me look again at my plate and wish I hadn't taken so much.

After supper, we all followed Luke to his office to examine the latest discoveries. When we were inside, Luke shut and locked the door, then turned to one of the worktables. We gasped as he swept off the cloth covering the statue we'd found in the room revealed by the cave-in.

The gold statute of Krishna gleamed so brightly, it might as well have been moulded yesterday. The intact eye glittered with ruby fire as though the god could see into our souls. The empty eye socket radiated malevolence. One hand curved over the headdress and the other followed the sensuous curve of the body as if the god had been caught in the act of dancing. Every shred of clothing, every bangle, every tassel, every detail of finger and face displayed unbelievably intricate craftsmanship.

My mouth hung open as I gazed at the statue. With only ancient tools and techniques at their disposal, how could the sculptors have fashioned such a masterpiece? How long had it taken? And this was but one example of thousands of images, friezes, and temples scattered throughout the Indian subcontinent.

I began to understand some of the appeal of idolatry. To their devotees, images such as this one must have seemed miraculous—as though created by the gods. Mesmerizing, the graven images of Hinduism—and other religions—gave visible shape to the mysteries of faith. They provided devotees with a tangible focus for their supplications, while the God Christians worshipped (in common with Jews and Muslims) *lived in unapproachable light, whom no one had seen or could see.*

The statue before me gave shape to the never-ending human struggle to make visible and understandable and controllable the one who was infinite, incomprehensible, and sovereign. No wonder God, in his wisdom had sent his Son to reveal himself to mankind.

A distorted voice suddenly broke the silent spell cast by the statue. Luke snatched his walkie-talkie from his belt and spoke into it. "Yes." The answer came back in Chinese, no doubt from one of his security guards.

After listening a moment, he clicked off and turned to me. "Josh, someone is at the gate asking to see you. A young man on a motorcycle. Are you expecting anyone?'

My brow puckered. "No. Can't think of anyone."

"He seems very agitated. The guard tried to send him away, but he insisted on seeing you."

Outside the gate, I found Padri Fazal's son Caleb pacing back and forth. As soon as he saw me, he rushed over. "*Salaam,* Mr. Radley. Please can you help? My father is missing."

"Missing? How long?"

"Since this morning. Early."

"Do you know here he went?"

"With man in big car. I was at work. My wife tell me that a man in big car came to ask *abba ji* about *injil*—the gospel. *Abba ji* talk to man, then get in car and go off with him."

"Did he tell Rahima—*apki bivi*—where he was going?"

"He had her fetch a New Testament to give the man. Told her he be back before lunch."

"Did she see the man?"

"No. Windows of car..." He seemed at a loss for the right word.

"Tinted?"

"Yes, tinted."

I patted Caleb on the shoulder. "I'm sure he's okay. Probably he was so excited to tell the man about Jesus that he forgot the time."

Caleb shook his head. "Not forget. Very thoughtful. He would have called my wife. Please, *bhai ji*, can you help us look? Use your Land Rover?"

"Have you tried calling some of his fellow pastors, or church members? Maybe he went to see someone else."

"He not go without motorcycle. But we call everyone. No one see him."

I scuffed the sand with my shoe. "What kind of a car did he go away in?"

Caleb scrunched up his eyes. "Wife say big; green or blue." He threw up his hands. "Wife not know cars."

"Okay, I'll get my Land Rover and follow you back to your house."

CHAPTER THIRTY-THREE
Infidel

Streamers of saffron and salmon had begun to tint the clouds building on the western horizon as I followed Caleb on his dad's motorcycle. I felt sure there would be a perfectly natural explanation for Padri Fazal's absence, but I could hardly refuse his son's request for help in finding him.

I'd declined Luke's offer of one of his Chinese guards to ride along and assured Stephanie that I'd be back by nine o'clock. With limited daylight left, we'd need to hurry.

A cluster of Padri Fazal's neighbours—mostly Christian, but a few Muslim—were gathered in front of his courtyard when we drove up. Several asked if there was any news.

Caleb shook his head, wheeled the motorcycle inside, and then joined me in the Land Rover.

"Caleb, could his phone battery be down?"

"No, Sahib. I just charged it yesterday. I'm careful to keep it charged... he always forgets."

"Can you think of any place where your dad might go and forget the time?"

He stared out the window for a minute or so. "Sometimes he goes to Dhera Sufi, Sahib. The Marwaris there often keep him a long time explaining the Bible."

"Is that on the way?"

"Yes, just outside Nowshera."

"Okay, we'll stop there first. Anywhere else?"

Caleb frowned as he stroked his moustache. "Teashops. He often takes Muslim friends into teashops."

"Good... keep thinking."

At Dhera Sufi Sahib, we skirted the elaborate shrine and parked near the entrance to a cluster of Marwari huts surrounded by a thorn brush fence. The Muslim shrine had been built on the site of a much earlier Hindu shrine, hence the proximity of the Hindu Marwaris who, I'd heard, venerated this Muslim mystic as though he was one of their own Hindu *pirs*.

Caleb announced our presence, although that seemed hardly necessary since a group of barefoot children had immediately appeared. A turbaned old man leaning on a cane hobbled up to us.

After the usual welcome ritual, Caleb showed him his father's picture and asked if he'd seen Padri Fazal. A smile creased the lined face of the old patriarch and he launched into a lengthy monologue. I couldn't understand more than a few words, but I did gather that he thought highly of the Padri.

As we drove away, Caleb laughed. "Elder want us take tea. Hard to stop him. Haven't seen *abba* for weeks. Say, 'He come back soon. Answer more questions.'"

While there was still light, we drove up and down the streets in the more affluent sections of Nowshera, hoping to spot a parked car that might indicate a home where Padri Fazal was visiting. It was a bit of a lost cause, since most houses had high walls and gates to protect their vehicles from thieves. But we needed to try.

272 • CAPTIVES OF MINARA

When that search proved fruitless, we started canvassing the *chai* shops. Five or six of the main shops recognized Fazal, but none had seen him recently. The officer in charge of the downtown police substation also responded in the negative.

By this time, it was dark. I parked in the roundabout near the station and passed my cell phone to Caleb. "Why don't you check with your wife? Maybe he's back home by now."

After a brief conversation with his wife, he handed back the phone. "No news. Mr. Radley, I very worried."

The vain words of assurance given at times of crisis—promises of health, safety, long life, and success—had always annoyed me, so I was slow to reassure Caleb. Instead, I asked, "Can you think of anywhere else we can inquire?"

He ran his hand through his hair. "Villages... often visited villages... but on motorcycle... and he tell us. We called fellow pastors. Nothing." He shook his head. "No, Sahib."

We were interrupted by a rap on the window of the Land Rover. I turned to see the boss of the coolies—the big man who called himself the Chairman—standing there grinning. "You need coolie, Sahib? Remember me. I watch car good, no?"

The Chairman had reason to remember me after the hefty *baksheesh* I'd given him when we'd seen Janice off on the train. I reached over to take the photo from Caleb. "No need of a coolie, but have you seen this man today?"

He took the photo I offered and screwed up his eyes as he studied it. Suddenly, his eyes opened wide. "Good man. Padri Sahib. Laugh much... but I no see today."

He pointed to the cluster of coolies gathered at the entrance to the station. "I show them?"

I nodded. We watched, hoping for something positive as he passed the photo from man to man. A few minutes later, he came back, returned the picture, and shook his head. "No one see him today. Next time you need coolie, you use me."

With that, he waved and headed back toward his compatriots. We sat there a few more minutes trying to think of other places to search. Nothing. So we headed back toward Caleb's village.

Silence reigned on the drive back, except for the occasional blast of a horn. Twice I almost collided with bullock carts creaking down the middle of the narrow roadway without any lights. One turban-clad farmer perched on the tongue of his cart to balance his huge load waved his goad at me when I careened past on the shoulder blowing my horn angrily.

On the outskirts of Caleb's village, we could see a pair of red lights flashing off and on and the headlights from two police jeeps illuminating a cluster of men.

"Caleb, why would the police be over there?"

"Not know, Sahib... village rubbish pile."

"I'll take you home, then I'll find out."

"I go with you."

"Okay."

I parked beside the police jeeps on the edge of the village refuse pile. The group, made up of six police officers and a few villagers, stood looking down at something.

Caleb went over to one of the men and whispered, "Sardar Sahib, *kya hai?*"

Sardar jerked around and moved to block his view. He replied in Punjabi. "Caleb, something terrible has happened. A great evil... your *abba*. You go home. We'll care for him."

Caleb pushed him roughly aside, stared at what they had hidden from his view, and shrieked, *"Abba!"*

The body of Caleb's father lay sprawled in the refuse. A series of livid bruises and cuts disfiguring his father's face. One eye was shut. The other stared up at the sky. Dried blood darkened his grey hair. The red gash encircling his throat indicated that his throat had been cut. Blood spattered his white shirt. A word was written in blood across his chest—*kafir*—infidel.

The circle of men drew back as Caleb flung himself onto his father's body. He screamed again and again, "No... no... *abba*... no." His cries became great gulps of distress as he cradled his father's head in his arms.

I knelt beside him, took out my kerchief, and spread it beneath Padri Fazal's head—in an attempt to shield it from the filth littering the ground. The stench made my eyes water and my nose quiver. I looked around. Rotting fruit and vegetables, maggot-ridden meat scraps, plastic bags, pieces of rusted tin, broken bricks, and not ten feet away from where I knelt lay the rotting carcass of a dog covered with flies. The ultimate indignity—to be dumped beside the most ceremonially unclean of animals. The malevolence indicated by the malicious way Fazal's body had been thrown on the garbage heap made me shudder.

Near one of Fazal's outstretched arms lay a pile of charred paper which was immediately identifiable. Not only had his assailants murdered him, but they'd burnt his copy of the New Testament. An attempt to divert attention away from the real motive? I glanced around the circle. The police stood back from the group of villagers in a cluster by themselves. A couple of them were smoking while the rest of them whispered among themselves. Several tried to hide smirks behind the hands they used to cover their noses.

Caleb gently laid his father's head on the kerchief and stood up. He looked around the circle slowly, face screwed into a mask of anguish. "*Kyun*—why? What has he ever done to hurt anyone?"

Heads shook. "*Kuch bhi nahi, bhai Caleb*—nothing, brother Caleb."

An aged *maulvi*, whom I assumed to be the village Muslim priest, stepped forward. He shook his head. "Caleb, your father was a good and godly man. The whole village loved him. Our hearts have been deeply cut by this great evil. No true Muslim could have done this to a man of the book. He will be greatly mourned."

The *maulvi* pointed toward the burnt pages of the New Testament. "This is a desecration—burning the *Injil.*"

If only that kind of respect could have been shown between Muslims and Christians throughout the country—indeed, throughout the world. Sadly, it was rare.

The *maulvi* went over to the officer in charge and shook his finger in his face. "I will hold you personally responsible to find the murderers of this righteous man."

The officer threw down his cigarette and frowned. "Righteous? Looks like a *kafir* to me... discarded on a garbage dump. Quite appropriate."

He fixed the *maulvi* with a stare, then turned to his men and began to give orders. One fetched a camera and began to take pictures. Another brought a plastic bag to collect the charred remains of the New Testament. Taking out a notebook, the officer began to question the growing crowd of villagers.

I fetched a blanket from the Land Rover and threw it over the body. A few minutes later, one of village Christians appeared with a string bed. While Caleb stood by, apparently frozen in grief, four villagers gently lifted Padri Fazal's body onto the *charpai*. At a nod from the officer, they hefted the *charpai* and set off for Caleb's compound. Caleb trailed behind, his head hanging down onto his chest. A silent file of villagers trailed behind.

I returned to the Land Rover, but instead of following the mourners, I sat there fighting emotions. I thought of Padri Fazal's kindness to me as a boy, the sonorous cadences of his preaching voice, his tireless visits to scattered Christians on his bicycle, his advocacy for those unjustly chewed up by the corrupt bureaucracy, his organizational skills... A great wave of grief washed over me. To be murdered and then dumped like a dead dog on the village rubbish heap. Tears began to course down my face.

I brushed away the tears with a swipe of my hand and ground my teeth as a sudden tsunami of fury overwhelmed me. *Someone thinks they can get away with murder, and kidnapping, and slavery, just because their victims are powerless. Well, they won't get away with it! They can't.*

I snatched up my cell phone and called Luke. Without explaining, I asked him to get Stephanie. When Stephanie came on the line, I told her as briefly and starkly as I could what had happened.

"I can't believe it," Stephanie said. "Padri Fazal struck me as such a godly man."

"The local Muslim priest said the same thing, but the police just smirked as if they got some pleasure out of seeing him dumped on a rubbish pile. They called him an infidel."

"That's horrible."

I smacked the dashboard. "I warned the Superintendent of Police that something like this might happen. I'm going in right now to confront him—the dirty rat."

"No, Josh! Don't. Come back."

"I'll be there shortly."

"Josh, please. It's too dangerous."

I flicked the phone off, started the Land Rover, and drove over to Padri Fazal's, where I jumped out and threaded my way through the crowd that had begun to gather. The news had galvanized all the village's Christians. In the center of the courtyard, Padri Fazal had been laid out on a *charpai* under an embroidered sheet. Off to one side, a group of women gathered around Caleb's wife Rahima and tried to comfort her and her two children. On the other side of the Padri's body, Caleb sat on a *charpai* with his head in his hands. Neighbours had already begun to bring in more beds to seat mourners.

I expressed sorrow again to Caleb, offered him any help I could give, then quickly took my leave.

CHAPTER THIRTY-FOUR
Arrest

I left Padri Fazal's and raced toward Nowshera, blowing my horn at any driver who got in my way. The fleeting thought that I might be out of control only goaded me to drive more recklessly.

It was all too much. Jan, my blonde-haired, blue-eyed sweetheart—and now, the uncle who had taught me cricket. Yes, he had been as surely an uncle as any flesh and blood relative.

I screeched to a stop in front of the SP's office, slammed the car door, and ran up the steps. I'd given no thought to whether the SP might be in or have gone home by now. I'd not even attempted to cool my anger. It burned white-hot.

Before I could reach the veranda, a stentorian voice stopped me. "Mr. Radley. What are you doing here?"

278 • Captives of Minara

I jerked my head in the direction of the voice. The Superintendent of Police stood off to one side of the veranda talking to several of his officers.

"Reporting an outrage, that's what."

"You're always reporting some outrage or other." The police officers around him snickered. "What is it this time?"

I spit out the words. "A vicious murder. The murder of a kind and gentle man."

The SP tapped his pant leg with his swagger stick. "Who?"

I put my hands on my hips and glared at him. "Padri Fazal Masih... his throat cut."

"Oh, him." The SP turned away. "We know about him... good riddance, I say."

Murmurs of affirmation issued from his officers. "Troublemaker... *Kafir*. He got what he asked for."

My mouth fell open as I pointed my finger at the SP and stuttered, "I warned you. You took no action. You could have stopped it."

He slashed my extended finger with his swagger stick. "You warned me! Who do you think you are to tell me what to do? I am the authority in this district."

"Ow!" I massaged my injured finger with my left hand. "I'll report you to Islamabad. I'll—

"Shut your mouth. I've had enough from you." He turned to one of his officers. "Arrest this man for obstruction of justice and..." He fingered his moustache and frowned. "And trespassing."

Two policemen grabbed me by the arms and marched me into the station. Inside, they led me to a cell, but the SP stopped them. "No, not here. Take him to that holding cell in Tibi. And Sardar, you follow in his jeep. Abandon the jeep in the canal on the way. In Tibi, leave two *sipahis* to stand guard."

●●◆●●

I looked around the cell. A single barred and shuttered window let in a few rays of light, but not enough to dispel the gloom. Brick walls. Packed dirt floor. Heavy steel door. No light fixtures, no table, no chair, no latrine—nothing but the sagging string bed and dirty mattress on which I'd been thrown—and a stained coverlet. Cobwebs hung in festoons from the rafters.

My nostrils quivered at the overpowering odour of human waste. My eyes followed my nose to a corner of the room that must have been used as a latrine once.

My head throbbed both from frustration at being stupid enough to confront the SP and from the blow one of his officers had delivered to the back of my head.

Tibi? Where was I? They'd handcuffed me and thrown me into the back of a jeep. When I'd tried to sit up to see where we were going, one of the policemen had smacked me on the head with his nightstick and covered me with a blanket. They'd taken my watch, so I had no idea of how long the trip took beyond the general impression that it was longer than half an hour but under an hour. My impression could have been exaggerated by shock and the roughness of the ride. Nor did I have any clue of the direction the jeep had taken from Nowshera.

Stupid. Stupid. Stupid. How could you be so dumb to let your rage overwhelm your common sense? I guess the temper you thought was under control still simmers below the surface. The SP warned you not to stick your nose in his business.

How can you help Janice now? No one knows where you are. Stephanie will be frantic. And Nadia can't help her, nor can Colonel Nasri.

You've really blown it this time.

With a rusty screech, the bolt on the door was thrown back and the door swung open. A policeman stood to one side glaring at me over the barrel of an ancient looking Enfield rifle.

Should I jump him?

Just when I was giving thought to luring him inside, his compatriot appeared with a *ghurdha*—a terracotta water pot—which he plopped on the floor by the door. As he turned to go, he flung down a tin cup which rolled across the dirty floor. In a moment, the door was closed and the bolt shot home.

At least I'd have water. I picked up the cup, wiped it with my shirt tail, dipped it in the *ghurdha*, and walked over to the window where I held the cup to a tiny shaft of light. It looked fairly clean, although it smelled slightly, or was that the overpowering odour that pervaded the room? By this time, I was thirsty enough that I didn't care.

After quenching my thirst, I wet my kerchief and wrapped it around my head in an attempt to lessen the throbbing pain.

I tried the bars on the window. Set in concrete. No hope there. I peaked out through the tiny crack between the shutters, but it was so narrow that I couldn't see anything but a bit of dusty roadway and what looked like a mango tree.

I turned away from the window and wandered around the room, looking for some weak spot. The room was almost a perfect cube, about ten feet square with the ceiling at least ten feet above the floor. The walls appeared to be very solid, constructed of two layers of brick. The ceiling was made of tiles laid on steel rafters. The dirt floor might have provided a route of escape if I could dig a hole under the wall, but that would mean digging it deep enough to get under the footings, and all I had to dig with was the tin cup. How would I hide any hole I made? Even if I could disguise the hole, it would take days—maybe weeks—to dig a tunnel. Did I have days? Did Jan?

Hopeless. I collapsed on the *charpai* and tried to still the pounding of my head and the panic that seized my chest in waves. I pulled the soiled coverlet up to my neck and willed myself to relax. I stared up at the ceiling and began to count the tiles. In the corner, I spotted a *chipkilli*. At least I wasn't alone.

Alone? Wasn't God here with me? Of course, he had been in the SP's office, too. After all, he was everywhere. Then why had he let this happen? Okay, I guess I'd been pretty lackadaisical about my faith, even after he'd rescued me from terrorists the year before. Was that it? Did I find praying convenient when I was in a jam—like now? I was beginning to sound like a whining kid who only came running to his parents when a bully threatened to beat him up.

Of course, Stephanie was different—genuine. She'd be worried... praying... and God would be hearing. But would he answer? Why should he?

Maybe my stubborn determination to keep my log retreat on Rice Lake had plunged us into this mess. I could have taken the job Stephanie's father offered, even if it had put an end to my freelance writing dream. Then Janice would be safe. Had the thought of writing a series of articles that would propel me into the international spotlight blinded me to everything else? Blast! How could I begin to understand the machinations of my own heart?

Had those terrible dreams, the premonitions of danger, been God's voice? Warning me?

I moistened the kerchief from the cup of water I'd brought over to the *charpai* and retied it around my head.

Lord, I hadn't wanted to come back. Really, I hadn't.

I must have drifted off, because the next thing I remembered was waking to darkness and the sound of rustling. Rats? A snake?

I sat up. From outside, I heard someone cough, then spit. Through the chink between the lintel and the door, I could make out a faint glow that faded and brightened. The guard must have started a fire. I shivered, pulled the coverlet around me, and tried to see into the dark corners. Near the door, I could make out some scattered fragments of brick. I retrieved a dozen or so to throw at whatever was making the rustling sound.

I slept little during the rest of the night, unable to shake off the thought of a cobra seeking the warmth of my body by climbing the legs of the *charpai*. Warmth, hah! When I wasn't sleeping, I shivered and whenever I heard a rustle I threw a fragment of brick in the direction of the sound. That failed to discourage whatever it was for more than a few minutes.

Finally the weak light of early morning began to creep through the crack in the shutter. By that time, I was beginning to itch all over. At first, I had thought it a natural reaction to my situation, but when I rolled up my pant leg I discovered a bunch of red welts. Bedbugs.

I took out my comb and ran it desperately through my hair, examining it at every stroke. I squashed every dark speck. Whether animate or inanimate—I could hardly tell. Then I took off my shirt and examined every inch. My eyes began to spy movement everywhere. In spite of the cold, I stripped off my clothes and examined every part of my body that I could see.

I wasn't sure if my actions made any difference. At least it gave me something to do besides sink into melancholy or yield to scratching the bites until they became infected. I even knelt down on the floor and began to examine the bed.

The hours dragged by as a new agony began to overshadow the fiery itch. Hunger. I hadn't eaten anything since the morning of the previous day. I began to pace up and down, back and forth.

Around mid-morning, I heard the screech of the bolt being thrown back. My two guards stood in the doorway, one pointing the rifle and the other bearing a tin bowl, which he set down on the floor. He plopped two *chapatis* on top of the bowl, leered at me, and turned away.

At the sight of food, my stomach gave a lurch and I began to salivate. The *chapatis* were dry and scorched on one side while the bowl held a watery lentil curry. Who was I to be picky? I broke off a fragment of *chapati,* dipped it in the bowl, and stuffed it in my mouth. Immediately, my tongue caught fire and my mouth began to burn. I gingerly put down the bowl and ran to the water pot. A whole cupful of water did little to soothe the sensation of having swallowed live coals. I gagged and spit.

Great gusts of ribald laughter came from just outside the door. Taunts of *"Kao, ji, kao. Bahut muzedar"* were followed by more snorts of glee.

In response, I called them a couple of piglets, *sewer ke bacce*. I was losing my grip on civility.

Something hard hit the door. *"Khabardar."*

I took a cup of water back to my bed and stood looking down at the fiery curry and dry *chapatis*. They'd skimped on lentils and doubled the chillies—but it was food. The ache in my stomach intensified as the burning sensation in my mouth began to ease. I had to eat to keep up my strength, so I willed myself to ignore the fiery taste. Didn't they hold contests in Louisiana—or was it Mexico?—to see who could eat the hottest chilli peppers? Didn't the farmers of Pakistan and India routinely eat flaming hot curries?

I took a deep breath, broke off small fragments of *chapati*, and tried to scoop up the lentils while draining off the red sauce that floated near the top of the bowl. Little by little, with much gagging and many cups of water, I consumed the *chapatis* and most of the curry.

The day dragged on. I tried to avoid thinking any more about my stupidity or the anguish Jan must be experiencing. Instead I counted the number of steel rafters in the roof, the number of tiles, the number of courses of brick in the wall, the number of cobwebs in the room... anything to pass the time and keep me from scratching my bites. I reviewed a list of my favourite authors. I recited the Twenty-Third Psalm and the Lord's Prayer. I prayed for Jan and for rescue. I listed the books of the Bible and endeavoured to remember the characters and themes of each. I watched my *chipkilli* and gave him a name, Alexander. The thought of Alexander the Great set me searching my memory for dates of history.

The day passed without any further contact from my guards, beyond their appearance to refill the water pot and retrieve the tin bowl. I could occasionally hear snatches of conversation or hoots of laughter. Near evening, the smell of frying meat wafted through the chinks in door and window.

I was sitting on my bed and imagining an evening meal of gently spiced lamb curry when I suddenly realized what they were about. Part of their torture. I jumped up and began to pace the room.

The night went by in fits of exhausted sleep and starts of waking agony. Fears gripped me. No matter how tightly I curled up under the filthy coverlet, I couldn't get warm. The bedbug bites itched mercilessly. My stomach felt, by turns, empty and queasy. By first light, my head felt warm and my eyes swam with pain.

Sometime in the morning, I succumbed to despair. This was it. The end. No one would find me. I'd die in this stinking hole from typhoid or dysentery. Stephanie would be widowed. Janice would be sold as a white slave to a brothel in Lebanon.

Mid-morning, my guards brought my daily meal. I stared at them through bloodshot eyes, wanting to fix their images in my mind. The one with the rifle had a luxuriant black moustache and a face cratered by smallpox scars. The other had a head that seemed too small for his pudgy body, as if he'd been given the wrong head at birth. He perpetually cocked his head to one side as if listening for something. His eyes flashed with laughter and his mouth seemed set in a perpetual grin. His wasn't the humour of a Santa Claus. I could imagine him pulling the wings off dragonflies as a child.

After they left, I approached the tin bowl and dry *chapatis* with trepidation. I dipped a fragment of bread into the lentil curry and gingerly touched it with my tongue. No tingle at all. I broke off a bigger piece and scooped some of the lentils into my mouth. Strange—tasteless—as if they'd cooked the lentils without salt or onions or spices of any kind.

Suddenly, something hit the door with a resounding smack, followed by gales of laughter. "*Khao, ji, kao. Mazedar, hai nah?*"

So that was their game. Confuse me first with curry so hot it would set my mouth on fire, then give me utterly tasteless gruel. They were toying with me. No matter, it was food. I finished off every morsel.

By mid-afternoon, paroxysms of pain seized my stomach. I retched until nothing remained of my meal. Even so, I could barely stop the dry heaves that racked my body. Bile burned my throat. I stumbled over to the water pot, rinsed my mouth out with water, and returned to the *charpai* where I collapsed. I huddled beneath the coverlet, curled up in a ball to get warm, but I couldn't stop shaking with fever. Soon, perspiration drenched my clothing and the bed on which I lay.

Typhoid? Cholera? Dysentery? How long could I last without medical attention?

Hours of misery crept by, then darkness fell. I lapsed into a stupor as I lay in my own filth, unable to leave the *charpai*. Light filtered into the cell. I dimly remembered my jailers bringing my daily meal, laughing at my condition, and leaving, slamming the door shut behind them.

CHAPTER THIRTY-FIVE
Nowshera Hospital

I blinked and shook my head. Clean sheets. Blanket. Ah, warmth. Pastel green walls. I stared down at my arm and pondered the IV tube fastened with tape. Where was I? I frowned as I tried to remember.

Car door slamming. Shouts. Then the steel door of my cell had flown open and I'd been carried to a jeep. Then... nothing.

"You're awake. How are you feeling, Mr. Joshua?"

I turned toward the voice. A young man in a light green *shalwar-qamiz* stood there, holding a clipboard and smiling at me. "Where am I? Who are you? How did I get here?"

"Ah, many questions. Very good. You are in Nowshera Memorial Hospital. I am Anwar Masih, one of your nurses."

"But how...?"

"Your friend in the army bring you. Very sick."

I struggled to sit up, then collapsed back on the pillow. "My friend in the army?"

He laid his hand on my arm. "Please, Mr. Joshua, rest. You've been very sick. Your friend Major Nadia Khan brought you in."

I screwed up my face in puzzlement. "Major Nadia Khan... is she here?"

"She was here. She and your wife left to get some breakfast. Back soon."

I grabbed the side of the bed, sat up, and made to swing my feet over the side. "Police?"

Anwar Masih frowned as he gently pushed me back down. "Mr. Joshua, pleased to lie back. Relax. No police. This is a private room. You have a military guard outside your door."

He went over to the door, opened it, and beckoned. An army MP in full uniform cradling an Uzi appeared. He nodded in my direction and smiled.

I relaxed into the pillow. By Anwar's last name, Masih, I could tell he was from a Christian background. I lay there trying to stem the flood of fears that lapped at the fringe of my consciousness. How had Nadia found me? Would the police be searching for me?

Perhaps the very fact that Nadia had chosen a Christian nurse to attend me demonstrated that she understood that I'd feel insecure. Or it could have been a coincidence. Christian nurses, mostly women, were much higher represented in the profession than their Muslim compatriots. Few Muslim families allowed their women in a profession that many considered either unclean or too likely to expose them to naked men.

Anwar offered me a thermometer, which I stuck under my tongue. How long had I been here? I pointed to his watch and raised my eyebrows in a question.

He held it out for me to see. "Nine-thirty."

I indicated by signs that I wanted to know when I'd been brought in.

He frowned, then smiled. "The day before yesterday. After-noon. About four."

He retrieved the thermometer. "Ah, very good. Fever almost gone." He made a notation on the clipboard, filled a glass from the jug of water on the bedside table, and held it out to me. "Drink much water."

He turned to go. "I return soon."

"Before you go, tell me what day it is."

"Why, Sahib, it is Saturday."

I took a long sip of water. Saturday! Was it Tuesday when I'd been arrested? Five days ago? Couldn't be. I must be missing a day. And Jan... almost a week since she'd been kidnapped. I had to get out of here. I groaned and tried to sit up, but beads of perspi-ration broke out on my brow and my stomach felt queasy. I fell back on the pillow.

I must have fallen back asleep because the next thing I re-membered was someone holding my hand. I blinked and tried to focus. "Steph, is that you?"

"Josh, sweetheart." Stephanie kissed me gently.

I let out a long sigh. "Got any more of those?"

She kissed the tip of my nose, my eyes, my cheeks, my lips. "Honey, I thought I'd lost you." She sat down on the side of the bed and began massaging my hand as if she was afraid to let it go. "You came in with a high fever and were terribly dehydrated. You were delirious most of yesterday."

The door opened and Nadia came in dressed in her army fa-tigues. "Our patient is awake, is he?" She pulled up a chair and sat down on the side opposite Stephanie. "You gave us quite a scare."

"But how? What?"

"I rushed back to Nowshera the minute Steph called me to say you were missing. I'd been planning to come back anyway, as soon as I could countermand orders. It seems Chaudri Gujar Mo-hammed has powerful friends in Islamabad. Fortunately, mine are more powerful—at least for now."

Steph helped me sit up. "Nadia arrived back Thursday morning."

Nadia ran her fingers through her inky black hair. "I immediately went to the SP's office. He pretended to know nothing about your disappearance, but one of his officers came to my billet later. Told me what had happened and where you were being kept."

I frowned. "Why would one of the SP's officers do that?"

Nadia smiled. "He's one of ours. A plant. That's all you need to know. As soon as I found out where you were, I arranged for a squad of soldiers to liberate you... and here you are."

Stephanie held a straw to my lips. "You've got to keep drinking water."

"My guards?"

"Don't worry, they can't tell the SP. They're locked up in the base stockade, held incommunicado. Besides, our men treated them a bit rough. Scared 'em." Nadia wrinkled her nose. "That cell was a pigsty. I can't believe how they treated you. You were in terrible shape, dehydrated, delirious, with a raging fever. We rushed you to the hospital, had one of the military doctors treat you, and put a guard on your door."

Stephanie wiped my forehead with a moist cloth. "They hooked you up to IVs and pumped you full of medicine. You're a hundred percent better... well, almost."

I turned toward Nadia. "So now you can arrest the SP, find Jan?"

Nadia looked away. "Not quite. Unfortunately, Chaudri Gujar and his cronies, including the SP, have this area under their thumb. The army can't interfere in civilian affairs unless they are asked to during an emergency. Especially right now, with so much resentment of martial law in the country."

I pushed away the straw Stephanie offered. "But..."

"Don't worry," Nadia said. "We're making progress. Let me bring you up to speed. Under the army's national security mandate, we've raided three of the smuggler's locations and released hundreds; men, women, and children. What a nauseating business. Most of those we freed were from poor families. Some had been forcefully enslaved to clear family debts. The men would be sold to brick kilns, factories, or farmers. Many of the women and children were destined to become domestic servants or sex slaves."

Nadia massaged her forehead. "We even found twenty-three young boys from two Christian villages. They'd been abducted to service the huge demand for homosexual sex slaves. I can hardly bear to think about it without my stomach churning.

"It looks like this is a full-service gang trading in arms, drugs, and slaves—anything that will turn a profit. And we're talking about multiplied millions of dollars.

"Fortunately, we're slowly strangling the gang's ability to move their illicit cargo. Yesterday, we intercepted a truck smuggling drugs from Afghanistan to Chaudri for transhipment somewhere."

"So you can arrest Chaudri then?" I asked.

Nadia grimaced. "He seems to have disappeared... but don't worry, we'll nab him. There is a nationwide warrant out for his arrest. As we get a clearer and clearer picture of his organization, we're tightening the noose. One of these days, he'll step right into it."

"Yeah, and he'll buy his way out." I turned away from Nadia and looked into Stephanie's eyes. "Jan? Any clue about her whereabouts?" My voice caught. "Or is the trail getting cold?"

Stephanie avoided my eyes and looked across at Nadia, who reached over and touched my hand. "Josh, we'll find Janice. I know we will."

I made to swing my legs over the edge of the bed. "Can't lie here," I mumbled.

"Josh." Stephanie pushed me back onto the pillows. "You must get better first."

Nadia pulled her abbreviated military *dupatta* into place, carefully tucking in any stray locks. "I've got to check out a few things. Josh, when I get back I don't want to find out you've been *zidi*, giving the nurse a hard time. Not taking your medicine, not drinking enough water, not resting. Okay?"

"Yeah, sure," I said. "And... thanks." My voice caught. "I owe you... a lot."

"Keep positive. Colonel Nasri is trying to get reassigned here. We'll find Jan."

After Nadia left, I lay back and tried to think. I'd forgotten something. Something important. But what? Some clue, or...

I turned to Stephanie, only to find her wiping her eyes. "Worried about Jan?" I asked. She nodded. I reached out and gripped her hand. "Stephanie, I love you."

"I love you, too," she whispered.

She pulled the cover over our intertwined hands, hiding them from anyone who might come in. For some time, neither of us said anything.

Finally, Stephanie broke the silence. "I feel certain we'll find Jan."

I sighed. What could I say? Perhaps it was just my personality. I'm more naturally pessimistic than Stephanie, but I couldn't conjure up the feeling that Janice was safe. Fear skated around and round the surface of my mind. Bad things happened to people all the time. Why not us? Look what happened to me.

"I've been praying," she said, "and God has given me this deep assurance that she'll be okay."

I squeezed her hand. "That's great, honey... I've been praying, too."

I quickly changed the subject. "What about Luke? Does he know where I am?"

"No, just that you've been found, are being treated, and kept safe."

Time passed. The nurse came and went a few times to adjust the IV and take my temperature. Late in the morning, the doctor arrived and after checking my vitals gave permission to detach the IV. I began to feel hunger in the pit of my stomach.

"I think I could eat some plain cookies or crackers or something like that."

"That's a good sign," she said. "I'll go get you something from the hospital shop."

She picked up a garment and began to put it on.

"What's that?"

"A *burqua*," she said, as she did up the buttons down the front. "The police are looking for you. Nadia thought it would be better if I disguised myself. I'm glad she didn't suggest I wear one of those white tents with the grill to see through."

"Police? Maybe you better just stay here."

"No one would dare challenge a *begum sahiba* from a wealthy family."

The *burqua* was made from beige satin with large cloth-covered buttons down the front and a head-covering of the same material that could be adjusted to hide as much of the head and face as the wearer thought modest.

"Wow," I said. "That's quite fashionable."

After she left, I tried to clear my head so I could think. Where could the gang have taken Janice? I reviewed what the girl we'd found in Janice's train compartment had seen: four big SUVs and an expedition jeep used in the hold-up. I'd found an American cigarette butt where the jeep had been parked, the butt from a cigarette like those used by the head security guard at Pattan Minara. I'd also seen tracks leading off the main highway heading east.

East, toward the desert and India... that was it! After abandoning us in the cave-in beneath the tower, Ali had fled east from Pattan Minara. And Raju knew of an ancient fort in the desert, a fort being used by smugglers.

As soon as Stephanie returned, I blurted out, "Raju! Did you tell Nadia about Raju and the old fort?"

Stephanie threw me a box of Peek Freans Nice cookies and began to unbutton her *burqua*. "Raju? Never thought to tell Nadia about him. We were sort of preoccupied with taking care of you."

"I need to call her now," I said.

She draped the *burqua* over a chair and sat down. "You think the old fort is significant?"

I explained my reasoning as I opened the box and took out a cookie.

She retrieved a cell phone from her purse. "Okay, I'll call her." Partway through dialling, she stopped and glanced at the door. "Do you think the police have spies here in the hospital? I didn't like way the shopkeeper looked at me. I disguised my voice, speaking in broken English, but—"

I frowned as I munched. "Possible, but I wouldn't worry about it. The guard looks competent and the nurse is a Christian."

She pushed a lock of hair behind her right ear. "Do the police monitor cell phone traffic?"

"Mmm, I doubt it. The army might."

"I'm getting paranoid." She finished dialling and walked to the far side of the room, away from the windows.

After every few bites, I took a sip of water. I was finishing a second cookie when she shut off the phone and came over to sit by the bed.

"Nadia is willing to give your idea some thought. She said that east, into the Cholistan Desert, is the only direction they haven't searched. She doubts they would have gone where it's so desolate, but she's willing to give it a shot. Later today or tomorrow. Right now, she's with a squad raiding another warehouse. She did sound more hopeful than she's been in days. Evidently, those they've arrested have given them a ton of leads. And the evidence against Chaudri is overwhelming."

"About time."

"Oh, I almost forgot. Chaudri was detained at the Karachi airport just as he was about to board a plane for Dubai."

"I wish I felt better about that. That slimy character can weasel his way out of anything. He'll just wave some rupees around."

The day dragged on. Stephanie had bought a couple of magazines, so we tried to pass the time by catching up on news. By noon, my fever was gone and I felt well enough to eat some scrambled eggs and toast. A couple of times, we joined in praying fervently for Jan's rescue.

Partway through the afternoon, we heard a commotion in the hallway. I immediately recognized the SP's loud voice demanding in Urdu to see the patient. I signalled to Stephanie to put on her *burqua*. I slipped out of bed and stumbled into the bathroom where I shut the door, climbed into the shower stall, and pulled the curtain closed behind me.

CHAPTER THIRTY-SIX
Desert Search

I pressed against the wall of the shower stall and tried to still my thumping heart. The sounds of a loud argument came to me from the hospital corridor. Finally, the voices stilled and I heard the clump of retreating boots. Then silence.

After a few moments, the bathroom door opened. "You can come out now, Josh," Stephanie said. "The SP has gone."

When I came out of the bathroom, I found Nadia standing by the foot of the bed, frowning. She had dark circles under her eyes. "That was close," she said. "He's no dummy. He'll probably bribe a nurse to get information about who is in this room."

"But you have proof of his abuse of power," I blurted. "You saw what he did to me. Why can't he be suspended, arrested... something?"

Nadia pushed her *dupatta* back until it rested on her shoulders. "It's not that easy. Things in Pakistan are in a state of flux, almost chaos. The civilian government views the army as the bad guys while the police are on the side of law and order."

"Hah," Stephanie snorted. "That's a joke."

Nadia began to pace back and forth. "To be honest, the army hasn't been lily-white either. And I'm not sure whom I can trust in the ISI, my own department. The more smugglers we arrest, the more evidence we get implicating corrupt officials, including dishonest army officers. It's like cutting into a block of Swiss cheese and finding it full of holes. I guess I shouldn't be surprised. It's one of the reasons I left the country."

"Is it really that bad?" I rubbed my stubbly jaw. "I'm not feeling very safe here."

Nadia stopped pacing and came to stand by the side of my bed. "Don't get me wrong. The majority of men in the army are honest and patriotic to a fault."

"Men like Colonel Nasri?" Stephanie asked.

"Exactly. He knows who can be trusted and who is on the take. I'm hoping he'll get transferred back here by tomorrow. Meanwhile, we've got to keep you safe."

For a few minutes, Nadia did nothing but continue her pacing. Suddenly, she stopped, took out her cell phone, dialled a number, and gave some murmured instructions. Then she turned to me. "The nurse tells me your temperature is down, you're off IV, and starting to eat again. So I've called for a couple of MPs to transport you in the base ambulance to the army barracks. Okay?"

It was certainly okay by me.

As soon as the spit-and-polish guards saluted us at the entrance to the cantonment, I felt the knot in my stomach begin to loosen.

Other government departments might have shown the marks of neglect due to perpetual shortage of funds or prevalence of fraud, but not the armed forces. Since independence, the military had remained Pakistan's single stable institution.

Whether in Pakistan or India, army cantonments, such as the one in Nowshera, stood out as islands of discipline and order in the midst of a society that often seemed chaotic. We drove along roadways marked by whitewashed stones past a neat parade ground before turning into a residential area containing a cluster of neat officers' bungalows with well-kept gardens.

Nadia dropped us off at the base guesthouse and told us she'd be back shortly. We'd scarcely seated ourselves on one of the leather sofas in the living room before an orderly brought us tea in a bone china tea service.

"Do you feel like tea?" Stephanie asked.

"Actually, I do, though I'm not up to coffee yet."

Fifteen minutes or so later, Nadia rejoined us, loosened her *dupatta*, and collapsed into an armchair.

Stephanie passed her a cup of tea. "Here. You look beat. Have you slept in the last day or two?"

"Thanks." Nadia dumped two spoonfuls of sugar in her tea and stirred it methodically. "Sleep? Not much. But give me forty winks and a good strong cup of tea and I'll be good as new."

"I hate to bother you," I said, "but have you thought any more about checking out that desert fort?"

Nadia raised her eyebrows. "Actually, that's what I was doing. Finalizing arrangements for a squad to reconnoitre the area. It's leaving at 16:30 hours."

I looked at my watch. "Four-thirty? Less than an hour away?"

"Right."

"Great. Let me get a bit of a nap and I'll be ready to go."

Nadia snorted. "You? You're staying here where you'll be safe."

I ignored her protest. "Do you know where the fort is?"

"We can find it. The army has ordnance maps of the whole border area."

"But aren't there a string of old forts? How do you know which one without Raju to guide you?

Nadia stood up. "Raju? But he's disappeared. Look, this is an army operation. This is what we do. We'll check them out until we find the right one. No way are you going."

I stood up to face her. "Nadia, please. Raju trusts me. He promised he'd appear when we need him."

Nadia looked over my shoulders at Stephanie. "Can you talk some sense into him? He's just been deathly ill."

"You've seen how stubborn he is, and... Janice is our daughter. I don't think anything I say will change his mind."

Nadia threw up her hands. "I don't want either of you to get hurt. This could be dangerous."

Stephanie traced the gold rim of her teacup with her finger. "Been a lot of that lately. Don't think we can escape it. Janice can't... Besides, Josh is much better and I'll go with him."

"What!" Nadia paced back and forth, frowning and muttering under her breath. Finally, she came to stop in front of us with her hands on her hips. "You two are a pair. I guess I should have expected something like this." Her mouth softened. "If I had a daughter who had been kidnapped, I'd do the same—but at least I have the training. If you're coming, you stay in the background and follow orders. Agreed?"

We both nodded.

She pointed toward the first door along the hallway. "Use that room to get some rest. But be ready at 16:30 sharp."

She disappeared down the hall to another room and closed the door.

We left Nowshera with a squad of sixteen rangers commanded by Corporal Ijaz, the officer Nadia had sent to guard us in our canal bungalow. Seeing Corporal Ijaz in this setting, obviously highly trained in counterterrorism, did much to ease our anxiety.

The convoy consisted of modified jeeps, Hummer look-alikes. As a major, Nadia outranked Corporal Ijaz, but true to Pakistani custom she deferred to him. And yet the respect all the men accorded her indicated their awareness of her unique position as an influential operative in Pakistan's intelligence community.

Nadia remained an enigma. A highly educated woman from a culture that treated many women as chattel, a major in the Pakistan army, and a practicing psychiatrist seconded from the ISI to the Canadian Security Intelligence Service.

Twenty minutes out of Nowshera, the convoy stopped near the Marwari village I'd visited during my search for Padri Fazal. I walked in alone so as not to alarm the villagers. I asked the grizzled elder who met me to spread the word that I urgently needed Raju Moro's help. Before I could rejoin the convoy, a young Marwari man sped past me on a motorcycle, heading east on the same road we were taking.

Half an hour later, we skirted Pattan Minara and headed into the desert on a bone-jarring, pebbly track. At first, the track wound its way through a landscape of squat rocky ridges, studded with stubby grasses and thorn bushes. Then we pushed on into a desolate expanse of low rippling sand dunes where the trail all but disappeared. Our driver had to engage four-wheel drive and gear down to power through long stretches of clutching, wind-driven sand.

A few miles further on, we entered a surreal region of towering dunes. Partway through this Cholistani sahara, we came upon a village of round mud huts with conical grass roofs perched on the very top of one of the highest sand hills. Children and camels stared down at us as we crawled by in low gear.

As the light faded, we descended into an area of salt flats sparsely covered with squat vegetation. Our speed picked up where the track bore left on the edge of the hard pan. Then, without warning, the convoy lurched to a stop. Nadia got out and joined the officer who stood by the lead jeep staring first left, then right. Stiff and sore, I joined them at the head of the convoy where I saw that the track branched off in three directions, all showing evidence of vehicular traffic. At the very junction stood a post with a bleached board lying at its foot—all lettering long since erased by sand and sun.

Men got out of the convoy to stretch and smoke. Nadia and the corporal consulted a map they spread out on the hood of the lead jeep. Anxious to work out the kinks from the jarring ride, I wandered up the left track, which seemed to show the marks of slightly more traffic.

Suddenly I stopped as a rank odour assailed my nostrils. Camels. I looked around slowly. Ahead of me, in the deep shadow of a *kikur* tree, where they would be hidden from the convoy, stood two camels. Why hadn't I heard the tinkle of camel bells betraying their presence? The camels' obsidian eyes glinted in the dim light. Two turban-clad men sat atop them, immobile. We stared at each other for a moment, then one of the figures flicked the reins on his camel and it moved toward me. I stepped back.

"Mister Joshua Sahib."

As I peered closer, I realized that the turban-clad figure who had addressed me was Raju Moro. I folded my hands and bowed my head toward him in a gesture of greeting. *"Salaam,* Raju Sahib."

A loud click behind me caused me to spin around. Two rangers were loping toward us, their MP5s trained on Raju and his companion. I turned toward the soldiers. *"Roko. Yih dost hain."*

They lowered their weapons and relaxed. Raju flicked the rein leading to the plug inserted in the tender nose of the camel. With a grumbling sound, it knelt and Raju hopped off.

"I'm very glad to see you," I said, "but..."

He smiled. "We've been waiting. I came by better trail, on motorcycle. Borrow camel from relatives in nearby village." He pointed back to his companion. "Munnoo, my brother."

By this time, Nadia and the officer had joined me, so I introduced them. "This is Major Nadia Khan and Corporal Ijaz."

Raju frowned, but returned their *salaams*. The officer pointed to the map he was holding and rather imperiously requested Raju to show him the location of the fort. Raju leaned over the map a few minutes, saying nothing. Then he picked up a stick and began to trace a rough map in the dust of the road, explaining important landmarks along the way.

He looked from the corporal to Nadia and then to me before waving toward his camel. "You will get lost in the darkness. I will show you."

"How far?" Nadia asked.

"An hour. Maybe more."

Our convoy crept along behind the loping camels through a barren landscape magically transformed by the silvery light from thousands of stars. The cloud-enshrouded, inky blackness of the nighttime sky common to more humid climates was foreign to the desert. The starlight turned this land of shifting sand and salt flats into a shadowy canvas of ethereal beauty.

I stared at the panorama out the window of our jeep and breathed David's verse. *The heavens declare the glory of God, the firmament shows his handiwork.* I took a deep breath. *Are you out there, Lord? I know you are. Watch over Janice, I pray.*

Stephanie squeezed my hand as if she knew I was praying.

I must have drifted off, because the next thing I remembered was awakening to silence. I looked through the windscreen at the motionless convoy, engines stilled, lights off. I could dimly make out the two camels and a cluster of men in front of the lead vehicle.

I yawned, gently easing away from Stephanie and slipping outside. The sound of the door closing splintered the silence and echoed off the towering dunes that surrounded us. As I turned to walk toward the group at the head of the convoy, I saw that they were all staring in my direction. Nadia was running toward me with a finger to her mouth, motioning me to silence.

She stopped in front of me and whispered, "Gotta be quiet. The fort is only a mile away and sound carries far in this environment." I lifted my eyebrows in a query, but I kept quiet as she went on. "The corporal has sent a couple of men ahead to reconnoitre. We'll wait until after midnight to take the fort."

I glanced at my wrist, then remembered that the police guards had taken my watch from me.

"Nine-thirty," she said. "Couple of hours to kill. Here, take these and share them with Stephanie." She handed me a couple of energy bars.

The corporal came down the line of vehicles, stopping at each. Like ghosts, soldiers drifted from their jeeps to walk up and down, collapse on the sand, or light up cigarettes. One enterprising soldier started a fire with sticks from a stunted bush. He soon had a billycan of tea boiling away.

By the time I got back to our jeep, Stephanie was awake. I tossed her one of the energy bars and explained what was happening and the need for silence.

She slipped out of the jeep and joined me, rubbing her hands to warm them. "A cup of hot *chai* would go down good right now."

"I'm afraid you're out of luck... unless I can beg some from that soldier." I pointed toward the fire.

Raju and his brother, atop their camels, came toward us along the line of vehicles. Raju stopped beside us and raised his hand in salutation. "*Salaam, Sahib. Memsahib.* May *Baghvan* protect you and lead you to your daughter. We leave now."

We watched them lope away until they disappeared among the shadowed dunes.

At midnight, Corporal Ijaz gave the signal to suit up. The rangers donned their flak jackets and helmets, adjusted their night vision goggles, and clipped on heavy belts weighted down with grenades, extra clips of ammunition, walkie-talkies, and mysterious pieces of equipment I couldn't identify. They tested their walkie-talkies and took up their MP5s, ready to move.

In spite of vigorous protests by Nadia and the corporal that we stay with the vehicles, we both insisted on following the squad at least to a vantage point overlooking the fort.

With a hand signal, we moved out, Stephanie and I in the rear. Two men stayed with the lead jeep, the only one with a heavy machine gun mounted on a roof port.

Beyond the occasional clink of equipment or creak of strained leather, the squad marched in silence.

When the shadowy outline of the fort came into view, Nadia motioned us to a position high on the summit of a towering dune where we could overlook the scene. For the first time since Jan's kidnapping, I felt confident as we lay in the sand and peered down at the crumbling fort below us. This was it. We'd find Janice. Envelop her with our love. Life would be good again. No flea-bitten gang of smugglers could stand against an assault by one of Pakistan's elite counterterrorism units.

In its day, the square fort must have been almost impregnable with its huge semi-circular bastions at each corner and a parapet running around the top of the wall. In size, I'd guess that the fort could have contained two football fields side by side. The massive walls were at least thirty feet high and twelve feet thick. However, all along its walls the fort showed the marks of centuries of neglect. Two piles of rubble were all that remained of the bastions on either side of the gaping entrance. In many places, the brick facing of the walls had eroded, leaving the mud brick core exposed.

Inside the fort, starlight glinted off the chrome of several vehicles parked in a row. To the left of the vehicles loomed some kind of structure built against the wall. No light showed anywhere, except for the occasional glow of a cigarette on the parapet. A sentry?

I smiled grimly as the corporal deployed his men by hand signals into positions ready for an assault. Except for the yawning opening where the gate had once stood, the fort still looked unassailable. So it was in front of this opening that the corporal arranged his assault team. Bloodthirsty as it sounded, I couldn't wait for them to give these fiends a taste of their own medicine. But with only sixteen men, plus Nadia and Corporal Ijaz?

Stephanie and I watched as two groups of four men silently took up positions against the wall on either side of the open gate. Two more men with sniper rifles covered the fort from camouflaged positions high on the dunes, surrounding the fort on three sides. Using night scopes, they would be able to detect any movement. Two other men slipped into position against the back wall, where they could cover any unforeseen retreat.

After strictly warning us to stay where we were, Nadia went to join the corporal in the ruins of a small building a hundred yards from the gate. Suddenly, the crack of a rifle split the silence and the sentry on the top of the parapet collapsed like a sack of flour.

"You are surrounded," shouted the corporal into a bullhorn. "Come out with your hands up. Resistance is futile."

His warning sparked a pandemonium of shouts and curses, followed by a few random shots. Corporal Ijaz repeated his warning as our lead jeep roared into position about fifty yards from the entrance. The roof folded back and a trooper appeared wielding a heavy machine gun.

One or two smugglers began to fire toward the jeep in earnest. The gunner ducked back inside. The corporal had obviously not yet given the order to fire. He'd explained to us earlier that he hoped the surprise nature of the attack would move the smugglers to surrender without a bloodbath. In that way, he could spare the victims within the fort from further trauma.

As the corporal raised his bullhorn for a third time, an engine sprang to life. I sidled along the dune into a position where I could look into the fort through the entrance to see what was happening. A truck roared to a stop broadways across the entrance, sealing off easy access.

Before Ijaz could give his third and final warning, one of his troopers near the gate shouted a warning: "RPG!"

I heard a swoosh, followed by an enormous explosion. The jeep disappeared in a blinding flash of flame and smoke.

CHAPTER THIRTY-SEVEN
Desert Fort

From our vantage point, the sight of the wrecked jeep left me stunned. Shrapnel continued to whine through the air as ammunition inside the wreck exploded.

"Those poor men," Stephanie groaned.

"And the heavy machine gun destroyed."

Suddenly, a flare lit up the sky. We watched as the rangers prepared to assault the truck blocking the entrance. A couple of grenades tossed under the truck set it ablaze. Three or four men immediately stormed the gap left between the front of the truck and the crumbling wall.

The echoes of automatic rifle fire reverberated from the surrounding dunes. The smell of cordite drifted on the breeze. Smoke obscured our view. When it cleared, I saw that two of the rangers were down. Several of their buddies came under intense fire as they dragged them toward safety. When they finally gained the protection of the wall, I could see that one or two of the rescuers staggered from wounds they'd received.

My focus shifted to the parapet around the top of the wall. I saw the snipers down two men racing along the parapet to positions overlooking the entrance. Three more smugglers ran to take their places. Smarter than their dead comrades, these men ducked below the parapet wall and must have crawled toward a position where they could lob grenades down on the rangers clustered near the gate.

I shouted a warning, but my voice was lost as renewed explosions rocked the area around the entrance. The rangers had begun lobbing grenade after grenade through the entrance or over the wall while the snipers kept firing intermittently at the defenders on the wall to keep them pinned down.

Stephanie's fingers dug into my arm. "I hope Janice, if she's here, is safe."

"So much resistance."

Corporal Ijaz sounded a loud whistle and the assault team retreated, carrying their wounded. They regrouped behind the dune where we lay.

We slithered down the slope to join them. The rangers clustered in a group around the corporal. He knelt beside one of their buddies and helped the medic staunch the flow of blood from a head wound. The other two wounded men sat in the sand, pressing bandages to their lacerations. Fortunately, none of the wounds looked life threatening.

Nadia stood off to one side, talking into a satellite phone.

I shook my head. Four dead. Three wounded. One of the four Hummers destroyed. That left nine able-bodied soldiers, plus two officers out of the original squad. But two of the men patrolled the rear of the fort and another two manned the sniper positions. If I included the officers, that left only seven for any kind of assault. Bad odds.

Corporal Ijaz stood up and stared at the ground for a few moments. Then he looked around at his men and began to speak in Urdu. "In due time, we will avenge the deaths of our comrades. Obviously, the intelligence on this operation has been faulty. We face a larger gang than anticipated and they are better armed. But we've been trained for just such a situation. And trained to never give up. We won't.

"This is what we are going to do. Mumtaz, Iqbal, and Sadiq, you three go back and bring the vehicles—double time. As soon as you get back, be sure everyone is resupplied with ammo, including Rahmat and Waheed in their sniper positions.

"Mohammed and Anwar, you spread motion sensors around the fort, especially across the front. We'll notify Ahsan and Rafiq that you're coming. Bring them back with you when you're finished."

He turned to one of the injured men who was holding a blood-soaked compress over a wound on his left forearm. "Hussain, can you still fire your weapon?"

"Yes, sir. Absolutely, sir."

"Good, when the medic has you patched up, I want you to join the major and me in setting up an observation post over there, about two hundred yards from the fort." He pointed toward a brush-choked defile that might have carried water during the rains.

He turned toward the two more seriously wounded men. "Mahmood, I want you and Umer to stay here to guard the jeeps. Can you do that? I'll task you to keep track of our ammo."

"But, sir—" One of them struggled to rise, but fell back. "Yes, sir. Very good, sir."

Corporal Ijaz looked around his squad like a football coach willing them to win. "*Insh 'allah*, they will taste the wrath of God. *Allah-hu-akhbar.*"

They echoed, "*Allah-hu-akhbar.*"

"Okay. Let's get to it."

The men scattered to their assigned tasks.

I went up to Corporal Ijaz and pointed at the MP5 slung over his shoulder. "Sir, if you give me one of those, I could help."

He looked at me. "Ever used one of these to kill a man?"

"No, but I've killed a deer with a hunting rifle."

He frowned and looked away. "A bit different."

After a moment, he said, "There is something you can do. When the jeeps arrive, we'll get you binoculars and a portable radio. Then you and your wife can return to your position up there on the dune. Keep scanning the fort. Look for any signs of movement, the location of defenders, how many—that kind of thing. You and your wife can take turns using the scope until morning, so neither gets too fatigued."

I nodded. "Very good, Corporal."

As we hunkered down to wait for the vehicles to be brought up, Nadia came over and squatted beside us.

She tucked several stray locks under her abbreviated, khaki *dupatta* and sighed. "Josh, I hate to admit it, but you were correct about this fort. Obviously, it's a key stopover in the smuggling pipeline. I should have learned by now to listen to your hunches."

"It was a guess," I said. "What now? The squad is decimated."

"We've called up reinforcements. They'll come by morning."

"I know nothing about military strategy, but wouldn't it have been better to come with a much larger force in the first place?"

"In hindsight, I agree. Unfortunately, the brass thought this expedition was futile. We had a hard enough time convincing them to even send the few we brought. But now..." She scuffed the sand with her boot. "With four men dead, they're convinced. Sadly, that's the way it often goes."

Stephanie reached over and gripped Nadia's arm. "What if Janice is in there? And other victims? Isn't an all-out assault going to endanger them?"

"Corporal Ijaz is keeping that uppermost in his mind. That's why he used a bullhorn and repeated his demand three times during the initial assault. Don't worry, he'll be careful. Lay siege to the fort. Destroy their water supply. Strangle their ability to escape—then negotiate."

She stood up. "Look, I've got to go." She smiled down at us. "Keep hope alive. We won't give up until we find Janice... Here, take these."

She passed us a couple more energy bars and strode away.

Stephanie and I took turns scanning the fort with binoculars throughout the remainder of the night. Even wrapped in a blanket, I could feel the desert chill. I had to rub my fingers to warm them before I could adjust the scope. Nothing, though, could warm the icy fingers that gripped my heart. Was Janice in there somewhere? In spite of Nadia's assurances, I wondered how she could survive an assault on the fort. Should we have offered a reward? Negotiated? But how? *Josh, stop speculating and pray.*

During one of my watches, I noticed that sniper fire had punctured their water tank. Good, they'd soon be out of water. The intermittent whine of bullets from our two snipers forced the defenders to stay out of sight.

An hour into our stint, I saw a couple of shadows flit across the compound toward the line of vehicles. Fortunately, the snipers saw them, too, and began to direct a steady line of fire toward the vehicles, peppering them and apparently cutting down a couple of the men.

The defenders responded by probing for the snipers with automatic rifle fire and a couple of RPG rounds. Wisely, our snipers kept moving to different positions along the crest of the dune.

For the last two or three hours of darkness, comparative silence fell over the scene. Finally, the eastern horizon began to lighten. That's when Stephanie spotted shadowy figures entering the brick structure built against the far wall of the fort. She transmitted the information to the corporal, suggesting it might be where they stored their weapons.

Moments later, we hear the swoosh of RPG rounds from the snipers, followed by an enormous explosion. The structure disappeared in a cloud of smoke and fire. For some time, exploding munitions lit up the sky and echoed off the surrounding dunes. The explosion left a huge crater where the structure had been and badly damaged the far wall of the fort.

A figure emerged from the fort waving a white flag. He pushed in front of him a woman with her hands bound behind her. Corporal Ijaz rose from his observation post and strode toward them with a scrap of white cloth tied to his helmet. They stopped about three feet from each other. After five minutes or so, they parted.

I saw the corporal speak into his radio, then start back toward his position. Suddenly, the smuggler whipped a pistol from somewhere on his person and shot Corporal Ijaz, and then the woman. Ijaz staggered and fell. The woman collapsed like a puppet discarded by its handler. The killer raced back toward the fort.

I screamed, "No!" as I stared at the scene through binoculars. The woman sprawled on her back, immobile in the dirt. Corporal Ijaz lay facedown, shot from behind.

Nadia leaped from her position at the observation post, raised her MP5, and loosed a hail of fire at the fleeing smuggler. Then, she flung down her weapon and shouted into her radio.

Almost immediately, the squad began to lay down a screen of fire mainly directed toward the walls and entrance to the fort. A jeep roared across the sand and slid to a stop beside Corporal Ijaz. A figure leaped out and lifted him into the jeep, which then sped back to its shelter behind the dunes.

I lay there in the sand for some time cradling Stephanie's head on my arm. My sleeve was wet from her tears. She shuddered a couple of times. I felt numb at the treachery we'd witnessed.

The orb of the sun had begun to rise in the eastern sky when our ears detected a distant whisper that quickly coalesced into the *chop, chop, chop* of helicopters. We stared in the direction of the sound, but saw nothing until two military choppers roared toward us, barely a hundred feet off the crest of the dunes. The swirl of sand they kicked up as they passed stung our eyes, but lifted our spirits.

The Apache choppers swooped low over the fort before hovering briefly in a position beyond the far wall. From there, they poured rocket and cannon fire down on the smugglers who had been taking shelter from the rangers' fire under the lee of the wall nearest us. In an instant, they broke away to circle the fort from some distance so they could blanket the compound with overwhelming firepower from other directions.

Within a few minutes, the siege appeared to be over. Under the watchful eye of the hovering choppers, five or six men struggled through the entrance with their hands held high. From her position in the observation post, Nadia raised a bullhorn and ordered them to lie facedown on the ground. A Hummer emerged from behind the dunes and raced across the sand to take them into custody.

One of the choppers swooped again over the compound and dropped what appeared to be stun grenades. Before the echoes of the explosions had died away, six heavily armed rangers slid down ropes from the second chopper onto the wall. The first chopper then dropped its contingent of rangers on the ground off to one side of the fort and sped away to hover at a safe distance. This fresh contingent approached the fort's entrance with care, but meeting no resistance raced inside past the burnt-out hulk of the truck.

We heard a single burst of submachine gun fire, and then silence. Five minutes passed. Ten. Fifteen minutes ticked by in agony before we spotted a ranger waving his submachine gun from the wall. A couple of soldiers emerged from the entrance, prodding a prisoner. Behind them staggered a bedraggled file of women flanked by rangers.

Stephanie cupped her hands together and shouted Janice's name. Getting no answer, we jumped over the crest of the dune and half-ran, half-stumbled down the side. I landed at the bottom in a heap with Stephanie on top of me. We righted ourselves and raced toward the fort, only to be halted by two submachine gun wielding rangers.

Nadia strode over and explained to the soldiers that we were with her. Turning to us, she shook her head slightly.

Impossible. Nadia must have missed her. We walked slowly toward the women, searching their haggard faces. Two soldiers were in the process of distributing blankets to enable them to preserve some measure of modesty. All the women were young. Most stared at the ground. Three or four wept silently. Some had the vacant looks of women much abused. With few exceptions, all wore cotton *shalwar-qamizes* that were torn and soiled. Obviously, the gang chose most of its victims from poorer families.

Janice was not among them.

I turned and walked away, kicking the dirt as I went. I'd only gone ten or twenty yards when I heard Stephanie calling.

"Josh. Josh!"

I looked back. Stephanie pointed toward a woman emerging from the fort followed by a ranger. "Could it be?"

I joined Stephanie in racing toward her. Janice saw us coming and ran to meet us. We collapsed into each other's arms and time stood still.

EPILOGUE

A week later, Steph, Jan, and I sat beneath an umbrella overlooking the pool at the Holiday Inn in Lahore. None of us felt like swimming, even though the bright sunshine felt warm within the confines of the bougainvillea-shrouded courtyard wall.

Jan sat between us, her tea untouched, staring into the distance. We often found her like that, as if her eyes were fixed on something only she could see. She had rejected outright our appeal that she fly home immediately with Stephanie, stubbornly refusing to wipe the sandy soil of Pakistan off her feet so easily. She had muttered something about driving a car soon after a serious crash, and Pakistan deserving a second chance. In spite of her brave face, we knew that her healing would take time. Sudden noises still made her jump and, although Stephanie had taken to sleeping in the same room with her, Janice seldom slept through the night.

Her rescue and the freeing of the twenty-three young women held at the desert fort had captured the imagination of the world press, who descended on us like locusts. Our plan to spend a quiet two days at the canal bungalow while we pondered options turned into a nightmare. Colonel Nasir, who had commanded the choppers involved in the rescue, tried to insulate us from the clamour of reporters by stationing a military guard in front of our bungalow, but nothing protected us from their shouted requests for interviews and pictures. Several even camped out in the trees along the canal.

Fortunately, Luke Wu came to our rescue. He smuggled us out in an expedition van and got us on a plane bound for Rawalpindi, but told us to get off in Lahore where he had booked us rooms in the Holiday Inn. And he insisted on picking up the tab.

I smiled thinly as I thought of the reporters' chagrin. They had probably spent days searching for us around Nowshera and in the Rawalpindi/Islamabad area. As a reporter myself, I could understand their frustration. My own paper, the *Toronto Times*, had offered to take me back if I gave them an exclusive. I took perverse pleasure in telling my former boss to jump into Lake Ontario.

I reached over and touched Jan's arm lightly. She jumped. "Sorry, honey," I said. "I just wanted to ask if I can get you something; a *samosa*, a curry puff, an éclair?"

She turned toward me, her face pale and her eyes dark-rimmed. "No thanks, Dad."

Stephanie set down her cup of tea. "The water's warm. You might enjoy a swim."

"Swim? And have those men across the pool leering at me? I've had enough of that for awhile."

She leaned her head on her mother's shoulder. "Mom and Dad, I know you mean well." Her eyes were wet with tears. "But this is going to take some time... and I have to do it my way."

"Of course, sweetheart," I said.

"Take as much time as you need," Stephanie said. "Just know that we love you and will do anything to help. We can still get a flight back to Toronto, if you want."

She wiped her eyes. "I know that. But I don't think that'll help. If possible, I'd like to go back to the dig... spend some time with Parveen."

When we'd first returned to the canal bungalow after Jan's rescue from the fort, Parveen had been one of the first to arrive. She'd embraced Jan and they'd cried together before talking for hours.

"Being in Pakistan is not the problem. I think I feel more love for the people than before this happened. I... I just can't get the picture of those women out of my mind. They raped two of them... in front of me. Thought I was next."

She began to shudder with great spasms of grief. Stephanie enveloped her in her arms and they clung to each other for several minutes. I knelt in front of them, wanting to embrace them both, but uncertain of Jan's reaction. She'd not yet become comfortable with my hugs, as if the whole male gender had somehow been besmirched by her experience.

Suddenly, she sat up, grabbed a towel, and daubed at her eyes.

Stephanie blew her nose into a tissue. "Can you talk about it?"

Jan shook her head. "Not yet." She gave us a thin-lipped smile. "I'm going inside."

We watched her leave, then Stephanie turned to me. "Are you sure we shouldn't insist on flying home with her? I know she really clicked with Parveen, but..."

I shook my head. "I honestly don't know. To be home, surrounded by her grandparents and brother, loved by her church, might be the best thing. Or..."

"Or she may not yet be able to face them, answer their questions, and see the pity in their eyes."

"Yeah," I said. "That's the thing. We're feeling our way here."

"Yet I see the beginning of healing." Stephanie pushed a stray lock of hair behind her ear. "This is the first day she's said anything about what happened; the first time she's really cried in front of us. I think our visit to Faria's home helped. They're kindred spirits and, like Parveen, Jan seemed able to open up to her."

The day before, in spite of misgivings, we'd visited the home of Faria, the college friend Jan had been on her way to visit. When Faria had heard of Jan's rescue, she immediately offered us the hospitality of her parents' Lahore estate. We'd politely declined. Then, a couple of days after checking into our hotel, gifts began to arrive for Janice: flowers, a box of imported chocolates, a silk outfit. We learned that Jan and Faria had begun an e-mail correspondence. Somehow through that contact, Faria had learned our location. Finally, the day before, Jan had agreed to visit her for lunch if we accompanied her.

Faria's home turned out to be an opulent estate, not the typical Lahori bungalow. Stephanie and I dined with Faria's mother and father in a room reminiscent of Buckingham Palace. Faria and Janice had opted to eat in a secluded gazebo in the garden. We didn't see Jan again until we left.

Faria's parents had immediately dispelled any nervousness we felt at dining in such palatial surroundings. They spoke flawless English and showed a surprising interest in archaeology. We soon felt at ease, as though being entertained by a neighbour back home. When we left, Faria's father insisted that we use one of his Mercedes for the duration of our time in Lahore.

"Visiting Faria helped," I said.

"I guess it's natural," Stephanie said, "for her to open up more easily to young women her own age."

"But to revisit the Nowshera area?"

Stephanie fingered the pearl earring in her left ear. "Certainly not by train."

"She loved the dig and might feel comfortable there... with Parveen."

Stephanie nodded. "Could speed her healing. It worked for you, although I'm not sure if what works for a man would work for someone like Jan."

"I'm not sure I know what you mean."

Stephanie reached over and touched my arm. "You were adamant about not coming back to Pakistan. Do you still have those nightmares?"

I scratched the stubble on my chin. "No. So you think facing my fears made them dissipate?"

"Something like that. I'm not saying that Jan needs to face her trauma, so soon."

"Hard to see how anything positive can come from this terrible experience—but it has."

"You mean, the nightmare..."

"Not just that." To be closer to Steph, I moved into the chair vacated by Janice. "You and me. I'm so thankful that you stuck with me... that our separation didn't end in divorce. I think I love you more than even a week ago."

"Oh, Josh." She looked around, then brought my fingers to her face. "Sweetheart, I love you more, too." Conscious of curious stares, she dropped my hand. "I can't imagine life without you."

"And faith..." I shook my head. "When you said that God had given you assurance that Jan would be rescued, I had my doubts."

"I could have been wrong. It wasn't as if God actually spoke to me... just that, I... I felt peace as I prayed."

"But that's it, isn't it? God was there all the time, listening to your prayers. He may have even heard my feeble cries."

"But God is always there, listening," she said. "Jesus promised to never forsake us."

"Yes, but back in Canada that was always sort of... theoretical to me. Something to sing about in church. But out here—now?"

"And now?"

I ran my fingers through my hair. "Now God is... well, real. I felt his presence with me in that cell when I thought I was dying.

Oh, some would say any feelings I had were just the result of the trauma, but it was more than a feeling. It was as if the veil hiding unseen reality had been pulled back. Suddenly, my faltering faith has become... what? As real as gravity, or...?"

Steph leaned forward. "The writer of Hebrews said that faith is the evidence of things not seen."

"Exactly. And I'm going to commit myself to nurture what little faith I have."

Steph smiled at me. "I'm glad, Josh."

I signalled for the bearer to bring us a fresh pot of tea and plate of curry puffs.

"What about my contract with Asian Archaeology? Should I beg off?"

Stephanie adjusted her lounge chair so she could lean back. "Couldn't you write the articles from here in Lahore. Or back home?"

"Probably. I have tons of pictures, lots of notes."

"And couldn't Luke send you e-mails about any new discoveries?"

I nodded. "I don't see why not. He's been tremendously understanding. He even said to take a week off, two weeks, a month... but I still feel responsible to finish the series of articles. To make them authentic, I probably need to visit the site again."

"Understandable. After all, he paid for this hotel."

"And he was so excited to get the stolen artefacts back. Using the recovered tablet, he thinks he'll be able to decipher the Indus script. He'll want me there to cover that... pictures and all."

"Maybe you could return after Christmas?"

The bearer arrived with tea and pastries. I was in the process of pouring tea when we heard a familiar voice.

"Here you are."

We turned toward the voice. Nadia strode toward us, dressed in a sleeveless black *qamiz* and matching *shalwars*, embellished with vertical bands of white embroidery. An abbreviated black *dupatta* covered her shoulders, but not her head, allowing her dangling crystal earrings to sparkle in the sun. The shock of seeing her out of her military uniform left us speechless for a moment.

"Nadia," Stephanie said, rising to embrace her, "it's so good to see you."

Nadia pulled up a chair. "I'm on my way to the airport. Thought I'd see you guys before I left. Find out your plans."

"Where're you headed?" I asked.

"Back to Toronto. Then on to Vancouver. Some kind of a threat they want me to investigate. How's Janice?"

"Some better," Stephanie said. "It's going to take time."

I signalled the bearer for another cup.

Nadia frowned. "Jan has been through hell. I'd love to see the whole gang lined up and shot."

"What about Chaudri?" I asked. "Did they get the goods on him?"

"You know that security guard at the dig—Ali? He survived the attack on the fort. He squawked like a parrot. Implicated Chaudri, the SP, and a bunch of his officers."

"What'll happen to them?"

"Public trial, then probably the death penalty...except Chaudri."

Stephanie frowned. "Not Chaudri?"

"He got out on bail. Must have bribed a judge. Skipped the country. Dubai, I hear."

"What?" I jumped up, slinging my arms out and knocking over a teacup, which shattered on the tile patio. People turned to stare at us. "Sorry," I muttered, sitting back down.

"I know how you feel, Josh. Colonel Nasri is going to have Chaudri shadowed, try to extradite him. But even without getting Chaudri, the gang is smashed. We raided two more warehouses and freed hundreds. The drug pipeline has been blocked, the stolen antiquities recovered. Oh, and you know that young woman you saw being brought into the jail in Nowshera?"

I nodded. "Yeah."

"She's been freed and her attacker charged."

"Praise the Lord," Stephanie exclaimed.

"So with the SP gone, what's going to happen in Nowshera?" I asked.

"A new SP takes over next week. Vetted by Colonel Nasri. I'm not saying you'll see an end to *rishvat*, *risookh*, and *rishtadari*, but it's a start. There's more and more men and women like Nasri Sahib, allergic to both corruption and extremism."

The bearer brought two more teacups and knelt down to clean up the mess I'd made. "*Mu'aff kijie Sahib*," I said.

We sat in companionable silence for awhile, sipping our tea and munching on the savoury pastries.

Nadia set down her teacup. "So when are you heading home?"

"We're not sure," Stephanie said. "We're taking it a day at time."

I sighed. "Jan even wants to go back to the dig."

"Is that wise?" Nadia asked.

"Wish we knew," Stephanie said.

Nadia stood. "Well, I've got to go if I'm going to catch my plane. Oh, one more thing. The murder of your padri friend? Arranged by the SP through some *goondas* he hired. I went to the memorial service." She shook her head. "Must have been a thousand there. Too bad I never knew him. I could have asked him some of my questions... Well, give my love to Jan."

I felt my eyes moisten as I stood. "Nadia. We can't begin to—"

She interrupted me. "Anytime. That's what friends are for. Call me when you're back home."

I watched as Stephanie accompanied her out, then sat back down and stared into the distance. A hoopoe searching for grubs bobbed up and down on the grass along the courtyard wall. A light breeze feathered the fronds of the palms, bringing with it the scent of jasmine. In spite of everything, I felt a connection to the land and its people. A connection I'd lost—and found again.

GLOSSARY OF URDU TERMS

Note: Urdu terms have been transliterated using the sounds common to English speakers in North America for those characters. Although differing spellings may be found by diverse writers, this method seemed to best suit the flow of a fictional text and enable the reader to sound out the Urdu words.

Urdu term	English meaning
Abba	Father.
Afsos	Sorrow, generally used of the ritual of offering condolences at a bereavement or tragedy; also, *bahut afsos*, literally, very sorrowful.
Ammi	Mother.
Acha ji	Okay.
Afeem	Drugs.
Allah-hu-akhbar	God is great!
Amrikan	American, commonly used for all Westerners.
Angrez	Foreigner, originally for the English.
Azan	The call to prayer from the local mosque, issued five times daily in Arabic.
Babu	Clerk.
Basti	Distinct cluster of houses in a town, a suburb.
Burqua.	The head-to-toe tent-like covering worn by strict Muslim women. Some *burquas* are made more fashionably.
Begum Sahiba	Honorific title for a lady, usually the lady of the house.
Bahut mihrbani	Thank you very much,
Beiziti	Dishonour, loss of face.

Bevukoof	Stupid, idiot.
Bhai	Brother, used also to address fellow Christians.
Bidi	Hand-rolled, inexpensive Pakistani cigarettes.
Bivi	Wife.
Baksheesh	Tip given to coolies, alms given to beggars, sometimes even used for bribes.
Chacha, chachi	Uncle, aunt.
Chai	Tea, especially of tea made by boiling milk, tea leaves, and sugar together; sometimes called *deci chai.*
Chapati	Circular, flat, unleavened bread made from whole wheat flour cooked either on a grill or in a clay oven. The staple bread of Pakistan.
Chaukidar	Night watchman, security guard.
Chipkilli	Small house lizards, like chameleons, that scoot around the walls to catch insects.
Charpai	The common, portable string beds; constructed of a woven string (often jute) mesh on a wooden frame.
Cleaner	Name given to the helpers—usually young—employed by truck drivers to fetch and carry, polish and clean, and generally be at the beck and call of the driver.
Dakoo	Bandit.
Dhardi	Beard, *dhardi wala,* bearded one.
Dost	Friend.
Dupatta	Long gauzy scarves worn by women, wrapped around their heads and over one shoulder to maintain their modesty.
Deg	The huge pot used to cook curry for large gatherings; often two and a half feet wide and as deep.
Ek dum	Immediately.
Ghardhas	Large terracotta water pots often covered with burlap which is kept wet. The evaporation cools the water inside.
Ghulab	Rose.
Goonda	Thug.
Hooka	Water pipe, tobacco smoke is drawn through a water-filled bowl.
Injil	Gospel .
Insh'allah	God willing.
Izat	Honour.
Jaldi	Quickly; when repeated, it means especially quickly.

Janab	Sir, more honorific than *sahib* or *ji*.
Janab-e-ali	Sir, even more honorific.
Ji	Sir or mister, often inserted after various titles such as, *Sahib Ji*; a less honorific title than *janab*.
Jin	Evil spirits.
Jirga	Council.
Kafir	Infidel, heretic.
Kao	Eat .
Khana taiyar hai	Dinner is ready, the meal is ready.
Khadavand zinda hai	The Lord is alive.
Khush amdad	Welcome.
Kya hua	What happened?
Kya bat hai	What is it?
Latti	Long bamboo or cane riot sticks.
Muaf karna	Forgive me, sorry; a more honorific form, *muaf kijie*.
Mahavrah	Proverb, saying.
Munna	Forbidden.
Maulvi	Muslim priest who leads the regular prayers.
Mazedar	Tasty.
Memsahib	Mrs., honorific title for a married woman; plural—*memsahiban*.
Mihrbani	Honorific form of thank you. See also *shukria*, which is more common.
Numberdar	The headman of a village, often unofficial but recognized by villagers.
Pakorda,	Vegetables such as potatoes rolled in a spicy dough made from chick pea flour and deep-fried.
Panchayat	A village council.
Pir	Religious mystics whose tombs are often venerated.
Prata	*Chapati* slathered with butter cooked on a hot grill.
Prebu, prebu Jesu	Word for lord used by Marwaris and those with a Hindi background; *Prebu Jesu*, Lord Jesus.
Purdah	The Muslim practice of keeping women in seclusion, hidden from the eyes of all men except close relatives using walls or by requiring them to wear the *burqua*.
Rishvat, risookh, and rishtadari	The three r's said to be used to get ahead: bribery, influence, and relatives.
Roko	Stop.

Roshandan	Small windows near the top of a room with high ceilings that can be opened or closed to aid air circulation.
Rupeah	Rupees, the currency of Pakistan.
Subar	Patience .
Sag	Curried spinach and/or mustard greens, often with pieces of homemade cheese (*paneer*).
Sahib	Sir, mister. Very common. More honorific than *ji*, but less than *janab*.
Salaam	Hello or goodbye, depending on the context; the common greeting used by Christians.
Salaam alay kum	Muslim greeting to which the reply is *Waalay kum as salaam;* generally meaning, peace be upon you.
Samosa	Vegetables or meat deep-fried inside a five-inch triangular pouch of thin pastry.
Shadi	Wedding.
Shalwar-qamiz	Common Pakistani wear; *shalwar* is the pair of baggy cotton pants while the *qamiz* is the long-sleeved shirt with long tails worn outside the *shalwar*.
Shukr	Thanks, thankfully.
Sipahi	Policeman or soldier of lower rank.
Tuva	A beehive-shaped clay oven set into the ground or into a raised platform. *Chapatis* plastered on the heated sides cook quickly.
Tonga	A two-wheeled horse-drawn carriage with a canvas roof and seats facing front and back.
Wah wah	Wow! Expression of delight over something impressive.
Waalay kum as salaam	Reply to greeting, used by Muslims meaning generally, and peace be upon you.
Zidi	Stubborn.
Zina	Immorality, adultery.
Zindabad	Long live.